W9-ABS-821

Also by Robert Boswell

DANCING IN THE MOVIES

CROOKED HEARTS

CROOKED HEARTS

Robert Boswell

Alfred A. Knopf New York

1987

THIS IS A BORZOI BOOK
PUBLISHED BY ALFRED A. KNOPF, INC.

The first chapter appeared in slightly different form in Dancing in the Movies *(University of Iowa Press). Copyright © 1986 by Robert Boswell. "Edward's Story" and "Jill's Story" appeared in slightly different form in* The Georgia Review.

Grateful acknowledgment is made to the following for permission to reprint previously published material: Harper & Row Publishers, Inc.: *Stanza, p. 107, from "The Man Watching" from* Selected Poems of Rainer Maria Rilke. *Translated from the German by Robert Bly. Copyright © 1981 by Robert Bly. Reprinted by permission of Harper & Row Publishers, Inc.* Random House, Inc.: *Excerpt from the poem "As I Walked Out One Evening" from* W. H. Auden: Collected Poems, *edited by Edward Mendelson. Copyright 1940 by W. H. Auden. Copyright renewed 1968 by W. H. Auden. Reprinted by permission of Random House, Inc.*

Library of Congress Cataloging-in-Publication Data

Boswell, Robert.
Crooked hearts.

I. Title.
PS3552.08126C7 1987 813′54 86-46001
ISBN 0-394-55706-9

Manufactured in the United States of America
FIRST EDITION

I would like to thank Dorothea Oppenheimer for her support and patience and good faith.

FOR ANNELLE AND ALBERT

AND FOR TONI

O stand, stand at the window
As the tears scald and start;
You shall love your crooked neighbor
With your crooked heart.

—W. H. AUDEN

CROOKED HEARTS

TOM'S STORY

ONCE WHEN I WAS eleven years old, my father asked me not to buy him cigarettes, even if he begged. We had just moved back to Kentucky and were staying with Aunt Hannah, Mother's big sister, while Dad tried to find work. Her white clapboard house had two bedrooms, but the room that had been Grandfather's was not used and the door was locked. The house overlooked Highway 60 from a steep but short hill. Across the two-lane highway, set close to the road, was Hale's Cafe, a rectangular building with huge windows on either side of the front door and an immense gravel parking lot flanking it. A pole near the highway held a neon sign high above the building. HALE'S was written in cursive red neon, CAFE in thin yellow neon, and around them both, a glowing blue oval. For my brother Ask and me, the cafe was the only source of entertainment.

During the day we went over to Hale's six or seven times to buy sodas, play the jukebox, or push nickels through the pinball machine. Jennetta worked there. She knew our father and let me buy cigarettes because she knew they were for him. When Dad took me aside that Friday night and asked me not to buy him cigarettes, he meant he didn't want me to go to Hale's the next day and stick a quarter in the machine for Kent regulars. He had decided to quit smoking.

It had been a summer for decisions. Just a few weeks earlier he had decided to return to Kentucky from Arizona. He said he needed folks he could talk to. He was making a new start in an old place, and I guess that made him think it would be a good time to quit smoking. He hadn't liked Arizona. We'd lived in a small town on the Gila River and he'd taught government to eighth graders. Something had dissatisfied him—the administration, he said once; the desert, dry as asphalt; the puny trickle of water they called a river. Mother told me it was something else, something I was too young to understand. Whatever the reason, he announced one day that we were leaving, and not long afterward we left.

Charley was the only one mad about it. He was just a year away from graduating high school and wanted to finish with the kids he knew in Arizona. Ask and I had friends too, but no one took the friendships of eleven- and nine-year-olds seriously. Mother's people were still in Kentucky, so she was willing to come back. Cassie was only five and happy wherever she was, although she was the reason we'd moved to Arizona in the first place. The doctors had said she needed drier air, so we'd headed west. Since her breathing problems had cleared up, my father assumed we could return.

Charley was the loudest complainer. He was our brother for certain, but you couldn't tell from looking. Ask and I were sometimes mistaken for twins, even though I was two years older. We both had high foreheads, light skin, and domed skulls. I was so skinny my head looked like a watermelon on my neck, but because of the shape, kids in the first grade had labeled me Peanut Head. My major concern about returning to Kentucky was that someone would dredge that name up again. People in Arizona had just called me Tom and I'd been happy with that. Ask's head was normal and he was heavier, but we still looked alike. Charley, on the other hand, was real handsome, like Elvis Presley without the sneer.

Supper was at six at Aunt Hannah's always. At our real house, supper had been whenever it was ready, but Aunt Hannah liked things to have order. She used to say, "The top should be on the top." So we ate at six.

Any trips to Hale's had to be before then. Father said he didn't like the crowd that gathered there after dark. The night he asked me not to buy him cigarettes, we had made one last run at five forty-five. The neon sign was already on and Elvis was singing "Jailhouse Rock." In Arizona, everyone in the sixth grade had a favorite Beatle, but in Kentucky Elvis was still the king.

A big boy, nearly grown, with a package of Kools rolled up in the arm of his T-shirt, had the bases loaded on the pinball machine. Jennetta leaned over the counter and smiled at us.

"How's my little men?" she said. "Cokes?"

I nodded and we climbed up on the stools. They were perfectly round, supported by one chrome leg, and could spin either way without stopping. Ask had taped a penny to the edge once, and I had spun while he counted over a hundred revolutions before my arm got tired and I quit.

Hale's had nine booths with red vinyl seats and green tables trimmed with polished aluminum. Each booth had a miniature jukebox with the songs listed on cards like a menu. Every Elvis single I could remember was there, plus Bobbie Gentry singing "Ode to Billie Joe." But every jukebox had them; what Hale's also had was Sam and Dave, the Doors, Aretha Franklin, Jimi Hendrix, the Temptations, and even Little Richard, music our father wouldn't let us listen to. And at night it was loud. Ask and I could hear it clear up the hill, across the highway.

Jennetta brought us our Cokes. She had the blackest hair imaginable, black like paint, and blue eyes, the kind of blue the sky gets at night. I couldn't say she was beautiful, but with her hair tied back in a red handkerchief, a few strands teasing across her forehead, I understood even then that something about her was magical. I could see it with my own eyes. Ask couldn't. He liked blondes like Marilyn Monroe (who was dead), Ann-Margret, Nancy Sinatra. He *knew* they were pretty, everybody said so. To me, Jennetta had the same something Marilyn had, whatever that was. She was about five years younger than Mother, which made her thirty-three or -four, but she talked to us like we were real people, not just kids, asking how we liked being back in Kentucky, if Dad had found work, whether the Beatles were better than the Stones.

We had to hurry to get back to Aunt Hannah's before six. After supper we lay on the grass overlooking Hale's and talked about the differences between Arizona and Kentucky. What we missed most were the lizards. My favorites were the striped ones you could chase for an hour. If you caught one by the tail, it'd snap off and squiggle around in your hand. Over the next couple of weeks you'd see a bare-butt lizard hustling around until its tail grew back. Ask liked horny toads. They depended on camouflage for protection. Once you spotted them, they were easy to catch. He had tried keeping one in a shoe box, but it died, which led to a lecture from Mother about the wild being wild. That night I told Ask the difference between him and me was the way we liked to catch lizards.

We counted cars on the highway. I had the northbound and he had the south. With him leading 36 to 18, I conceded, secretly happy I was behind, because he would never have given in. I'd have had to look into my hands or stare at the moon whenever I heard a northbound vehicle until we were tied. Ask never conceded anything. That was why Dad always asked me to buy him cigarettes. Ask wouldn't do it. He didn't like smoke. Of course, Dad could have bought the cigarettes himself, but he avoided the cafe.

Back inside, we listened to the Cardinal game. They were the reigning world champions and Dad said we'd better enjoy the glory while we could. Charley had gone to a Pony League baseball game with Limber Watkins, and I could tell our parents were relieved.

He was becoming reacquainted with old friends and might start acting less hostile. By the fifth inning, the Cards trailed the Phillies by seven. We gave up on them. Mother suggested that Ask and I get ready for bed. It was then my father made his request.

My mother and father were both tall and thin. Mother had dark wavy hair and her top lip turned up when she smiled, a kind of proof that she was friendly. Her name was Jill (which didn't sound like a grown-up name to me or Ask). Dad's hair was dark red and his eyes were blue. His name was Edward, and he didn't like people to call him Eddie. He had a serious face (there were creases in his forehead from thinking so much), but he liked to laugh and I liked to listen to it. We all did. His laughter made me laugh, a good thing for a laugh to do. Our last name was Warren, and Mother would sometimes say it was the only thing we all had in common.

That night, my father came to me with his hands in his pockets, wearing his green hunting shirt, tan slacks, and the brown wingtips he'd had for years. He was fifty-one then, only a little older than the astronauts—a fact he often pointed out. "Tom," he started, gesturing for me to walk into the kitchen with him. "I don't want you to buy cigarettes for me tomorrow. Even if I ask you to do it."

I was a little puzzled, but I nodded.

"No matter how much I ask. Can you do that for me?"

I nodded again and that was the end of it.

IN THAT TINY HOUSE made tinier by the locked-up room, Mother, Father, and Cassie slept on Aunt Hannah's bed, leaving her to sleep on the couch. We boys slept on the front porch. Ask and I got into our pajamas and crawled into the makeshift bed—two quilts beneath us and a sheet on top. Since Aunt Hannah went to bed early on the couch, our parents had to do the same. By ten fifteen we were able to sneak out to the edge of the hill and watch Hale's.

A pretty good crowd milled about the checkered floor. Others ate burgers and fries in the booths. One couple danced near the back, and a group watched a boy in a yellow shirt rack up points on the pinball. The parking lot filled with station wagons borrowed from worried parents, pickups, a couple of Bugs, shiny Mustangs, and always two or three hot rods with chrome pipes and grilles, their bodies painted candy-apple red or metallic sparkle blue. Boys gathered around the side of the building to drink beer bought in Illinois (our county was dry) and tell stories so loud we could catch parts about racing their cars, beating up their friends, or feeling up their girls. If there was nothing real to talk about, they'd dream about Jennetta.

After working most of the day behind the counter, Jennetta waited tables at night. She was the star of Hale's Cafe. Even Ask admitted he couldn't keep from looking at her, especially when one of her favorite songs came on the jukebox and she pulled some lucky boy up from his seat to dance. She liked Little Richard, who became my favorite—Ask preferred Elvis, who he knew was good.

Then what we never would have guessed could happen happened: Charley arrived at Hale's.

He and Limber Watkins must have pulled in while we were watching Jennetta, because suddenly there he was posing in the doorway, the collar of his shirt turned up, sleeves rolled to his elbows. Jennetta clapped her hands when she saw him and gave him a big hug.

"Did you see that?" Ask said.

"She hugged him," I said.

Charley walked like the other boys we'd seen, swiveling his hips a little, leading with his chest. He sat in a booth facing us, next to a girl with a ponytail. She was cute enough, but after Jennetta hugged you, how could you be interested in anyone else?

We watched for almost an hour until we were both about to fall asleep. Just as Ask suggested we go back to the porch, Charley walked out of Hale's, stopping at the door to wave and say something. He had taken only a couple of steps in the parking lot before Jennetta came hurrying after him. She took his arm and leaned up close like she was whispering. They paused for a moment, and we paused with them, not even breathing. Ask and I both leaned closer, although we had no chance of hearing. They began walking around the corner of the building on our blind side. We had to run across the yard to see them—dangerous because it put us in front of our parents' bedroom window, but a risk we were willing to take.

Jennetta leaned against the white wall, but only her shoulders touched Hale's. Her body slanted away from the building toward Charley. He flattened his palm on the wall beside her head and leaned on that arm. One of her hands, on his chest, fooled with his shirt or his buttons or something we couldn't quite see. He bent slowly forward, closer to her. We knew at any moment it could happen—our brother was going to kiss Jennetta *on the lips.* Somebody put "Love Me Tender" on the jukebox and they both laughed.

Then something funny happened. Even though she still fiddled with his shirt, his head started creeping back until he stood straight. He pulled the hand away and shoved it in his pocket. Jennetta took his arm at the elbow, but he shook his head and walked away from her. At the neon sign he stopped and turned back. Ask and I expected something like in the movies where the man gives in, says he loves her, and they rush into each other's arms. That didn't happen. Our brother called out to Jennetta and we heard what he said.

He said, "Fuck you."

Charley came straight across the highway. We had to run back to the porch, jerk the sheet up around us, and pretend to sleep. He must have flown up the hill, because we barely shut our eyes before he was there, sitting on the steps, staring out at the cafe. We lay silent as bricks, barely breathing—almost always the way people pretend to sleep is to pretend to be dead. We were so quiet that when Charley muttered under his breath it sounded like it had come over a loudspeaker.

"Hicks," he said and lay back against the floor.

I couldn't take it anymore and looked at him with my best

sleepy face. His feet were on the top step, his back flat against the porch, hands behind his head, knees wide apart forming a diamond.

"That you, Charley?" I kept one eye only half opened.

"Go back to sleep," he said.

Ask jumped at that. "What's going on?" he said, scratching his head as he raised up. I gave him a mean look for overacting. He just scrunched up his face at me.

"Go back to sleep," Charley said again.

"Good ball game?" I asked.

He didn't say anything.

Ask sat up straight. "What's wrong, Charley?"

"Nothing's wrong with me. Why aren't you guys asleep?"

"You woke us up," I said.

"I didn't wake anybody up." He finally turned and looked at us, propping himself on one elbow. "Stay up late listening to the Cards?"

I nodded. "Phillies beat them."

"I hate baseball," he said. "I just wanted out of the house."

Ask and I looked at each other, then Ask said, "Where'd you go?"

Charley shrugged. "Places. A bar, maybe. What would you think of that?"

"How could you get into a bar?" I asked.

"Some people think I look pretty mature. Some people think I'm full grown. You going to run to Mom with this?"

"Heck no," I said. Ask was too offended to reply.

"We went to Cairo in Limber's Chevy. He's got it souped up and cherried out. I ought to have a car like that." He looked back at the cafe. "Everybody ought to."

"You went to a bar." Ask didn't want the story to fizzle out.

"Kind of. We got this guy to go into a bar and buy us a six of Budweiser. Me and Limber drank all of them. But there's nowhere to go in this hick town."

I waited to see if he was going to offer more. "There's Hale's," I said finally. Charley narrowed his eyes at me. "Me and Ask like going there," I added. Charley relaxed but Ask seemed tense. I elbowed him under the sheet.

"We went there too. After the beer." He sat up and looked at the cafe. I hooked my head around the porch railing, but all I could see was neon red, yellow, blue.

Nobody said anything for a long while. I thought we might wind up going to sleep without knowing. I expected Ask to be close to gone since he could never stay awake for anything, even Jerry Lewis movies, but he was wide awake, staring at our brother. Charley finally broke the silence.

"Wouldn't be a bad place except for that woman."

My heart started to beat like I was scared. "I like Jennetta," I said. He didn't seem to hear me. "I think she's all right."

"You're too young to understand," he said.

Ask had this look on his face, like his eyes had turned into marbles, a look he got whenever he was trying to fight off doing something he knew he shouldn't do. This time I was sure exactly what it was. He was close to asking Charley outright. I poked him with my elbow to snap him out of it. He didn't even turn his head. I hit him again, a mistake, because the words just popped out of his mouth.

"We were watching," he said. "We saw you and Jennetta from the hill. We heard you too."

"Heard what?"

"What you said to her," I said.

Charley didn't do anything but stare at us, then back at the cafe.

"What happened?" Ask said.

"You're not old enough to understand," he said.

"Fuck you," Ask said.

Charley and I snapped our heads around to look at him. His eyes weren't marbles anymore. I don't know if Charley realized when I did, but he must have soon afterward, that Ask wouldn't quit until he got an answer, even if it meant asking Jennetta. That's just the way he was, even hitting him wouldn't change anything.

Charley lay back again and scooted closer to us. "She wanted me to give a message to Dad. She said I was mature enough to understand." He moved even closer until I could feel his breath when he whispered, as if the words themselves were pushing against my face. "She said I should tell Dad she'd wait for him to work things out."

It was a funny thing then. I started crying. Ask didn't; neither did Charley. Just me, my face in the blankets, Charley going, "Shh," and Ask running his hand through my hair the way Mother always did. I didn't cry long and lifted my head to wipe my eyes and nose.

"What was that all about?" Charley said.

"I don't know," I said. "I couldn't help it."

"Maybe she can't help it either," Ask said. I could tell from the way he said it that he was trying to make me feel better.

The next day Ask and I went to Hale's. Jennetta was there by herself, frying eggs for her breakfast behind the counter. "Too early for Cokes," she said, smiling at us, then looking back to the eggs. "Your daddy'd skin you alive, drinking Coca-Cola this early."

It should have been the same. Her voice floated like it always did, she talked with us like we were real people, but we both knew it was spoiled. Even though we'd come not for sodas but to play pinball, we turned around and left.

Just before noon, my father stepped out onto the porch and called me. Ask and I had been playing baseball according to who picked the snazziest car to come next on the highway. He was ahead 6 to 3. I walked up the porch steps and my father offered me a quarter and two dimes.

"Pick me up some Kents," he said. "You and Ask get yourselves Cokes."

I shook my head. "You told me not to."

"I'm telling you to do it now."

"Last night . . ."

"Forget what I said last night. I changed my mind." He slipped coins in my shirt pocket, patted me on the shoulder, and gave me a lopsided nod. "Come on, partner."

By this time Ask had walked up behind me. He stared at us all marble-eyed, which scared me. I must have been shaking my head no, because Dad said, "Am I going to have to go across and get them? You boys run over there all day."

Ask climbed the porch steps beside me. "I'll get them," he said.

The two of us walked down the hill and across the highway to Hale's together. Jennetta called out as we entered. Neither of us paid her any attention. We walked straight to the cigarette machine. I gave Ask the quarter. He slipped it into the slot and pulled the knob. When the package fell into the tray, he pulled out the tail of his shirt and picked it up with his shirttail between the package and his hand. Jennetta stared funny at us walking out. Ask held the cigarettes away from his body and had to walk limp-legged, his face screwed up like he'd been eating lemons. I helped him up the hill and waited on the porch while he walked in the house and dropped the Kents on the couch next to our father.

WE DIDN'T STAY in Kentucky long. Cassie started choking on the air again, and by the end of the summer we were in another little town in Arizona. Our father never stopped smoking. Whatever it was in Kentucky he'd returned to look for, he never found in Arizona. I don't know what it was, although I'm pretty sure it wasn't just Jennetta. The last time I asked my mother, she shrugged her shoulders. "Sometimes people want to be happier than anyone has a right to be," she said.

And once while I was in high school and Charley was going through a tough divorce, he asked me to hide his gun and not to give it to him no matter how hard he asked. He dropped it on my bed, a big revolver. I took a towel from the bathroom after he left and wrapped the gun. I rode my ten-speed to school where Ask was in the middle of a Science Club meeting. We rode together to a park. I showed him the gun. We made a plan.

We biked past the edge of town, beyond the citrus groves, to the county dump. Ask picked a spot full of rotting vegetables and crushed glass. We dropped the gun there, then dragged a stained mattress over it. With him on the seat and me standing, pumping the pedals, we rode all the way downtown. I called Mother and told her we were going to the movies. Normally she would have been angry with us for missing supper, but she seemed happy to have us out of the way. We saw *Big Bad Mama* twice, then rode home in the dark.

The light in my room was on. The sheets and blankets had been ripped off the mattress. The mattress was turned sideways on the box spring. All the drawers in the dresser were pulled out, with shirt sleeves and socks hanging over the lips. On the floor, in the center of the room, Charley lay asleep. Ask threw a blanket over him. I turned off the light.

It was a tight squeeze, the both of us in Ask's bed, and I couldn't help but think about Aunt Hannah's porch. I asked if he remembered.

"Of course I do," he said, offended that I had to ask.

PART I

Cara vemos, pero corazón no vemos.
(We see the face but not the heart.)
En la casa uno tiene su propio enemigo.
(One finds one's truest enemy in one's own house.)

—GUATEMALAN PROVERBS

COMING HOME

I

It was a custom in the Warren family to celebrate failure, and they had their share of it. They were prone to excesses of imagination that made the impossible appear likely and the merely difficult a matter of course. They bought raffle tickets with the confidence of grifters. They took beginning violin lessons picturing the tuxedos they'd wear with the Philharmonic. They believed George McGovern could pull it off.

And they had their share of the big disappointments, too: betrayal, divorce, humiliation, sickness, sadness, death. Failure had become as much a physical part of their lives as the Sunday box of doughnuts on the kitchen table, the daily paper that waited dutifully on the lawn each morning.

Jill was the arbiter of ruin, weighing each failure secretly and announcing her verdict by pulling the tangle of Christmas lights from the hall closet and depositing it in the center of the living room floor. Ask strung the colored lights around the room and made banners with butcher paper and watercolors. Cassie hauled the ladder out of the garage and taped strips of crepe paper to the ceiling. Together, they inflated balloons, rubbed them against their heads, and stuck them on the walls, where they hung like huge cold capsules.

Edward stocked the refrigerator with Budweiser and made endless toasts. The breakfast bar became a liquor bar, and Ask, who believed mixology would help him become a lawyer, became bartender. Jill called a caterer and had the kitchen table adorned with a great tray of shaved ham, roast beef, and turkey, arranged in concentric circles and bordered by piles of sliced cheese—Swiss, Cheddar, American, Gouda.

Charley took charge of the salad, one of the few domestic chores he performed, and created it according to color, insisting on blood red tomatoes, terra cotta carrots, jade fresh spinach, and always a wild card: mushrooms, avocados, snow peas, popcorn.

Tom had only to select the music and, at the right moment, pull his mother or Cassie onto the living room floor to dance, or, if he could find no partner, begin dancing by himself, knowing Ask would soon join him, jumping and swaying, fingering an imaginary guitar, kicking the fallen balloons.

Riding the bus back to Yuma after dropping out of Berkeley, Tom had no reason to believe he would escape a party celebrating his failure. Images of past parties had haunted the long ride. He remembered when Ask's eighth-grade science project, a plaster of Paris volcano, had failed to erupt until the judges were three tables away, then exploded, spewing sewage-brown "lava" on the ceiling and knocking Ask against the wall, breaking his arm—his family had thrown a party. Charley had gnarled radishes for the salad and claimed they looked like igneous stones. Jill created a bubbling drink she called El Volcano, providing Ask with his first drunk. But what Tom remembered most clearly was Ask sitting in the living room, smiling and drinking left-handed, his right arm covered with a brilliant white cast.

Ask enjoyed being the center of attention at the parties. No one else did. When Cassie forgot her lines in a sixth-grade play and decided to let her character die on stage, she was so embarrassed she lay under her bed in the dark. Ask had to drag her out by the ankles to join the party. He made a banner that read AN ACTRESS MUST DIE ON STAGE BEFORE SHE CAN LIVE ON STAGE. Edward bought a book on improvisation and forced everyone to act like bees in a hive, vegetables ripening, farm animals in a slaughterhouse. Tom remembered playing Monkees albums, swing dancing with his sister to "Hey, Hey We're the Monkees," singing along with Mickey Dolenz.

When Edward's affair with one of his American History students became common knowledge and he was humiliated at a faculty get-together, they had a subdued party. Cassie recited the epigraph from "The Rime of the Ancient Mariner," which she'd memorized for extra credit in school. Tom played old Louis Armstrong and Boots Randolph records. Jill danced barefoot with Charley, spilling a Bloody Mary in Edward's lap, staining his pants and the floral couch with a dark red exclamation.

When Charley's wife left him and he ransacked the bedrooms and garage trying to find his gun, the Warrens had a party and just drank a lot, sitting outside, staring at the stars, listening to Edward tell war stories.

Tom, slouched in a seat in the back of the bus behind two noisy children, alternated between sleeping with his head propped against the window and staring out the same window at the darkening desert. He was nauseated from movement and exhaust fumes, an ache behind his eyes from sleeping sitting up. Everyone on the bus showed evidence of recent or recurrent failure, and he took some consolation in being among his kind.

An unshaven man in a suit coat that drooped down his shoulders like an apology lay sideways in a seat, his mouth open and slack with sleep. Beside him, a woman, purple and green about the eyes, her lips red as a blister, pulled a hand mirror from her purse every ten minutes to check her frazzled hair that smelled of eggs and sulfur. Across the aisle, a human so old as to be sexless, strapped about the chest to the seat, neck supported by a chrome bar, head bald and flecked mud-brown, moaned the names of movie stars. "Elizabeth Taylor," he said, "Robert Mitchum, Frances Farmer, Lionel Barrymore." The smelly children who sat in front of Tom argued about the armrest they shared, elbowing and whining, their eyes as flat and stupid as a trout's.

And there was Tom himself, a junior college transfer humbled by the big university, wearing a crumpled gray shirt, jeans, and, for the past one hundred miles, an erection, dreaming intermittently of the woman in Yuma who had just dumped him, shifting in his seat to hide the persistent hard-on, staring at the blur of desert and his faint reflection imposed over it, the image marred by a circle of fog and drool where his open mouth had slept. He thought he should invite the people in the bus to the party. "Friends from school," he'd say. There should be a commune for losers, he thought, but who would cook?

The woman in the seat beside him, middle-aged and thin as a root, had been reading an issue of *Cosmopolitan* for six and a half hours. She was on page 96, an article titled "How to Catch a Man Worth Hanging On To!"

Don't ride Greyhound, Tom thought. He held his breath and attempted to count to ten thousand, a family cure for tension. He made it to forty-one.

"Are you finished yet?" The woman stared at him, waiting to turn the page.

"Just browsing," he said.

"I read every word," she said. "It's the only way I can feel I'm getting my money's worth. Where you headed?"

"Yuma," Tom said.

"Lucky you," the woman said. "I'm going to Dallas. Another thousand miles at least."

"You'll have to buy another magazine," Tom said.

"Sometimes people leave them lying on the seats. What's in Yuma? You have family there?"

"Yeah." He nodded and she turned the page. A family who would be waiting to drink to his status as dropout and cuckold. Charley had once said the custom stemmed from an undying familial urge to drink. "Any excuse for a party," he said. However, the truth was they had parties only in response to catastrophe. Ask argued that their parents wanted the family together whenever there was trouble, and once together, they could never think of anything else to do. "It's not like we could pray or something," he said.

Tom wanted his brothers to be waiting at the bus station with a huge blanket. As soon as he stepped onto the pavement, they would leap from the darkness and wrap him in it, then carry him to an unmarked car and throw him in the trunk. The trunk would smell of cat urine. The car would take a circuitous route to their house, arriving after midnight. They would secrete him through a window into his room, which would be stacked to the ceiling with unmarked tins of unidentifiable foods. He'd hole up there for several weeks. Dropping out of college was no justification for a party.

Ask was outside the bus station leaning against an orange pole, one foot on top of the other. For Tom, one of the few enjoyable things about coming home was knowing that Ask would be exactly as he'd left him. He waited with his arms crossed, his shirt and pants perfectly pressed. When he spotted Tom through the bus window, he bit his lower lip so he wouldn't smile too big.

"You cut your hair," he said as Tom stepped off the bus.

Tom grunted and put his arm around him. Ask's hair was almost long, not quite to his shoulders, and parted in the middle. Tom had cut his hair the day he decided to drop out. It had reached his shoulders and identified him as a holdout against conformity. To return to live with his parents meant giving up that pretense.

They waited for suitcases to emerge from the bowels of the bus. Tom watched the few others disembark, the woman with the frazzled hair, the children who appeared to be with her. The station smelled of oil and exhaust, but the evening was cool, clear. Traffic whined through the streets. The moon, almost full, shone dully, like an incomplete thought.

COMING HOME

"Let's go for a drive," Tom said when the suitcases appeared. He looped one strap of his backpack across his shoulder.

Ask grabbed a suitcase and shook his head. "They're expecting you at home."

Tom imagined his family standing in a semicircle around the living room door, waiting for him to enter, eager to celebrate his return to the fold after making an ass of himself at college, proving he should never have left.

"I need the drive," he said.

"You've been on a drive. All the way from Berkeley."

"Don't argue."

Ask shrugged. "Nothing's changed." They threw the suitcases into the back of the family station wagon, a white 1968 Impala that Cassie had dubbed the Ancient Mariner.

Yuma, Arizona, sprawled across the great flat desert like a gaudy carpet, and not a single thread had raveled while Tom had been gone. It was the same collection of trailer courts, chain stores, fast-food restaurants, gas stations, and tract homes. It embodied failure as other cities embody light or reason.

Twenty miles to the west were sand dunes so perfect in their desolation as to be elevated to the level of spectacle. A hundred miles to the east were saguaro forests, each cactus twenty or more feet high, hundreds of years old. But the desert that made up Yuma was a cauterized scar—wiry creosote, tumbleweeds, emasculated mesquite, shriveled prickly pear, blunted and yellowing barrel cactus, cholla as thin and dry as antlers—vegetation so coarse and harsh to the eye that only the fact of its survival gave it any appeal, living proof of the earth's insufficiencies. The landscape brought to mind images of life after the ozone layer was gone or after the bomb's startling mushroom.

The Colorado River, powerful enough in the north to carve the Grand Canyon, muddled by Yuma, shallow and tired, swallowing the city's sewage but not digesting it, letting it float and foam in even the best swimming holes, a river defeated by water skiing and blasphemed by the London Bridge, which crossed the Colorado a hundred miles above Yuma, moved block by block to attract the idle and addled.

The city itself was no better, a western strip city whose aorta was blocked daily by aging out-of-towners and nightly by insane adolescents and insomniac truckers. It was surrounded by mazes of trailer courts that filled in the winter, nearly doubling the city's population, and emptied in the summer, everyone returning home, like people who come to a party just to drink your liquor.

Yuma had once been a prison town and was known in the Old West as the Hell Hole. The prison, long since closed, had become a tourist attraction, and the city was given over to the individual links in those great chains known as Pioneer Chicken, Handyman, Village Inn, Safeway, McDonald's, Jack-in-the-Box, True Value, Texaco, Avis, Long John Silver's, Nautilus, Kentucky Fried Chicken, Sizzler, Wendy's, Shakey's, Sears, Frederick's of Hollywood, a city so anonymous as to defy location if not for the stultifying heat from May to October. Even the respectably old downtown buildings had been vulgarized by false white fronts and Mexican tiles in a failed effort to impersonate a shopping mall.

Movie-set architecture, Tom thought, as they drove through the abandoned downtown. A pear-shaped man in a Day-Glo orange sweat suit jogged in place waiting for the traffic light to change. Tom hated people who ran in place. Couldn't they quit moving for thirty seconds until the light changed?

"Satisfied?" Ask turned toward home without waiting for an answer.

The roof tilted more than he remembered. Except for that, the house, the neighborhood, the entire city were the same. One story, with a large attic that held heat like a thermos, the house was forty years old, wood frame, and located in a neighborhood that was otherwise entirely stucco, flat-roofed tract homes. As a result, it was a landmark of sorts, although in another neighborhood it would have been unremarkable. The roof was pitched steep for a desert house and sloped south, as did the floors and counters at the south end.

COMING HOME

The house felt like home to Tom, but he had trouble believing the people who inhabited it were really his family. As a kid, he'd toyed with the idea that he'd been adopted. Ask, however, looked so much like him people often mistook them for twins, and Ask was too much a part of the family for Tom to think they'd both been adopted. He'd given up the idea, but still felt like the family dog—loved and cared for, but not really one of them.

"To having the whole family together again," Edward said as soon as Tom opened the door. He raised a tumbler of Seven and Seven high above his head. Christmas lights twinkled behind him.

Suitcase in hand, backpack slung over his shoulder, Tom stopped at the doorway, hesitating as if he had a choice about entering. Ask pushed from behind. "Go on, for chrissakes. You're making me miss the toast." Tom moved aside to let him pass. He thought he might be unable to step across. They might have to come out after him. Crepe paper fluttered from the ceiling. Most of the balloons had already found the floor and huddled near the walls. *Wrap me in a blanket,* he wanted to say. *Let me return to the bus people.* He held on to the illusion of choice another moment, then crossed the threshold into the house of his parents.

Jill rushed into the room from the kitchen with her glass raised. She was forty-seven and a fellow college dropout. Her dark hair was glazed with an increasing amount of gray. "You're back," she said.

"Hey," Tom said, but it came out a whisper. "I'm back." He felt he was lying, as if he'd left his important parts in California and returned only a shell.

Charley stuck his head through the kitchen doorway, then leaned against the wall. The sleeves of his shirt, olive with black pinstripes, were rolled to just above his elbows. He raised a bottle of Budweiser face high. "Began the party without you," he said and drank, which started Jill and Edward drinking to finish the toast.

"Wait a minute," Ask said, walking toward the kitchen. "I need a beer." He stepped around Charley and through the doorway.

Christmas lights hung from the front window and gathered in a bunch at the corner of the room. Another string ran along the back of the couch, looped through an arm of the rocker, and around the knobs of the antique dentist's chest that Jill had found in a warehouse. Strips of chartreuse crepe paper hung almost to Tom's knees. The blinking of the lights and fluttering of the paper strips reminded him of the movement of the bus. He became mildly nauseated and imagined that he could smell exhaust. Across the kitchen doorway was a butcher paper banner with blue and yellow lettering. YOU MUST KNOW HOME TO BE A TRAVELER, the banner read. It was unmistakably the work of Ask. He loved making aphorisms.

Jill put her arms around Tom, hugging him for only an instant. "Drop those bags immediately. You look like you're about to leave." She hugged him again. "Someone wake Cassie. Ask, get her."

"I'm getting a beer," Ask yelled from the refrigerator. "Charley can wake her."

Charley ducked out of the doorway into the kitchen.

"I'll get her," Tom said. He carried his suitcase and backpack into the hall before anyone could disagree. He paused at Cassie's door, then walked on to his room.

The room was exactly as he'd left it, down to the unmade bed and white sock on the floor. It was eerie, as if he were looking at the ruins of an extinct civilization. He dropped his suitcase in the closet and tossed his backpack on the bed. He locked the door. Let them have their party without him. Here, he felt comfortable, close to his family but not too close.

On his desk lay a large white envelope, his name in familiar script. Eileen Ingham, his girl friend of two years, who had married while he was at Berkeley, had sent him just two letters, the first full of missing him and apologetic that she'd taken so long to write, the second, a wedding invitation. The handwriting on the envelope was hers. By its weight, he judged the letter to be just one page. There was no stamp or return address.

Even the skimpiest "Dear Tom" letter should be two pages, he thought, and dropped it back on his desk. He had enough to deal with for one night.

Eileen's photograph had disappeared from the bulletin board over his desk. He wondered which member of his family had been angry enough to remove it. His father, maybe, or Cassie. Or his mother could have taken it, trying to be considerate. But who delivered the letter in the first place? Who had spoken with Eileen, listened to her explanations? No one should know her reasons before he did, and he didn't want to know them. He felt like a bit player in a bad movie, the one whom all the other characters talk about while they're in bed but who is on screen only thirty seconds, seen through a car window or through the haze of memory.

The square of cork where the photograph had hung was a lighter brown than the rest of the bulletin board, a visible sign of loss, something he needed, something the party would deny him. He decided it didn't matter that the photo was gone. He only wanted to mutilate it, anyway. He picked up the envelope and tore it instead, then dropped the ragged halves into the waste basket.

He wanted to blame dropping out of college on Eileen. So far he couldn't do it, but with time, if he persevered, he was confident he could come to blame everything wrong with his life on her. A sizable endowment, he realized. He had plenty of time to decide why he'd failed.

The walls of his room were bare except for the bulletin board and a poster of Little Richard, who grinned at him, hands on the glistening ivory keys of a baby grand. Tom yanked the poster down. The relief he'd felt at finally being in his own room had passed.

Cassie's room was dark and the wall switch did nothing.

"Cass," he called out. "I'm back, Cassie."

The floor was so littered with clothing Tom felt he was walking on bodies.

"Cassie," he said and twisted his ankle on a balled-up sweater, almost falling. "God, Cassie."

She lay diagonally on the bed, wrapped to her neck in a jungle-design sheet. He worked his way across the room and touched her shoulder.

"Cass," he said. "Come on, Cassie."

"Fluoride," she called out.

"Wake up, Cassie. You're wanted."

He sat on the edge of her bed and jostled her. She was a notoriously slow waker, who talked, walked, and occasionally threw things in her sleep. She was the only blonde on either side of the family as far back as anyone could remember. Edward used to tease Jill by wagging a handful of Cassie's blond hair and saying, "There were never any somnambulists in my family either." To which Jill would reply, "*Everyone* in your family is a somnambulist." What Cassie had received from her father's side was height—she was already five seven at age fifteen—but she had the dark eyes and complexion of Jill. Only her blondness was a mystery.

Tom shook her again.

"The big flapping ones," she said, "and the fluoride smile."

"You're talking in your sleep."

"He did," she said and sat up. "He had big, flapping balls." Her eyes were open, and she stared at Tom for a moment. "Tom?" she said. "Was I sleeping?"

"Dreaming about flapping balls." He smiled, expecting her to be embarrassed.

She put her arms around him. "Jennie had a book with naked men. How can you put up with them?"

"Naked men?"

"They had balls that hung down like floppy drapes. I know about penises, but I never thought about balls. I baked a cake for the party." She threw off the sheet and crawled out of bed. She was wearing a yellow blouse, tan corduroy pants, and penny loafers.

"Your clothes are a mess," Tom said.

"I was only going to nap a minute. What time is it?" She pushed against the wrinkles in her pants and continued without waiting for an answer. "I never got the icing on. Ask is the only one who cares about icing. He cares about everything." She turned on the lamp next to the bed.

The room was layered in clothing. Mounds surrounded her bed like sacrificial offerings. Even the lampshade had a green blouse, a checkered sock, and white panties draped across it.

"You could clean once in a while," Tom said.

"Don't start nagging until the second hour you're home, please." She grabbed the panties on the lampshade. "How embarrassing," she said, without any sign of embarrassment, and stuck them under her pillow. "Don't tell anyone about Jennie's book. See these?" She held up salt and pepper shakers shaped like butterflies. "A boy gave them to me. He thought he was being romantic."

In the living room, the family had gathered like campers crowding around a fire. "Here they are," Jill said, as if Tom and Cassie were newlyweds emerging late from bed.

"To having the whole family together again," Edward said and raised his tumbler.

"Not yet." Ask carried drinks to Tom and Cassie. "They don't have anything." Edward and Charley drank anyway.

"Do I get wine?" Cassie asked as she took a glass from Ask.

"Kool-Aid," he said. "Cherry." He handed Tom a beer.

"You get beer and you're young," she said to Ask. "I hate cherry."

"It's your favorite," he said.

"I just *said* that. I didn't mean it."

"Oh, for chrissakes." Ask raised his glass and looked back to his father. "Now."

"I'm dry," Edward said, staring at his tumbler. He seemed amazed it was empty.

"That was the last of the Seagram's," Jill said and began riffling through her purse, a mammoth rat-colored bag, for money.

Charley, leaning on the wall of the kitchen doorway again, tipped his bottle straight up and guzzled the last of his beer. He pivoted and threw the bottle. The plastic trash bucket fell against the wall as the bottle hit, then righted itself, spinning slightly. "Be out of beer by the time you get more booze," Charley said.

"Ask," Jill said, still rummaging through her purse, "see what we have left and I'll make a quick run."

Cassie moaned and slapped her leg. She was ready for the party to begin, but Jill disliked driving anywhere by herself, especially at night. Cassie trudged to her room to get a sweater.

"I'll help Ask," Tom said to no one in particular and followed his brother into the kitchen, swiping at the crepe tentacles. Each time he left the living room, he felt he was escaping.

Ask opened the cupboard door under the breakfast bar, revealing a disarray of liquor bottles. "What's the matter with you?" he said, looking up at Tom. "You keep hiding." Ask never failed to mention what others tactfully avoided.

Tom sat on a barstool and stared down at him, but Ask had turned his attention to the bottles. "I feel stupid," Tom said. "Ashamed, maybe. A student's failure reflects on the whole family."

"No it doesn't," Ask said. He sat flat on the tiled kitchen floor and pulled bottles out of the cupboard. They gathered around him like ducklings who'd imprinted badly.

Tom squatted next to him to get his attention. "Sure it does." He squinted his brows in order to make Ask see the seriousness of the problem, but he was too engrossed in his flock of bottles. Tom always had trouble making Ask see what was really important. It was an annoying chore he felt obligated to perform. "If I was on the dean's list, they'd brag about me," he said. "So when I drop out, it makes them look bad."

"What's this?" Ask lifted a rose-colored bottle. He had begun sorting according to color, with the darkest bourbon at one end and vodka at the other.

"That's sherry. It goes with the wine."

White wine was at the vodka end, red wine just a row short

of bourbon. Ask put the sherry in the middle. "They'll find some way of bragging about you dropping out. We're having a party, aren't we?"

"Put the wine with the wine," Tom said, dimly aware of what his brother was doing. "We always have a party. It's their reaction to anything. Anything bad. There's not a full bottle in there." The bottles in their varying degrees of incompleteness bothered him.

"We're nibblers," Ask said.

"Sippers. They're sippers, not nibblers."

"There," Ask said, standing. "We're low on darks and middle colors, but we've got plenty of lights and clears."

"God, Ask. How can anyone shop for a party with that kind of information?"

"Mom'll understand," he said and closed the cupboard door.

Tom didn't argue. Sometimes he felt there was a secret language everyone in the family understood but him. He relaxed his face. Being annoyed never got him anywhere with Ask. "What do you suppose I'm going to do here?" He sat again on the barstool.

Ask took the stool next to him. "I've been checking since you called. You could be a waiter. Stag and Hound needs a waiter."

"I don't want to wait."

Ask took his beer from the bar. "You could hang around and figure out what you really want to do."

"Ask?" Jill was in the doorway.

"Low on dark and middle colors," he said.

"Check," Jill said. Cassie appeared next to her, pulling on her sweater. "You coming, Cass?"

"When are we going to eat my cake?" She looked first at Tom, then her mother, who just took her hand and led her out of the house.

The table had the traditional tray of meats and cheeses, but something was wrong. Tom wondered if the lighting in the room had changed, if the furniture had been rearranged. What did he really want to do? Go to college, he thought, see Eileen. These were not options he had selected, these were his premises.

There was no salad. Tom was happy to be able to name what was missing. Before he could ask what had happened to it, his father yelled for him from the other room.

"Son," Edward called. He stood at the window watching the taillights of the Ancient Mariner.

Tom knew he was the son in question.

"Son," Edward called again and watched the taillights until they disappeared around the corner. Tom stepped to the window just as they vanished. "Son," Edward said, softly this time, and put his hand on Tom's neck affectionately. He nodded toward the hall and Tom followed.

"Wise father routine," Charley said as they passed. "Right on schedule." He finished another beer and tossed it at the bucket. The bottle shattered against the wall.

"You wouldn't do that if you had to clean," Ask said.

"I'll help," Charley said. "Get the broom. I've got something to show you."

Near the end of the hall, Edward began patting Tom's back. "Tom," he said. "I'm sure, I imagine anyway, that you're, well, *down* right now."

That you've let us down, Tom thought, was what he meant. He wanted an opportunity to forgive Tom for dropping out of Berkeley. This would probably be the worst moment in a bad night, his father letting him off the hook. *Don't even think about the expense,* his father would say. *If you're going to drop out, you may as well drop out of the best.*

Edward stared at him a long while, then moved his hand from Tom's back to his own hip, finally putting both hands in his pockets. That he needed to tell Tom something, a story, maybe, or give some kind of advice, was so clear that it frightened Tom. Worse than his willingness to forgive, his stories went on forever and their meanings were cryptic.

"You want to talk?" Edward said finally.

"No," Tom said, too quickly and too firmly, but he didn't want to leave any room for misinterpretation.

Edward nodded, shrugged. "But when you do . . ."

"Yeah," Tom said, and they walked back to the living room.

Charley and Ask were laughing.

"Charley's got a surprise for you," Ask said. "He's got to give it to you before Mom and Cassie get back." He bit his lip to keep from smiling too big.

Charley produced a package the size of a paperback novel. The wrapping paper was divided into squares and each was filled with a drawing of a naked woman.

"Charley," Edward said with mock disapproval.

"Open it," Charley said.

The box held a fat red pocketknife.

"Everything you need to survive," Charley said.

Ask shoved Charley at the hip. "You told me it was rubbers."

Charley took the knife and began explaining. He loved gadgets. "All the basics, of course: scissors, screwdriver, can opener." He flipped each utensil out as he spoke. "Nail clipper, tweezers, toothpick, corkscrew, bottle opener, ice pick. And three blades—one for filleting, one for whittling, one for stabbing."

"Charley," Edward said again, his voice more stern.

"A potato peeler here." He had to work to pry it out. "An apple corer, a razor if you're ever able to shave. Compartment with three wood matches, double-headed. And if you close it all . . ." He pushed all the blades and accessories in. "For nights you can't get it up—a dildo for your sweetie."

"Charley, goddamn it," Edward said.

"Here." He put the knife in Tom's hand. "He's just jealous he doesn't have one." Charley turned and walked into the kitchen.

"Thanks," Tom said. Charley didn't seem to hear.

"I don't know what gets into him," Edward said to Tom, as if Charley weren't his brother but someone who called for an explanation or apology. Edward lit a cigarette and walked to the antique dentist chest, trailers of crepe paper running over his shoulders.

"What is a dildo?" Ask whispered.

"A fake dick," Tom said.

"For people who lose theirs?"

"Something like that. Charley been moody lately?"

Ask shrugged. "He seems the same to me."

While Jill and Cassie were gone, it was impossible for the four of them to be in the same room. There was nothing to say that wouldn't cause trouble. They didn't know how to behave. Charley leaned against the breakfast bar with his arms crossed while Edward stepped to the front window and peeked through the curtains. Tom stood next to the doorway that separated them, watching Ask, who moved back and forth from kitchen to living room.

"It's a great knife," Ask said to Charley, "even if it's not rubbers." When Charley only grunted, he stepped past Tom and said to his father, "Did you read my banner?" Edward mumbled that it was very nice without turning his head.

"Did *you* read my banner?" he said to Tom.

"What does it mean?" Tom said.

"Just what it says. You have to know home to be a traveler," he said. "You can't go somewhere until you know what you're leaving."

"What does that mean?"

"It's technical," Ask said.

They needed Eileen, Tom thought. When Cassie had lain under the bed to avoid her party and Jill had gone to convince her to come out, Eileen had made it possible for them to wait together. How had she done it? He couldn't remember exactly, but she had a way of talking that commanded attention and a gift for finding the right tone. Tom pulled the knife from his pocket. He pried open the corkscrew. It looked like a weapon, a fierce weapon.

"Tom's opening the knife you gave him," Ask said, stepping into the kitchen again.

They were hopeless, Tom thought, the four of them. Without at least one of the women in the family present, they weren't a family at all. They were more like a band of disillusioned thieves, sticking together only because everyone knew too much. Following this thought was its corollary, that Eileen had been a part of the family.

Jill and Cassie finally returned with three dark bottles and a case of beer, and they were a family again. "There was an awful boy at the liquor store," Jill said as she approached Tom. "He had one of those mustaches like Hitler."

"They're called toothbrush mustaches," Edward said.

"It was uneven." Jill rubbed her finger across her upper lip. "The right side was longer than the left. It made his face look lopsided. He stuck his head out the store window—we went to the drive-through liquor store on Ninth—and he stuck his head out, and said, 'Hold on, lady,' then disappeared. He took forever to get the beer, and to top it off, he didn't give me my change. I had to honk the horn to get him to come back. He was a mess. They'll be advertising for a new clerk in a week."

"Don't bother him with that," Edward said.

"Oh, I'm not saying you should work there," Jill said.

"I don't know what I want to do," Tom said.

"Take some time," she said. "When I dropped out of college, I got a job as a bank teller—it was terrible, but we needed the money, and I never did get back to school."

Edward pointed at her with the glowing end of his cigarette. "Don't bother him with it."

Jill glared at Edward. "No one's talking to you," she said.

When Cassie started school, Jill had begun classes at the local junior college, but the family was always short of money and she had left school for a series of short-term jobs. Tom remembered her as a bank teller, file clerk, receptionist, cashier, travel agent. For the past few years, she had sold real estate and enjoyed it, contributing an erratic income from the sale of an occasional house or lot.

"How's your work?" Tom said.

"I'm showing a house tomorrow," she said, "to a nice young couple."

"Quit bothering him," Edward said. "He doesn't want to talk about it."

"Seven and Seven," Ask called out and held the tumbler high as he entered the room. Edward snatched it.

"White wine," Ask said and handed the glass to his mother. "Charley's got the beer." He pointed with his thumb over his shoulder.

Charley passed a beer to Tom.

"A toast," Edward said.

"Wait," Ask said.

Cassie walked into the living room with a piece of cake in one hand and a glass of Kool-Aid in the other.

"Now," Ask said and nodded to his father. But it was Jill who spoke.

"To Tom," she said, raising her glass. "We're so proud you decided to come back to us after school didn't work out."

Everyone drank.

The beer stung Tom's throat like an accusation. He had made a choice, whether he'd been conscious of it or not. He hadn't been forced to come home. He could have taken a job in San Francisco, hitchhiked to Canada. Coming home was the product of a decision. He was here because he chose to be.

Ask elbowed him. "I told you they would brag," he whispered. "What are you worried about?"

In his room, after the party finally ended, Tom undressed and picked the pieces of envelope out of the garbage. He was tired from drinking and dancing and the hours on the bus, but the party had left him mildly happy, and the bed welcomed him home, soft and cool, familiar. He held the envelope fragments to his nose. They smelled of pencil shavings. Naked, with the sheet to his neck, he adjusted his foam pillow. He had hated the flat feather pillows in the dorm, the stiff mattress of his bunk.

He loved his room, his bed, with the unthinking love of drunkenness. He had masturbated here dozens of times. Hundreds?

Thousands? He couldn't be sure. Most of his important love affairs had taken place here—in his head, in his hand. He reached between his legs and felt the smallness, shrunkenness. If he didn't read the letter, he could believe whatever he wanted was inside. What would that be? He tried to imagine the perfect letter from Eileen, but he was too drunk to concentrate.

She looped her *T*'s like a junior high girl with a crush. He traced the swoop of her pen. Several of her annoying habits came back to him: ordering nothing in a restaurant, then eating half his sandwich; switching the radio station in the middle of a song; the way she sometimes withheld sex to manipulate him.

Her wedding invitation had included no note, just a printed card that said she was marrying Sam Crawford, a pale, quiet boy who had been her friend in high school, a friendship that had baffled Tom even then. All of Sam's friends had been girls—not girl friends, he never seemed to have a girl friend—just friends. Whenever Tom tried to talk to him, he'd fidget and say something Eileen had told him, "Eileen says you're a good dancer," or "Eileen says you're going to Berkeley." Tom had always wondered what Sam could talk about with Eileen. That she had married him didn't surprise him so much as confuse him.

He pulled the torn letter from the halves of envelope and fitted the pieces together.

> *Dear Tom,*
>
> *I still love you. I work Monday through Thursday until ten at the drugstore by myself. Come by and I'll explain. Everything has an explanation.*
>
> *Love,*
> *Eileen*

An explanation, Tom thought, pulling the sheet around him. Was that what he wanted? He tossed the letter off the bed. The pieces fluttered down, landing on the crumpled poster of Little Richard. He lay his head against the pillow and pulled a second pillow close. When he shut his eyes, he saw Eileen as clearly as if she shared the bed with him. And then he slept.

2

JILL SAT IN THE DARK of a strange bathroom wishing she smoked. The tub rim was cold and uncomfortable, and the room smelled of stale water. She lowered the toilet lid and moved to it, a wooden lid that was hard against her bones. What did you call those bones, she wondered, bottom bones? Tailbones? There would be a long scientific name for it, she guessed, one she'd never know.

Smokers needed only a cigarette to be occupied. She wanted to be alone, smoking a menthol, giving up the world entirely for the duration of the cigarette. Although she had never tried it, she was sure that was the appeal of marijuana—no more houses to sell, no children to worry about, no oil shortage, no A-bomb, no ache in the nameless bones she rested on. A three-minute escape.

She had been showing the house to a couple, the Stanleys, and both the house and the Stanleys were depressing her. They were in a neighborhood known as East Mid-Town North, a mishmash of old decay and new—aging houses of powdery brick crumbling at the corners, or weathered clapboard with once-white paint that flaked and dropped like filthy confetti. She associated the old houses with worn trails through linoleum, alkaline-laced coolers, bulges and hollows in heavy couches and too-soft mattresses.

The cheap new apartments depressed her even more—shoe-box duplexes and triplexes with stark yards of fingerbone maples and straw shrubs. They had carpet that stuck to rubber soles, gathering around the shoe like a beard, and thin walls that allowed neighboring lives to crowd in with muffled arguments, television chatter, and the drone of refrigerators, coolers, light bulbs, pacing feet, restless limbs. The thin walls were left bare except for an occasional poster of a rock singer or a calendar with large X's through days just past.

Scattered around the neighborhood were old houses that had been renovated by optimistic young couples who planted grass and plumbed walls. She had shown houses to several such couples and knew the type. They spurned carpet for hardwood floors, painted doors and windows blue, filled rooms with ferns and ficus. They rescued mutts from the pound and drove trucks or old cars. They dug gardens in the backyard and raised tomatoes, squash, and watermelon. They loved rattan and stereos with huge speakers and had at least one album to show visitors, an obscure singer whom they abandoned once he became popular. They had little children with silly names and long golden hair. They were the kind of people Charley could have turned out to be, she thought, if she and Edward had been better parents or if they had just been luckier.

Jill hated luck, despised randomness, which was why she usually enjoyed selling houses. They were monuments against chance, as solid and enduring as faith was supposed to be. She and Edward had lived correctly, more or less. There were plenty she knew who had lived worse. They didn't deserve the bad luck, the failures, the relentless animosity of Charley. At some point Edward had turned to Charley and said "Stop" when he should have said "Go," and Charley was lost. Cars brought to mind randomness for her, and she hated them, often refusing to drive even to 7-Eleven by herself. Houses were more reliable. Build one well and it would last a lifetime.

The house whose bathroom she sat in was an anomaly. It was thirty years old, had never been renovated, but was not decaying. White and bulky, with thick block walls and a solid overhanging roof, it had small bedrooms and, in the center of the living room, a monstrous, bulging, stone fireplace. For lack of a defining architectural scheme, Jill called it Neo-Muscular.

She had shown the Stanleys several houses during the week—an Early American stucco model, a pink pseudo-Victorian with a two-car garage, a pretentious Neo-Colonial with brick floors in the kitchen and dining room, even a fifties Modernistic with a plastic staircase. Mr. Stanley found something wrong with each. "Too crisp," he said of the brick floors. "Too blended," he said of the pink Victorian. She had tried to decipher each of his statements but came to understand they all meant "Too expensive."

Frieda Stanley was in her early thirties, her first few months of her first pregnancy, and so obviously in love that Jill felt jealous, believing it must be a remarkable love to survive with Mr. Stanley as its recipient. A tall man with hunched shoulders, a narrow head, and large ears that lay flat against his skull, Mr. Stanley trailed behind Jill and Frieda as they walked through the house, lurking in corners, finding fault with electrical outlets, bathroom moldings, room acoustics. Jill hypothesized that he'd stuck his head in a trash compactor and lost the interesting parts of his brain.

"It's very structurally solid," Jill had said as they entered the house. She pounded against a wall. The place had been impossible to sell and the asking price steadily declined. Frieda Stanley swept her eyes across the room quickly, then smiled at Jill, the kind of smile sales people hate—wrinkled and mousy—the smile that says, "I'm feigning interest because you've been nice." Jill couldn't blame her. Whenever she was in the house, she thought of Burt Lancaster in *Birdman of Alcatraz* having to make friends with sea gulls to endure imprisonment. *An attractive Neo-Alcatraz model,* she thought, *bars on the doors optional.*

"I'll show you the kitchen," she said to Frieda. Mr. Stanley was still outside "sizing up the planes."

She made a cursory run through the appliances, pointing out that there was no trash compactor, as if that were an advantage. She opened each of the cabinet doors, lauded the counter space, and made a brief pitch for morning sunlight, knowing Frieda had no real interest. She found herself imagining their life together—Mr. Stanley must be an early riser; Frieda, she guessed, liked to sleep late. She pictured Mr. Stanley perched beside the bed trying to think of an excuse to wake his wife. Did Frieda call him Mr. Stanley? She couldn't remember hearing a first name. When Jill had been pregnant with Charley, she had felt uncomfortable with

"Edward." It sounded so formal. She had called her husband Eddie. She couldn't remember when Edward had become easy for her. She pictured herself just married and pregnant, calling Edward "Mr. Warren."

"Dear God," she said aloud.

Frieda, staring at the kitchen, nodded, then looked to Jill and smiled again.

Jill felt a sudden ripple of tenderness for her. "There are plenty of other houses," she said.

"Oh, this is a fine kitchen," Frieda insisted, shaking her head.

"But not what you had in mind?"

"Well, not really. But it is a fine kitchen." Frieda stooped to look in the cupboards to prove her interest.

Jill heard Mr. Stanley enter the front door. What did Frieda see in him? He wasn't charming or interesting, but Frieda loved him, had somehow fallen in love with him. Perhaps they'd gone dancing and there was a moment during a step when she felt she was flying. It didn't necessarily take much. For her, it had been seeing Edward step off the train. He'd turned his head from side to side, looking, she found out later, for his parents. He was in uniform, returning from Italy, the war. Seeing Jill, he smiled and took off his dress hat. She was there to look for her brother, who was missing in action and would never come home. She was fifteen and checked her brother's bedroom each morning and the train station in the afternoon, knowing he wouldn't be there but going anyway. Then Edward smiled at her, took off his hat, and ran his hand through his hair. They married when she was nineteen, and before she was twenty-one, they had a little boy of their own. "Fell in love with a uniform," her father said, but he accepted Edward when Charley was born, a beautiful boy who charmed everyone.

Jill watched Frieda lean over the sink and reach for the cord to the kitchen curtains. The swelling in the dress troubled her store of images, calling to mind rooms lighted by the sun and sheets fresh from the line, images so slight and fleeting as to be unintelligible but with a residue of sweetness. She touched the swelling in

Frieda's dress with her open palm, then laughed at herself. Frieda turned and laughed with her. They walked back to the front room with their arms around one another.

Mr. Stanley stood in a corner, his back to the walls. "I like a house to be close," he said.

Jill had to stop herself from laughing again. He seemed to be praising the house. "Close to what?" she said. "Schools? Work?"

"Close to itself, like this place here." He opened and closed his arms quickly, a flapping motion.

He's a pterodactyl, Jill thought.

Frieda's face drooped visibly. "We'd have to paint," she said softly. She swept her eyes across the room again. "We'd have to paint," she said, louder this time.

Jill disliked the sound of Frieda's voice. She was either too passive to argue or too much in love to fight. Jill loathed the thought of a miserly reptile forcing the house on Frieda. She hated to see a person take advantage of another's love. On the other hand, her job was to sell the house.

"Painting is fairly inexpensive," she said to Frieda. The walls, she realized, were the same gray as the walls in her own house. "It can be a family project."

"One good picture on this wall." From his corner, Mr. Stanley patted a wall. "That deer one—with the stream—Mother gave us. Make the whole place sprightly."

Frieda put her hand on her throat. She was wearing a string of wooden beads of various colors, the kind that had been stylish in the sixties. She held the beads with her fingers and flipped through them with her thumb. "I'd better sit," she said and looked to Jill. "Morning sickness, I think."

Jill directed her to a stool in the living room, the only furniture in the house, then led Mr. Stanley through the cell block of bedrooms and bathrooms. He fiddled with doorknobs and stuck his fingers in vents, smiling. She wondered if Frieda knew the real reason he liked the house. Did *he* even know? He didn't seem very aware. She considered walking into the living room and taking

Frieda by the shoulders. *He likes it because it's cheap,* she'd say. *He's cheap. He's a pterodactyl.* She glared at him, then caught herself. "Excuse me for a moment," she said, and it was then she ducked into the bathroom.

She sat on the toilet lid, envying smokers and loathing the man in the next room. To rid herself of the Stanleys, she thought of her family, what they were doing at that moment. Edward, Ask, and Cassie were all at the high school. She glanced at her watch, but the room was too dark for her to see. She guessed it was near eleven, third period. For Ask, that meant P.E., his least favorite class. He'd never been athletic like Tom and didn't have the easy grace of Charley. However, the class was going better than he'd expected because he had developed a "strategy," as he called it. "I volunteer for everything, so the coach likes me and the guys think I have guts." He explained this to Jill after coming home with a mat burn across his neck from demonstrating a wrestling hold.

Cassie's third-period class was called Rudimentary Psychology, a term that amused Jill. "You're so anal," Cassie said when Jill asked her to clean her room. Whenever she thought of Cassie being in high school, she felt startled anew. If there were light in the bathroom, she would look at her hands, her face—she didn't feel any older, at least she didn't feel any more mature than she had twenty-eight years ago when she'd married Edward. "Eddie," she said aloud.

But Cassie was in high school, and next year she would have Edward for Driver's Education, which was what he was teaching at that instant—what you should do if a ball bounces into the street, how many inches square the red flag must be to mark an overlong load, who has the right of way in an intersection if everyone arrives at once. He taught the same class five times a day. She could see him age visibly from week to week since he'd been transferred to Driver's Ed.

She shifted her weight on the toilet lid, crossed her legs. Mr. Stanley was in the next room talking to himself. He was probably a better conversationalist when alone, she thought. "Straight as a sparrow,'' he said. Jill pictured him hunkered down next to the wall moldings, eyeing them. The image was comic, but she couldn't muster a laugh. She thought of Charley in the warehouse, directing the coming and going of seed and grain, watching the clock as lunchtime neared. One of the reasons she was glad Tom had returned was that she could worry about him instead of Charley. Tom's problems were much more concrete—he needed a job to keep him busy; otherwise, he would wallow in his failure at Berkeley. And he needed to start dating new girls—women, Jill realized, startled again—he needed to date new women so he wouldn't dwell on Eileen's marrying so suddenly.

What Charley required she couldn't be sure—to be somewhere else, maybe to be someone else. She'd tried to convince Edward that they should ask Charley to leave the house. "That's just what he wants us to do,'' Edward had said. She believed he could use a push. Edward argued that he needed time. He couldn't stand to let Charley go. Charley had been his favorite from the beginning, those first years when it was just the three of them—he, his young wife, and his handsome boy. None of Charley's anger changed that—it just made Edward more determined to change Charley. Change him how? She wondered. Into what?

She preferred worrying about Tom. She could define his problems and approach them—"tackle them,'' Edward would say, but she preferred to think of it as approaching, offering the problem a carrot. She would ask around about jobs. She would find a woman to introduce him to. Until Tom had a job and a girl friend, she would not worry about Charley.

She heard breathing outside the bathroom door. Mr. Stanley, lurking. She flushed the toilet and opened the door quickly, bumping him solidly on the head.

"This hall is narrow,'' Jill said. She led him to the living room.

Frieda was slouched on the stool, her face gray as the walls, staring strangely at the fireplace, hands folded across her lap. How was she going to reconcile herself to living here, Jill wondered. Maybe she would come to resent Mr. Stanley without understanding why, or why she resented him most on cloudy days when the house became dank and dreary as a dungeon. Maybe she would begin to see the other repulsive traits of the man, and the crack in the shield would widen with time. For an instant, Jill thought of Edward and Charley and wondered at the source of Charley's resentment and how magnified it had become over the years. But she'd promised herself not to worry about Charley.

"I'm not sure this place is right for you," Jill said finally, almost a whisper. She needed to sell the house. She couldn't afford to lose a sale. But she had to acknowledge Frieda's disappointment. The rest was up to Frieda.

Mr. Stanley slapped the wall. "Very solidly structured," he said.

Frieda ignored them both, still staring at the fireplace. Her face was curled, as if she were trying to solve a puzzle. Jill stepped to the fireplace and ran her hand down the stones where they bulged around the opening. She made one last offering. "You'd probably have to do some repair here."

Frieda seemed to understand Jill's intention and shook her head. Suddenly her mouth opened. She pointed at the fireplace. "It's smiling," she said and laughed. "Honey, the fireplace is smiling." She laughed so hard she had to stand. Mr. Stanley laughed with her. Jill was surprised at how pleasing his laughter sounded.

Frieda walked to Jill and hugged her. "I think we'll like it fine here," she whispered. "Don't worry."

Jill clasped Frieda's shoulder and stared at the bulges in the fireplace, trying to think of it as a smiling face. All she could see were loose stones. The effort tired her strangely. "I have a daughter in high school," she said.

Frieda, in her excitement, didn't hear.

3

ASK ENTERED THE BARBERSHOP carrying a woman's hat. He had been vacillating about the haircut until he saw the hat, round and dark blue with black netting. He found it on the pavement in the Bayless parking lot. For the past few weeks he had been considering a haircut for several reasons:

1. Lawyers kept their hair short.
2. Short hair was more stylish now.
3. Long hair had become a sign of being a redneck instead of a hippie (even the word "hippie" was outdated and embarrassing).
4. The girl he liked preferred boys with short hair. At least, the boys she stood next to during lunch had short hair.
5. Tom had cut his hair in California, where all the new trends began.

Still, he had been reluctant to get it cut. Haircuts made him sheepish, as if he were giving up a secret part of himself. He had thought of his long hair as a political statement. Cutting it meant that he was retracting the statement, something he hated to do. Besides, the barber was sure to make wisecracks.

The hat had given him a strategy. While his barber gave a good haircut and hadn't taken on any of the pretensions of a hair stylist, he never left hair full on the sides. Ask decided to carry the hat and when the barber asked why, he'd say, "So if you cut it too short on the sides I can hide the whitewalls."

The barber stood at the first chair, his back to the window, clipping the hair of an old man in overalls. There were no other customers. Ask swaggered in, letting the door go as if it were the door to a saloon. A mechanical arm kept it from swinging shut, destroying the effect.

"Hey," he said, a little too loud. "I need a haircut, but I don't want it short on the sides. You always cut it too short on the sides. Now, can you give me a cut without making it too short on the sides?" He was overacting, something Tom often accused him of.

The barber turned, waved his scissors as if dismissing the whole idea. "I don't think we've been introduced," he said. "I think you've got the wrong barber." The man in the overalls leaned forward to frown.

"This is the place," Ask said. "You're the barber." He dropped the hat on a table of magazines and sat in a chair. Why would a barber lie to him? Or did he just have a forgettable face?

"I'll be with you in a little bit," the barber said and turned back to the man in overalls, who grunted something Ask couldn't make out. The barber shook his head once in reply.

Ask picked a magazine from the table and pretended to read. His strategy was backfiring, making him more self-conscious with each moment, but he couldn't abandon it now. He wondered if Tom had any trouble getting through his haircut. He doubted it. Tom was capable of caving in on any issue at any moment. He had, after all, dropped out of college, something Ask had found inconceivable at first. Now he believed he knew the true reason Tom had returned. He lifted the magazine higher to cover his face because he had begun to smile. Ask believed Tom had come back to be with him.

The notion made perfect sense. Tom was a good student. Berkeley was a good school. Why else would he have quit? Why had he spent a year at the local junior college to begin with?

He acknowledged that Eileen's suddenly dumping Tom and marrying Sam Crawford was an intervening variable. But, if anything, that should have made him even less interested in coming back to Yuma.

"Okay, young fellow," the barber said.

The old man in overalls was staring into the mirrored wall, flattening his hair against his head. He watched Ask through the mirror.

Ask stood and tossed the magazine to the table, returning to his strategy. "Give me a regular man's haircut. Leave the sides full." He climbed into the chair, turned to get the barber's attention. "That's full on the sides."

The barber nodded, taking mild offense, and covered Ask with a cloak, spreading it over him as he might spread a sheet over a bed. He called out to the old man, "Let me know what the boy decides."

The man paused at the door. "The kid's no-account," he said. "Never decided a thing in his life. Looks like that one." He raised a bony finger to Ask. "Got all the answers in the world and all of them wrong." He coughed and brought a white handkerchief from his back pocket to his mouth. "This one"—he pointed again to Ask—"is cleaning himself up at the least."

"Your boy'll come around," the barber said. He took a comb from a jar beside the sink and waved with it to the old man as he left. "He's from the old school," the barber said. The comb moved through Ask's hair, from forehead to crown, easily, despite the length.

Ask tried to imagine why the barber did not recognize him. The length of his hair? Would he recognize him after the cut? He thought of Superman putting on a blue suit and glasses and never being recognized. What were the details that determined who you were? Surely not hair length, but why then had he been so reluctant to cut it? What would Tom or Charley have to do before he would be unable to recognize them? If Cassie had an operation and became a boy, would he be able to pick her out of a crowd?

The barber cleared his throat. "Why," he asked, "did you bring that hat with you?"

"It was on sale," Ask said and began laughing. He turned around to look at the barber. "That was a joke," he said.

"You have to keep your head still if you want a decent cut."

"None of you barbers have any sense of humor at all. The one I usually see, the one I thought you were. He has no sense of humor at all. And he always cuts too much off the sides. That's my sides you're cutting now, isn't it?" Ask persisted with his strategy. He hated to give up a plan.

"Relax. You've got enough hair here for two. You want the shaggy dog look, you got it. It's your head."

"It's my head." Ask watched him in the wall-sized mirror. The barber cut the sides, inches of hair falling at his feet, then returned to the top of the head. Would he recognize this man outside the barbershop? Did he know him just as a barber? He imagined the man chopping meat, directing traffic, walking a collie.

"So," the barber said, looking in the mirror to catch Ask's eye, "why do you go to this barber anyway?"

"To get my hair cut."

"No, I mean, why go to him if he's got no sense of humor and never leaves your sides alone?"

"That was another joke—'To get my hair cut.' When you say the obvious, it's funny. For chrissakes." Ask folded his arms, disgusted now with his strategy. He would have to give the barber an honest answer, he decided, and began considering the question. Why did he come to this man?

"Forget it," the barber said. He measured lengths of hair with his fingers.

"I like his hands," Ask said suddenly. The truth had unexpectedly presented itself. "He has comfortable fingers." He remembered his mother holding him in her lap, running her hands through his hair. Whenever he was upset, she calmed him that way. "Do my hair," he used to say and sit at her feet.

The barber lifted his hands from Ask's head. "I can put two and two together," he said.

"What does that mean?" Ask said.

The barber lifted the electric clipper, made it whir. "The hat, the long hair, liking a man's fingers." He ran the clipper over Ask's neck, then by his ears.

For Ask, the electric whine became an extension of his own frustration. "I'm not gay, if that's what you mean," he said.

"It wouldn't be any of my business, now would it?" He dusted Ask's collar with powder. "As long as you don't do anything weird in my chair."

"For chrissakes, I found that hat. It was in the Bayless parking lot. I brought it in as a joke. I thought I'd tell my barber I brought it in case he cut the sides too short no one would see. Then you said you weren't you and I figured, he's too nervous and has no sense of humor at all, so what's the use?"

The barber looked at Ask through the mirror. Ask stared back at him. They looked at one another this way for several moments as a man might stare at his own reflection.

"That old fellow," the barber said, still looking into the mirror, "has a kid in Canada. Went there to avoid the draft." He parted Ask's hair with his fingers once and again. "My boy lost a digit, a finger on his left hand, over there, in Viet Nam." He raised his index finger to show Ask in the mirror, then parted his hair again. "You can't be a barber without that finger. You'd be surprised the things you can't be." He ran his hand through Ask's hair once more, and the part was perfect. He pulled an arrow of hair over one of Ask's ears, measuring.

"How about those sides?" he said. "Trim them back just a little?"

"A little," Ask said, and the barber went to work.

4

WHILE IN his fifth-period class, watching a gory Driver's Education film for the fifth time that day, the hundredth time in his life, Edward finally hit upon the right story to tell Tom. In the film, the boy driving the car (who looked a lot like a young Robert Redford) had a flat on the freeway. When he opened his trunk, it was so full of junk—beer bottles, loose tools, matted clothes, month-old groceries, a battered leaking ice chest, a stuffed dog, a jar full of marbles (which he promptly spilled)—he couldn't find the jack or tire tool. At first, Edward thought he would tell Tom the story of the film, about the dangers of holding everything in (the driver was eventually run over by a truck). Tom was certainly one who locked things in, who never opened up to the family. Edward imagined the driver opening up the trunk at home and letting each member of his family retrieve the junk he or she had left there, freeing the driver and, in the long run, saving his life.

Much too corny, he decided. Tom was wary of corniness. It often had the opposite effect of the one desired. He was like Charley in that way. The last shot in the film was of the stuffed dog on the shoulder of the highway, blood splattered across his big polyester ears. Edward suddenly thought of the golden retriever they'd had years before, a floppy-eared dog named Squirrel. He decided at that moment to tell the story of Squirrel and the hunting trip. It was perfect, although he couldn't say exactly why. It just felt right.

He was the first to seat himself at the dinner table. He smoked a Kent and drank from a tall glass of Seven and Seven while Cassie and Ask made sandwiches of leftovers from the night before. Ask also threw together a quick salad because Charley refused to. "I don't do that anymore," he had said. Edward ignored Charley's obstinacy because the night was full of good news.

Jill had sold a house and would have a commission coming with the conclusion of the paperwork. And Ask had cut his hair, finally giving in to his father's wishes. Over the years the boys had flaunted their hair as a means of angering and annoying him. It had been a source of friction between Charley and him, although the boy had never been a real long-hair. The day of Charley's graduation, right after they'd had a shouting match, Charley shaved his head. "Short enough now?" he'd said and bowed. Edward remembered scraps of bloody toilet paper dotting the bald head. He had been too angry and humiliated to go to the graduation. With Tom and Ask, he changed his approach, and it was finally working.

He waited until everyone was seated and the mustard and mayonnaise had made the rounds. All he needed was a little quiet and an opening to begin the story, but Jill started before he had a chance.

"Tom, I need you to do me a favor," she said. She put her elbows on the table and rested her chin on her fists.

"Don't start nagging him about work. He's hardly been home a day," Edward said.

"I'm not talking about work and don't interrupt me," she said, then smiled at Tom. "You remember Marriet Shacterly? Bob and Erin's girl?" *Woman*, Jill thought, *at least twenty-three by now*. She picked up a napkin and began bunching the paper between her fingers.

Charley covered his mouth with his hand and turned to Tom. "Shack-up Shacterly," he said.

Jill glared at Charley. She wished he would just be quiet for once. Tom sat between his brothers, nodding. Ask was biting his lip to keep from smiling, his hair cut short, almost identical to Tom's. He had always followed Tom's lead, she thought, even when they were little.

"I remember her," Tom said. In a red sweater, books pressed against her breasts, she ran across the high school breezeway in his memory. She was two years older than he, beautiful. He had masturbated once in his room, staring at her photograph in the annual. The memory embarrassed him. He folded his arms.

"She's had a rough time of things." Jill dropped the napkin and put her hand to her neck to touch her necklace. She wasn't wearing one, hadn't worn one for years. She remembered Frieda flipping through her beads. As they had been leaving the house, Jill had run into Erin Shacterly, who was visiting her daughter in one of the shoe boxes across the street.

"She's back in Yuma," Jill said. "Most of her friends are gone or married."

Charley put his hand on Tom's shoulder and whispered, "I'd fuck her if I were you."

"Watch your mouth, Charley," Edward said.

"Be nice," Jill said to Charley. "Marriet is a nice girl."

"I don't feel comfortable with blind dates," Tom said. Charley leaned next to him to whisper again. Tom pushed him away. He had developed a twitch in his stomach the moment his mother had mentioned her name. At the same time, everything he could say held the possibility of humiliation, especially with Charley there. He was angry with Jill for bringing it up in front of the family.

Cassie, who had been eating quietly, could hold back no longer. "She got used on in California," Cassie said. "Have a heart."

Edward stuck his hand on Cassie's blond head and turned to Jill. "Do you tell this child everything?"

"Yes, I do. Hush," Jill said.

"This is not something we need to talk about at the table," Edward said. He shook Cassie's head for emphasis. "We ought to talk about other things."

Jill ignored him. "You don't have to think of it as a date," she said. "Take her bowling or skating. Think of it as being neighborly."

Tom shook his head and stared at his plate. His parents were capable of making him uncomfortable in an infinite number of ways. That she would offer to set him up with one of the two or three women he lusted most after while he was in high school was exciting. That she would bring it up as a topic for the whole family to comment on was infuriating.

Ask waited for Tom to reply, chewing a mouthful of bread and roast beef, staring alternately at Tom and his mother. Finally he said, "Don't worry, Mom. If he won't do it, I will."

Charley began laughing. "Ask . . ." he started, but Tom elbowed him hard in the ribs. His anger had shifted to Charley.

"I could take her out," Tom said, without looking up. "Sure."

Cassie clapped. "Where are you going to take her? Bowling is the pits. Take her to San Diego."

"We don't really have to go into all the details," Edward said.

"Not till afterward," Charley said. "Then we get a blow by blow account."

"Tomorrow night," Jill said. "Eight o'clock. I took the liberty.

Another sandwich?" She began laying ham on a bun. Her only chance of appearing nonchalant was to keep busy.

"You can take my car," Charley said.

Cassie hit the table with her palms. "I don't believe it," she said.

Charley had owned a series of fast cars, the most recent a silver-blue Firebird. He never let anyone else drive it.

"I'm serious," he said. "Help get your mind off what's-her-name, the bitch."

"Drop it," Tom said.

"I'll even wash the goddamn thing for you," Charley said.

"Drop it is right," Edward said, annoyed by the whole line of conversation. Jill seemed to do things specifically designed to anger him.

"Take her to San Diego," Cassie said. "We women love the beach."

"It's almost two hundred miles," Ask said. "Take her bowling and you'll have something to do."

"This isn't a group decision," Tom said. He took a vicious bite of his sandwich. The room quieted.

Finally, Edward thought. Now all he needed was a transition.

"I'll even fill the goddamn tank," Charley said.

Edward ignored Charley. He'd have to work around Charley to tell the story anyway. Unable to think of a transition, he chuckled. It elicited no response. He chuckled again and looked at Ask. He could always rely on Ask for help, just as he could always depend on Charley to hinder.

Ask looked at his father and grinned. "What's so funny, Dad?"

"I was just thinking," he said and laughed again.

"Does the front seat of your car fold down?" Cassie asked Charley. "They could take a nap before they come back from San Diego."

Charley snorted. "No such luck."

Cassie was becoming as bad as Charley, Edward thought. He was determined to get the story rolling. "I was just thinking," he said again, "about old Squirrel. Charley's the only one of you kids old enough to remember Squirrel."

"Kids are baby goats," Cassie said.

Edward put his open palm on her head again. She could be worse than Charley, he thought, and gave her one firm shake. "Big golden retriever with long, fat ears and a habit of taking shoes out of the bedrooms and dropping them in his bowl. Whole family would have to go in our stocking feet to his dog bowl and select our shoes each morning." He laughed.

"Cassie did that once sleepwalking," Ask said. "She threw my shoes in the sprinkler."

"I was wide awake," Cassie said. "They stank."

Edward shook Cassie's head again. She slapped his arm away. He went on as if unbothered. "First time I ever took Charley camping, he was about seven and Jill was too pregnant with Tom to go. We took Squirrel and set up tent near a stream the locals called Hazlip Creek. The tent was one of those old canvas jobs that needs about a thousand stakes and it took the better part of two hours to get it in place. Charley wanted a campfire, but we'd brought a Coleman stove and I didn't see any call for one." He looked directly at Charley to fend off any argument. "It wasn't really cold," he said, as if there were still some controversy. "I was frying steaks on the Coleman while Charley and Squirrel went for a hike. 'A short one,' I told them because steaks don't take that long to cook, and like I said, Charley was only seven."

"He was six. I remember that trip," Jill said flatly. "I didn't want you to go."

Now Jill had turned against him, Edward thought, but the story was for Tom. At least he and Ask could appreciate it. "A half hour comes and goes, I've already eaten my steak and his is about to turn black, when Squirrel comes back without Charley. 'Charley,' I yelled. 'Char-ley,' I kept yelling, but no Charley. I rousted Squirrel. 'Where's Charley, Squirrel? Come on, boy. Where's Charley?' " He gestured as if the dog with the fat ears were beside the dining table. "Squirrel walked around the camp in circles a few times, sniffed at the dirt, took a longing glance at the steak, then started off into the woods. I followed him. It was getting dark and I couldn't tell whether Squirrel knew what he was doing or was just playacting, but what else could I do?" He directed the question to Tom, who did nothing. Ask, beside him, shrugged.

"There wasn't a trail and the branches were low, so I had to duck, even crawl, and really push myself to keep up with the dog. I was afraid to slow him down—he seemed to understand what I wanted and I didn't want to confuse him. Then I got stuck."

"Like we're stuck listening to this," Charley said under his breath.

Edward felt the comment physically in his throat as if he'd swallowed a knot of air. He pretended to be undisturbed, but his face flushed and he stared at his lap. "There was a puddle of ugly-looking mud I wanted to avoid," he said softly. "So I pulled myself up on a branch and threw a leg out to another, planning on stepping over and then down on the opposite side of the puddle, but for some reason I couldn't move. For a second I was scared, thinking there was a hand pulling me back. What it really was, was a stub limb that had caught the collar of my jacket. I tried to squinch my head down, but I was caught between the two branches and couldn't get low enough."

Charley tipped his beer bottle straight up, chugged the remainder, then slammed it to the table.

"I'm trying to listen to this," Ask said to him.

Edward paused, thinking Charley might walk out. Instead, he folded his arms and leaned back in his chair. Edward continued. "Finally, I fell. Splat into the muck, hands and knees first, mud splashing everywhere." He slapped his open hand on the table to illustrate. "I got out and wiped my hands and face as clean as I could, which took awhile because I was a mess. By this time it was dark and Squirrel was long gone. I hadn't thought to take a flashlight, so I called for Charley and then for Squirrel before I decided to go back to camp to clean up and see if Charley was there. I had to walk right through that miserable puddle to get back. I hate being dirty."

"You were so muddy when you got back," Jill said. "Filthy."

"This whole time, Hazlip Creek had been rising and was near the tent already. I ran around, pulling up stakes, yelling for Charley and cursing. And there on the other side of the tent was Squirrel eating the steak. 'Damn you, dog,' I cried at him and went to give him a swat. But when he cringed I saw Charley's little boot under his front paw. It was right then I got really scared."

At the moment in the story Edward felt was most dramatic, Cassie leaned over into her mother's lap to sleep. " 'Charley,' I screamed again." He yelled to wake Cassie. She just frowned and resettled in Jill's lap. "I started shaking the boot at Squirrel. He finally got the idea and we went off back through the woods, but this time I brought a flashlight and ran through the puddle and found Charley tangled up in a brier bush, sound asleep. 'Damn you, Charley. Scared hell out of me,' I said." He waggled his finger at the grown Charley across the table. "I wrenched him loose and put his boot back on and followed Squirrel back to camp."

Edward paused and brought his hands together beneath his chin. "We lost the tent and the Coleman. The creek was about to take the ice chest, but I saved that. We hiked back to the bridge and across to the car. For some reason, Charley was mad at me." He glanced at Charley again. "So we just went home. Me crusty with mud, him not saying a word. A three and a half hour drive and there was no one home when we got there. Just a note—your mother had gone into labor." He looked directly at Tom. "By the time I got to the hospital, you were several hours old. In fact, I looked at the birth time and figured back and guessed that you were born while I was stuck in that damn tree and Charley was sleeping in the brier bush."

Edward smiled at Tom and waited for him to respond. Ask, who loved family stories, was beaming. Cassie was asleep.

"So?" Charley said to Edward.

"Uh huh?" Edward said, still smiling.

"So? What does it mean?"

Edward couldn't decide what Charley was up to. He looked to Ask, then Tom, for help, finally to Jill, but she had her head down. "It doesn't mean anything," he said. "I was just thinking about old Squirrel."

"You always mean something," Charley said. "What does it mean?"

"Charley, I don't. I really don't." Edward shook his head.

"What does it mean? I get stuck in the brier bush, you in the tree, the tent's washed away, the stupid dog takes my shoe, all while Tom is being born. What am I supposed to make of that?"

"Charley, please," Jill said. She cradled her forehead in her palm. With her other hand, she brushed Cassie's cheek.

Edward pointed at Charley but spoke to Tom. "Sometimes I think he's stayed mad at me since that trip," he said. "I didn't understand it then, and I don't now."

Tom looked from his father to his mother and back to Edward. "You left Mom when she was that pregnant?" He could see Edward's face fall. He didn't ask why he'd worried about the tent while Charley was missing, or why he let Charley go off by himself in the first place. The whole story was full of mistakes. Had he heard this story before and never questioned it? Tom stood and put his hands in his pockets.

"What does the goddamn story mean?" Charley said.

"That we're a family," Ask said. He shoved his chair back from the table and opened his arms. "For chrissakes."

Charley glared at Ask, then his eyes softened. "Yeah," he said. "Of course. We're a family." He stood, turned his back to the table, and in swift, graceful motion threw his beer bottle over the breakfast bar and through the kitchen window. Glass sprayed onto the counters and into the sink. A ragged oval in the window let in the dark.

Charley walked out of the room and out the front door.

"You come back here," Edward yelled.

The breaking glass and yelling woke Cassie. She rubbed her

face. "Did I miss something?" No one said anything. "You guys never wake me for the good stuff."

Tom sat again. "Charley got mad," he said.

"Oh, *that.*" Cassie lay back in her mother's lap.

"I don't know what's gotten into him." Edward stood, and as he stood he felt an intense burning in his chest. The sandwich, he thought, the Seven and Seven. It felt like a comet had fallen into him and lodged. He held himself rigid. The comet burned, sizzled. When the pain subsided, he walked to the front window and parted the curtains. He looked out into the night for his son.

TOM MOTIONED TO ASK with his head. "Let's go get Charley."

"He likes to walk by himself," he said.

"Since when?"

"Ask is right," Jill said. She looked through the kitchen doorway at Edward peeking out the window. "Your father will sleep it off. Charley walks it off."

As Tom stared at her, the room stretched out of shape, asymmetrical and foreign. Even the kitchen chairs cast strange shadows. But she was normal, calm, bent over the table as she ate to keep crumbs off Cassie. Why was he the only one who felt an urgency to act? Had he been so unhappy at school he'd forgotten the family problems, or had something happened while he was gone?

"Was it like this before I left?" he asked.

"Charley just lost his temper." Ask put his dish in the sink and came back to the table. "Forget it. We'll patch everything in the morning." He put his hand on the back of Tom's chair. "I got my hair cut," he said.

"I noticed." He had probably wanted to cut it months ago, Tom thought, but waited until Tom cut his. He never gave in on anything.

"Tonight's a particularly bad night," Jill said. "For some reason, your brother believes your father is a son of a bitch." She took another small bite of her sandwich. "I don't think any longer it's something he'll grow out of. Nothing's changed, except in degree." She put her hand on Cassie's head and ran her fingers through the blond hair. Tom remembered that she used to do the same with Ask and him, and how much they enjoyed it. He tried to remember a moment like that with his father—they'd played catch; they had listened to the Cardinals on the radio.

His brother leaned on the back of his chair, waiting for a comment on his haircut. His mother smiled at Cassie, her lip turning up. His father stood in the other room by the window, smoking a cigarette. *As if nothing happened,* Tom thought, and he could believe nothing had happened except for the window, the reflection of the kitchen distorted by cracks, invaded by a black oval. And the fist in his stomach, the throb in his temples.

"I let him trim the sides back a little too much," Ask said. "Otherwise, I'm happy with it."

"Doesn't this upset you?" Tom looked from Ask to his mother. "Shouldn't we do something? It's like something's come loose."

"No, it isn't," Ask said. "Dad told a story, Charley got mad, and I got a haircut. We'll remember the story, tape cardboard over the window, and decide whether I look good or not."

"You look fine," Tom said.

"Good," Ask said. "I've got cardboard in my room." His shoulder scraped against the doorway as he left.

"I wanted to throw Charley out." Jill lifted her head, still smiling. "That surprises you, doesn't it? Your father wouldn't hear of it. Besides, Cassie would have a fit. Ask would fight it. And you. Tom, I don't know what you would do."

"It's not my decision, is it? One brother can't decide whether the other can stay." He put his hands to his eyes. He tried to remember home as it had been: Charley got angry, but his anger had fit. The anger tonight didn't fit. "Is he a son of a bitch?" Tom said.

"Your father?" She stared again at Edward in the family room, still at the front window, hands on the curtains. "I don't think so. But I'm not Charley. What it is between them that causes all this, I don't know. Maybe it was something silly to start with, random."

She lifted Cassie upright in her chair. "Charley will be home. Maybe you can talk with him." She thought of her brother, how he never came home. How some men survived the war and others died or disappeared, how much chance laid waste to plans. "You know, we named you after my brother."

"I know," he said. "The soldier. What does that have to do with Charley?"

Jill shrugged. "I don't know why I brought it up. If you don't want to see Marriet, it's okay."

"I said I would. I don't mind. I'd like to meet her."

"I just want you to be happy," Jill said. She shook Cassie gently to wake her.

"There's a face in my soup," Cassie said, opening her eyes.

Jill shook her again. "Wake up enough to get to bed."

TOM SAT at the kitchen table a long time, eating, then reading. His father came in and inspected the broken window. He assured Tom it would be no trouble to fix. Ask taped a flat of cardboard over the hole in the window and cleaned the glass from around the sink. "I thought you'd have this done by now," he said, depositing the shards of glass in the garbage. "You live here, you know." He came in twice more for water, obviously looking for Charley, who didn't get home until after midnight. Everyone but Tom was in bed.

Charley walked into the kitchen swinging his arms, taking long loping steps. "What are you doing here?" he said and sat next to Tom.

"I'm not sleepy," Tom said.

"No, what are you doing *here*? How come you couldn't make it up there?" He put both his elbows on the table and leaned against them.

Tom didn't want to talk about himself. He wanted to find out what was going on in the family, give himself a reference point in order to make sense of the evening.

"Who knows?" he said.

"*You* know. Tell me. You were out of here. You were gone. Why on earth did you come back?"

"You came back. After your divorce."

Charley was startled for an instant. "My wife left me." He dropped his chin into his hands.

"I don't want to argue with you, Charley." Tom felt he had left chaos in California and returned to chaos in Arizona. Charley was the last person he could talk to about dropping out of college.

"I didn't have any choice," Charley said. "I was broke. I was torn up."

Their mother wanted to throw him out, Tom remembered. He considered telling Charley. "You've got a job now. Why don't you move?"

"It's not that simple. What difference does it make whether I'm here or across town?" He scooted away from the table. "I'm still here wherever I am. But you were out. You made a clean break. *Out.* Believe me, if I could get out clean, I'd be gone. I'd never come back." He jumped up from his chair and walked to the refrigerator.

"I don't know what you're talking about," Tom said.

"You're smart enough," Charley said. He took a beer from the refrigerator and pointed it toward the bedrooms. "They think Ask is the bright one. I've known all along it was you. Cassie knows it too. She told me. So it wasn't smarts. What was it?"

"I couldn't get adjusted. I couldn't dig in."

"Twelve weeks?" He twisted open the bottle. "You expect to dig in in twelve weeks?"

"I don't know."

"Yes, you do."

"I was lonely," Tom said. "My roommate was a jerk. The classes were oppressive. I caught a cold and got behind. I started sleeping all the time. *I don't know.* You may have all the answers but I don't. I couldn't hack it, so I quit."

"You were out." Charley pointed the bottle at him. Beer dribbled out and foamed on the floor. "It won't be so easy next time. I know. This family is a drug. And you're a junkie."

"They're just people," Tom said.

"Jesus," Charley said and dropped into a chair. He let his head fall to the table.

Tom tried to picture him as the little boy in the woods with the dog, sleeping in the brier bush. He couldn't make an image he could reconcile with the man in front of him. He realized it must have been Charley who left the letter from Eileen. Anyone else would have said something by now.

"You know anything about the letter in my room?"

"That bitch you used to go out with sent it," Charley said into his arm. He looked up. "I read it. Haven't you read it by now?"

"Yeah."

He dropped his face back to the table. "Good, wouldn't want to spoil it for you."

"How'd it get here?"

"I was at the drugstore." He raised his head again. "She cornered me."

"What about the picture from the bulletin board?"

"She's a cunt."

"What did you do with the picture?"

Charley took his wallet from his pants pocket and removed the photograph. "I thought you might want it back." He tossed it across the table. In the photograph, Tom and Eileen stood side by side, arms around the other's waist. The sun shone in their faces. Tom squinted, Eileen smiled. She was pretty, prettier, Tom knew, in the photograph than in reality.

He took the photograph and stood. "If you read my mail again, I'm going to punch you in the mouth."

Charley nodded. "Yeah, yeah. You going to see her?"

Tom had avoided thinking about that decision, but the answer suddenly seemed clear to him. "No," he said. "I'm not going to see her. I don't want to ever see her."

Charley stood beside him. "You really can use my car, you know. To see Shacterly. I'm going to bed."

Tom stopped him. "What makes you think I was out? If you could be across the country and not be out . . ."

"You're better than me," he said and walked to his bedroom.

Tom took the beer Charley had opened and walked to the bar. He still felt there was something that had to be done, that he had forgotten. Who would he side with if his mother tried to kick Charley out? What he hadn't said was that he would stay out of it. Not that he didn't care, but that he didn't think he earned a vote. He didn't want to deny Charley so much as he wanted to deny them all. The family dog, he thought, gets no vote.

"You're still up."

It was Ask, carrying the glass he kept on the desk beside his bed.

"Charley's home," Tom said. "He's gone to bed."

"I told you," Ask said. He turned around and walked out of the room, the water glass still in his hand.

5

WAITING FOR EILEEN, Charley sat beneath the awning at a corner table, stripping the label from a bottle of Budweiser and watching the happy hour crowd feel one another up—a hand on the waist, a pinch on the arm, one body brushing against the next. It looked ugly from his corner, but he was a master of happy hour talk and touch. It was the number of amateurs in the crowd that annoyed him. He had never been good at waiting; if his energy were visible, the table would be scarlet and light the corner as it poured out of him.

By the time Eileen arrived, he felt drained and awkward. She stepped from sunlight into the shadow of the awning and her blond hair washed dull as grass. Her face was solid, middle American. Charley believed that this was her beauty: strong, drab features, a sexy plainness.

"Over here," he called. She gave no flash of recognition but moved toward him in long even strides, weaving through the tables, the couples, completely separate from them, aloof, as if she were royalty.

"You look like hell," she said flatly and positioned a chair opposite him, settling into it by degrees, a slow collapse from knees to waist, waist to shoulders, finally rolling her head from side to side and resting her arms on the table.

"I thought I was stood up," he said, a lie she wouldn't acknowledge, staring at him impatiently, plaintively. "I thought you'd look pregnant by now," he offered and imagined her—dark and fleshy, growing, a part of her becoming someone else. Scraps of beer label littered the table like unfinished thoughts. They embarrassed him. He collected and wadded them in his fist. "I thought . . ."

"I feel fat," she said. "Even if I don't look it. Have you quit sleeping?"

Beneath his eyes were spoons of flesh; his lids were heavy and thick. He had studied his face that morning, as he did every morning, in the bathroom mirror, imagining that this was how he would look in twenty years, his face puffy and dark, his eyes just visible below their hoods.

"You really look awful," she said.

He drank from the bottle, throwing his head back, posturing—something to shut her up, to make her stop pretending she cared about him.

"Did you give Tom my letter?" she said.

He wiped his mouth with the back of his hand, a knuckle meshing with his parted lips—posturing again, a lie, but how was he supposed to act with her? She had moved so quickly from talking about him to talking about Tom, it had made him angry.

"He's not going to see you," he said.

"Is he mad at me?"

Now she was struggling, looking at her lap, rubbing the table with her palms, self-consciously calm, as phony as the happy hour crowd behind her. He liked seeing her shaken; it gave him the edge.

"He's got a date with someone else," he said, and she became visibly disturbed.

"You're lying. What did you say to him?"

"You're old news," he said. "Old married news."

"Stop it."

"I'm even letting him take the Firebird." Taking pleasure in meanness, he thought, was as natural as falling in love.

"You are not." She said the words so firmly, she startled them both. The couple at the next table turned and stared. Eileen touched her forehead and closed her eyes.

What if she miscarried, Charley thought. Weren't miscarriages brought on by worry? His mind lodged on the word miscarriage: to carry badly. He had never thought of her as a carrier, exactly. His wife had miscarried their son, and this thought led to a memory: sitting in the drugstore while Eileen wiped the counter, telling her how he'd cried at the hospital, how the baby—almost seven months along—should have lived, how tiny he had been.

"Hey," he called to a waitress a few tables away. He waved his arm. "Two beers," he said.

"One," Eileen said and turned to the waitress. "Just one." She looked again at Charley. "I'm pregnant, remember?"

"I won't let him have the Firebird," he said. Any pleasure he'd taken in tormenting her was gone. He shifted his weight forward, elbows on the table, and tried to change the subject. "His last chance though. I'm trading the Firebird tomorrow. Tonight, if Tom's not taking it."

"He's not."

"What's so great about Tom?" Charley said.

"You love Tom," she said. "We both do."

It wasn't Tom he was after, he thought. None of this was meant to hurt Tom. But his motives were too difficult to explain, sometimes too difficult even for him to keep straight.

"I've already made the deal on the Firebird," he said. "I'm getting a VW bus, an old transporter, no windows." She had no interest in the bus, he thought, no interest in him. "You can come with me if you want," he said.

"You're insulting."

"Because I want you with me?"

"You don't want me. You want whatever will hurt your family."

"No," he said. "That's not it."

The beer arrived. Eileen smiled at the waitress, told her she wanted nothing. He liked the way she handled it, glad she didn't order soda water or juice to have something to hide behind. She was exceptional.

"I just want out," he said and drank from the bottle.

"Walk away. Get an apartment near the warehouse. Forget your family."

"Could you do that?"

"I don't want to do that. I like my family. I like *your* family, for that matter." She locked her fingers together on the table. "You're the sick one."

"Don't be a bitch."

She reached across the table to slap him, but he leaned away. She swiped at the air.

"I'm sorry," he said, hands raised. "You see how I am? I have to get out of there. I can't even sleep."

"You look like hell."

"I should have left before Tom came back. I should have known I couldn't be in the same house."

"Why won't he see me?"

"You betrayed him," he said, thinking, *You betrayed us both.*

"Yes," she said, her voice just audible. "All right." She touched her chest just above her heart with her fingertips. "You're terrible," she said.

"What does that make you?"

He had taken her to bed two weeks after Tom left for Berkeley. He'd begun by going to the drugstore daily to see her, talk, relay information about Tom. At some point, he talked about himself, his view of their family which she found so different from her own, his marriage, his divorce. He took her to lunch. He took her dancing. He took her to bed.

She had disowned their lovemaking, as if there had been someone else in the bed, and she had just watched. Then she cried and said it was terrible, but slept with him again, several times, denying each time that it meant anything. She wrote long letters to Tom, threw them away, wrote again. "Marry me," Charley had said. "I'm the one, not him." When they discovered she was pregnant, he thought she would agree. Instead, she refused to see him at all. He'd expected her to get an abortion and still didn't understand why she hadn't, why she'd married Sam Crawford, whom she referred to as a buddy.

Now, sitting at the table across from her, he wished he had told her everything—why he hated his father, how long it had been going on, how perfect the payback would be if she'd marry him. "Think of the symmetry," he'd have said. Didn't everyone love symmetry?

"What are you going to do?" Eileen said.

"I'm getting the van to stay in until I can find a place to live," he said and began peeling off the new label. "I'm going to work tomorrow—hell, I may do it now—and I'm telling Arnsburger to fuck off, punch him if I feel like it. Then I'm getting out. Somewhere in the East. I'm not sure. I'll write you."

"I thought you liked Arnsburger."

"Friend of the family. Used to teach with my father. That's the point. I tell him to jump, then disappear. Can't go back to the job or the house. Sleep in the van. Get free."

"That's a stupid plan. Just get an apartment."

"Won't work."

"You're a jerk."

"Yes. I look like hell and I'm a jerk. Get it in while you can because you'll never see my face again. I'm going to be out of here, and I'm getting out clean. No fight with the old man, no indication of where I'm going. Let the son of a bitch fret. I'll be gone. No job to come back to. No family wanting me back. That was my problem last time, while I was married, seeing Tom and Ask and Cassie. No more."

"Arnsburger isn't that important to your family," she said.

"Tom is."

"He'll forgive you," she said. "I have to tell him. But he'll forgive you."

"Maybe," Charley said. "But they won't. Not Father, not Mother, not even Ask."

"What about Cassie?"

Charley drank again. "I'll talk to her before I go. I'll explain." He leaned across the table, whispered. "Want to know something? The iris of my father's eyes are not round."

"Of course they are," she said.

He stuck his hand in her face, extending his little finger. "This fingernail, flattened out on one side. That shape. You don't notice it, but they are." He sat back in his chair, pulled at the collar of his shirt. "Reason enough to hate the bastard. His blunted iris." He looked away. "Out of round like a bad tire."

"I only remember them being blue."

"Except for you"—he faced her again—"I don't look women in the eyes. If I move my hips, they don't even know I have eyes. Women love me, the stupid shits. I roll my shoulders, smile." He rolled his shoulders against the chair, smiled at Eileen. "Push the sleeves of my shirt up." He rubbed a hand against each forearm as if pushing up sleeves, although his sleeves were already rolled to the elbow. "Touch her cheek, her ribs." He thought of the happy hour amateurs, clumsy and cowardly.

"Stop it."

"I'm irresistible. Even you, Eileen." His eyes pinned her. "And you know why? Because you never really look at my eyes. The filthy brown fingernail floating in my eyes." He stared hard at her, watched her focus on his eyes. "Look too close at somebody and he gets ugly. Look at me and you see my father. I can't get rid of that easy. I can't just get an apartment and be free of that. Easy doesn't work. I have to burn bridges. Get out clean."

"Your eyes are just like anyone's," she said. "You just don't use them."

"Don't see Tom until I'm gone." Finally he said what he'd come to tell her. "I want to get away clean. Once I'm gone you can tell him, tell the whole world if you want."

Eileen dropped her stare to the table. "Doesn't sound like I'm going to see him at all. Who is this date of his?"

"Mom set him up. It doesn't mean anything. They're going bowling, I think."

"Who is it?"

"Shacterly."

"Marriet Shacterly?" She crossed her arms. "I never liked her."

"You don't know her."

"I don't need to."

"You won't come with me?" He pressed, knowing her answer, almost enjoying her refusal.

"No, Charley. I'm going to stay here and have our baby and get Tom back."

"You're the only woman I ever loved," he said.

"How many women have you said that to?"

He shrugged. "A few." He laughed. "I meant it every time. It's like the new one erases the others, and I wonder what got into me. How could I have thought I loved her? You know that feeling?"

"I've only loved your brother," she said.

"Then you fucked up," he said and pushed himself away from

the table, pausing a moment to give her a chance to stop him before standing and walking away.

6

AT THE LAST MINUTE, Charley withdrew his offer of the Firebird and drove away. Tom was relieved. The Firebird was too flashy, making promises he didn't know how to keep. Even worse, it was Charley's car and carried Charley's reputation with it. Being Charley's younger brother on a date was something like being Reggie Jackson's little brother on a baseball diamond, or so it seemed to Tom. The less he reminded Marriet that he was Charley's brother, the happier he was. Besides, the Ancient Mariner was messy. Cleaning it was a good way to kill an hour. He always gave himself more time to get ready for a date than he needed, then paced his room or the house until it was time to leave, often arriving early, a trait he discovered women disliked.

"So where are you going?" Ask had volunteered to help him clean out the old Impala wagon. He crawled into the back with a huge brown paper bag and began filling it with beer bottles and newspapers.

In the front seat, Tom crammed a tissue box into the glove compartment. "I'm going to take her to Stag and Hound to eat, then there's some group playing at Bozeman's. I thought we'd dance." The tissue box crumpled into the compartment. "Jesus, why do we need so many maps?"

"Mom sells real estate, remember? Put them under the seat."

"How can she show people around in this heap?" Tom shoved the maps under the seat. "What's this?" He removed a wad of material. "It's underwear." He held four pairs of panties.

"Cassie stashes them everywhere," Ask explained. "Mom says getting your period is traumatic for some girls. She's got three sweaters back here." He lifted the sweaters, matted into the shape of a rhomboid.

"I guess getting cold is traumatic too." Tom stuffed the panties back under the seat.

"So you think Stag and Hound is a good place to take someone on the first date?" Ask said.

"I had to get some money from Mom. It's expensive."

"What if you weren't old enough to drink?" Ask pushed the trash down inside the sack and moved to the backseat.

"We're both old enough to drink. She's older than I am."

"But what if you weren't?" Ask said. "You could take her to Stag and Hound, and then what?"

Tom stopped cleaning to face his little brother. "What's she like?" he said.

Ask shrugged and continued cleaning. "I was being hypothetical."

"If you weren't being hypothetical, what would the girl be like?"

Ask picked up a pair of Cassie's shoes from the floorboard, bending lower than necessary. "Just this girl from school," he said into the carpet.

"Take her to a movie," Tom said.

Ask quickly raised his head. "What if she doesn't like movies?"

"Find a girl who does." Tom ran a rag across the dashboard. "Everybody likes movies. She say she doesn't like movies?"

"I haven't completely talked to her yet." He tossed another beer bottle into the bag. "I haven't worked out a strategy."

"Try this." Tom leaned over the front seat close to his brother. "Keep an eye on her hair, then if it changes tell her it looks good. Girls like that. It means you're attentive."

"What if I don't like her hair? What if it's one of those punk cuts that look like shrubbery?"

"Doesn't matter. Another thing." Tom threw the dirty rag out the window. "Look at her eyes and think of something that looks like them."

"We're just going to have to pick that up," Ask said, staring at the rag on the lawn.

"If her eyes are blue, you could say they look like the sky."

Ask pried a Tootsie Roll Pop loose from the back of the seat. "You ever do that?"

Tom laughed. "Never. Too corny."

Ask hit him on the shoulder with one of Cassie's shoes.

"Charley's the ladies' man," Tom said. "Talk to him."

"I already did. He said to look right at her and when she looked back to smile and keep staring and do this." Ask nodded with his chest and waggled his head.

"Anything works for him," Tom said.

"I practiced for a week. She never even looked back at me."

"What's her name?"

"Julie. You think Cassie could help?"

"Only if you're willing to go to San Diego on the first date."

Ask laughed. "I'll be waiting up," he said, then pulled the sack of garbage and clothes from the car. He picked up the rag from the lawn and walked into the house.

Tom took the long way to Marriet's apartment and was still five minutes early. He drove around the block twice. Her apartment was part of a triplex across the street from a house his mother had just sold. "The one that looks like a mausoleum," she had said.

Marriet answered the door before the bell stopped sounding. "Hi, Tom." She stuck her arm straight out in one quick motion and gripped his hand firmly. "You remember me at all?"

Her hand was as cold as an Eskimo Pie. "Sure," Tom said. She was wearing designer jeans and a V-neck blue and gold blouse, but he saw her in the red sweater, schoolbooks pressed tight against her breasts, running across the schoolyard. It was unbelievable that he could be here with her now. "I'm surprised you remember me," he said.

"Of course I do." She grabbed her purse and stepped out onto the concrete porch. "Who could forget Charley Warren's little brother?" She walked past him toward the station wagon. "How is Charley?"

Tom's expectations fell so sharply, he could believe the thud was audible. "He's alive," he said, remembering Charley at the dinner table making snide comments about Marriet. He thought he might race to the car and drive off without her. Instead, he stuck his hands in his pockets and walked to the Ancient Mariner. "I didn't know you two were friends."

"Oh, we're not," Marriet said across the car roof. "But all the girls were in love with him. He's positively the cutest boy I ever saw." She jumped into the front seat.

Tom slammed the car door.

Halfway to the restaurant, Marriet apologized. "Forget that 'Oh Charley' stuff, okay?" She put her hand on his shoulder as he drove. "Sometimes I'm an asshole to avoid being nervous. I figure I may as well get in the first shot."

Tom couldn't decide whether she was sincere or not but nodded anyway. She pulled her hand away and put her fingers to her mouth, withdrew them, smiled. He hadn't expected her to be nervous.

"Charley was just one of the older boys who was handsome and dangerous." She put her hand back on his shoulder and tapped with her fingers. "I do remember you. You played basketball. Whitest legs on the team, very cute."

Tom was pleasantly embarrassed. He relaxed. She turned away from his gaze, but he could see her face reflected in the dark window, smiling. Her hair was pebble yellow. "What are you doing now?" he asked.

"Coagulating." She laughed. "I hate to say, 'Getting it together.' *Regrouping*—how's that? I've got a job with Sears in TVs and stereos. I was in LA for eight months. Awful experience." She flapped her hands in the air, then slipped them under her legs. "Fell in love with a piranha. Who was married, of course. Slept with my boss. All the basic mistakes, except getting pregnant. It's a shame in a way. I had the chance to be the perfect fool. Now, all my old friends are gone or cosmic assholes. I use that word too much, don't I? I have nothing against that part of the anatomy." She leaned closer to Tom. "You've got something on your face."

She picked at his cheek. "A black fleck of something. It was driving me crazy." She examined the fleck, then put her hand out the window and flicked her fingers. "What are you doing?" she asked.

"Getting it together," Tom said.

She laughed. "You are so hip."

A wooden bench rimmed the lounge at Stag and Hound. Tom and Marriet sat across from a family of redheads—two redhead little girls, an adolescent redhead boy, and redhead parents separated by a cigarette machine. The mother's hair was brassy, the father's, copper. Their children were various mixtures, strange alloys. Beside Tom, a teenage boy told bad jokes to his smiling date. Next to Marriet, a small man, whose ear was clenched shut like an angry mouth, held hands with a tall, heavy woman.

"He was a boxer," Marriet whispered to Tom as the little man and heavy woman left. "I heard them talking," she explained. "He was a bantamweight. Like a rooster. I saw a cockfight once. It was awful, but I couldn't look away."

"How did you wind up at a cockfight?"

"I wanted to see one." Her nostrils flared when she spoke. "I guess I thought it would be sexy." She laughed.

Early in the meal, Tom realized he was infatuated with her. Her voice reminded him of a marimba. He enjoyed listening to her talk, watching her eat. She told him that she'd tried a hundred diets and none of them worked.

"Nothing on earth can change my weight," she said. She put her fingers to her mouth, then curled her hand and lowered it to her lap.

Tom considered reaching across the table to hold her hand, but neither of them was visible. He wasn't ready to be that bold anyway.

"You look perfect," he said.

She glanced at her lap, her hands. "I guess I was fishing for that. But that's sweet of you." She drank from her water glass. "I wanted to be model-skinny. I'm over that. You remember my hair? Peroxide Shacterly? I cut that out too."

Tom thought she might be looking for another compliment. He couldn't say he liked her hair better now because he didn't remember her hair as it was in high school. What he remembered was the red sweater, the books pressed tight against her breasts. Already, he liked the woman across the table from him better than the high school girl in his memory.

When the bill came, Marriet insisted on paying half. She pressed so hard, he began to think that she was just interested in him as a friend. "It's one of my quirks," she said and took his arm as they left the restaurant.

He managed to find a table at Bozeman's that faced the Cuban Missiles, a "new wave bop" band from Phoenix. The bar was one huge room packed with little, round tables. A small dance floor and a haze of cigarette smoke separated the Missiles from the tables. Red and yellow lights lit the band, but the rest of the bar was dark, so dark the far walls were invisible.

"Budweiser," Tom called out to the waitress. The band had just begun playing. He had to yell. "And a screwdriver."

The waitress, a chunky woman chewing gum, shook her head at Tom. She leaned over and yelled. "Tap beer only. Pabst," she spit in his ear. "Okay?"

He nodded.

"Screwdriver and a Pabst," she spit again and left.

"They look Third World, don't they?" Marriet said, nodding toward the band.

"What?" he said.

"Third World," she said. "The band."

The three band members were grotesquely thin but very neatly dressed. "More like emaciated choirboys," he said.

"Huh?"

Tom shook his head. "Unimportant," he yelled. "You like this kind of music?"

"This music?" Marriet said.

Tom nodded.

"Yeah," she said. "It's good to dance to."

"Dance?" Tom said.

"What?"

He shook her off, smiled. The waitress returned with two plastic glasses. "Screwdriver and Pabst." His beer bubbled where her spit landed. "Three fifty."

Marriet paid the waitress before he could get his wallet. She smiled at him. "They don't serve anything in glass," she said.

"What?"

She pointed to the plastic. "No glass. No bottles." She acted as if she were going to hit Tom over the head. "Too much fighting."

He smiled, nodded. He could taste cigarette smoke in his beer. His eyes burned. The Cuban Missiles were singing, "Nuclear hammers, nuclear nails, put nuclear hardware in nuclear jails."

Sitting without talking was too uncomfortable. He motioned toward the dance floor. She nodded, gulped her drink, and they danced through the entire first set.

Tom believed he was a pretty good dancer. He and Ask used to play records in their room and practice dance steps. He still liked to watch "American Bandstand." When he felt loose, he could get lost in the music, let his body find a rhythm of its own and keep him moving, surprising him with a sudden spin or kick. Marriet was much more polished. She knew specific steps and had set gyrations and hand movements.

They drank a plastic pitcher of beer between them before the second set began. "You're a wild dancer," she told him. She ran her hand across his forehead to clear the sweat.

The second set became an endurance test. The floor filled and they found themselves in a dark corner near the band. Tom began jumping and shaking his head. Marriet jumped with him, hopping from foot to foot, shifting her weight. He lost himself in the movement. He no longer felt tired. In fact, he felt weightless, as if the music alone were holding him up and at the same time holding him, just barely, to the earth. When the second set ended, his shirt and hair were drenched with sweat. Marriet fell back against the wall and motioned to him. A ring of sweat stretched from her neck to her breasts. She pulled him by the collar to whisper in his ear.

"I'm going to show you something very ugly," she said.

Her face angled up at him, mouth slightly open, hair wet with sweat. He kissed her, and although he'd planned just to brush across her lips, he kissed her hard and touched her tongue with his. He straightened and lifted his head. "What are you going to show me?"

She lifted her right hand to his face. The fingers were stubby, nails chewed to the quick. "I used to hide my fingers," she said. "In my pockets, behind my back, on a boy's shoulder or neck. There are a thousand ways. Boys aren't so observant." She pushed herself away from the wall, put her arms around Tom's neck, and kissed him again. "I'm not going to hide them anymore," she said.

He took her wrist and lifted her hand. She flashed the V for victory sign.

He laughed and gave her a hand sign in return, the "horns," holding down his middle two fingers with his thumb.

She flipped him the bird. He stuck his thumb out as if to hitchhike. She put her thumb to her nose and wriggled her fingers. He flipped his fingers up from his chin toward her. She pinched her fingers together and kissed them, then twisted them out. Desperate, Tom picked his nose.

"Let me. Let me," Marriet said and stuck her little finger in his nostril.

THE COUCH in Marriet's apartment was blue with tiny white stars. It looked new. Tom sat at one end of it while Marriet went into the kitchen for water. An old rolltop desk against the adjoining wall was the only other piece of furniture in the room. There was not even a chair for the desk. The walls were blank. There was no clutter, no magazines or clothes strewn about, no knickknacks, no television, no radio or stereo.

"Water," Marriet said, walking into the room with two tall jars of ice water, "is the best way to avoid a hangover. I hate hangovers."

"I knew a guy who took aspirin before bed," Tom said as he took the clear jar from her. "I told him once that it had to be psychosomatic, that aspirin couldn't be working eight or ten hours later when he woke. He said, 'So?' He didn't care why it worked, as long as he didn't wake with a hangover."

"The why of things always catches up with you, I think." She leaned against the wall opposite the couch. "You look good sitting. Some people look great standing but their bellies stick out or their legs get flabby when they sit. You ever notice that?"

Tom smiled, shook his head, drank from the jar.

"That sounded silly, didn't it? I'm getting nervous again. I have an overwhelming desire to chew my nails. It's such a moronic response. Why do you think people chew their nails when they're nervous?"

"Why are you nervous now?" He wanted to set the water down. There was no table. The gray carpet looked too lumpy.

She smiled, stepped over to the couch, and sat beside him. "I like you," she said. "That makes me nervous. Very."

"I'm a little nervous too."

"Does that mean you like me too?"

"Yeah, that and I'm worried that I'm going to spill this water."

She laughed and took the jar from him. "I've been meaning to get a coffee table. And glasses." She began walking to the kitchen.

He followed. There was a tiny table opposite the sink, two straight-back chairs, a stove, a refrigerator.

"You just move in?" he said.

She set the jars on the counter beside the sink. Hers was still full. "Everybody says that," she replied. "I decided to cut myself off from the clutter. I wanted to become someone new. You ever have that feeling?" She leaned against the sink, crossing her arms. "I had stuffed animals that I took to LA with me. Can you believe that? And ceramic figures, monkeys mostly. A postcard collection. You name it."

"What did you do with all of it?"

"I left it in LA. I'm trying to be more careful this time. That's why I'm drinking out of jars. I can't find the glasses that are right for me. The new me."

Tom laughed.

She punched him in the arm. "I did buy a couch. You like my couch?" She began walking to it. "I looked at a hundred couches." She plopped down on one end.

Tom sat beside her, kissed her.

"One of the things I've been working on," she said, pulling away slightly, "is being open. Forthright. That's why I told you that I liked you. I used to always wait, hoping the boy would say it first."

Tom kissed her again. She pushed him gently away. Her nostrils flared, but she said nothing. "Wheels are turning," he said.

"What if I wanted an agreement," she said, "just something between reasonable people, about us, not that we're an 'us' yet. Wait a minute. Let me get this right. I'm just trying to be forthright." She twisted on the couch, put her hand on Tom's knee. "What would you think if we made a deal before we go to bed?"

"What do you mean?" he said. The word "bed" had startled him.

Marriet chewed her nails and looked to her rolltop desk. "People have different ideas of what's expected. Wait." She stood, walked to the desk, lifted the rolltop an inch, then turned back. "I'd better explain first," she said, jerking her hand from her mouth. She sat next to him again. Her hand went back to her mouth. Her eyes were watery. She slipped her hands under her legs.

"I've worked up a contract," she said. "For lovers."

Tom just stared, waited. He wanted to think this was a joke, but he could see it wasn't. His blank face seemed to disturb her.

"It sounds crazy, I guess." She began to stand, then resettled on the couch, leaned back, sat up straight, her hands on her knees. "It's just something where we agree to call one another, to spend the night if we have sex." She stood again, took a step toward the desk. "It protects you too." She stared at him, and he realized that she was about to cry. "Wait," she said and held up her two hands, open, flat.

At that moment, Tom wanted more than anything to be out of the apartment. Desire left him so quickly, he felt the void in stomach and limbs, a hollow pain.

"You don't know exactly what I want," she said and sat next to him again. "I mean, this is just saying we'll be nice to each other." His blank face seemed to panic her again. "It's not *legal* or anything. Not a commitment, exactly." She began crying. "This is a modern approach."

Tom touched her arm. She pushed it away and stood.

"Maybe we're going too fast," he said, and stood beside her but a step closer to the door. "Maybe I should go."

She looked quickly around the room as if she were taking inventory, but there was only the desk, the couch. "Please leave," she said and wiped her eyes. "Please leave. Leave."

"We could talk. I could stay and we could talk." He saw on the desk a single sheet of paper, typewritten. "Or later. We could talk."

"Get out," she said calmly and walked into her bedroom. She closed the door. Tom heard the click of the lock.

7

THE FASHION MODELS in *Vogue* would not permit Cassie to clean her room. That morning the librarian's assistant at school, a heavy-set woman with a too curly perm and braces, had said that Cassie could be a model. "You're so tall," she said. "And slender. And you have such a pretty smile." The woman had rolled a magazine into a tube while she spoke. "Models have the best clothes. You could be one," she said, wringing the magazine until it tore.

The models in *Vogue* let Cassie know otherwise. They stared out of their pages, not quite at her but just past her, at something elegant and sophisticated. They were so perfect looking, so distant from any human she knew. Makeup and diets, lighting and air brushing couldn't account for the differences. She decided the librarian's assistant was wrong—none of these women smiled, anyway, except the ones in kitchens who weren't fashion models but real women making advertisements.

She tried to look at the clothes without looking at the models, but it was they who interested her, who glued her to the couch and kept her turning the pages. She was supposed to be cleaning her room. Charley had withdrawn the Firebird after promising Tom, making his date less romantic and forcing Tom and Ask to clean the Ancient Mariner, which resulted in Ask's dumping a sack full of clothes in her room, which led to an ultimatum from her mother to clean the room or be grounded for a week.

"*Sieg heil,*" Cassie had said, snapping her heels together and raising her arm. Her mother hadn't seen the humor in it. If her room wasn't clean by morning, she would be grounded a full month.

Cassie began to think of all the ways her family made her look bad: Ask was impossible to please so everyone found out she couldn't make icing, her father was so long-winded she couldn't stay awake during his stories so everyone thought she was rude, her mother hated to drive so she always had to go along even if it was during her brother's homecoming, Tom slept so late every day they made a big deal if she slept later on Saturdays, her mother was a clean freak so she looked messy in comparison.

Charley interrupted her list of grievances. He walked in the front door smiling, sat beside her on the couch, and whispered in her ear. "I bought a new vehicle."

"Another one?" She was mad at him and didn't want to sound encouraging or interested. She closed the magazine and let it drop to the floor.

Charley motioned for her to come with him.

"I can't go. I've got to clean my room because you wouldn't let Tom take your stupid Firebird," she said. "I always have to pay for others' mistakes."

"I'll help you clean," Charley said. "Come on. I've got news."

"All right." She knew Charley's offer was honest but worthless. He liked to talk to her about things. She liked to listen. She had been the first to know about his engagement and about his divorce. She was the kind of person people told things to. No one ever told anything to a model, she guessed. They were the kind of people others just looked at and wondered about. Why would anyone even want to be a model?

The van was old but handsome, all white and no windows on the sides except those next to the front seats. It looked like an elephant without a trunk. She thought she could make this into a joke, since cars didn't look like elephants but had trunks. A joke was in there somewhere but she didn't have the mind for it. Ask could have made it into one. Tom might even have made it into a funny one.

She sat in the passenger seat next to Charley and stared back into the rear. "It's like a tunnel in there," she said, twisting in the seat. The back part of the van was covered with gold shag carpeting and wood paneling.

"It was a florist's van." He turned the ignition. "For delivering flowers. Some kid bought it and fixed it up but got busted for dope. I got it cheap." He shifted into first, eased away from the curb.

"This car doesn't seem like you," she said.

Usually he accelerated fast enough to leave marks, especially when they were in front of their house. He called it laying rubber. The term had some strange sexual meaning, she was sure, but she didn't know what. That was the thing about her brothers, and especially Charley—no matter how much she found out about sex, they would say or do something that indicated there were other parts she hadn't even imagined. Ask had said he wasn't going to be a "lay person," which sounded either commendable or prudish and she didn't know which. Once she had heard Tom talking about "blowjobs," and she couldn't imagine what blowing on a penis would do, although she pictured the boy inflating like a raft.

With Charley, it was more the way he moved around girls, the way he looked at them as if he knew what they were thinking, how he would be walking and Cassie would just see her brother walking, but if one of his girl friends was there, that girl would see something else and her face would flatten and flush and she'd have to move all her limbs. If they were even half-decent brothers, they'd just tell her the secrets and get it over with. She was good at keeping secrets.

The engine made a putt-putt noise as they slowed for the corner. "This car doesn't seem like you," she said again.

"It's not a car. It's a van," he said.

"This van doesn't . . ."

"Or you can call it a bus, a VW bus." He checked the mirror and wheeled around the corner.

"Charley."

"I'm leaving, Cass," he said.

"Not again." She was bored with Charley's routines.

"I'm going to live in this van. Go east. New York, I think. I already quit my job. I made a special trip to tell Arnsburger to bite it. By the time anyone misses me Saturday, I'll be hundreds of miles away."

"Stop it, Charley. It won't work. You'll come back."

"I'm cutting myself off."

"You'll still come back."

"There'll be other news." He shifted gears. "I can't come back. If there was a way I could see you and not the rest, I'd do it."

She was suddenly scared. "What about Ask and Tom, at least?"

"That was my mistake last time. I shouldn't have let them

come over. They're too tied to him. You have to promise to keep all this to yourself. I'm not telling anyone but you."

She crossed her arms, frightened but indignant. "I'm no snitch. What other news?"

He shrugged. "You'll hear soon enough. I don't want a blowup before I leave. I'm getting away clean, with him worrying and me free not to think about it or about what I should have said." He turned at the corner to circle the block.

"Him who?" she said, although she was sure he meant their father.

"Because if we have an argument, and I can't think of the right thing to say, I'd think of it an hour later, and then I'd have to turn around and come back and say it. Then we'd have another argument and there you go. I've got to do something big enough to erase the old arguments and then vanish before we can argue again—this will do it. For sure. It has to work, or it'll take something even bigger. You understand?" He looked over at her. "It's like getting a new life."

"What's wrong with your old life? The one where I'm your sister?"

"You'll still be my sister. Don't get stupid about it."

White stucco houses, neat and tidy, lined the street, one almost exactly like the next. She'd always wished they had a house like everyone else's in the neighborhood. But they had to have the one weird house, so old it was sinking on one end like a leaky ship.

"You're deserting the ship," she told Charley as they pulled up to the house.

He stopped the van and killed the engine. "This is like my own little ship."

"It looks more like an elephant. Without the trunk, which most cars have. Which makes it funny." She knew she couldn't make it into a joke.

"Uh huh," he said.

"Oh, Charley, why don't you just make friends with Dad and forget about it? He never did anything to you he didn't do to the rest of us. He's just so . . . *him,* so Dad-like, which is annoying. But he is our father. We came from his blood or sperms or however it works." On their lawn, the garden hose looped around a tree and squiggled across the yard like part of a foreign alphabet. "I know," she said. "We should get a dog. A puppy." She surprised herself with this idea. It seemed like the perfect thing. She and the boys could play with it and their dad could tell stories about it.

"You can have anything you want from my room. Just don't tell anyone," Charley said. Headlights flared, lighting the inside of the van. "Especially Ask."

"I never tell him anything, anyway," she said and tried to think of another way she could bring up the idea of getting a dog. The Ancient Mariner pulled into the driveway, disturbing her concentration. "Do you think Tom fell in love?" she said. She watched him put the car in park and open the door, trying to see if there was any visible change in him, a telltale gesture that would give him away.

"It's only midnight," Charley said. "You don't fall in love before one."

"Midnight?" She panicked. "You've got to help me with my room."

"I will. Let me take Tom for a spin first."

"No."

"One little drive. I may never see him again."

"Tom," she called out the van window, stretching his name into two syllables.

"Whose is this?" Tom said.

"If you don't help me, I'll be grounded for a month." She leaped out of the van and grabbed his elbow.

Ask, who had been waiting for Tom to get home, stepped out of the house.

"Take you both for a ride," Charley said. "How was the date?"

"What about my room?" Cassie said.

"It was okay," Tom said. "More or less."

"More or less?" Ask said.

"More?" Charley said. "Or less?"

"I don't want to talk about it," Tom said, climbing into the van.

"Definitely less," Charley said.

There they went again with the talk she almost understood. "My room," she said. "Charley, you promised."

He started the engine. Ask climbed in after Tom. "You can begin without me," Charley said. "We'll be right back."

Cassie slapped her legs as they drove away. Each of them would have to drive it and talk about its bearings and grease sockets and other stupid car things. She trudged into the house, through the hall to her room. She hated the idea of cleaning as much as the actual act. Rooms were a means of expression, free-form art. Her mother had no imagination.

She scooped up mounds of clothing and stuffed them into the closet. As she began the specific work of cleaning, she became less worried, although it was clear she had no chance of finishing before morning. The fact of doing something made it less scary.

One thing Charley had said disturbed her. Not the part about leaving. He was always telling her how he needed to get away, to become somebody else, like he was a pod from another planet about to go body snatching. Once he'd even told her that his marriage was just a way to get free of the family. He couldn't explain why in terms she really understood. The words she could understand, but what they meant to him was a mystery.

The disturbing part was when he said that there would be other news that would keep him from coming back. She liked having Charley around, even though he was mostly mean. She should be riding in the van with him right now. She might never see him again, all because her mother had a fixation on cleanliness. She pushed against a wall of clothing, then leaned on it, sliding down to a reclining position.

A sweater from the top of the pile fell into her lap. Charley had given her the sweater. It was wool with a low neckline. Some girl had left it in one of his cars. She rolled it into a ball and put it beneath her head. She thought of the slides her Humanities teacher had shown last week. He had set up a little screen, then turned off the lights, scurrying around, talking about art. The slides were of paintings and they were pretty, but when she looked at them she just saw what was there—people and animals and ships, the ocean, a field, some old buildings. The teacher kept insisting other things were there, meaningful things about the way people lived and what happened when you died. She had gone to the school library that morning to look at the paintings in a book, but the librarian's assistant had distracted her, saying she could be a model.

She wished she had found the book. She imagined the paintings, remembering some of them in detail, and imagined the artist with brushes and a beret standing in front of an easel. He began painting, in her imagination, the inside of a house, the furniture and plumbing, a towel on the bathroom floor, a red skirt draped across a rocker, a dog sleeping on her back beneath the kitchen table. Then he painted the outside of the house, wooden planks and a tile roof, a long porch with white columns. He painted over the inside until it was completely covered although still there, invisible. Cassie felt a small rush of excitement and anticipation, believing she was close to discovering something about the paintings or about her brothers or about being a model. She could feel her body tingle first with knowledge and then with sleep as the house became an image in a dream, and the painter, the dreamer.

8

IN JILL'S DREAM, she sat at the kitchen table drinking coffee, listening to jazz (it might have been Charlie Parker, definitely a saxophone). Sunlight poured through the windows, reflected off the walls and floor, shimmered along the table. A car pulled into the driveway. She could see it clearly, as if she were looking across no distance at all. It was an old car with rounded edges, not like the new ones, corners so sharp they could tear skin. An old car with an elaborate chrome bumper, dark green paint—the color, even the approximate shape of an avocado.

A man climbed out of the car, a young man in uniform, smiling. She set her coffee down. He pulled a duffel bag from the passenger side. Handsome, smiling. At first she thought it might be Edward, as he had been when he'd stepped from the train years ago. But it wasn't Edward. A vibration began just beneath her sternum. "Tom," she called out. "Tommy." Her brother Tom, home finally. "Tom," she called again. He opened his arms. She ran to him, the dream collapsing just before they touched.

She woke disoriented, suspended between the world of the dream and the world of consequence, drifting momentarily before accepting the blue sheets, the icy plaster ceiling, her snoring husband. The dream was quickly displaced by a memory: she and Edward at Kentucky Lake, the sky overcast and low, Charley only two and a half in tiny red trunks running across the beach, falling, running, falling again, laughing, covered with sand. "He's a pistol," Edward says, not to her. They're with friends, another couple, childless but trying. "He's darling," the woman says. Edward says, "He's all boy." The man, holding hands now with his wife, says, "Good coordination for being so young."

Why had this memory suddenly returned? A Sunday more than two decades ago, a trip to the lake ruined eventually by the weather and short tempers. The rain forced them inside a tavern. The men drank too much. She remembered how their friend ordered when the waitress came to their table. "Redeye," he said, pointing to his chest, then at Edward. "Redeye," he said again. He pointed at Jill and his wife. "Clear eye, clear eye," he said and laughed as if he'd said something terribly funny. The rain clinked against the window, Charley fell asleep, and she and the other woman talked about a boy they had gone to school with who had come back from Korea missing part of an ear, how he would still be a handsome man if it weren't for that flap of skin where his ear should be. "Looks like a seashell," the woman had said.

Jill could hear her voice and taste the cheap red wine that the tavern had served chilled. But she couldn't place the couple, couldn't quite see them. Who were they? How were they friends? The man and Edward began arguing about something foolish—clothes, what clothes meant, and that led to personality, what kind of personality was trustworthy. At some point Edward had stood and said, "I want nothing to do with you," and the man yelled something back. She and the woman had been talking quietly, occasionally making a funny remark to ease the tension. Once the men started yelling, the woman had turned to Jill and said, "I despise you. You and your prissy boy."

Why this memory had suddenly come to her, she couldn't say, but what baffled her were the inconsistencies, how she could remember the woman's voice, the taste of the wine, but not her face or name; how she could remember their conversation about the boy's ear but had no clear recollection of how the men had become angry or why her friend had turned against her. She rose and dressed, leaving the dream, the memory, and her husband asleep in the bed.

She no longer bothered with a big breakfast on Saturdays. Charley either worked early or slept late. Cassie always slept late. Ask rose before she did, cooked his own meal, ate, and cleaned so thoroughly afterward that the sparkling sink was the only sign he'd eaten. Tom didn't eat breakfast food. If he was hungry, he would drive to the A & W and buy a cheeseburger. Edward enjoyed breakfast, but he could fend for himself.

She picked two oranges from the tree in the backyard, put bread in the toaster, sliced cheese. Her favorite breakfast: fresh-squeezed orange juice and a sharp Cheddar cheese and honey sandwich. She wondered if Tom was up, wanted to talk to him, find out about his date without prying, at least without seeming to pry.

She liked Marriet and could tell they would be good together. She wished she could take control, tell them to marry, have children, get on with it. Unfinished things made her tense. A tenseness she could sometimes enjoy but not today.

Sunlight glinted off the aluminum toaster, recalling the kitchen as it had been in her dream. It had been a pleasant dream, but reminded her of that great unfinished part of her life. She thought she should go to Africa where her brother died, to stand there and feel the finality that was missing because there had been no body. She needed a feeling of completion, but her life kept tossing things up in the air while she held her breath and waited for the thuds.

The gate to the backyard rattled. She took the last bite of her sandwich and stepped to the window. Tom and Ask faced each other, walking aimlessly. Tom's hair was misparted and stood out in places. Ask's hair was still wet from the shower, looked shorter wet than it had when he'd returned from the barber. Tom was barefoot, in jeans and T-shirt. Ask's shirt was ironed, buttoned to the collar. To a stranger they might have seemed like an unusual pair, unlikely brothers.

She opened the window to invite them in to hear about Tom's date, but she heard part of their conversation and was too startled and embarrassed to call.

"Fucking is too big," Tom was saying. He spread his arms as if to include the whole world. "I wasn't sure I wanted to anyway. Not right then, the first time we've ever even spoken to one another."

She thought she should close the window, but it might draw their attention. They would think she had been eavesdropping.

"You liked her, though. You said she was nice." Ask swept his shoe over the grass, hands in his pockets. "Maybe she just wanted insurance."

If they were younger, she could just call out to them, ask them what was going on. She should leave the room, or call to Tom as she'd planned, pretending she'd heard nothing.

"Some things have to be *understood*." Tom pivoted, facing the window. "Would you want a girl to sign a contract agreeing to like you, no matter what?"

"Sure." Ask moved to keep facing him. They walked in circles. "It'd be great."

Tom laughed, a low laugh from his chest, an adult laugh, she thought. "We could make a contract for Dad: no stories at dinner," he said.

"I like his stories. The contract would be for Charley to quit acting like he's mad all the time."

"Acting? That was no act."

"Why do you keep going on about that? We fixed the window," Ask said. Jill ducked out of the window. "He's only human," he added.

"He's *barely* human," Tom said.

She stepped back to the window, flustered and almost out of breath. As she began again to call them, they spoke again and she listened.

"We could make Cassie sign one to clean her room," Ask said.

"And the car," Tom said.

"Contracts sound like a good idea to me," Ask said. "I sort of have one for myself. My list of rules."

"You still have that? You made that when we were kids."

"I update it," Ask said. "I cut out the kid stuff. I keep it in my wallet in case I think of something new while I'm out."

"Like what?"

"Well, if you wear a colored shirt, you should wear socks to match. Like that."

"That's one of your rules to live by?"

"All I'm saying is a contract can be a good thing. You have to have an open mind to new ideas."

"I liked her," Tom said. "She was . . . I liked her. Who'd have thought Mom would set me up with someone like Marriet? Mom, who started nagging at me about a job the first night I was back, who wants to throw Charley out, who throws parties whenever things go bad. She's as hard to figure as Charley."

Embarrassed, Jill stepped to the breakfast bar, drank her juice. And listened.

"Oh, come on. We should make a contract for you to quit moping," Ask said.

"Yeah? What about for you?"

"Well," Ask said. "I should ask Julie out. Or at least *talk* to her."

"Raise your right hand. I, Edward Askew Warren, promise to ask Juliet . . ."

"Julie."

"Julie out before the week is up."

"Or at least talk to her."

"Or at least talk to her before the week is up."

"Okay," Ask said.

"Repeat it."

"If you want this to be a contract, you have to write it out. Otherwise, you'll just have to take my word. I'll do it."

Jill slipped quietly away from the table. How could Tom think she'd nagged him? She couldn't talk to him about it without making him realize she'd been listening. Which, of course, she had, but she hadn't meant to. The difference was blurred but significant. She decided to wake Cassie and see if she'd cleaned her room.

A pathway had been cleared to the closet. "Cassie?" She looked beyond a mound of sheets at the bed. Empty. A ball of clothing tumbled onto her feet when she opened the closet door. On her knees, she checked under the bed. It looked like the face of the moon. But no Cassie. She stood again. "Cassie?" she called. She checked the room once more. Sleepwalking, Cassie had once curled around a post on the back porch and stayed until morning. Another time, she had been wakened by the paper boy under a neighbor's blue spruce. Usually she just traipsed around her room.

Jill walked back to the kitchen, calling ahead of her for Ask and Tom to avoid further embarrassment. "Have either of you seen Cassie this morning?"

"She's asleep," Ask said, through the window. "She's never up before eleven on Saturdays."

"She's not in her room," Jill said. "Help me look."

Ask and Tom ran through the garage and front rooms calling for her. Jill looked in the master bedroom. Edward was pulling a sweat shirt over his head. "Is Cassie in here?"

He surveyed the room, stooped to look under the bed. "Check the closet," Jill said and walked to Charley's room.

She knocked. There was no answer. "Charley," she called and opened the door.

The bed was made. The dresser was bare. The trash had been emptied. The room scared her.

"Cassie," she called and searched the closet.

"Think she went with Charley to work?" Edward said, sticking his head in the room. "I looked in the boys' rooms."

Jill, on her knees, looked under Charley's bed. The floor was perfect, immaculate. "Call Charley at work," she said. "Now. Quickly."

Edward responded to the urgency in her voice. He ran to the phone.

Jill looked again in the closet. She paged through his shirts on their hangers. Three, four, perhaps five were missing.

Charley was gone, she realized. Cassie was with him.

EDWARD DIALED the warehouse. Arnsburger's voice came over the line. "Edward, this is Arnie. I can't believe Charley didn't tell you."

"Tell me what?" Possibilities flooded his mind: he had been fired, he was arrested, he'd lost an arm or leg.

"He quit. Last night. Not pleasantly either. Said I should cram this job up my you-know-what, among other things. Worse things."

"Arnie, check. See if he's there." Edward's voice became a whine. "Or outside."

"He's not going to show his—"

"Please," he said firmly. "Just check."

"Charley's gone," Jill said. "Cassie is with him. I'm sure."

"No you're not," Edward said. "We're not sure of anything. Don't act like you know more than you do."

"They could be at the library," Ask said. "They could be on a drive. Charley wanted to show off his van."

"Van?" Edward said.

No one spoke. They were embarrassed. He could see it.

Finally Tom said, "Charley sold the Firebird. He bought an old VW van."

"Oh Jesus," Edward said.

"No sign of him," came the voice over the phone. "When you see him—"

Edward hung up. A chip of ice formed inside him, at the base of his throat. He could feel it grow, the passageway becoming solid. "They'll be back," he said, the ice tearing at his Adam's apple. "We wait."

9

TOM STEERED the Ancient Mariner through the library parking lot—a yellow Camaro, a pair of old square Fords, a few pastel Toyotas and Datsuns, a dilapidated Dodge pickup. The truck's dented bumper held a faded bumper sticker: IN YOUR HEART YOU KNOW HE'S RIGHT/GOLDWATER FOR PRESIDENT.

"What would Charley be doing at the library anyway?" Tom said.

Ask scanned the lot for the van. "Cassie could have wanted a book." He leaned back in the car seat and crossed his arms. "Besides, I can't think of any other place to check."

Tom pulled into the street and stopped. "Where to?"

"You can't just stop in the middle of the road." Ask turned to look behind them.

"I don't know which way we're going." Tom glanced in the

rearview mirror. "No one's coming." The asphalt, black and blank, reminded him of the futility of their search. Even if Charley was still in the city, which Tom doubted, how could they possibly find him? They had no idea where he hung out or with whom.

"Come on. Don't stop here." Ask rocked forward as if to move the car.

"I looked in Charley's dresser," Tom said. "His jeans were gone. His underwear too."

"The lake," Ask said, looking behind them again. "They probably went there. A van is coming."

Tom turned. "That's a Chevy van."

"It's in this lane."

Tom stuck his hand out the window and motioned for the van to pass. "You have any idea where Randy Holmes lives?"

Ask nodded to the van driver as he passed. "I hate this," he said. "Who's Randy Holmes?"

"He was Charley's best man." Tom took his foot off the brake. The car edged forward. "He's the only friend of Charley's I can think of."

"He's got other friends. We just don't know them."

Tom braked and turned to Ask. "Do you ever wonder who he is?"

Ask sighed, looked behind them again, reached for the seat belt. "Who?"

"Charley. Don't you sometimes wonder who he is?"

"No." Ask buckled his seat belt. "I do wonder where you learned to drive."

"Jesus, Ask. He's quit work. He's always angry. We're his brothers and we don't have any idea who his friends are."

"So? Look, a station wagon is coming." His head was turned again. "There are *kids.*"

Tom stuck his hand out the window to motion them by without looking back. "I've lived with him my whole life, but we're strangers."

"Oh, you are not." Ask waved to the children in the station wagon as they passed. "Who are my friends? You don't know any of my friends. Do you think we're strangers?"

"I know your friends." Tom thought for a moment, then named two boys Ask had known since elementary school, a girl and her little brother who lived down the block, a brother and sister who used to live near them, a girl who was the president of the Law Club, and the girl he wanted to go out with, Julie Mayhew.

"She is not really a friend. Yet." He folded his arms. "Okay, the others are my friends, but you didn't name my best friend."

"I didn't? Someone new?"

"I've known him a long time. The point is you can't know everything about a person, but that doesn't mean you don't know him."

"Who is it?"

"I'm not telling."

Ask turned again to look behind them, but it was self-conscious, a gesture. "I guess Eileen was your best friend," he said, still looking back. "There's a police car coming."

"I guess she was."

"I'm not kidding about the police car, Tom."

Tom motioned for the car to pass. It pulled into the next lane and stopped even with them. The window in the police car lowered. Two bare-headed blond men, each with reflector glasses, faced them.

"We're looking for my brother and sister," Tom said before the cops could speak.

The near one took off his glasses. "How long have they been missing?"

"Since morning," Tom said.

"You can't report them as officially missing until they're gone twenty-four hours," he said, putting his glasses back on. "Good luck." He raised the window. The police car drove on.

"Clowns," Tom said. He turned to Ask. "You're my best

friend." He let his foot off the brake. "Far as I can tell, you're my only friend."

"Cassie," Ask said. "Mom. Dad. Charley."

Tom snorted and drove. He stopped at a Quick Mart and paged through the phone book while Ask bought Cokes. "No Randy Holmes in the phone book," Tom said.

Ask handed him a Coke. He bit his lip to keep from smiling.

"What?" Tom said.

"This reminds me of when we used to play Hardy Boys, looking for clues."

Tom laughed. "I'll be Joe."

"You can't be Joe. Frank was the oldest. Now, what would the Hardy Boys do to solve a case like this?"

"Look for their chums," Tom said, "Biff and Chester, then examine something under a magnifying glass."

"Chet," Ask said, "not Chester."

"Yeah, Chet, the fat one. I'm kind of short on chums and I've never owned a magnifying glass, so why don't we go home?"

Ask shook his head. "You give up too easily."

They decided to go to the Arzate house. Tony Arzate had been one of Tom's closest friends in high school and a teammate on the basketball squad. Early in their final season they started several games together, Arzate at point guard and Tom at shooting guard. Tom was the first to be benched, for poor shot selection and a bad attitude. Arzate was demoted for eating a hot dog half an hour before game time. They had been disappointing players on a bad team.

Tom had avoided old friends by staying home. He didn't want to answer questions about Berkeley or Eileen. Arzate, however, had done a hitch in the navy just out of high school. He would know little about Tom's humiliations and care even less.

"Strangers," Arzate called out as he opened the door. He yelled as if someone were listening, but no one else was home. He clapped his hand against Tom's arm. "I thought you were in prison."

"College," Tom said.

"Yeah," Arzate said. Two years in the navy had given him a thicker chest and bigger arms. He had been the smallest player on the team and the only Chicano. He headed for the refrigerator and beer. Tom and Ask followed.

"Here's what I want to know," Arzate said, sticking his head deep inside the refrigerator. "Was there some kind of epidemic or something? All the girls I knew are gone."

"California fever," Tom said. "They all live in San Diego or LA. There's something like three point four women to every two men in Los Angeles. I read that."

"That's a woman and a half each." Arzate retrieved a Schlitz for each of them. "Plus change. What are we doing here?"

"Looking for Randy Holmes," Ask said. Tom explained.

"I know where Randy Holmes lives," Arzate said. "I used to play softball with him. Just a couple of blocks. Why is your brother friends with that dude? You ever talk to him?"

"Couldn't pick him out of a crowd," Tom said.

"He's a pretty good hitter," Arzate said. "Played right field. I didn't like to have him on my team, though. I'd rather lose. You'll see—Mr. Zero."

They finished their beers and crowded into the front seat of the Ancient Mariner. "Don't one of us have to get out and crank this thing?" Arzate said.

"It's a perfectly good car," Ask said.

Randy Holmes lived only a few blocks away. "Over there," Arzate said, "the yard that looks like tundra."

In the barren front yard of the Holmes house, a blue plastic wheelbarrow held a yellow shovel and a doll's smiling head. Tom searched for a doorbell, then knocked. A shirtless little boy opened the door. "Go away," he yelled and shoved the door, but Tom caught it.

"Randy," he called.

"Go away," the boy said. Chocolate smears made parentheses around his mouth. "You stink."

"Anybody home?" Arzate yelled.

"Hold on," said a voice somewhere in the house. The door opened. Randy Holmes stared at Tom. "Who are you?" He looked to Arzate. "What's up?" His hair, the yellow of aging paper, stood up on one side, lay flat on the other.

"We're Charley's brothers," Tom said, motioning to Ask who stood behind him. "We're looking for him."

"I remember you guys," Randy said. He smiled, but Tom didn't see it as a friendly smile.

A woman holding a baby on her hip appeared beside him. She wore an orange bikini top and khaki shorts. Her hair, brown and stringy, fell to her shoulders. "Ask them in," she said.

Randy shrugged, stepped away from the door. He was barefoot, in P.E. shorts and a green T-shirt. He dropped onto a mottled pink couch.

"We're looking for Charley," Tom said. They stepped into the room. Beside the couch was a director's chair, a low coffee table, a deep bookshelf supporting a small color television. The bookshelf was full of plastic toys.

"Let's see," Randy said. He had both feet on the couch, knees up. "The Mustang Bar, about a year and a half ago."

"Yeah?" Tom said.

"Would any of you like something to drink?" his wife said. "My name is Carol."

"They don't want anything," Randy said. "The Mustang Bar, that was the last time I talked to Charley. What gave you the idea we were still friends?"

Tom shrugged, reached behind him for the door.

"You were his best man," Ask said. He had been standing quietly in the corner.

Randy laughed. "That was years ago. Fuck." He shook his head. "What's he done, anyway? Are the police in this?"

Arzate walked up to Carol and tickled the baby under the chin. "What's his name?" he asked.

She shook her head and stepped away from him, through a doorway. Arzate looked back to Tom and Ask. "What'd I do?"

Randy laughed. "I don't know where Charley is. He could be dead for all I know. He could be in China. He could be president of the *You*-Knighted States."

There was a crash in the next room, the sound of glass breaking. A collie pup ran into Arzate, head low, tail between his legs. He hurried down the hall. Arzate stuck his head through the doorway. Another crash.

"Fuck," Randy said and stood.

The little boy ran from the hall, naked, and stood next to Arzate, looking into the kitchen. He slapped Arzate's leg. "Go away," he said. "You stink like poop."

Randy lifted the boy off the floor by one arm, pushed Arzate to the side, and walked out of the room. There was another crash.

Tom opened the front door, nodded toward it, and they left.

"She was throwing glasses against the floor," Arzate said, pulling the car door shut.

"Why?" Ask said.

Arzate shook his head. "Very weird."

Without any plan, they drove to the lake. Twenty miles from Yuma, Martinez Lake filled a star-shaped gorge with Colorado River water. Saturday swimmers lined the beach with folding chairs and umbrellas. The Ancient Mariner wove in and out of the parking lots. There was no sign of the van. They parked, walked to the water's edge, and sat in the sand.

"I've been home a few months," Arzate said, responding to Tom. "Working part-time for a landscaping company. I water and mow, plant a few things. I've got my name on the hiring list for Parks and Rec."

"Was she throwing the glasses against the wall or the floor?" Ask said.

"The floor," Arzate said. "She took them out of the cupboard and threw them down."

"I've got to get a job, or do something," Tom said. "Otherwise I'll get as nutty as her."

"Carol," Ask said.

"You should have come with me in the navy. You would have liked it. Played hoops on the ship. You've got to make some adjustments in your shot, your dribbling. Lot of good players. That girl is beautiful." He pointed to a short, dark-haired woman in a bikini walking out of the water. A tall balding man followed her.

"I don't see how the navy would do anything for me." Tom shifted in the hot sand. His jeans clung to his knees.

"I spent one night in Cambodia. We were shipped in and shipped out just like that. Went to the Philippines. Guam. Japan. A lot of women in the Philippines have those kind of looks." He looked steadily at the woman approaching the beach.

"Was she still holding the baby?" Ask said.

"Who?" Arzate said.

"Give it up," Tom said. "There's no explaining it. She was a crazy woman. It was a crazy house."

"She asked us if we wanted to drink something, then . . ."

"What difference does it make?" Arzate said. "She's looking at us."

The woman's bikini was vertically striped, blue and white. Her dark hair hung over her forehead almost to her eyes. She smiled at them, then walked down the beach with the bald man.

"We probably look like jackasses out here in our regular clothes," Tom said.

"Yeah, but we've got hair," Arzate said.

"Were the glasses cracked or chipped or anything? Were they perfectly good glasses?" Ask stared earnestly at Arzate. "I can't figure it out. There must be a reason."

Arzate looked at Ask a moment, turned to watch the woman in the striped bikini open a lounge chair and sit. "I knew this guy in the Philippines. His name was Koseck. We called him Kotex. I worked with him, so we were kind of friends. We'd all ride in and out of town from the base on this big truck. There were benches along the side walls to sit on.

"On the way back to the base, most of us would be pretty drunk, laughing and giving each other shit, yelling to be heard over the truck. Kotex, every time, would be tanked up and start saying how screwed up his life was and how he didn't have any friends. Then he'd say he was going to jump out of the back of the truck—we were going pretty fast—jump out of the back of the truck and kill himself." Arzate looked to see if the woman in the bikini had moved.

"We'd have to talk him out of it. Sometimes we'd have to hold him back while he struggled to get loose. Then this one time we were coming back. I had won fifty dollars playing poker and was pretty happy. Kotex starts threatening to jump again, and I wasn't really paying any attention. So he grabs my shirt and says he means it. He pissed me off. And I said, 'Go ahead, Koseck. Jump. Get it over with. Quit bugging me.' "

Arzate sat up, erect. "The whole truck got quiet. Kotex kept saying he really meant it. He started running toward the tailgate. Nobody did anything. He stopped just in time and started crying.

"The next day he says to me, 'Arzate, you prick, you son of a bitch, you were going to let me jump.' And I said, 'You didn't jump, Koseck.' But he was all mad at me, and he never forgave me. In fact, he started hating me." Arzate looked around at the woman, the lake. "I thought this story had something to do with that woman throwing down the glasses, but I forgot how. Except that Kotex was a nut too."

"They both knew you," Tom said, laughing.

"Sometimes my stories don't pan out." He pointed at the woman in the bikini. "Why would she be with a bald guy? She could go out with anyone she wanted. Even me." He looked at Tom. "What about you?"

"I'm available," he said and looked to Ask.

"What I want to know," Ask said, "is why that lady started throwing glasses. Did we do something? Did the dog have something to do with it?"

"You're impossible," Tom said. The sand burned through his jeans and blew in his hair, but they sat in the sun another half an hour before starting home.

10

EDWARD THOUGHT of himself as a good American man, a veteran of the Second World War who had earned a good conduct medal, a family man who had held a paying job all his adult life, a father who had raised his children to be straight thinking.

As a soldier, he had disliked the army but felt he was part of a common effort that was real, more real than school had been or work or even his family. When he returned home, the communal feeling had remained; everyone was still pitching in, and he was a part of it. America was not just a country but a community as well. The nation had seemed young to him, as young as he, as young as his new wife.

Which was why he'd wanted Charley to enlist (something Charley never considered), and why, when Charley was turned down by the draft board, Edward had wanted a party. Jill, who, in one of her longest-running charades designed to spite him, had joined groups and stuffed envelopes and carried signs opposing the war, refused to have a party. "It's no disgrace to be turned down by the draft," she had said. "I'm happy that he was. I'm delighted. You should be, too. It's no call for a party."

Years later, after the war was lost, she refused him again, saying there'd be no party after Viet Nam. She said that national failures would not be celebrated, and she had been consistent, taking the McGovern returns with a glass of wine and a sigh (she had worked daily for him; Edward had voted for him reluctantly and only because he had never voted anything but a straight Democratic ticket).

Their parties, she said, would only be over personal matters, and that disturbed him. He believed it was why the country had grown suddenly old and feeble. People couldn't see that the war was a personal issue, that the workings of the country, like the workings of a family, were blood and bones and gristle.

Charley had never been a part of even the most inconsequential group effort, which was why he needed the war. He was never on a team in junior high or high school. He didn't join clubs. He didn't protest the war or support it, didn't seem to think it affected him. He wasn't part of a clique, was never a hippie or a hippie hater. He wasn't really a citizen of the United States, never bothering to vote or read about candidates or the issues. And worse, Edward admitted, he wasn't even a member of the family, not in any way but the merely physical.

The draft board had said his teeth were bad. Charley with the perfect smile had bad teeth? It made no sense. What did teeth have to do with being a soldier? Edward had questioned them. They had been evasive, as if there were something else. But, as far as he could determine, there wasn't.

What he hadn't been able to make Jill understand was that whether they were right or wrong in Viet Nam meant nothing. Young men were fighting and dying. Everyone should have pitched in, no matter what the cost, and the country would have been whole again, young again, one people, a community.

Charley had been denied the war by foolish bureaucrats. Now Jill wanted to deny him the family. "He should get a place of his own," she had said. "We should make him move."

"That's just what he wants us to do," Edward told her.

"Then let's do it," she said. "Tell him to be out by the end of the week. Force him." She had spoken with the same fervor she had when denouncing Lyndon Johnson. At a demonstration on the university campus in Tucson, she had chanted, "Hell no, we won't go," a woman who swore perhaps once a year, who had traveled 240 miles to carry a placard that read NO WAR NO MORE, who was not being asked to go at all. Edward would not let his family fall apart as his country had. He would not lose Charley. Not Charley. Here was a battle where he could make a difference.

When the van appeared outside the window, he left the curtains and ran into the yard. He yanked open the passenger door. Cassie sat closest to him, Charley, behind the wheel.

"Don't say anything," Charley said, pointing at Edward. The engine was still running.

"The hell," Edward said. "You pull a stunt like this then expect . . ." His rage swallowed his words. The van rocked as he pulled on the open door.

"I was sleepwalking," Cassie said to Jill, who stood behind Edward. "I balled up beneath his clothes to get warm. He didn't see me."

Jill ducked under Edward's elbow and took Cassie by the arm. "Let him go," she whispered in Edward's ear, ducked again, and led Cassie to the yard.

"What did you say to Arnsburger? He's a friend of mine. Doesn't that mean anything to you?" Edward was screaming. Charley said nothing, the engine idling. "What does this stunt mean? This is your family."

"Let him go," Jill said again.

"Shut up." He turned to her, pointing as Charley had. "Get in the house."

The van began moving forward. "Stop that," Edward said, walking then running along.

"Fuck off," Charley said and accelerated.

Edward grabbed the open door, pulled himself to the van, standing on the short running board, one hand on the swinging door, the other on the back of the seat. Pavement slid beneath his shoes. He pulled his head inside, gaining his balance. Charley turned right at the corner without stopping. The door swung out. Edward was thrown back and leaned out with the door.

Children in a green yard looked up from their dump trucks to watch them wheel by. Edward pulled himself in again, able to sit this time, to shut the door. "Now," he said, "go where you damn well please. But we're going to have this out." Charley only glared at the road. Edward looked there too, the asphalt, a crumpled grocery sack, an approaching Buick. "You're going to talk to me, goddamn it. Look at me." His hands became fists. He punched Charley in the shoulder. "Look at me," he said. He put his knuckles to Charley's chin but only pushed against it, a gentle cuff. He turned back to the road and caught his breath, calming himself, ready for the next confrontation, a good soldier.

EDWARD RETURNED in the van that evening. He came in the door saying, "Charley walked off. I don't know where he is." Ask and Tom stared at him as if he were the tax man and they didn't know whether to confess or keep quiet. Damn them. Tom was ruining Ask—and the next thought came to him quickly, without time for reason to intervene—*as Jill had ruined Charley.* "No," he said aloud, shaking his head, feeling the word shake in his mouth until it became a growl. He marched into his bedroom, Jill appearing suddenly behind him, following him into the room.

He turned to her, shoving the door shut. "You know what he was doing?" His whisper was coarse, fierce. "He was running away. Twenty-four years old and pulling a junior high stunt."

"Twenty-six," Jill said. "He shouldn't even live here."

Edward screamed. "This is his home."

"You just said it." She folded her arms, walked away from the door. "He's too old."

"If this doesn't prove it, I don't know what will." Couldn't she see the truth? "He may be twenty-six, but he's still a kid, a brat, a little boy." *Our little boy*, he thought, *our first born, our best*.

"You're suffocating him," she said. "We all are."

"What in the name of hell do you mean?" He grabbed her arm as she turned away. *As Jill had ruined Charley,* the thought insisted.

"Let me go." She jerked her arm away. "Let him go. Make him go. If you love him . . ."

"If I love him? How can you say that?"

"Then kick him out."

Edward slapped her across the cheek. Hard. "Don't you say that." His voice trembled. He pointed fiercely, made a fist. "Don't you ever say that."

She turned, walked to the doorway. "You're the brat, Edward." Her cheek reddened. One eye filled with tears.

His knees grew suddenly feeble. He sat on the bed, a collapse. "I'm sorry I hit you," he said. "Does it hurt?"

"Go to hell," she said and left the room.

He pulled a pillow into his fist and slapped it against the bed. "If you love him," she had said, as if there were a question. What had he done in his life but love Charley? Anger flared in his chest like a flame. He bent forward in pain, slapping the pillow against the headboard.

If Charley wanted privacy, he could get an apartment. Edward would not stop him, would not try to talk him out of it. But Charley was trying something more. He wanted to abandon the family, and that Edward would not permit. He would not kick Charley out, giving him the excuse that he had been shunned. Charley was one of them by blood, by bones, by gristle, and until death, and beyond death. He slapped the pillow against the headboard and held on against the pain until it passed.

TOM PLAYED Crazy Eights with Ask while they waited for Charley. He returned at midnight. Edward, who'd been chain smoking and watching through the window, walked to his bedroom before the front door opened.

Charley stumbled when he entered. He quickly righted himself and pushed the door behind him but failed to close it. He walked to the dentist's chest and leaned against it.

Ask got up and closed the door.

"Where were you?" Tom said.

"Cassie all right?" he said.

"She thinks you're mad at her," Ask said. He sat next to Tom, who had already put his cards on the coffee table. "We should finish this hand anyway," Ask said and spread his cards in his hand.

Tom stacked his cards with the deck.

"I'm not mad at her anymore," Charley said.

"You all right?" Tom said. Cassie had told them that Charley cried for almost an hour coming home, cursing every car that passed them. She had been frightened.

"He wants me to kill him," Charley said. "If I could do that I wouldn't need to do all this."

"All what?" Ask said. "Why were you leaving?"

"I hate it here," Charley said. He kicked the table. The cards fell at their feet. The ashtray hit Ask in the shin, coated his shoes with speckled ashes. "I hate him." He pointed down the hall. "God, I hate you, you prick," he said to Ask. He looked at Tom. "You too, you fucking coward."

"So go," Tom said. "Get out."

"I will," he said. "It's just going to take more than I thought. *He*"—Charley pointed again—"keeps raising the stakes." He took off his shirt, threw it against the front door, and walked to his bedroom.

"Mom's right," Tom said. "We should kick him out."

"No, we shouldn't." Ask had picked up the cards and was stacking them to return to their package. "Will you do me a favor?"

Tom imagined himself walking into Charley's room and demanding that he leave. "You have ten minutes," he would say. He could picture it, but he couldn't do it.

"Tom."

"Yeah?"

"I have ashes in my shoes."

Tom looked at Ask's shoes and socks, gray as death.

"I hate cigarette ashes," he said. "Would you mind?"

Tom untied his brother's shoes and pulled them off. A Kent

butt rolled to the heel, nestled in the ashes in the first shoe. The second held a mound of ash among the strings. He tugged Ask's socks off.

Ask held his feet in the air and scooted to the end of the couch, beyond the spill of ashes. He stood. "I can vacuum after I shower," he said.

Tom shook his head. "I'll get it."

"We should be happy Charley's come home," Ask said. His hands were at his thighs, bunching his pantlegs, pulling them up off his ankles as if he were wading through shallow water. The cuffs of his pants were white with ash.

Tom snorted, then smiled. He scraped a handful of cigarette butts and ash from the carpet and raised the hand over his head. "To having the whole family together again," he said.

Unable to raise his hand, Ask did the next best thing. He curtsied.

CASSIE'S STORY

WHAT I REMEMBER most about Charley's wedding was that Mom slapped Dad on the face and called him a wretched child, and Ask wouldn't let me wear my white go-go boots. And the phone call to Brenda. I did that. I don't know why. I was really young, like ten or eleven. And mixed up, the way people are before they get to high school. I liked the idea of a wedding and I liked Brenda, but at the last minute I got panicky. Things started shooting around inside me, like there was a school of fish, those little quick ones—neons. I wrote a paper at the beginning of this semester on anxiety. I called it "The Aquarium Syndrome," but high school teachers have no imagination.

My stomach was a fishbowl and Ask hid my go-go boots and Charley was already dressed and looked perfect, like the Great Gatsby, which I just read, so I couldn't have thought that back then, but that's the way he looked, and I was scared all of a sudden and wanted to stop the wedding, so I called Brenda and asked if she knew about the family secret.

III

"It probably won't change a thing," I said. "I shouldn't even bring it up."

"Cassie, is this a joke, Cassie?" Brenda's voice had holes in it, like for a second she would be somebody else, a little girl maybe. "It's not so funny. I've got pins all in me."

I thought she meant she was on pins and needles like in that old saying. I almost told her I had swallowed an aquarium myself. Then I remembered she had to let out her dress. There were real pins. That made me picture her as a voodoo doll with pins in her knees and boobs.

"Your dress," I said to her. "It was late or something." I knew the truth. Charley had told me. "She's what's late," he'd said and I didn't get it, so he explained. I couldn't tell anyone Brenda was pregnant, even Brenda. I wasn't supposed to know.

"So what is it, Cassie?" In the background I heard Mrs. Horne, Brenda's mother, telling her to turn, stand up straight, hold still. Her voice was nothing like Brenda's. It was pointy like that sound the water pipes make just before they rattle.

I tried to think of a good secret, like Charley had only six months to live, or we had another brother who was on death row in Kentucky, or there was this disease in our family that you could catch if you got married to one of us. None of them sounded good enough to say out loud.

"It's nothing really," I said.

"Ow," Brenda yelled into the phone. "You did that on purpose." I could hear Mrs. Horne deny it.

"See you at the wedding," I said and hung up. It was a stupid idea to start with. I liked Brenda, partly because of the way she looked. She had blondish-brownish, stringy hair and slopey shoulders. She wore baggy clothes and didn't have those huge breasts like all of Charley's other girl friends, who wore their boobs like they were gold medals from the Olympics. Her breasts were more human-sized. She never called me a cute little girl and didn't change her voice when we talked like I was a cat. She even showed me how to frug, this dance she saw in a movie. It made no sense at all to call her. I wouldn't have done it except for all those neons schooling around inside me.

I had used Mom and Dad's phone, which was the only one where you could get any privacy, and I had just hung up and was lying on their bed when Dad stomped into the room like he had mud on his feet. I rolled off the bed to the floor where he couldn't see me. He's a nuisance when he's mad.

"Never," he yelled and I rolled right under the bed. "*I* decide what I do, and I have decided."

"You're punishing Charley, not Eva." I recognized Mom's voice. It was her edgy voice, the one that comes just before she yells. Eva was Mrs. Horne's name, Brenda's mother.

"He's punishing me," Dad said. "He's getting back at me through that woman."

"He's marrying her daughter, not her. You're so . . ."

"Where's he going to live? We've got enough room here for the both of them. The baby. A dozen babies. I could build onto the back porch."

He wasn't supposed to know she was pregnant. I hadn't told him, but for a few seconds that's what I worried about, that I would get the blame for Dad knowing, then Charley would quit telling me things.

They kept yelling for a while, moving over near the closets. All I could see was their shoes, his old wingtips and her black heels. The shoes faced each other, then turned away. The wingtips stomped. The heels tapped, then slid, angled out and angled in. They could have been dancing or playing a game—it seemed like there was a pattern. I had always wanted to know what adults did, why I would have to go to bed, why they would lock the doors. Those shoes were like an answer.

Dad kept saying he wasn't going to the wedding. When Mom slapped him and called him a wretched child, I rolled out from under the opposite side of the bed and kept rolling right out of the room. I didn't think they would see, but Mom called after me even before I hit the doorjamb with my head. She's got that Mom-vision. I kept rolling, then ran outside.

My dress was a mess, covered with those little balls of under-the-bed stuff. Ask and Tom were standing in the yard with their hands in their pockets and I ran to them. For some reason the sight of them made me start crying. I was really young. The only good things to come out of it were that Tom knocked the dirt off my dress, and Ask relented and said I could wear my go-go boots. I didn't feel like changing my shoes by then, but the fact that Ask said he'd get them meant a lot because he never gives in on anything.

THE WEDDING WAS at a church next to the library, a new church with carpet and concrete and little speakers on the walls above the pews. We sat near the front, me and Mom and Ask and Tom. There weren't very many people. Mrs. Horne sat across the aisle from us by herself. *She* had on go-go boots and a white blouse with ruffles and a light blue miniskirt. She kept talking across me to Mom, except for once when she said I had a dust ball in my hair. "You're such a cutie," she said while Mom dug it out. I wanted to puke.

There were a few other people there. Some of Charley's friends, I guess, and their girl friends. A bunch of dopey-looking girls who must have been Brenda's friends. One of the dopey girls tapped me on the shoulder and said the bride wanted to talk to me.

Brenda was in this little room in the side of the church standing beside a big built-in bathtub. Her white satin dress stretched so tight across her stomach, it looked like a movie screen. Her slopey shoulders were bare and pretty. Her stringy hair was done up high. She had on white lipstick. "You look grand," I said and I put my arms around her. The satin against my cheek was smooth and slick as a balloon.

"Cassie, you're making me nervous, Cassie." She held my shoulders at arm's length. "The secret? Is that a joke? If it's a joke, it's no joke."

"No," I said and I knew just then it was no joke, even though I couldn't explain it, the way you can know how to get to someone's house but can't give directions to it.

"What then? Why are you making me nervous? I'm already sweating like a monkey."

I had my pearl-lined hand purse that Aunt Hannah had given to me, which I was finally getting to use. I'd put Kleenex in it in case one of us wanted to cry. I'd heard a lot of that goes on at weddings. I gave Brenda some tissues, which she stuck under her arms. The whole time I was trying to think of what the secret was.

Our family is like a family of lepers, no, a family of elves, I thought. *If one leaves, none of the rest of us grow up.* Then I realized what it was, what it really was—*my father hates your mother,* I thought, and decided to tell her. But somehow I got confused. What I said was, "My father hates your husband."

Brenda squatted and I thought her dress was going to burst. She put her hands on my cheeks and nodded. "Charley told me," she said. There were tears in her eyes. "You don't fret, Cassie. He doesn't have to love Charley. We can love him enough to make up for it."

I hadn't meant to say what I said and didn't believe that Dad didn't love Charley. But when she said *we* can love him, I threw my arms around her and we held each other until the "Here Comes the Bride" music came on. Everybody laughed when I ran down the aisle to my seat.

The ceremony was quick. When the minister said, "You may kiss the bride," Brenda threw her arms around Charley and the wads of tissues fell from her armpits. Otherwise, it was real beautiful.

After the I do part, Mrs. Horne started patting Brenda on the belly, which clued everybody in that she was pregnant, except Ask, who can be so dense. Mrs. Horne kissed Charley on the lips, really sickening. Then we stood around for a while, like you do when you're waiting for someone to go but the engine has to get warm first.

When Charley and Brenda started out to his car (he had a red Mustang back then), Ask said, "Wait," and threw up his hands. He and I ran to the Ancient Mariner to get rice to throw on them, but Ask had read where rice gets eaten by birds and expands in their stomachs and kills them. When Charley and Brenda came out of the church with their arms around each other, Ask and I threw trail mix at them.

DAD WAS STANDING at the window when we drove up. I could see his hand on the curtains. It made a fist. When we walked in, he was by the kitchen doorway, trying to fool us, as if we hadn't seen his fist. We all stood around in the living room for about a minute, and that was it. The wedding was over.

I lay in my bed for a while thinking about getting married, but I couldn't really picture it. Things kept interfering. Like my dad. How he hadn't come to the wedding. How we were all dressed up and he hadn't shaved. How dark he looked. How I'd seen his hand on the curtains and nothing else, just his hand. How there seemed to be mysteries that I wouldn't ever be able to solve. Like those shoes—my parents' shoes, facing each other, turning. If I had a paper due right now, I'd write about the mysteries in shoes and hands and shaving, the little mysteries that always get overlooked.

SEX AND SHELTER

I

THE TWO RUNAWAY GIRLS spending the night in Charley's van told Tom they were seventeen. They looked younger. The dark one, Gin, was thin as a rope and made popping noises with her bubble gum. She took a quick liking to Tom and made a point to touch him each time she spoke. When the boys decided to skinny-dip in the river, she shed her jeans and panties but wore her elastic tube top into the water. Her friend, Cathy, was shorter, lighter, and had evidence of breasts beneath her white T-shirt. She had small features and spoke so softly she had to say everything twice. Around one wrist she wore two red rubber bands. When finally coaxed to wade in up to the ragged edges of her cutoffs, Cathy used the rubber bands to knot her hair up off her neck.

Cathy wrapping her hair into a bun, Tom discovered, excited him more than the glimpse of brown goatee between Gin's legs. His sense of desire was more attuned to movement than image. Girlie magazines had never interested him in quite the way he thought they should. He liked to see women doing things—Eileen, loaded with popcorn and sodas, walking confidently down the darkened theater aisle, shuffling past seated people, pivoting into the seat beside him. How beautiful and complicated those movements were. Her strong hands operating the cash register at the drugstore, fingers moving over the rows of buttons as if it were a keyboard. He thought of Marriet dancing at Bozeman's after she'd given up her rehearsed steps, or as she had been in high school, books pressed tightly against her red sweater, running across campus. And now Cathy's raised hand, pirouetting at the wrist as she twisted her hair.

Tom had spent the afternoon standing in muddy water, drinking beer and explaining his early return from Berkeley. People who had said nothing to him when he left were curious about his unhappy return. Everyone loves to hear about the failures of others.

"Things just didn't work out," he said. If pressed, he added, "The place gave me the willies." To acquaintances, he said, "I didn't know anybody up there." To those who had lousy jobs, he said, "Too expensive." The more people asked, the more the question nagged at him, until he finally told the truth.

"I don't know," he said to Arzate. "For some reason, I couldn't stand it."

Arzate nodded. "You get laid up there?"

Tom didn't answer.

"Must not have, you'd still be there." Arzate crossed his arms, water lapping against his elbows, and smiled.

Tom crossed his arms as well. Naked, the water just above his hips, he had nothing to do with his hands. An especially hot Saturday during an unusually warm winter had inspired the river swim. Arzate had insisted Tom take part. "You've got to be more social," he'd said.

They stood in the deepest part of the Colorado. Slow and shallow, the river, banked by salt cedars and desert, flowed as aimlessly as thought, swirling and pausing in little coves, but eventually moving on.

"Once," Tom said. "There was one girl."

"Yeah?"

"Tell you about it some other time," he said.

"There's two chicks interested in your van," Arzate said.

They swam to a wide spot in the river, where Gin stood talking to the few remaining people, all boys but her.

Gin, it turned out, had been living with Cathy's family for almost a month. Her parents moved to Chicago but agreed to let her finish the semester in Yuma. At four that morning, Cathy's father had crawled into Gin's bed, drunk and naked. "His dick was up to here," Gin said and slashed her hand across her eyes. She had stuck her foot in his face and run with Cathy out of the house. They were looking for a place to stay just for the night. "I have a friend who will be back from San Diego tomorrow. I can stay with her then," she said, her hand on Tom's chest.

Cathy nodded and said, "My father . . ." trailing off to a whisper.

"Was that important?" Arzate said.

"My father would never touch me," she said and pointed to Gin. "She's the only one . . ." and trailed off again. After standing in water up to her thighs for half an hour, she had walked into the deeper water when the conversation turned to the van. Her cutoffs were submerged and water lapped against her T-shirt above her breasts. Her nipples, hard and round as toothpaste caps, pointed skyward.

"I guess it's all right," Tom said. He had custody of the van for the night. Charley had been promising to let him use it in order to make up for withdrawing the Firebird weeks ago. Tom had finally taken him up on it.

Walking out of the river, Gin stepped on a broken beer bottle and cut her foot. She slipped on her jeans and tied her panties around her foot as a bandage. "It's nothing," she said, tapping the bandaged foot against Tom's ankle. "You like my toes?" Her toenails were painted purple.

Arzate bought four Big Macs. Tom parked the van in the McDonald's lot and opened the doors. They ate on the carpeted floorboard. Arzate, Tom discovered, knew the girls no better than he did.

"Who took you to the river?" Arzate said.

"This guy," Gin said. "We met him at Taco Bell. What a creep." The Taco Bell was the local hangout. People met there to go elsewhere.

"We used to go there," Arzate said and nudged Tom.

When they had been in high school, the hippies went there and the cowboys to Der Wienerschnitzel. Those distinctions had changed, Tom was sure. Although only a couple of years past, his high school years were separated from him by a huge black gap, the same gap that separated him from the two girls.

By the time they'd eaten and dropped off Arzate, it was almost dark. *"Cuidado,"* Arzate said to Tom as he got out. *"Peligrosas."* He pointed at the girls.

Tom parked in front of his house. They sat silently for several moments, Tom in the front seat, Gin and Cathy in the back.

"I could get you some blankets. A pillow," he said, looking straight ahead, out the windshield.

Gin sat up, put her chin in the shallow of his shoulder. "It's plenty warm," she said.

Tom looked in the rearview mirror at Gin's face and past her to Cathy, who was saying something. He turned, dislodging Gin. "What did you say?"

"They'd see you," Cathy said, pointing to the house beyond the van door, "if you got pillows."

"Yeah," Gin said and ducked back behind the seat. "You sure you can't see inside here?"

The van had only a rear window, which was covered by a curtain. Another curtain separated the front seats from the bed. "I'm sure," he said and stepped into the rear of the van. He shut the front curtain.

Gin untied the panties that bound her foot. They were splotched with blood. "I should wash this," she said, poking at the cut.

"I'll get some water," Tom said.

"In a glass," Cathy said, loud enough to be heard. "So no one will think . . ." She drifted off.

Gin nodded. "A glass is less suspicious."

Than what? Tom wondered—a pan? a bowl?

"Walk out like . . ." Cathy twisted the ends of her hair, hand pirouetting again at the wrist.

"What?" he said.

"When you walk out of the house, act like you're doing something," she said. She smiled awkwardly. "I don't want anyone to know," she whispered. "About my father."

"Don't worry." He lay his hand on her shoulder. She put her hand over his.

Stepping out of the van, he spotted his mother directly across from him bending to turn the knob on the water faucet. He hopped out and let the door fall shut behind him.

Jill straightened. "Your father left the water on the bougainvillea all day," she said smiling. "It's like a marsh over there." She nodded toward the side of the house.

Tom followed the trail of the green garden hose to where it disappeared around the corner.

"How was the river?" she asked.

He shrugged and walked toward her. "Nothing special." He felt like a kid, hiding things from his mother. He enjoyed the feeling.

Jill took a step toward him, then walked past. "You left the door open," she said. The side door to the van was ajar.

"I'll get it." He ran past her to the door and pushed it shut.

She laughed at him. "Did Marriet go to the river with you?"

He thought he might be blushing. "Nah," he said, stepping away from the van. He hadn't seen Marriet since that first date, although he had resolved to call her several times. Once he had even dialed the first three numbers before returning the receiver to its cradle.

"Oh." She crossed her arms, waited to see if he would offer more.

"I may go for a walk," he said. "Need to do some thinking." He saw his father open the curtains at the front window. "Pop wants you," he said.

"Maybe we can talk later. After your walk."

He nodded, watched her go to the house, his father drop the curtains. He opened the van and jumped in.

"They're both right next to the front door," he said.

"Who?" Gin said, putting her hand on his knee.

"My parents. How's the foot?"

"It's dirty."

"I'll get some water," he said. "Keep this door closed."

Cathy said something too low for Tom to hear. He nodded at her. He could tell from her expression she was telling him to be careful.

Ask's room was lit. Tom tapped on the window. It faced the street, separated from the front door by a large pyracantha bush. When he'd been in high school and stayed out too late or come home too high, he'd tapped on Ask's window and crawled in, then crossed the hall into his own room, or, sometimes, passed out on Ask's bed.

Ask pulled the window open. "What's up?" he said.

"Listen," Tom whispered. "There are two girls in the van. They're spending the night, and I don't want Mom and Dad to know."

Ask nodded. He bit his lip.

"They want a glass of water. Can you get it?"

"There's two of them?"

"Yeah."

"Don't worry. I'll be right back." Ask shut the light and left the room.

Tom heard the front door open and ducked behind the bush. He leaned out to see his father walk to the water faucet, stoop, and turn it on, then walk back into the house. Cautiously Tom raised his head.

Ask's head appeared in the darkened room. "I did better," he said, smiling. "Look."

He raised two glistening bottles of Coke.

"They need water to wash with," Tom said. The front door opened again and he ducked. Jill walked out and turned off the faucet. She quickly went back into the house. Tom stood.

Ask's face had fallen. "Wash? Aren't they dressed?"

"She cut her foot." Tom reached through the window and took the Cokes. "I'll see if they want these."

"I'll get the water," Ask said.

Tom slipped back into the van. "My brother thought you might be thirsty," he said.

Gin laughed, covering her mouth. Cathy spoke.

"What?" Tom said, handing each a bottle.

"That was sweet," she said and took the Coke.

Ask produced a tall glass of water and a washcloth. Tom found a flashlight behind the driver's seat. The gash in Gin's foot was long and shallow, crusted with dirt. He dipped the washcloth in the water and gently wiped at the cut.

"That hurt?" he whispered. He had his back to them to treat the wound.

"A little," Gin said. He felt a hand along the back of his leg.

The batteries in the flashlight were weak, the light dim. He tried to keep the light contained as he wiped the area around the cut, the dirt and dried blood. Her foot was soft and small. He moved the washcloth to the ball of her foot, the base of her toes. He ran the cloth between each of her toes, carefully, slowly.

The hand moved up his leg to his butt, around in a circle, back to his thigh and forward, almost to his penis. Tom ran the cloth over the tiny nails—purple, he remembered, but in the bad light, black—and the top of her foot and toes. The hand went beneath his shirt, lightly touching his spine, shoulders, ribs, around his chest. Fingers tweaked a nipple and withdrew.

He concentrated on the foot, wiping carefully but firmly until the wound was real again with new blood. He pulled off his shirt. The hand touched his back again. He wrapped the wound carefully with his shirt as the hand moved in arcs across his back. He knelt closer to the foot, clean now, tiny. He kissed the exposed heel, ball, toes. He took each toe in his mouth, running his tongue in the spaces between them, sucking gently. Gin giggled.

Tom turned off the flashlight. He took hold of the hand from his back and pulled her close. It was totally dark, but he knew he was kissing Cathy. He ran his hands over her thin waist and small breasts, her large, hard nipples. He dropped his hands to her thighs, ran them up her legs, under her cutoffs as far as he could reach. Then he stopped, released her, cautiously opened the van door, and stepped outside.

"I'll be here," one of them whispered. He was unsure which.

He didn't want to go through the front door without his shirt. He tapped again on Ask's window.

Ask held out a beach towel. "I figured you'd be back," he said.

"Look out." Tom pulled himself up and through his brother's window.

TOM LAY IN BED considering the van. His body argued for exploring the possibilities waiting there. Desire manifested itself in his legs and arms, as if their cores were charged, and in his chest, a dry churning, and in the sweet readiness of his groin. But he wasn't sure the desire was for either Cathy or Gin, although they had awakened it. He found himself thinking of Marriet, whom he should have called but hadn't, and already a month had passed. He thought also of Eileen, the texture of her tongue, both soft and rough. The width of her hips.

He sat up in bed, leaned against the cool wall. An image of the van sprang into his head, idealized and beautiful. It shone white on the darkened curb, the asphalt a perfect black, the lawn an unreal green. The doors to the van suddenly flew open. Cathy and Gin framed the opening, naked in soft white light. Perfect.

Tom got out of bed and paced his room. His erection knocked

against his thighs. Marriet had wanted a contract before sleeping with him. It had offended, even frightened him. Eileen wanted to see him and explain her betrayal. She wanted, Tom thought, to be understood and forgiven. The girls in the van wanted nothing from him but his time, he thought, and took a pair of pants from the dresser. And his body. He smiled and opened his bedroom door very quietly. And a place to spend the night, he realized, and stopped in the dark hall. His breathing was quick. Goose bumps covered his bare chest.

He didn't want to be like Cathy's father, trading shelter for sex. The circumstances were different, he thought. They *wanted* him to come to the van, separately and, perhaps, together. His desire, however, seemed less specific. A general horniness? Seeing Cathy wrapping her hair had excited his desire through association, he reasoned, which was why he had lain in bed thinking of Eileen. And Marriet. Neither of whom was in the van.

He stepped back into his room, closed the door silently. Cathy's father was a pig. He was sure of that. Did he want to spend a lousy night awake in his bed, lusting after someone who was waiting for him to come to her, or would he rather be a pig? A pig is an animal with dirt on his face, his shoes are a terrible disgrace. If you don't care a feather or a fig, you may grow up to be a pig—he'd always hated that song.

Pushups would exhaust him. A couple of thousand would probably be sufficient. He pulled off his pants and lay in bed. Pushups wouldn't do. Would he think of Gin or Cathy while he masturbated? Marriet or Eileen? "What does it feel like," Eileen used to ask, "to be inside someone else?" He pictured her freckled breasts, the mole just below her rib cage. "It feels wet," he whispered to her. "Dark. Sweet."

Before he could finish answering Eileen, Marriet had slipped in beneath him and taken her place.

TOM WOKE EARLY. As he walked to the van, he spotted Ask's head in his bedroom window. Tom waved to him, guessing that he hadn't slept very well either. The girls were still asleep. He closed the door quietly.

The engine turned over and caught. Gin stirred but didn't wake. Cathy sat up. Tom shifted into gear and the van began moving. As soon as they were around the corner, Cathy pulled herself into the passenger seat. Her cheek was red and reticulated from the carpet. Her hair was bunched and crossed, her eyes and mouth slack from sleepiness. She was astonishingly beautiful.

"I waited up for you," she said, just audibly.

He nodded.

She pushed and tugged at her hair. "Why didn't you come?" she said, louder.

He shifted into fourth gear unnecessarily and tried to think of a reasonable answer. The van lugged. Gin, from the rear, moaned. He down-shifted, looked at Cathy's soft sleepy face, and unexpectedly stumbled across the truth.

"Because I hardly know you," he said.

"Oh," she said. "I thought . . ." She trailed off.

"What did you say?"

She shook her head. "Not important."

The streets were nearly empty. In the early morning light, they were almost handsome. A bread truck made a left in front of them. SUNBEAM was written in bold red letters across its side.

"I know your sister," Cathy said. She glanced back at the sleeping Gin. "Gin said I shouldn't tell you. You might think . . ."

"What? I didn't catch that."

"I'm fifteen," she said. "Gin will be fifteen in . . ."

"Yeah," Tom said. His voice sounded calm, but his lungs were momentarily weighted and swung inside him. "I thought you might be young."

"Turn here." She pointed to a street bordered by gas stations.

"You're really very beautiful," he said, following her directions. "Lovely."

She smiled at him and crawled in the back to wake Gin.

2

FOR A MONTH, Charley lived across town. Eileen promised to stop trying to reach Tom if he would move out. "Try being rational," she had said. "New experience. Do you good."

He withdrew his savings, rented a furnished apartment, part of a large complex, and bought two orange rugs for the bathroom, a mirror for his bedroom door. He subscribed to the paper, read through job listings daily, and never found one worth calling about. He bought a color TV, began watching "General Hospital," "The Young and the Restless," "Wheel of Fortune."

He met a woman in the bar where he'd talked with Eileen, a weekend weather woman on a local television station. She had dark eyes, a nervous habit of shaking out her hair, and slept with him the same afternoon they met, in his double bed, on clean, new sheets, still creased from their package.

They shopped after they made love. She cooked him dinner. They watched "Barney Miller," "Three's Company," then went to bed again. His cock went limp inside her. She said they should talk about it. He blamed his family. "They're not the kind of people you can move across town to escape," he said.

She said that was stupid. She propped her head up with her elbow and pulled the sheet to her neck. "Everybody's got a fucked-up family," she said.

Surprised, he backtracked, said the real truth was that he liked to bring women to his parents' house because he either had to sneak them in behind their backs or walk them through the house, flaunting them. He felt bold telling her this. He was revealing himself to her.

She said that was stupid too. "I used to like sex in public places. Half public, anyway. Like in a restaurant but hidden," she said. "I got over that. You get over those things. You grow up."

"You're making this all sound simple," Charley said.

"Not simple. Stupid was what I said." She laughed. "I'm teasing. But it sounds so sixties—LBJ era problems. No one feels that way anymore. It's tacky."

Charley told her the story about Squirrel, how he'd gotten lost on the camping trip and caught in a brier bush, how his father ate before bothering to look for him then bawled him out, how scared he had been, although the truth was he didn't remember the episode, only his father's telling of it.

"He brags about that day," Charley said.

"Why should I feel sorry for you?" she said. "My old man left me and my sister in the backseat of a Corvair once and forgot about us. Big deal. You don't live with your family anymore and . . ."

"And what?" Charley said, pulling her closer.

"And you're beautiful," she said.

Eventually they made love again. Charley took a long time. They were both sore by the time they finished. Lying in bed together, she began humming a song. "What is that?" he said.

"I don't know." She sat up and shook out her hair. "A waltz, I think. I don't know why it came into my head. Sometimes I think the weirdest things."

"Like what?"

She covered her breasts with her hands, crossing her arms. "I was thinking what it would be like to be married to you," she said. "Isn't that weird? We just met."

"It's not that weird," he said. He pulled her arms away, stared at her breasts. "What do you imagine it would be like, the two of us?"

Her fingers entered her hair just above her ears. She lifted her hair high on her head and arched her back, rising to her knees, sighing. "What would it be like?" she said, considering the question. Charley kissed her just below her navel and again, in the dark pubic triangle. She took his head in her hands and pressed him against her. "We'd be happy," she said. "For a while. Then we'd be miserable. Just like everybody else." She released him, slid down beside him, and pulled the sheet up to their necks.

CASSIE AND ASK VISITED, bringing fresh fruit. "This was his idea," Cassie said and set the fruit on the kitchen table.

"A housewarming gift," Ask said, poking around the apartment. "It's traditional. This is a nifty place, Charley. It's very modern. Do you have a garbage disposal?"

"I don't know," Charley said. He took an apple from the box of fruit.

"Dad says you're going back to the warehouse." Cassie opened the refrigerator. "Where's your food?" There were five bottles of Budweiser, a half-eaten Sara Lee pound cake, ketchup, and a jar of Picante sauce.

"Ice cream in the freezer," he said.

"Tom would be here, but he was busy," Ask said.

"Oh, he was not," Cassie said. She stared into a frosted bucket of ice cream. "I hate vanilla. No one in this family has any imagination."

"What are the folks up to?" Charley said.

"Mom said we shouldn't come." Cassie put the ice cream back in the freezer and shut the white plastic door. "She said to give you time to yourself. Dad is waiting for you to come visit. Or something like that. Where are your other rooms?"

While Cassie and Ask looked over the unmade bed and disheveled dresser in the bedroom, Charley turned on the television. He found a black and white movie, a jungle story. A white woman with blond curls was talking and making signs to a tall black man in a loin cloth. He wore a bone around his neck like a bow tie.

"I've seen this before," Cassie said and sat beside Charley on the couch.

Ask carried a chair from the kitchen into the room. "What have we missed?" he asked Cassie.

"She's in love with this professor who has a stutter and who wants to give the natives a bunch of shots. Then there's this bad guy who wants their ceremonial diamonds and elephants' tusks and he loves the girl too, but she loves the professor and she wants to make the natives wear clothes and cut their hair and quit wearing bones." Cassie curled up on the couch. "I can put my feet on your couch, can't I?"

"Whatever you want," Charley said. He walked into the kitchen and returned with the bucket of ice cream and a spoon.

On screen, a white man in a loin cloth and wavy hair dropped from the trees beside the white woman with the curls. The black man dropped to his knees at the white man's feet.

"Is he the professor?" Ask said and accepted the frosted bucket of ice cream from Charley.

"This is a whole nother movie," Cassie said. "Tarzan, that's Tarzan, he's been watching this woman, she's Jane, and she's an actress who is making this movie about the jungle, but the producer wants to take the chimp, what's his name? Chico? He's so smart for a monkey that the producer could make a lot of money with him in America. Oh, and he's engaged to Jane."

And so they passed their time together.

DURING THE SECOND WEEK Charley lived away, he lay on the couch in the dark, listening to the radio. There was a song by someone named Elvis but not *the* Elvis. The lyrics were hard to make out, something about a dance, something about a mystery.

Charley had discovered that he liked songs best when he knew some of the words but not all of them, when his mind had to fill in the gaps. Once he knew all the words, he was inevitably let down.

A figure appeared on the sidewalk outside his window: his father. The walk was dimly lit and he looked mysterious, a shadow dividing his face, lopping off a shoulder.

The doorbell sounded. Charley put his hands behind his head. He made no move to answer the bell. A new song had begun—Van Morrison. The doorbell rang again. Charley stared out the dark window, his father's shoulder and arm in a brown jacket—his father's bare shoulder and arm, pale skin with gray, curled hairs—long pink muscles of the upper arm, purple knotty veins, tendons taut at the elbow. Charley closed his eyes to stop his imagination and saw white skeletal bones linked by a rubber darkness.

Edward called, "Charley? Charley?" His voice sounded friendly; it was a friendly visit. "Charley?" The doorbell rang again, then he stepped from the door and looked through the window. He put his hands about his eyes and stared into the dark room.

"Do you remember when," Van Morrison sang, "we used to sing . . ."

"Charley?" His hands shielding his eyes made his head look enormous, like a pumpkin. "Charley?"

When he finally left, the window held an island of fog.

Two weeks later, packing his belongings to leave, Charley found a pair of pantyhose under his bed. The TV weather woman had left them. He held them up to the light, looked at them a long time, imagining her legs filling them, running his hands into them as if they were sleeves.

He suddenly stood, took off his shoes and socks, his pants and underwear. He pulled the pantyhose up his legs to his waist, pulled again at the crotch. He took the mirror from the bedroom door, propped it against the bed.

He looked silly and laughed, although the hose felt good, soft, secure, warm. He took them off, threw them in the trash, finished loading the van, and drove home.

3

Ask stayed true to his word and asked Julie Mayhew for a date. What he was ill-prepared for was her acceptance. "Sure," she had said, "what's your name?"

Surprised, he had trouble answering. "People call me Ask," he said finally.

"Cool," she said and introduced herself.

He began worrying about the date at that moment. First there were the mechanics to straighten out, and she waited while he removed his notebook from his backpack in order to write down her address and phone number. Then there was the date itself to plan. He turned to Tom and Cassie for advice.

"Just be yourself," Tom said.

"That never works," Cassie said.

The three of them sat on Ask's bed. "I don't want to take her to dinner, because I would have to eat in front of her. And at the movies I would have to worry about putting my arm around her, when to do it, how long to leave it there. I was thinking the last half hour of the movie would be good, but I can't read my watch in the dark, and what if she wanted to talk? People always tell me to shush if I say even one word in a theater."

"Take her to the drive-in," Tom said.

"For chrissakes, anything could happen there."

"Buy her flowers," Cassie said, "and don't be too polite. You can go overboard."

"She's right," Tom said. "Be yourself and don't worry about it."

"How can I be myself if I don't worry about it? I am myself and I'm worried."

"Don't buy her flowers, though," Tom said. "That's too much."

"We women love to get flowers from our men," Cassie said, indignant. She stood and walked to the door. "You think he knows anything about romance?" She left, slamming the door.

"She'll think you're a dope if you buy her flowers the first date," Tom said.

"What about a corsage?"

"To go to the drive-in?" He shook his head. "Just pick her up, a little late if you can, they hate it when you're early. Talk to her parents some, as little as you can. Then open the door for her . . ."

"The house door or the car door?"

"The car door, maybe the house door too, play it by ear. Then, when she's in the car, talk a little."

"About what?"

"Tell her she looks nice."

"That takes about three seconds."

"Stretch it out. Tell her her hair is nice. Her dress is pretty. She has a pretty smile. Improvise."

"I could talk about the movie, maybe."

"Sure, find out what kind of things she likes—movies, books, records."

"It doesn't sound very romantic."

"The romantic stuff comes later."

"That's the part that's worrying me."

"On the first date, all you are obligated to do is kiss her good night."

"When should I do that?"

"You take her home, walk her to her door, tell her you had a good time, and peck her on the lips."

"What if she wants more?"

"Then let her start things up."

"They'll do that?"

"Some of them. In high school it's hard to tell. Bring a couple of beers to the drive-in. She probably won't drink them, but she'll think you're dangerous."

"Yeah? Dangerous? That's good. We should clean the car." He stood with such a quick motion that the bed quivered in his wake.

"It's only Wednesday," Tom said. "You've got three days."

"Do we have any car wax?" He pulled Tom by the elbow out of the room.

. . .

HE TOOK HER to see a double feature: *A Fistful of Dollars* and *For a Few Dollars More.* Julie, as it turned out, liked beer. Ask had taken a six-pack from the refrigerator to make himself look extremely dangerous. She drank quickly. He had to guzzle to keep up.

"Clint Eastwood can't act," she said.

Ask nodded. "Who are your favorite actors?" This, he thought, was a good line to follow with.

"Dustin Hoffman is the most. He's a mature actor." She waggled her head. She seemed much thinner at close range than he had estimated at school, and her teeth were larger, but very straight and white. He liked the even layers of her dark hair, the mild pout in her lips.

"Did you ever see *The Graduate?*" she said. "I was too young but my sister took me anyway. He has an affair with this girl *and* her mother. It was a little gross but very mature."

"I saw *Little Big Man.* He was mature in that, old even."

"Do you smoke? I'm trying to quit. I saw this film where they put a tiny little camera into this guy's lungs who smoked like a pack a day and it looked like a gravel pit. I like pot, though. You smoke pot?"

Ask shrugged. "Sometimes." He had smoked once with Tom and thrown up.

"It's pretty cool you thought of the beer. Considerate and all."

"I thought the man should bring the beer," he said.

"Yeah, you'd be surprised what some boys are like. Look at that." Clint Eastwood outdrew three men and killed each. "He's like a Superman or something. You'd never see a mature actor do that. Two, maybe, but three?"

Ask found himself nodding a lot. He wanted to be friendly but didn't know what to say. So far, he thought he was doing all right. He was worried about what would happen when the beer ran out. He had to remember to thank Tom for recommending it.

"I'm going to Europe when I get out of high school. It's the backbone of culture."

"I'm going to study law."

"Oh yeah?" She put her hand on his shoulder. "Most guys don't even know what they're going to do. The thing about lawyers is they help people, which is good, and they dress good."

Ask bit his lip. "I've known since elementary school. I want to be in criminal law." Her hand on his shoulder packed a mild electrical charge.

"Lawyers are cute too. That's part of it. You got any gum? Beer makes me want to chew. My mother says I'm very oral. It's like being mouthy, only good." She leaned over and kissed Ask quickly on the lips. "I don't usually do that," she said.

He went out with her once a week, Saturdays, except for two weeks over Christmas vacation when she went with her parents to Lincoln, Nebraska, to see relatives. The quick kiss she had given him, plus the compulsory good-night kiss he had barely managed, grew to several kisses nightly, then making out, including a brief grope of her breasts. During this, he was surprised to discover himself bored.

His first thought was that he might be a homosexual. He wanted to keep an open mind, because he didn't think there should be anything wrong with being a homosexual; however, he didn't really like the idea. Then, a week before spring semester began, Charley let him borrow the van, telling him to park it backwards at the drive-in. Ask followed instructions, opening the back window and lying with Julie on the carpet to watch the movie. During a routine kissing episode, Julie stopped and took off her blouse.

Kissing Julie's breasts, Ask discovered a fascination and excitement that had been absent since the first date. They rolled on top of one another, and Ask slipped his hand down her pants to feel her ass, not quite brave enough to unzip her pants and look at her, touch her. But he knew that would come with time, and not a whole lot of time. Still, at the center of his excitement was a sense of something lacking. He felt he was bored and excited at the same time, something he had thought impossible.

Positive now he was not homosexual, he concluded that he just did not like Julie all that much. He was sure Charley would advise him not to let that get in the way. Tom, however, told him to hold off. "If you're not sure you like her," he said.

"I'm pretty much not sure. It's hard to tell. I look forward to seeing her, but sometimes that's the best part. If I keep going out with her, we're going to make love. Maybe soon, even. I want to. But . . ."

"Yeah," Tom said.

"On the other hand . . ."

"You'd really like to fuck her."

"Precisely."

"If you're bored while you're kissing her, then it's just a matter of time before you're bored while you're fucking her."

"On the other hand, I've never actually made love with a girl. It's hard to let an opportunity slip away."

"Don't be a slut," Tom said.

"That's easy for you to say. You slept with lots of women. A few, anyway."

"You could say lots."

"How many?"

"That's personal."

"I tell you everything."

"Seven."

"That's good."

"Charley is probably in triple figures," Tom said.

"It's like stamp collecting for him. He wants whoever he hasn't had." Ask folded his arms. "You think Charley is a slut?"

"He's got a certain style, but he's a slut."

"Maybe, but he's our slut."

"One slut in the family is enough. Cool off."

Ask nodded.

"In the meantime, you can give me her phone number. I could use a little boredom."

Ask smiled. "I like making decisions like this."

4

"WHAT MAKES a good bar?" Tom said, leaning back in his chair, looking from Ask and Arzate across the table to the pool tables just behind them. "I mean this place is not so much different from other bars, but it's better."

"The music," Arzate said. "Emmy Lou Harris."

"That's Bonnie Raitt," Tom said.

"Whatever. The pool tables."

"Every bar has pool tables," Tom said.

"These are good ones; the cues are straight."

The tables and cues at the Shanty, Tom acknowledged, were first rate. "That should only count when we're playing pool. Why's it a good bar when we're just sitting here getting drunk?" he said.

"What if a teacher from school comes in?" Ask said. "I could get suspended."

"The company," Arzate said. "I come here all the time because you do."

"We come together," Tom said.

"Exactly." Arzate smiled.

"Eighteen is the worst age to drink in public," Ask said. "You're a minor as far as drinking goes, but you're an adult in the courts. That's the kind of injustice I'm going to fight when I'm a lawyer."

"Undocumented workers," Arzate said. "They need lawyers. Even you."

"Draft resisters," Tom said. "I could have been one."

"You would have liked the navy," Arzate said. "That's Bonnie Raitt?"

"Since I fell-hell-hell for you-oo," Tom sang.

"You two would be contributing to the delinquency of a minor," Ask said.

"Coal miners," Arzate said, "who sue because they get black lung. They need lawyers."

"Copper miners," Tom said. "Unsafe conditions. Sue hell out of the company."

"Here's to miners," Arzate said, lifting his beer.

"And draft resisters," Tom said.

"And minors," Ask said.

"We already said that," Arzate said and dropped his bottle back to the table. "I don't want to drink to draft resisters, anyway."

"How come Charley never was drafted?" Tom said. "He was Viet Nam prime time."

"M-i-n-*o*-r-s," Ask said. "Charley has bad molars. You can't see them but they're rotten."

"That's dumb," Tom said. "I bet it was something else."

"He told me," Ask said.

"Here she comes," Arzate said, looking up at the waitress nearing them with their beers. He gave Tom a crumpled dollar under the table. Ask slipped him a five.

The waitress carried the tray with their beers at waist level. She moved effortlessly through the crowded bar. She reminded Tom of Eileen, although her frizzy hair and dark eyes did not resemble Eileen's. She smiled as she neared them. Her braces sparkled. "Three dollars," she said, setting the bottles on the table, shaking the ones they'd been drinking to see if they were empty.

Arzate lifted himself in his chair as if reaching for his wallet.

"I'll get it," Tom said, waving him off. The waitress smiled again. She was Tom's waitress. Whenever she waited on them, he pretended to buy all the drinks.

"You got the last round," Ask said, his mouth agape.

"One very generous guy," Arzate said, slapping Tom on the back.

"It's nothing," Tom said and gave her four dollars. "Keep it," he said.

"Thanks," she said and pivoted away from them.

"She's nuts about me," Tom said.

"I haven't seen my waitress all week. I think she quit." Arzate's waitress was boyish, short-haired, and pretty.

"That was a huge tip," Ask said.

"You were overacting," Tom said.

"Finesse," Arzate said, "is the key. Or she'll catch on. That was a big tip."

"She's worth it. Besides, we're drunk enough."

"You're right," Arzate said. "She's probably saving our lives by getting that big tip."

"A heroic woman," Ask said.

"Think I should ask her out?" Tom said.

"Nah. Spoil it." Arzate gulped his Budweiser.

"Spoil what?" Tom said and drank from his beer.

"As long as you don't know her very well, just as a waitress, she's perfect. You want to mess with perfection?"

"Platonic love is the ideal?" Ask said.

"I didn't say *that.*" Arzate drank again. "I don't know what *that* means. I said he shouldn't go out with her because then we'd have to find another bar. And this is the best bar in town."

"Why?" Tom said. "Why is this the best bar?"

"I thought we already covered that," Arzate said.

"We should write this stuff down," Tom said. "I lose track."

"We need secretaries," Arzate said.

"Do I look nineteen?" Ask said. "If she cards me, I'll say my wallet is in the car and walk out to get it. You guys meet me at the car, okay?"

"Would we date our secretaries?" Tom said.

5

EDWARD HAD ALWAYS SAID it would go up like a house of cards if they were ever careless. The fire started with the inner walls, causing them to fall in on themselves, one quickly following the next. Each fed the flames, and by the time the fire was out, nothing in the ashes or charred ruins resembled a house. Edward waited at a neighbor's for the fire trucks to arrive, only to see them appear too late to do anything but prevent the fire from spreading to other houses. He stood silently in his neighbor's family room, staring through a crack in the curtains. When the walls began falling, he said, "House of cards, I knew it."

A week before the fire, during the last days of Christmas vacation, the Warrens painted the interior of the house. Jill and Edward did the living room, dining room, kitchen, bathrooms, and their bedroom off-white, a color they hoped would lighten the rooms and resist smudges.

Edward started with the master bedroom, running masking tape around moldings, removing light switches and outlet covers. The room had striped curtains that had hung untouched in the desert sun so long they disintegrated like old documents in his hands. The curtains, the window, he realized, had not been opened in years. The window faced west, offering no morning sunlight. Afternoon sunlight was too intense to invite into the bedroom, so it had stayed shut. He stared out the window into his backyard, a view he had ignored for almost a decade. The yard, stolid greens and browns, had a strangeness about it, a foreignness. It became exotic, the edge of something, a border, like a beach, between what he understood and what he could only guess. Beyond his fence, in the limbs of his neighbor's citrus trees, the sun burned red as a tomato.

He moved furniture away from the walls, shoving the bed to the center of the room and stacking on it the bookshelf he'd already emptied, the folding tray they kept next to the bed, the rocker he'd taken from Kentucky. When he was a child, his father had rocked him in that chair, reading *Brer Rabbit.* He had wanted to read to his children in the rocker. They hadn't been interested, ruined by television—Huckleberry Hound, Quick Draw McGraw, Rocky the Squirrel.

He scooted the dresser next to the bed. Things had fallen behind it—wads of tissue paper, a tampon in its bullet container, a note in Jill's script, one she might have written years ago, that said, "Eggs, flour, Ivory, apples, popcorn, beer, vinegar, bread, a new color for . . ."

The note made him laugh. He wondered what the new color could be for and decided not to ask, to let it remain a mystery. There were coins beneath the dresser, a pencil, a fragment of glass. Their secrets remained secret, even to him. He became reluctant to paint but overcame it, working slowly, watching the new off-white cover the old gray. It seemed a more permanent change than just new paint. The roller made a sticking sound, like static from a radio, as the paint adhered to the walls.

A car entering the alley swept light across the room, startling Edward into awareness of the night, that the sun had set and he was painting in the dark. When he turned on the overhead lamp, the room was a waxy white, like the inside of a milk carton.

JILL TOOK A SHEET of wood paneling left over from an unsuccessful attempt to redecorate the den and cut out a piece the shape of a half moon. She began in the kitchen, pressing the paneling against the wall directly under her roller to catch any runs or spills. Cassie trailed with a soapy washcloth to wipe up any drops. The act of painting always made Jill think she should take it up professionally. She enjoyed the activity, the movement, the simple doing of it. And the disappearing, the past evaporating, the old becoming new. She worked quickly, adjusting her half moon, stroking and moving on.

"You think I could go to the McCartney concert in Phoenix?" Cassie stood beside her on the kitchen counter.

Jill protected the ceiling with the paneling and painted the top border of the wall. "No concerts until you're seventeen." Cassie was becoming uncomfortably sophisticated. Pulling the sheets from her bed a week ago, Jill had found a magazine with pictures of naked men, some with grotesquely large genitals. "Oh, I've had that for months," Cassie had said, taking the magazine from Jill's hand and throwing it in the garbage.

Cassie wiped wet circles on the unpainted portion of the wall. "You said sixteen last time."

"Then you should quit asking. I get more conservative as I age." She placed a foot on the rim of the sink, balanced herself, and kept painting. She'd like to paint Cassie, make her new again, a little girl with simpler requests.

"I like standing on the counter. Why do we only do this when we have to paint? Can you get high smelling this stuff?" She put her nose next to the freshly painted wall.

Jill glared at her. "That had better not be a serious question."

"Give me a break, Mom." She turned, the tip of her nose covered with paint.

Jill laughed. The dot of paint on her nose had turned her into a little girl again. For the moment. "Your nose."

Cassie rubbed her nose with the washcloth. "McCartney's a Beatle, Mom. He's harmless."

Jill ran the roller across the gray wall. "Get that drip."

"He's married. With kids. He's as old as you are. Almost."

"Not until you're eighteen."

"*Mom.*" She stretched the word into two syllables.

"Maybe we should become house painters," Jill said. "A mother-daughter team." She stepped down from the counter, moving quickly to the next wall.

By the time Edward finished the bedroom, Jill had painted the living room, dining room, kitchen, and bathrooms. Edward was the only one who could see any difference between her work and his. "There's a right way," he said, pointing to the grooves in a light-switch cover, now filled with white paint, "and a wrong way . . ." Jill had left the room, and he never finished the sentence.

CASSIE PICKED Yolk Yellow for her room and made a mess. She liked her parents' idea of lightening the house and chose the color she thought most resembled sunlight. On the gray wall, however, the paint took on a different shade, like jaundiced skin. Halfway through the first wall, she added a glass of water to the paint to lighten the color. The thinned paint ran down the wall faster than she could brush it, leaving watery yellow streaks that puddled on the tiled floor and in the cracks in the baseboards. She finished the half-painted wall and left the others unpainted, except for one long, diagonal slash above the bed, which she painted in her sleep. She woke with the brush on the pillow beside her, her cheeks and pajamas spattered with paint.

"I dreamed I was painting the lines on a road," she said, pointing at the long streak. "It was a no passing zone."

ASK BELIEVED the bedrooms should be the same color as the rest of the house. In order to convince the family, he gathered them and praised Sponge Cake, the official name of the off-white paint, and appealed for "harmony of hue." His final contention, that having identical walls would bring the family closer together, didn't carry the weight he'd hoped—even Cassie laughed. He decided that he needed to set an example and began painting his room.

It took longer than he'd imagined. His room was cluttered with things he couldn't throw away. He shoved his bed out from the wall and covered it with the small and various emblems of his life—science fair ribbons, the annual birthday photographs of the family standing around him, plastic fruit that he thought of as Pop Art, eight years of *National Geographic*, the ironing board and iron he'd been given for Christmas, National Honor Society certificates, a poster of F. Lee Bailey.

He stayed up all night moving furniture and painting his room. At five fifteen in the morning he finished. He waited until six, then woke everyone, gathering them in the hall. "Sponge Cake in every room," he said and opened his door. The family, one by one, stuck their heads in, then returned to bed.

TOM PICKED a brown that reminded him of wood. He pictured it as a walnut color and imagined living in his room as living inside a huge nut. The paint turned out to be darker than he intended, but in the three months he'd been back, painting the room had been his only activity that seemed remotely useful. Despite the depressing color, he never gave any indication that he was anything but entirely satisfied.

He finished at dusk. His bulletin board and Little Richard poster he threw away. In the center of the wall opposite his bed he hammered one long nail and hung his green jacket on it. The weather had turned cold, as cold as it ever got in Yuma, sometimes as low as freezing. He thought the jacket would be handy there. He pushed his bed back underneath the window. Standing on the bed to rehang his curtains, he spotted Ask in the backyard on his knees, digging in the garden with a hand spade.

"This room is ridiculous."

Tom turned. Ask stood in the doorway with Cassie. Tom looked into the backyard again. There was no one. They didn't even have a garden. Perhaps he'd seen Ask's reflection in the window or perhaps he'd just imagined it. He only considered the possibilities for a moment before dismissing them and forgetting the thing entirely. He hung the curtains and dropped to his knees on the bed.

"Completely ridiculous," Ask said.

Brown smears stained Tom's hands. The room looked like it was made of mud. He lay flat on his bed.

"Leave him alone," Cassie said. "A room is a kind of freeform art. Nobody in this family has any imagination."

"Art?" Ask said. He stepped in the room and stared at the wall with the jacket.

Tom pulled a pillow over his head. "Get out of here, will you?"

"You know what it makes me think of?" Ask held his chin in his hand.

Cassie stepped beside him. They stared at the brown wall and green jacket. "What?" she said.

"You can't see the forest for the trees," Ask said. "That's what I think when I look at this 'art.' "

"Beat it," Tom said and threw a pillow at them.

"You're the worst one," Cassie said to Ask as they left the room. "Free-form art doesn't mean anything, that's why it's free."

"Shut the door," Tom yelled.

CHARLEY CHOSE WHITE—"White White," the salesman had called it. When the family picked through the wreckage, the two cans of White White were positioned next to each other in what had been Charley's room. Warped by the extreme heat, the cans had exploded and white paint marked the ashes and bubbled still within the twisted containers.

EDWARD'S STORY

I'VE DONE EVERYTHING a man can do to make a good home. Nobody cares about that. It's the few times I've slipped that people focus on. So be it. I've borne that burden a long time.

I met Jennetta in the fall of 1966, the last year I lived in Kentucky except for the summer of '68, which I don't count. She was the waitress at Hale's Cafe, a little burger and barbecue place near the school. I'd eat there with one of the teachers or a problem student, with Jill for that matter—school cafeteria food is nothing to dedicate yourself to. Hale's was nearby and good.

I flirted with her. Everybody did. It was friendly and harmless. It was *southern.* And she was pretty. Beautiful is a better word for what she was. I'm trying to be honest. Her hair was dark, a natural dark. She wasn't tall but had that compact sexiness some women have. Yes, large breasts. Yes, blue eyes. She had all of that, and none of it meant a thing.

One day late in October I went there with Del Went, a fifth-grade teacher, for lunch. I ate there nearly every day, but this was the day that mattered. Keep in mind that by December Cassie was having breathing fits and by January I was teaching in Arizona.

Del and I sat in a booth. There were a few other people there, I can't remember everything, but we were the only ones in that booth and the only ones that matter to the story. Except Jennetta, of course.

Del was a wolf. That's what we called them back then, men that prowled the whole time for women to take to bed. To put it bluntly. Sitting in Hale's, waiting for Jennetta to come take our order, we talked about sex. It was what Del always wanted to talk about. A lot of men are like that and sometimes you just have to put up with them.

"For me," he said, "it's always a letdown. I get to thinking about a woman, get her image inside my mind, and I got to fuck her. Most times I do. By the time I get it in her though, hell. Then it comes back to me that a fuck is a fuck, and that's it."

"That's too bad," I said, acting interested, when the truth was he didn't have any right to think he could talk to me like that. I was the principal of the school. I had authority. Everyone knew I didn't go for that kind of talk, but sometimes you've just got to sit through it, even though the truth is you don't want to hear it.

"It's not like that for you?" he said. "The hell it's not. You're no different from me, I bet. You ever had a fuck that really made you happy?"

"Truth is," I said as Jennetta came near us, "I never had one that didn't."

I thought that would shut him up, at least make him move on to a new subject, but no luck.

Jennetta was wearing a short skirt with a red and white plaid apron. I can see that skirt and apron right now as clearly as I can see my hands. I remember that apron better than I remember her face. How do you account for that?

"What can I get for you two?" she said.

"This man says he's never had a woman who didn't make him happy," Del said to her.

I could have hit him.

"Can you believe that?" he said and laughed.

"You shut your mouth," I said. "Don't pay any attention to him." I looked up to Jennetta and smiled.

She nodded, rolled her eyes a little as if to say she knew how Del was. Then she said something that changed both our lives.

"I could make you unhappy," she said.

It was as if a plug came loose inside me. I became giddy, although I tried not to let on, but my sentences came out chopped and stupid. "I want a barbecue toast," I said, immediately wanting to laugh and say, "*On* toast," but she didn't react and . . . and what? I fell in love? I was infatuated? The label you lend to it doesn't much matter. That moment was profound.

Years later I would go to bed with a girl, a high school girl in one of my classes, because she made that moment come real to me again. That's later, but I wanted to mention it now because it all ties in. That's not making an excuse. I don't have an excuse for any of it.

I started going to the cafe without anyone else. It was still harmless. After all, even if I'd wanted more (and I didn't), my in-laws lived right across the street, just up the hill.

We'd talk. I could tell she liked me. God knows I should have left it alone, but I couldn't. I discovered that she had next to nobody in the cafe around nine thirty—breakfast crowd was gone, lunch group not there yet. I started going then.

One day in November, I came at nine thirty (I'd tell my secretary I was taking an early lunch so I could patrol during the school lunch period—a principal of a small school can do almost anything) and there was no one there but her. She had a barbecue sandwich on toast ready for me. I sat at the counter, but she walked right past me, put it on one side of a booth and she sat on the other. I joined her.

"You shouldn't eat the same lunch every day. Your stomach will get bored. We have a wide menu. You like tunafish? Egg salad? You don't look like a burger man."

Was that flirting? I thought it was, but I can't say exactly why. "I guess I'd like whatever you make." That *was* flirting.

"Lydia makes the barbecue. She's back there now mixing up new sauce."

A warning of sorts, I thought, to let me know we weren't totally alone. Then I said something strange. It just popped into my head.

"You ever heard a duck when it's been shot? I'm talking about a duck flying overhead and you're out hunting. You ever heard one when it's hit?"

She bit her upper lip, maybe trying to figure how to take this new line of talk. I didn't know where it was leading either.

"I used to hunt with my daddy," she said. *Daddy* sounds to me now like an affectation, but I was just getting to know her then. "It sounds," she stretched out the vowels, "like someone laughing while he's being strangled."

She was thinking about the quacking gaggle of a hit duck; I was thinking about the sound of the air through the feathers as it plummeted. I'd never heard anything that sounded like what she described, but what I said next wasn't a lie anyway. It was the truth because I didn't know it was coming.

"That sound went off inside me the other day, talking to you, something wild. Strange."

That sounds corny, stupid. It always does when you try to speak the truth and have to lie to do it, but Jennetta could tell I meant it. She nodded at me, slow and real, without any of her put on. We sat that way for a while and she said, "Tell me about your kids."

Every day I saw her and we talked. About my family. About hers. About Jill, and I never said one word against my wife. About her ex-husband, a blue-grass banjo picker who used to dance naked in the kitchen, then one day turned mean on her for no good reason. Some days we didn't seem to talk about anything, but the time flew. After a month of talking every day, during school, before, after, we talked about going to bed together.

I told her I couldn't.

If I had a Bible here I'd swear on it. I said no.

Two weeks before the end of the semester, Jill came back from Paducah with Cassie on a vaporizer. We had to move or Cassie would be sick all the time. I had known this was coming but hadn't admitted it to myself. Jennetta and I had talked about it. I couldn't put the move off any longer. I made some calls and found a job in Arizona starting in January. Only after I was sure I was leaving, only after I knew that I'd be a thousand miles away and she knew it too, did I make love with Jennetta.

Once.

In a motel in Paducah. One time. On a single bed in a room that smelled of rust and mildew. I never even kissed her on any other occasion. As God is my witness.

The day I arrived in Arizona, there were four letters waiting for me at the school. They had no return address on the envelope, but I knew who had sent them. She has written me every day since then. She could wait, she said. I wrote back to her regularly for a while. I told her I would never leave Jill. She said she could wait.

We moved back to Kentucky for one summer. I stayed up the hill from the cafe at Hannah's, Jill's sister's. I looked down there, across the highway, every day. I could see her move up and down the fry counter, in and out between the tables. She worked double shifts, wanting to be there when I came down.

I never did, although each day I was there I considered it. She never made any attempt to contact me. I had come the thousand miles, she should come the rest of the way, I reasoned.

How could she have? That one summer was the only time I didn't get letters from her. She had no place to send them. She wrote anyway. Once I saw her from the hill—she was sitting in a booth, bent over the table, writing. When we settled in Yuma, they all arrived. They were full of patience and love. I don't write her much anymore, not as much as I should. Her letters arrive at school every day. I don't read them. Occasionally, I do. As far as I can see, I ruined her life.

Sometimes I wonder why. Why she decided I was the one, why she has held on so long to so little. Much as I'd like to think otherwise, I know I'm just another man. Nothing went on in that single bed in Paducah that wasn't going on in a million other beds between two million other strangers. I asked her once, on a postcard. I wrote *Why me? Why do you love me?* I got a letter from her a couple of days later, the shortest letter she ever sent me. *Just because,* she said.

The high school girl, a senior and eighteen or God knows what would have happened, came to my room one day after class, sat in a desk in the front row and said she needed some make-up work to raise her grade. I checked through my grade book.

"You're getting an A," I told her.

"Then I need something to lower it," she said.

I laughed and it sounded like I was strangling. I was already lost at that point.

She was a child. I have weaknesses.

We went to bed several times. Many times. She let a friend know. It got around the school. I probably should have lost my job, my wife. They switched me to Driver's Ed, a class that teaches itself. I should thank them for it.

And Jill never said word one, except to let me know she knew. I should thank her too. I should tell you how I've loved her day in and day out for thirty years, how she's loved me, how we fell in love and married and had a baby boy that everyone in Ballard County envied. A boy so beautiful and full of promise, parents were pushing daughters on him in kindergarten. No one wants to hear about those happy years. No one wants to hear about a good man being good. It's the failings people want to hear.

So be it.

THE MORNING OF THE DAY OF THE FIRE

I

THE MORNING of the day of the fire, Tom, who had fallen into the habit of sleeping late, woke early, dressed in jeans, a blue cotton shirt, a bulky sweater, and waited in his room until he heard the Ancient Mariner leave the driveway, his mother taking his father, Ask, and Cassie to school. He stepped into the bathroom, adjusted the part in his hair, combed, parted again, shaved the scant black stubble from his chin, and slapped aftershave on his face and neck.

"She's going to make you miserable," Charley said. He sat on the living room couch in his gray robe, hunched over the coffee table. He turned a quarter over and over in his fingers, and stared at the revolving coin, his face pale, dark moons under his eyes. The hood of the robe was cocked oddly to the side of his head, a huge mouth just below his ear. He looked like an insane monk.

"I need to get it over with." Tom shoved his fists into his pockets. He was surprised to see Charley up. Since quitting his job, he usually slept into the early afternoon.

"Forget her," Charley said. The quarter tumbled through his fingers. "Let's get out of town. Go to San Diego."

Tom almost laughed. He could see, however, that Charley was serious. He tried to imagine them together in the van, or strolling down the boardwalk dodging skaters. What would they talk about? Where would Charley want to eat? What would he want to do? The prospect of finding out fascinated him, almost to the point of going. "Maybe tomorrow," he said.

Charley shook his head, dropped the quarter on the table, gripped his knees. "Be too late." The quarter spun on the table, settling finally. Tails.

"Too late for what?"

"Too late to go. Together."

"I don't get it."

"I can't explain myself. Never could do that." He released his knees, leaving white fingerprints around his red kneecaps like daisy leaves. "You still hung up on her?" He lifted his head to Tom, nodding as if under a great weight.

Tom moved to the door, put his hand on the knob. He was becoming increasingly uncomfortable. "Hung up is a good way to put it. I can't seem to do anything else until I clear things up with her."

"That's what you're going to do?" His head jerked back, his voice sharper. "Clear things up? You think *words* can do that?"

Tom suddenly believed Charley was right. He tried once more to picture the two of them in the van, sleeping side by side. He couldn't see it. He tried again, picturing them back to back, or facing one another, or on their stomachs. It could never happen.

"I've got to run," he said.

"Yeah, listen." Charley stood, hands in the huge pockets of the robe. "I never thought you were coming back. From Berkeley. Holidays, I thought, a long weekend, maybe even a summer—but not really coming back. I thought you were out. I figured . . ."

"So I'm not who you thought I was." Tom felt accused, although he couldn't name the charge.

"That's right. You're not," Charley said. "I may not be who you think I am either."

Tom opened the front door. The morning was cool, brisk. "What's the point?" he said.

Charley sat again on the couch. "Forget it. Take off."

Tom paused. Morning light shone through the door on the freshly painted walls, the graying hardwood floors, stopping just short of his brother. "You all right?" he said.

"No." Charley again lifted his stare from the coffee table to Tom. "I'm going to get well, though. Soon."

Tom nodded and stepped out onto the yellowing lawn. He inhaled deeply, smelling only his aftershave, and began the long walk downtown finally to see Eileen, watched by his brother, from the window, the curtains parted only a sliver.

TOM WALKED SLOWLY, imagining Eileen. She was pregnant, he knew, Arzate had seen her at the mall, but he couldn't adjust his image of her to account for the child. He hoped she was unreasonably large, huge, monstrously obese. He ambled along, picking up small objects and discarding them—bottle caps, a chip of green glass, a matchbook cover.

He had gone a long time without sex. Since the night the girls slept in the van, he had known he should call Marriet. He had enjoyed being with her. She seemed full grown—there were as many parts to her as there were to him. The girls in the van had been missing parts. What parts? He couldn't say exactly, a certain complexity, a sense of themselves.

He hadn't been able to call Marriet. Something would come up, or he would decide to delay the call until he got a job so he wouldn't have to borrow money. He knew he was rationalizing. He had done nothing more to look for a job than browse the paper.

The image of a contract, perfectly typed, a long dark line for his name, persisted in his mind. He thought of Marriet as damaged. He didn't like himself for it, didn't want to believe it, but he did. Even with this admission, he could have called her, but Eileen hovered above each possibility, freezing his finger on the telephone dial. He had known for weeks that he would have to talk with her before seeing Marriet again. Eileen left phone messages, wrote notes, sent cards. He, on the other hand, avoided the drugstore, the bars and restaurants they used to frequent, the mall, the theater. He could have talked to her a dozen times if he had wanted.

For a short while, Eileen had quit trying to reach him. It was a period of calm in the house, a respite. Charley had moved out, Eileen had given up, and Tom rested peacefully on the couch mulling over the paper for hours. Although the calm hadn't been that good, it had been quiet and easy, very easy. After a month, Charley returned, Eileen sent a Christmas card, an evergreen covered with snow and a note that said *Call Me,* and the calm was gone.

Yesterday, he and Charley had been the only ones in the house, he playing solitaire, Charley watching "Wheel of Fortune," when the phone rang several times and Tom finally left his cards to answer. "Tom," she said. He said nothing, his throat tight, his stomach tense. "Promise me," Eileen said, "you'll come by the store early tomorrow. No one is here early. Just a few moments."

"Yeah," he had said, "okay," and hung up.

He had slept with only one woman since Eileen, a pale girl with black glasses and a pretty smile. She had come to the dorm to sleep with his roommate Lance, a scraggly eighteen-year-old from New Jersey with pinched cheeks and wispy hair who smoked cigarettes and brought home a woman every night, most of them markedly unattractive and boring. At first Tom had stayed away nights when Lance had someone over, but once he realized that it was going to be every night, he insisted on sleeping in his bunk. Lance didn't mind at all. Each night he helped his new girl friend into the top bed, and Tom watched the springs depress, sometimes counting the depressions, until he fell asleep. "I'd fuck anyone who doesn't have teeth in her cunt," Lance said.

Tom had met Emma while sitting on the hall floor outside the door to his room. Inside, Lance was fucking a heavyset Bio major. "You don't have to sit out there," Lance yelled. The Bio major giggled. The bed rattled. A few minutes later, Emma appeared in the hall. Her face fell when she saw Tom. "Lock yourself out?" she asked, hopeful.

He shook his head. She stuck her ear to the door.

"He's a slut," Tom said.

She laughed. "Can boys be sluts?"

"No sweat," he said and stood. "I'll buy you a sandwich." He took her to a deli and fed her, walked her home, and spent the night. He told her about Eileen's engagement, how lousy he was doing in his classes. She listened and played albums by John Lee Hooker.

When he came home from English the next afternoon, she was in the top bunk with Lance. Later, she told him she loved Lance, but thanked him. "You really picked me up last night," she said. "I mean, I was really low." She kissed him and he dropped out of school.

He tried to quit thinking of women, to think instead about his future. He was sure he had one, but he didn't know what to do with it. He picked up a coin, a nickel with a gash through Washington's nose and the word "WE" of IN GOD WE TRUST. Tom looked the nickel over, then discarded it as he had the other articles he had found. He laughed at himself for throwing away money. The nickel skipped over the sidewalk, flying into a lush St. Augustine lawn.

"What are you doing?" The voice, gruff and ulcerous, came from the side of the house, a heavy man, bald with a graying mustache and watery yellow eyes. He walked toward Tom with quick forward thrusts of his elbows. "What was it? Gum wrapper? Beer tab? You thought no one was looking, didn't you? What was it?"

As he approached, Tom remembered his name. "A nickel, Mr. Davenport." He was the father of someone Tom had known since starting school in Yuma—Rita Davenport, a birdlike girl who wore glasses, sat in the back row of every class, and mumbled the correct answer when called upon.

"A nickel? Who are you? Should I know you? What are you

doing throwing a nickel on my lawn?" Even in the cool morning air, Mr. Davenport's arms were wet with perspiration.

"How's Rita, Mr. Davenport?" Tom felt oddly happy to see him, relieved to have a distraction.

He pointed at Tom, his finger jiggling. "You're a Warren. One of the Warren boys. Charley."

"Tom." He stepped into the yard, the St. Augustine thick and spongy, like a foam pad. He picked up the nickel and flashed it at Mr. Davenport. "A nickel," he said.

"My Rita is dead," Mr. Davenport said. His face flushed. He folded his arms, daring Tom to say something. He cleared his throat, spat. "You went to school with her," he said as if in explanation.

"Yes," Tom said. He tried to think of the appropriate words. "I'm sorry. I didn't know."

Mr. Davenport nodded fiercely, looking over his lawn. "Why were you throwing nickels?"

Tom shrugged. "I just picked it up and threw it away. I looked at it, but I didn't really think about its being a nickel. I knew it was a nickel—money, I mean—but then I just threw it."

Mr. Davenport nodded again, slower, an acknowledgment. "I threw away a twenty-dollar bill once." He smiled an awkward, painful-looking smile. "Spring cleaning. Made Rita . . ." He looked to Tom, eyes blank and frightened. He cleared his throat. "We found it in the trash. You want a cup of coffee?"

"I can't. I'm on my way . . ."

"Rita had a cancer. Right here." He put his hand to his chest, his almost womanly breasts. "They operated. She never come out of anesthetic." He nodded slowly, as Charley had a few minutes earlier, as if his head had suddenly become too heavy for the muscles in his neck.

"We had classes," Tom said, almost a whisper.

"This grass takes a lot of work," Mr. Davenport said. "To make it green all the year, that is. Fertilize. Water. Mow. Can't take the sun like Bermuda. Fragile. I didn't mean to bark at you."

Tom shook his head. "It's a good yard." He squatted, touched the grass. "It's nice, thick."

Mr. Davenport dropped to one knee, dug his fingers into the lawn. "Doesn't grow like other grass." He pulled up a loop of grass, a long rope with evenly spaced green blades on the top side and gray roots on the bottom. "These are called trailers. They spread out across the lawn slow. Little green trails, see?" He pulled another few inches of the green rope loose from the earth. "That's why they call them trailers. I can give you some clippings sometime." He patted the loop he had pulled loose back into place. "I love this goddamn grass," he said, pushing its roots back into the dirt. He stood, clapped his hand fiercely against his side, then wiped his fingers on his pantleg. "You get your nickel?"

Tom stood and held the scarred nickel up to eye level. It flashed for a moment.

"Stop again." He threw his hand up and charged around the side of the house.

Tom could see nothing of Rita in him. He turned the nickel in his hand as Charley had earlier turned the quarter, and began walking again, his thoughts, for the moment, free of Eileen.

2

THE MORNING of the day of the fire Jill wore a maroon dress, a Christmas gift from Ask and Cassie. When she had torn the gift wrapping off the box and seen the color, she had secretly hoped it would be the wrong size or have a hidden tear or stain. Red had never been her color. She had been disappointed that the dress fit, then surprised that it looked good on her.

Edward, across from her in the front seat, smoking a cigarette, flicking the ashes out a crack in the window, was quiet, distracted, distant. In the backseat, Ask and Cassie were up to something. She watched them in the rearview mirror—Cassie whispering in Ask's ear and smiling, Ask glancing back conspiratorially. The radio played songs from the 1960s. Mick Jagger shouted, "I can't *get* no!" The rest of the car was quiet.

The high school sprawled over a piece of the valley, one-story buildings connected by covered walkways. It looked more like a shopping mall than a school. She stopped in front of the main gate, a tall mesh fence on rollers topped with barbed wire, which made her think that the school also resembled a prison camp, but the children beyond the fence were dressed in such bright colors, she couldn't picture it.

Edward stepped out of the car without speaking. He shut the door and began walking to his class. "What's upsetting your father?" she said.

Cassie gathered her books in her lap. "Oh Mom, he's always like that."

"He is not," Ask said. "He's probably just tired."

"See you later," Cassie said, and they were out the door. They walked side by side, Cassie carrying her textbooks in front of her as she might a watermelon, Ask tugging at his underwear. A slip of paper fell from one of Cassie's books.

"Cass," Jill called, but the window was up and she was already too far away to hear. The paper was folded oddly, probably unimportant. Nonetheless, she shifted into park and retrieved it, a lined sheet of notebook paper tucked and folded into a triangle. She flattened it against the car seat. There were two colors of ink.

They sacrificed virgins? Cassie's handwriting in one corner of the sheet was in black ink. Below it, turned at a right angle and printed in blue ink, was *You'd think they'd* and nothing else. Jill shifted into drive.

Frieda Stanley was waiting on the stoop of Lynn's Odds and Ends. "My keys have legs," she said. "I can never find them."

Jill laughed and unlocked the door. The proprietor, Lynn, had died, leaving the shop to her daughter who lived in Truth or Consequences, New Mexico, and did not want to come to Yuma. Jill had agreed to pack up the valuables and have them shipped to New Mexico, to auction off the remaining junk, and to sell the store. She already had several people interested in the shop, but the clutter had been too much bother. She'd hired Frieda to help her box the cracked china and porcelain miniatures, old postcards, doilies, belt buckles. They had found the strangest things—a cardboard box filled with sunglasses, hundreds of them, jammed together, covered with dust; a walk-in closet on the second floor that held nothing but wire clothes hangers from floor to ceiling, tangled together like a modern sculpture; hotel soap, close to a hundred little bars, no two from the same place; a drawer of novelty pens, women who stripped when the pen was tipped, eyes that moved.

One room had been disturbing. The door had been locked and Jill tried a drawerful of keys before picking the lock with a bobby pin. The far corner was filled with little statues, the largest waist high, of black boys holding golden rings. Hitching niggers, her father had called them when she was little, made to hold the reins of a horse. They had survived in the South past the times of horses as a sign of old money. The sixties had all but eradicated them, except for Lynn's Odds and Ends.

In a dresser beside the statues, she found the tailored white drapes and stiff pointed hoods of the Ku Klux Klan, neatly folded, ironed. There were two drawers of them. The bottom drawer held obscene porcelain figures—a wide-eyed black man with an enormous erection, clothed only in comically oversized shoes and a noose molded around his neck; a foot-long figure of a heavy black woman lying on her back, naked, her knees spread, and a slot for coins between her legs. There were others, wooden figures that rocked into each other simulating sex when a handle was turned.

What should she do with these? Her first impulse was to destroy them, then she thought they should go to a museum, that there should be a record of the country's racist past, but what museum would have obscene figures in it? Finally, she decided to pack them up and send them to the daughter, except for the statues, which were too heavy. She would have them hauled to the dump. As she quickly wrapped the figures in newspaper and stacked them in a box, she came across the ugliest yet—a smiling (all the black figures were smiling) black man bending over, his erect penis in his own mouth, a placard extending out of his anus, which read *L.A./NiGGerToWn/1975*.

She threw the figure into the box. The date as much as the thing itself upset her. The figure lay broken on top of the others. She pulled the drawer out of the dresser and dumped the remaining ones on top of it, then lifted one of the smaller hitching statues by its elbows and hammered it against the other figures. She lifted again and let it drop, and again, several times. The action reminded her, strangely, of churning milk with her mother as a child, and that calmed her. She put a lid on the box of shattered porcelain and left the shop. She did not return until Frieda had agreed to work with her.

"I like that dress," Frieda said.

Jill first thought Frieda had come across a box of dresses, then realized that she meant her maroon dress. "It was a gift from my kids."

Frieda smiled and walked to a leather business chair that was on rollers. She spent most of her time in the chair, rolling from one stack of junk to another. Seven months pregnant, she wasn't the ideal person to hire, but Jill liked her and knew she was bored with being nothing but pregnant.

"I should be able to finish the files today," Frieda said. Three file cabinets had been filled with genealogical information, and the daughter wanted them. Frieda rolled the chair to the file cabinet.

Jill sorted through a stack of legal papers. She hated the paperwork portion of any job. She liked talking to people and showing houses. Something about houses delighted her, how people expanded to fill a large house—she thought really bright people most often grew up in big houses, as if the architecture of the house helped define the architecture of the mind.

"I had the funniest dream last night," Frieda said absently. She had an open file in her hands, a dozen in her lap. "I dreamed I was in an airplane, sitting next to a window, and you were a stewardess."

"I like that," Jill said. "Did I have on one of those stewardess miniskirts?"

"I can't remember, but I do remember what you said. You put a hand on the arm of my seat and leaned in. Oh, you even had on a little stewardess cap. You said, 'Miss Harper, your call has been completed.' "

"Why did I call you that?"

"That's my maiden name, haven't I ever told you? Anyway, I said, 'What call?' And you put your hands on your hips and started pouting. 'To your *friend,*' you said, 'Miss Warren.' 'But you're Miss Warren,' I said. Then you sat across the aisle from me and there were phones in the seats somehow and we talked to each other on the phones even though you were right across the aisle."

"What did we say?"

"I can't remember. I think we were the only ones on the plane."

"That's a strange dream."

"They say being pregnant gives you funny dreams, but I haven't noticed any difference dreaming for two." She lifted the file again. "Oh, another thing, the plane was on the ground. I looked out the window and there was grass."

Jill smiled and pushed the papers aside. She had decided to hire Frieda shortly after Mr. Stanley backed out of buying the house. She had heard he was backing out on her dead brother's birthday, an occasion that alternately depressed or elated her, depending on the direction of her thoughts. If she remembered past birthdays, she was depressed. The birthdays with him had been so few and so long ago. The birthdays without him were so numerous.

On the other hand, if she could avoid nostalgia, she might find herself in a very good mood, imagining him pulling into their driveway, still a young man, still in uniform, driving an old American car, the kind with rounded lines and huge chrome bumpers. The daydream was far enough from possibility to hold no sadness.

That day the house failing to sell had pushed her to think of other times when things had fallen through, which led her to think of birthdays without her brother Tom. She'd sensed her mood darkening as she drove into the parking lot of the Stanleys' apartment building. It would be a depressing day unless she was very careful.

The apartments were white, two-storied, with plenty of windows and a balcony. Perhaps Frieda had just decided to avoid dungeon living, Jill thought.

Frieda answered the door. "Oh, I'm so sorry," she said.

"Hi," Jill said.

"Roger decided we couldn't afford it. Come in. Do you have time? Let me fix you some coffee."

The apartment was spare and drab. His furniture, Jill thought, looking at the plaid couch, orange chair.

"Roger is afraid of the expense, with the baby coming and all." Frieda sat in the orange chair, forgetting the coffee. "I think he likes it here too much to move, too. He's lived here seven years."

Jill smiled. She was relieved to know Frieda didn't call her husband mister.

"I guess I have to try to fix it up." She rubbed the arms of the chair. "I was sure we were moving."

Jill scanned the apartment for something to compliment—yellow shag carpet, modern end tables around the green plaid couch. "That's a nice lamp," she said, a ceramic base, tall amber shade.

Frieda laughed. "I bought that last night. As soon as Roger said we couldn't afford the house."

Why did she put up with him, Jill wondered. What did she see in the cheapskate? "How did you two meet?" she asked, looking for clues.

"At an Elvis Presley concert. Roger loved Elvis. I was there with a girl friend. The concert was really late starting, and Roger entertained us with Elvis trivia. I thought he was such a fruit." She laughed, wistful, as if she were laughing at herself.

"I wouldn't have taken him for a rock and roll fan," Jill said.

When Elvis died, Ask had wanted a party. She had said no. She remembered that before the news of the drugs had come out, there was speculation that his death had to do with the anniversary of his mother's death. They had died on the same day a few years apart. Grief syndrome, or some such name.

"Roger had these terrible sideburns. Lamb chops, they're called."

"Mutton chops," Jill said, laughing.

"It's hard to believe now. Oh, I wish we'd bought that house, or some house. This apartment just reeks of bachelorhood." She looked over the room. "That night at the concert, Roger told me he was the head of a group trying to get Elvis made a saint—a real saint. Saint Elvis, the King. He seemed so fruity, I believed him."

"He was joking?"

"He has a great sense of humor. One time I came home and there was a big package with a bow on the coffee table. The box said Westinghouse Iron—I'd been wanting a new iron—but inside were carnations. He'd cut the stems to nothing so they would fit."

Jill had smiled, although she couldn't see much evidence of a sense of humor in the gesture. They'd talked for another hour, and by the time Jill left, she wasn't depressed. Frieda was the only person she had considered for the job.

Edward had wanted her to give the job to Charley. He had moved out of the house, and she was happy to see him go. If they could leave him alone for a while, she believed he could eventually come out of whatever condition he was in, that angry adolescent stage that most people abandon after a couple of years. "At least offer him the job," Edward had said. "He can always refuse." She wouldn't do it. "Leave him alone," she had said. She hadn't wanted to work with him.

She had thought of Tom, but had decided against it. She'd interfered enough by insisting he go out with Marriet. She couldn't understand why he hadn't continued seeing her. He, of course, refused to talk about it. At this moment Tom and Charley both were asleep, she thought, the drugged sleep of depression. She didn't know what to do with either of them. They shouldn't have let Charley move back, but he hadn't asked, just showed up, returning his clothes to his closet as if nothing had happened.

She helped Frieda with the files, then filled a box with old postcards complete with canceled stamps and messages from strangers to strangers. "Look at this one," Frieda said. A photograph of a red and white hot-air balloon high above a beach, and addressed simply to Pauline, who lived in Amarillo. "Reconsider," was the only message, signed "Love, Art."

The phone was ringing when they returned from lunch. Jill went to the phone thinking about the woman who had owned the store, how strong her urge to save, preserve the world must have been, thinking also how much she liked Frieda, not knowing that the call was from her husband, who, at that moment, was watching their house burn to the ground.

3

INGHAM'S DRUGS was an old-fashioned drugstore with a soda fountain and fry counter. It had weathered the decay of downtown and the influx of fast foods long enough to become quaint. Eileen's father owned the place and it was still a family business. Eileen worked by herself until ten, when the pharmacist came. When Tom walked in, she was behind the counter frying an egg for an old woman, the only customer.

"Tom," she said, flipping the egg.

"Hey," he said.

"Breakfast is on me." She put two hamburger patties on the grill and a serving of french fries in the deep fryer.

There was no reason she should have forgotten that he didn't like breakfast food, but the fact that she remembered reminded him how long they had been together, and he lost his calm. She was not as large as he'd hoped. Her hair was pulled back by a comb made of shell, one they had purchased together in La Jolla.

She was wearing makeup, and she was not wearing a wedding ring.

She shoveled a fried egg onto the woman's plate, then turned to him. "I'm glad you finally came. I'm glad I didn't have to beg."

"I remember that comb," he said.

She touched her hair, patting it twice before locating the comb. She smiled and the smile was so familiar it too seemed like a thing they had found together. She set the plate in front of the woman. "Well," she said, turning to him and putting her hands on the counter delicately. "*I* remember that sweater."

He glanced down at the bulky sweater. She had given it to him a year ago, a Christmas gift. He hadn't thought about it that morning. How had he managed to overlook that it had been a gift from her? He had dressed very carefully—wearing the sweater couldn't have been an accident—but he hadn't consciously planned to wear it, hadn't wanted to make any kind of statement with his clothes. Why did his mind play tricks on him? How could he ever possibly know what he really wanted?

He put his elbows on the counter. The bulge she carried was not a gift from him. "How far along are you?" he said.

"A few months," she said.

His nervousness and confusion took a turn toward anger. Couldn't she have waited a few months after he left to get pregnant?

He wanted to walk out. Instead, he dropped his head between his arms. His shoes looked like enormous gray rodents. The socks he was wearing, he realized, Eileen had given him on his last birthday along with—he touched his belt—a belt he never wore, until now. A mild panic descended into his chest. What did this mean? What would Freud say? Did he have a book on clothes interpretation?

Tom tried to think of innocuous conversation. "How's business?" he said.

"Aren't you a little curious?" she said. "About the circumstances?" She touched the swelling in her white apron.

He shrugged.

"Miss," the old woman said. "Could I have some salt, please? These potatoes need salt."

Eileen had waited so many weeks to see Tom, had rehearsed the scene so many times, she discovered she could not feel nervous. But as she lifted the shaker of salt, it didn't feel familiar, a foreign object, glass and metal, mushroom head, a geometry of holes. The weight in her hand was unreal. She thought she might drop it. Her movements became self-conscious. *This is how it always will be,* she thought, *at each of the most important moments of my life there will be an old woman who wants salt, a dog who wants attention, a child who wants to be fed.*

"I still love you," she said, standing above the woman, setting the shaker beside the plate of eggs and hashbrowns.

The blue-haired woman looked up at her, then over at Tom.

Tom was trying to remember what underwear he was wearing. Had she ever given him underwear? "How's Sam?" he said. "I never understood why you liked him."

"The baby's not his," Eileen said.

The woman salted her potatoes and eggs, turning her head slowly, back and forth, between them.

"You trying to say it's mine?" Tom said. Anger replaced confusion again. It began to build in his chest. He could feel the construction, the laying of bricks, the pouring of concrete, the flurry of labor. When the scaffolding was torn away, he knew, there would be an enormous monument.

"Pepper?" the woman said. "I'm sorry to interrupt but I can't eat eggs without pepper. Normally it's out in the open where I could just take some."

Eileen reached under the counter, lifted three pepper shakers, and set one beside the woman's plate.

"Doesn't it mean anything that I love you?" she said and set the other pepper shakers beside the first.

"Thank you," the woman said.

"Whose baby is it?" Tom said.

Eileen stepped away from him. She turned to the burgers on the grill and added squares of cheese. "It's *my* baby," she said.

"Goddamn you," Tom said, a hiss, an attempt to hold the construction in check. The old woman looked up at him and he stared back fiercely.

Eileen lifted the two burgers joined by melted cheese with the spatula. Her eyes filled with tears, which angered her, and she flipped the double cheese patty at Tom, who, staring at the blue-haired woman, didn't see it coming. Eileen had worked behind the fry counter eight years and was an expert flipper. The burgers hit him square on the side of his face.

The scaffolding fell away. His anger turned to hate and he leaped over the counter.

She took a swipe at him but was less adept with moving targets. He ducked, grabbed her arm, and jerked it so that the spatula flew over the blue-haired woman's head and into lipsticks and facial creams.

"Please," the woman called out, her open hand over her heart.

Tom shoved Eileen toward the double aluminum sink. He decided to drown her in the gray dishwater. He wrestled with her arms and pushed her so hard, the white blouse ripped from the back of her collar to the middle of her back. He bent her over the sink and pushed her face into the water.

She screamed, but the water muffled and bubbled the sound. She groped for his balls. He jumped back before she could locate them.

The blue-haired woman had disappeared. Eileen lunged for the half-empty plate, soap suds trailing her head, tiny rainbows in the bubbles. She slapped Tom in the face with the plate.

He bent over, wiping egg and potato from his eyebrows. Before he could straighten, a salt shaker bounced off his skull and the pepper whizzed by his ear. Through his arms he could see her lifting the deep-fry grease pan, where his french fries still sizzled.

He leaped back over the bar and squatted. The grease splattered against the counter and splashed onto his shirt sleeve. He jumped out of his squat, bumping the cosmetic shelves, pulling at his shirt. A shower of nail polish fell on him.

He ripped the shirt off and stood. Eileen was backed into a corner. He rocked back against the shelves, then swept his arm over the top. A dozen bottles of perfume, cologne, and deodorant fell onto the floor.

"All right," Eileen screamed, hands at her head. "It's not your baby. It's not your baby." She stepped to the dry end of the counter and fell over it, crying.

Tom walked to her, reached over the counter, and put his hand in the slit of her torn blouse. He ripped it open, raised his fist above her bare back, but it was a back he knew so well, had kissed and caressed, he could not hit her. He lay his cheek against her familiar back. Her sobbing rocked against his face. He pressed hard against her.

"That hurts," she said. Her crying subsided. "God, your arm. Get off long enough for me to fix your arm."

Seven bubbles of burnt flesh marked his arm. Eileen came around the counter, her torn blouse hanging below her shoulders. From the clutter on the floor she selected a jar of white cream.

He shook his head. "Ice." He followed her behind the counter to the soda fountain. The arm had begun to sting sharply. He lay the arm in the soda tray and Eileen shoved ice on it. "God," Tom said, as a shiver of pain passed through him.

"What hit here?" A man in a blue coat and tie stood in the aisle.

Eileen pulled her blouse together. "We're closed," she said. She shooed the man out the door and locked it.

Watching her, Tom realized that it was here, in the drugstore, that he had fallen in love with her, watching her behind the counter. He had liked her and come to see her, but not until he sat on a stool and watched her work had he loved her.

"How bad is it?" she said, stepping beside him, touching his arm. Her torn blouse dropped to her breasts which bulged over her bra. He pulled at the collar of the blouse and it tore again. He yanked at it until he had pulled it completely off her, then he stared at her swollen belly.

She pressed herself against his bare chest. "It's Charley's," she whispered and held him tighter. "The baby is Charley's. He wanted me to marry him. He said it was a way out for us both."

Tom lost the stinging of his arm to a throbbing of his throat. He felt anger begin to rise again but exhaustion held it back. "Out of what?" he said.

"I don't know exactly. Your family." She raised her head and kissed him on the cheek. "Don't hate me."

He stood, motionless, with his arm in the ice. Eileen pressed against him for a long time. *You were out,* Charley had said, pointing with the beer bottle, and then this morning, the quarter tumbling through his fingers. *Tomorrow will be too late,* he'd said.

"I've got to get home." Tom looked at her face, close to his, her eyes dry now. He kissed her as if it were the natural thing to do, as if there had been no time apart, as if he hadn't just heard she was carrying his brother's baby. "I'll call you tomorrow."

She shook her head. "Come by."

He looked at the mess. "How are you going to explain this?"

She shrugged. "I can clean it up. When you're pregnant, you can get away with anything." She touched his cheek. "Almost anything."

"I've got to get home. You have a car here?"

She shook her head.

He kissed her again quickly, let himself out the door, and began running home.

4

THE MORNING of the day of the fire, Edward struggled with conception and follow-through. He had conceived of the idea during the night and convinced himself he would follow through that morning, which finally permitted him to sleep. Now he was less sure about the plan—to drive to the warehouse and ask Arnsburger to give Charley his job back.

His students in first period hunched over their desks like old accountants. They were a lethargic group, sleepy and dull-witted, staring at their laps when he asked questions. "Gina," he said to one of the few in the class he could rely on to have completed the assigned reading. "What was the most convincing argument in the chapter for the use of seat belts?"

She put her elbow on the desk and her chin on her fist. "In an accident, the mosted sure way to die was to get thrown outa the car," she said.

Mosted? A sophomore in high school, one of the brighter ones in the class and she says *mosted.* "What do your parents do?" he asked her.

"Me?" Gina said. "I just answered one."

"I'm curious. Oh, never mind." He was in no mood to teach. "Yes, Rollie." A skinny boy who sat in the back had his hand raised.

"I saw when you got to school this morning," Rollie said. He smiled and brushed greasy hair off his forehead. "You didn't . . . you wasn't wearing a seat belt. I saw you jump out of your car."

Several of the students laughed.

"So what?" Edward said. "I have some bad habits. I smoke cigarettes, too. Does that mean I shouldn't tell you not to? Or let it go when I catch you and your friends lighting up in the john? You don't have any right to expect me to be perfect. They didn't have Driver's Ed when I was a boy; we didn't have a lot of what you kids have. I walked to school, and I respected my teachers. I've worked my whole life as an educator, and now you think you can tell me how to live?"

The boy had quit smiling. "I didn't mean nothing by it."

"You can't say one sentence correctly. I have some bad habits, but I can speak intelligently. Did you ever complete the reading, Rollie? Have you ever completed any reading assignment I've given you? What do your parents do?"

"My dad's a machinist. My mom lives in New York."

"My mother is a lawyer, Mr. Warren." Gina was standing beside her desk.

"She doesn't got a father," a boy next to her said, snickering into his jacket.

"Your father is a jerk," she shot back, then looked to Edward. "He was one of my mother's cases when she was just becoming a lawyer. He left us when he got parole." She crossed her arms defiantly.

"You can sit," Edward said to her. "You *may* sit." Who are these children, he wondered. And what was the point? In a few years he'd see them at the grocery pushing a cart full of diapers, a baby in the caged seat. They'd know no more than they did now, except that life could be hard. Was that all there was to learn?

"My daddy's no jerk, Mr. Warren. He's a motorcycle policeman, and he wears a helmet just like you say to, and he makes like this is the most important class in school, cause he says traffic can kill you if you don't know what you're doing, but what other class could kill you if you don't learn it? It won't kill you if you don't know shop, he says. It won't kill you if you don't know history. It won't kill you if you don't know health."

"Did you do your reading?" Edward said.

"No, sir," he said.

"It wouldn't kill you to read your assignments," Edward said. A few of the students laughed. "Silent reading, then. Get your books out," he said to the class, then looked back to the boy. "Steven, what does your mother do?"

"My real mother is an actress in Milwaukee. My stepped mother works at Safeway in meats. Do you have an extra book?"

Edward borrowed the shop teacher's Toyota at the beginning of third period. He started a film and instructed his aide to administer a quiz afterward.

The warehouse was near the tracks, not a real warehouse as he remembered them from his youth, but an aluminum barn with garage doors and a concrete floor. The parking lot was muddy, although it hadn't rained in weeks. He stepped over a puddle and across muddy tire tracks. Had Charley enjoyed working here?

The building smelled of dust and grain. A boy no older than Ask leaned against a forklift looking over a clipboard of papers. "Get me Mr. Arnsburger," Edward said as authoritatively as he could muster. The boy nodded, the underside of his jaw pocked with acne, and he hurried off.

"Arnie," Edward said when he appeared. "I meant to get over sooner."

Arnsburger walked with his arms close to his body, hands in tight fists. "Uh huh," he said. "I've got an office." He pointed to a paneled box. "How's Jill?" He walked in quick, even strides.

"Fine. She's just fine."

Arnsburger closed the door behind them and motioned for Edward to sit. The room was spare, a wooden desk, a few folding chairs, an aluminum file cabinet. On the wall was a photograph of his wife standing in their yard beside their daughter, who was in cap and gown. Charley had dated her once, briefly.

"I want you to call Charley," Edward said. "Give him another chance."

Arnsburger sat behind his desk, folded his meaty arms. "Not if the whole lot of you was starving," he said.

"Arnie, I know I don't have any favors coming . . ."

"Right. And neither does pretty boy."

"Hold on," Edward said. "It wasn't easy for me to come here. Don't get mad at me."

"Not mad at all. To tell the truth, I'm enjoying it. Glad to have the chance to tell you no." He opened a drawer, looked in it, his eyebrows raising and dropping like damaged wings. He shut the drawer hard. "Your son didn't just quit without notice, leaving me nobody to run the place, he called me every name in the book, humiliated me in front of my boss and employees. You can tell pretty boy if I see him out somewhere I'm as likely to punch his face as call his name."

"Let me explain "

"*You* are a goddamn weasel." He said "you" as if he were sneezing. "Don't care a thing about my feelings. You don't apologize for your son. Hang up on me when I tell you what he done."

"My daughter was missing. When I called. Charley and Cassie were both missing. I was worried. I was out of my head. She's fifteen years old. I couldn't chat."

"Well, she come back, didn't she? She showed up, didn't she? You could have gotten ahold of me. Explained. Three goddamn months you don't say one thing until you decide I should rehire pretty boy who tells me in front of my boss, my employees, goddamn it, in front of my wife, my daughter, to suck his goddamn cock. You don't give one damn about me or my feelings."

"All right, I don't." He was mad now, as he had been that morning when the boy had accused him of not wearing a seat belt. "I don't give a shit about your tender feelings. My son was good at his job and you should hire him again because he's a good worker."

"If he's such a hot number, he should have no trouble finding some other kind of work. Everybody wants a good worker. Fact is, no one wants that pretty boy. He thinks he's better than everybody else, thinks his goddamn shit don't stink."

"You don't know your head from your ass."

"I know this. You're no friend of mine, and your son is no goddamn good."

"That's just what he said about your daughter."

Arnsburger's chest jerked forward, his hands flattened on the desk. "What is that supposed to mean?" His fingers were thick and knobby as rope.

"Hell, Arnie, I don't know." Edward tried to lean back in the chair but it felt too rickety. *He's my son and I'm losing him,* Edward thought. *As one father to another* . . . "Look, it would mean a lot," he said.

"You get out of here."

"He never said that about your daughter. I was just angry."

"I know that. I don't need a weasel to tell me that."

Edward stood but didn't move toward the door. "I could pay you," he said, a whisper. "The first week's salary. A free week of work from him and if he doesn't act straight, you can fire him."

Arnsburger stood slowly, pushing against the desk. "No," he said. "Never."

"Please, Arnie."

"No."

Arnsburger stepped toward the door but Edward stopped him, a hand on his elbow. "Two weeks. I'll give it to you right now." Edward sat again, looked at his hands. They were fists. "Please," he said. His fists shook in his lap.

"You and your son can go to hell." Arnsburger walked out of the office leaving the door open. The door was hollow and a strip of the edge was missing. Inside were cardboard spacers and dark space.

Edward put his finger on one of the spacers as he walked out. The cardboard folded with the least bit of pressure. This was a pitiful excuse for a warehouse, he thought. A forklift raising a wooden bin groaned with mechanical arrogance. A radio played somewhere in the giant room. The echoing sounds were so muddled he couldn't tell what kind of song was playing—country or pop or whatever. This aluminum barn, he decided, with its hollow doors and icy concrete, was a kind of hell, a sort of tragedy, a flimsy, enormous nothing.

The sunlight surprised him as it did when he stepped out of the theater after an afternoon movie. It might be possible to escape hell unscarred, he thought, and hurried to the Toyota. His ankle was soaked before he realized he'd stepped in the puddle. He kicked at nothing to sling off the mud and water, then drove home to change his socks and eat leftovers.

He was met at home by the flames.

5

"WHERE IS SHE?" Cassie said.

Ask shrugged and folded his arms. "The bell only rang a minute ago."

They waited outside the door to the chemistry lab for Julie.

"What are you going to name it?" Ask said.

"It's a her." Cassie had been thinking about buying a puppy for almost three months. Her friend Jennie had visited the pound last week and recommended one, a golden Labrador and something else mix.

"I'm naming her Sheila."

"That's not a dog name."

"It's a woman's name, and this dog is a woman."

"Dog's aren't women. Dogs are female. You can't name her Sheila. Name her Squirrel Two, then Dad will let you keep her for sure."

"Only if I have to," Cassie said. She liked having a last resort.

Julie was among the first students out of the lab. "He is such a jerk. He always keeps us late. 'Lunch will still be there.' " She shook her head and deepened her voice to mimic the teacher.

Cassie thought Julie was a dope, but she needed the ride. She smiled until Julie slipped her arm in the crook of Ask's elbow. Cassie had never liked public displays of affection and Ask had always been someone she could rely on not to embarrass her in this way. He had a dozen other ways of embarrassing her, but they had seemed like teammates on this one until now.

Julie had her mother's blue 1964 Pontiac Bonneville, a huge flat car with a clothes hanger for a radio antenna. The interior was oppressively clean. Cassie secretly took tissues from her purse, wadded them up, and dropped them on the rear floorboard. She had been in the car once before and stuck gum to the backseat. She searched for the dried ball of gum and listened to Romeo and Julie in the front seat.

"I told Kerrie we'd come to her party Saturday night," Julie said. She touched Ask on the shoulder with one finger, a gesture that bothered Cassie. It was as if she owned him. She scanned the seat again for the gum wad. She hoped Sheila would pee on the floorboard.

Ask fidgeted in his seat. "I guess we could," he said quietly.

"Don't worry," she said. "We can have some time alone." She giggled.

Cassie disliked that kind of giggling. She spotted the gum. She had put it just behind the driver. It would be in Julie's hair if she didn't have one of those dippy short haircuts. No one ever rode back here, Cassie thought, suddenly saddened by the idea.

"I may not be able to go," Ask said.

Julie pivoted her head back and forth from the road to Ask. Her expression seemed to change slightly with each turn. She looked scared, and Cassie felt sorry for her. It was amazing that Ask could make someone worry.

She wanted to help them both out, so she lied. "He promised he would come to a surprise party I said I might throw, and it's going to be Saturday if I'm going to have it."

Julie's eyes in the rearview mirror questioned Cassie then shot over to Ask, who said nothing. He wouldn't lie, even to save his own neck, Cassie thought. She had to cover for him. "You can come if I have it," she said to Julie. "It would be for Mom and we'll play pin the tail on the jackass and bobbing for quarters—it's really hard."

Julie said nothing.

Ask shifted in his seat several times, staring out his window.

Cassie leaned back and took off her shoe. She knocked the ball of gum loose with the shoe's heel. She felt like clubbing Julie over the head while the shoe was off. Ask too, for that matter. But she had to have the ride. She'd had the money for weeks and had told all her friends at school that she was going to buy a puppy but hadn't gotten around to finding a ride to the dog pound. Until last night she hadn't been in a hurry.

Bored, she had opened Charley's door and looked in. He had lain in his bed tossing an orange up in the air and catching it. "What are you doing?" she said. He said nothing but tossed the orange, caught it, tossed again. "Charley, another human is talking to you."

"Close the door," he said.

Cassie stepped into his bedroom and shut the door behind her. She crossed her arms and leaned against the wall. "Well?" she said.

"Well," he said. The orange came within an inch of the ceiling then fell onto the bed, bouncing against Charley's ribs and settling against him. His hands were now laced together over his stomach.

Cassie wanted to sit, but the bed was the only place. Charley didn't have a desk like everyone else. There was no chair. He didn't have manners enough to sit up, and she didn't want to push his legs aside. She sat on the two paint cans that were positioned side by side—one for each cheek, she thought, and wondered if chairs would one day be made that way, if people in the future would have no embarrassment about their bodies. Then she thought of wooden chairs, how the seats were rubbed and worn with use to fit the human butt. This made her think of old stairs, how each step dipped in the middle from wear, and jeans, how they faded first at the knees and butt—knees on boys, butt on girls. Why were people so fascinated by butts? Why cover them if that was everybody's favorite part?

"Eileen reached Tom today," Charley said. He still lay flat on the bed, but he had turned his head to stare at her.

Cassie was imagining clothes that revealed your butt but hid the rest. Would arms become sexy if they were covered? Noses? What was wrong with her mind? It jumped around like a scratched record. "So?" she said and stood. She didn't like to be down so low when talking to someone. "Eileen's married now. They'll shake hands and be friends."

"He'll be depressed," Charley said, turning away from her,

groping for the orange, then bringing it close to his face, scrutinizing the peel. "He'll be angry and depressed."

She knew at that moment that it was time to get the puppy. Charley needed it and Tom would too after tomorrow. Before her mind could wander, she had to find Ask and convince him to help her. "I've got to do some stuff," she said and started toward the door.

"Wait a second." He sat up and stared at her, just stared at her, as if she were part of a test he had to memorize. Then he lay back in bed, studying the orange again with the same intensity.

"A second's up," she said and ducked out the door. Ask was in his room reading. She explained her idea. "A puppy would give Tom and Charley something to do all day," she said. "It would become a family project." She knew this was the best way to approach him. "Dad talks about all those old dogs we had. A new one is what the family needs."

"Squirrel, that was the other dog's name," Ask said. He had liked the idea and phoned Julie.

The pound, a flat concrete building, smelled of dog pee and medicine. A big woman with black-rimmed glasses and red lipstick told Cassie that Sheila was gone. "Newlyweds," she said, dragging a long black hose between the cages. "The day before yesterday. Took that yellow dog. Cute couple. Held hands the whole time they were here."

Julie, as if on cue, stepped next to Ask and took his hand. Cassie turned away from them quickly. "I'm going to find another dog," she said, and began down an aisle of cages. A full-grown German shepherd stared her in the face and let its tongue flap out. A Doberman in the next cage slept on its side. Across from them, a long-haired brown dog snarled at Cassie, then threw itself against the cage. Cassie jumped back.

"That one's mean," the woman said. She had dropped the hose and walked with her hands in the pockets of her overalls. "Been mistreated. Or just bone mean. Hard to say." She locked her fingers together on top of her head. Work gloves made her hands look huge. "Some dogs just bad to the marrow."

"I thought this would be like a pet store," Cassie said. "It's dog jail."

"That one," the woman pointed to the brown dog, "is on death row."

"Because he's mean?"

"Because he's been here two weeks." She snatched a white card off the dog's cage. "Look." A fat gloved finger pointed to the lines of information, where and when the dog had been picked up, its approximate age and breed. "Yellow tag means less than a week left. Red tag, less than forty-eight hours." She flipped her finger against the red triangle stapled to the card. "Can't keep them forever."

A black and white dog lifted a paw and wagged its tail. Its card also had a red triangle. "That's terrible," Cassie said.

"That one's sick," the woman said. "We get a lot of that. People abandoning their problems. Old dogs that are dying. Litter runts they didn't have the heart to flush."

"Down the toilet?"

The woman took off a glove and then her glasses. She rubbed one of her eyes and explained the practice of killing a runt so that the mother and the other puppies could be healthy. "When people bring them here. They say they found the runt. Never own up to it. You want to see puppies?"

Cassie chose a tiny, hairless puppy with bright but slightly crossed eyes. On the white card attached to its cage was a red triangle with the day's date. She hated the idea of the puppy being killed because she was too snobby to take a little, ugly dog. Besides, what better dog to rally round than a poor runt, small enough to fit in her palm, saved from extinction by the Warrens? It also looked like it was likely to pee on the floorboard of Julie's car.

"She's ugly," Julie said. "She's one of those Hispanic dogs, those little yappy ones."

"He's a he," Cassie said.

"I thought you were getting a she," Ask said.

"I changed to a he."

Julie had shown her a cage of fat gray puppies. "Look how cute," she'd said. Ask dragged her back to the cage with the German shepherd. He pointed to the white card. "The family had to give him up to move to Detroit. He's house trained, and watch—*sit,* Fred." The dog's ears stood up and he sat, raising one paw hesitantly.

Cassie insisted on the puppy. Outside, before climbing into the car, she whispered in Ask's ear. "They were going to kill him. Just because he isn't as pretty as the others."

"He's ugly," Julie said from across the car.

Cassie put the puppy on the floor, encouraging it to pee.

Julie drove them to their house, where Cassie thought she would hide the puppy until that afternoon when everyone was home.

The fire department had the corner blocked off. A black fog of smoke floated above the neighborhood.

"God," Ask said, staring through the car window.

Tom, shirtless, his arm blistered, walked through the ashes with a fireman and their father. Cassie began crying. She didn't want Julie, who was already crying, to see. It wasn't Julie's house. She had no right to cry. Cassie tucked the dog in her coat and jumped out of the car. She ran to the house across the street, past the neighbors who stood on their front lawn, and into their house, crying.

The television was on, "Gilligan's Island." "Gee, Skipper," Gilligan said.

"Shut up," she screamed at the TV. Gilligan stared back at her with a quizzical grin. Her house, visible through the window, was the black of decay, rutted like a bad tooth.

She remembered then what Charley had said to her, about there being news that would make it impossible for him to return. She pressed her face to the window. The van was nowhere in sight, and she knew that Charley had burned down the house.

The dog squeaked beneath her coat. "Shut up," she yelled again and pulled the dog out. It wet in her hand. Warm urine trickled down her wrist and into her coat sleeve. She ran to the bathroom, dropped the puppy onto a blue rug, and turned on the faucet. Above the toilet were pictures of each member of the family, the parents, the kids—all grown now, she hardly remembered any of them. Water splashed across her chest and sleeve as she tried to wash her hand. The dog was a mistake, she realized, a terrible mistake. Runts in a litter were flushed down the toilet to save the mother. She wondered how a person could do such a thing, how could they see that far ahead, how could they know the mother had too many puppies, how could they pick out the one to die? She sat on the toilet crying in fits that rocked her.

"Cassie?" Outside the door, Ask. She stood to go to her brother.

"Call her again." Julie's voice.

"Go away," she yelled. Where would they live? She would never see Charley again. She stomped her feet. Then she thought that *she* was the runt of the Warren litter. The littlest. The last born.

"Cassie, let me in." Ask again.

"Go away." The puppy had left a spot on the rug. An adult would flush the dog, she knew. That's how adults were. They drowned puppies and burned houses. Thinking that the dog would save the family had been stupid, childish, like kissing someone to make it better when the person had a broken arm. The dog had begun licking the spot it had left on the rug. "Go away," she yelled again, and picked up the dog.

She dropped it into the toilet, turning her head, but too slowly, the tiny legs were paddling, head up. She flushed and the puppy went under but did not disappear, legs now on the white porcelain as the bowl filled. It let out a yip, nothing more than a squeak. She flushed again and the dog sank again, clogged the hole, paws in a slow motion walk. Water rose dangerously high, to the brim of the toilet. She dropped to her knees, sank her arm into the water, which was cold, and that was what she would remember, her arm in the water, almost to the elbow. Not the touch of the wet fur because the puppy was still alive, coughing water, eyes closed, but the water itself as it touched her fingertips, palm, wrist, arm. There would be mornings she'd wake and her arm would still be asleep, not her whole arm, just to the point the water had reached.

She held the wet puppy against her chest, stared into the white toilet bowl, and quit crying. The water was murky with dirt and dog pee and little flecks that might have been fur. She flushed again as soon as the tank was full. The water cleared except for the fur, tiny dark filaments. She set the puppy on the rug and flushed again. Again. The tiny hairs would not disappear. Again.

She heard her brother's voice, Julie's, outside the door. And other voices, perhaps the people who lived there or firemen, Tom, her father. How was the world full of so many people? They seemed to press against her, poking through into her life.

The puppy had stopped breathing. She was as bad as the rest of them, as bad as anybody. They had made her one of them.

She wrapped the puppy in toilet paper and put him in an empty tampon box she found in the trash. She returned the box there, covering it again.

"Shut up," she yelled at the door, the voices. "Leave me alone."

6

THE MORNING of the day of the fire, Charley watched Tom walk away from the house until he disappeared. He took off his robe and draped it across the coffee table, then walked nude through the house. He showered and shaved. He dressed in his most comfortable jeans and a blue workshirt. He checked each room of the house to make sure he was alone. In Tom's room, on the dresser, he saw the Swiss Army knife he'd bought for him as a coming home present and decided to save it.

He walked through the rooms again, selected an item for each of his family, and put them in the van. He took a five-gallon can of gasoline from the garage. He started with the center wall nearest his bedroom, working his way back to the living room, pouring carefully—he hated the smell of gasoline on skin.

He took one of his father's cigarettes from a pack on the coffee table, lit it, smoking just long enough to get it burning well. He tucked the cigarette in a book of matches. He'd seen this in a war movie. When the cigarette burned down, the matches would light, which would light the gasoline-soaked magazine the matchbook rested on, which would light the gasoline-soaked carpet, then the inner wall.

Charley locked the front door as he left, knowing he would at last be out, completely out, without any possibility of returning.

The van started with the first turn of the key, and he drove away to a new life.

PART II

Winning does not tempt that man.
This is how he grows: by being defeated, decisively,
By constantly greater beings.

—RILKE

CROOKED HEARTS

I

TOM ASSUMED the salad-making duty. He peeled two price tags off the bottom of a wooden bowl and pushed vegetables to one side of the only available surface, the top of the color television, which sat under a long window, chained to a black ring in the wall. The front part of their kitchenette was shaped like the state of Utah. Tom pulled a head of lettuce from its plastic net, facing the window, the Nevada border, and looked out at the asphalt parking lot, the neon Oasis Motel sign, the flashing headlights in the street. What was Nevada but parking lots and neon?

To his left, the Arizona border, a yellow plank wall, was bare except for a small wood-framed painting of a mountain lake. Voices came from the Arizona side of the wall, muffled tones, television sounds, an occasional clear sentence. "I hate the way they make the women dress," a woman would say, and the man would mumble something deep and unintelligible.

An aluminum sink with short Formica counters on either side stood in the center of the Colorado border, with the refrigerator to the south and stove to the north. Above the sink was a small window flanked by identical metal cupboards. The window should have overlooked Grand Junction, Colorado; instead, there was a desert lot, vacant except for two rusting Chevrolets and several old phone books partially covered by sand. Ask lined new bottles of liquor on one side of the sink and clear plastic glasses on the opposite side. Each of the glasses held an inch of liquor. A sheet of notebook paper, attached to the refrigerator by a magnet, read HOME IS WHERE THE WARRENS ARE.

The bathroom was located in the Wyoming notch in the northeast corner. On the Idaho border was the door to the bedroom and a framed drawing of Christ smiling. Thinking of the room as Utah made it seem less tiny, Tom decided, made their loss seem less extreme. He dug his thumbs into the lettuce head and tore it open. Spinach was out. Charley had insisted on spinach because he hated lettuce. How could you hate lettuce? What is there to hate?

He had refused to buy spinach, but he had to have something unusual for the salad or Cassie would complain. "Charley always added a surprise," she'd say. His family didn't have the good sense to hate Charley yet. They expected him to show up, shocked about the fire. Tom had bought a sack of shelled pecans to mix in the salad. He dropped the ravaged lettuce into the bowl and made a row of cherry tomatoes along an edge of the television. The cardboard sheath protecting the knife blade guaranteed "Kitchen Perfection For Under A Dollar." He sliced the first tomato, tossing one half into the new wooden salad bowl and the other into his mouth.

EDWARD FINALLY RECOGNIZED the smell. The room held a permanent odor of cooking grease. He sat in the kitchen chair staring at Tom making the salad. The house was a complete loss, but Charley's disappearance troubled Edward more. He hadn't been in the house. The firemen had assured him there were no bodies. But where was he? Perhaps he'd just taken off again. He might even have left a note that was lost in the fire.

Across the room, Tom sliced tomatoes on the television set. Edward wanted to slap him across the face. The urge was so strong his arm jerked against the chair. They had gone through the ashes together. "Everyone is accounted for but Charley," Edward had said. Ask and Cassie were across the street, and he had telephoned Jill. "You don't have to worry about Charley," Tom had said, then added, "The van's gone." But Edward had seen the look on his face. Tom thought Charley had burned down the house. How dare he? Edward had not wanted to celebrate without Charley, and would not have gone through with it if Jill hadn't insisted. "It's what we do," she'd said. "We are not going to stop functioning because of this, all this." She had thrown her hands into the air as if everything, the very atmosphere, was at the root of their sorrow. He had agreed to go along but could think of nothing to do or say, and Tom making a salad, Charley's job, on the *television*, angered him.

"Do that somewhere else," he said to Tom. Hearing the anger in his voice, he tried to soften it. "You wouldn't make salad on our TV, you shouldn't here. We have to respect other people's property."

"We don't have a TV," Cassie threw in from the kitchen area.

He ignored her. "It looks good, though," he said, still trying to make up for yelling. "A good-looking salad." Lettuce instead of spinach leaves, another slap at Charley. Anger swelled in him again, but he did not express it.

"There's no place else," Tom said. "I'm not hurting the television, anyway."

Edward scanned the room. Bottles and glasses were strewn over most of the counter. "Here," he said and stood. "Take my chair."

Tom shrugged and acquiesced.

Edward walked to the kitchen counter. "You have a drink ready for your old man?" he said to Ask, aware of the false sound in his voice.

"You can be the first," Ask said, offering him a plastic glass. "The Firestarter," he said. The room fell silent. Ask put his hands on his hips. "The drink," he said. "It's strong. A hot one. You know, like your throat's on fire. We always have a theme, right?"

Edward took the glass and sipped from it. Hot and strangely bitter, the drink seemed to bead on his tongue before burning his throat. He shook his head and gave it back. "How about a Seven and Seven?" A toast, he thought. If they were going through with this, they should do it right, with a toast, something appropriate but that did not refer directly to their loss. And what was their loss? The house, their clothes, furniture, *things*, all the things they had accumulated. The photo albums that he never paged through but hated the thought of losing. Jill's dresses from the forties and fifties that she had been saving for Cassie. Ask's certificates and report cards. The suit Edward had married in. A lifetime of things. Tom's letterman sweater. Charley's old model planes and cars that lay jumbled on the floor of the attic. Charley himself? Had they lost Charley? Had he left them? There could be no toast. Nothing could hold it all.

He took the Seven and Seven from Ask and walked to the motel window—the dark parking lot, the Ancient Mariner, a blue Nova, a white Impala, a yellow Sunburst, each within the confines of the parallel white lines. Traffic on the avenue just beyond suddenly picked up. The view seemed mysterious to him. The rough black asphalt of the parking lot grew ominous. The blur of lights and cars on the avenue, a threat. Even the old station wagon they'd owned for years seemed part of the other side—savage and mechanical, heart of cast block, soul of vinyl. The human soul, Edward wondered, how was it different? Heart of muscle and tissue, soul of image and reason. *How could this happen to me*, he wondered. As if in answer to his question, the headlights of the Nova came on, lighting the motel window. A diesel on the avenue sounded its piercing horn. The Nova's engine started. Edward could see no one in the driver's seat.

He began to weep, wiping the tears quickly. His chest coughed forward. Seven and Seven ran down his arm. The Nova flashed its brights, blinding him. He put his hands out to lean against the window ledge, but this was not his home. The ledge was too narrow. He slid down the wall, bumping his head, crying openly, his heart clanking against its human cage.

JILL HELPED EDWARD to the bathroom and left him there to clean himself up. She had expected this, hoping it would happen while the others were gone. He was the weakest. Cassie had been hysterical when Jill arrived at the fire, or rather, at the site of the fire, the ashen lot. She had locked herself in the neighbor's bathroom, crying and screaming to be left alone, flushing the toilet. Jill picked the flimsy lock with a bobby pin. Cassie screamed, "This is my bathroom," and threw a bar of soap. Jill grabbed her and she began flailing. Unable to calm her, Jill dragged her into the shower and turned on the cold water, pressing Cassie to her chest until she finally gave in. She dropped to a squat in the tub and Jill dropped with her. They sat there several minutes, water spraying against the toilet, the sink, the photographs on the walls.

Later she discovered that the puppy Cassie bought at the pound had run off during the confusion. She was secretly relieved, although she promised they would get another puppy once they were settled. Cassie hadn't been interested. Jill had taken it as a good sign, that she would not whine for a new dog when there were other, more pressing, needs.

She had wondered then who of them would be next to break down, and had known it would be Edward. He was the weakest and he had lost the most. The happiest time of his life had been the early years of their marriage, with his beautiful young bride and beautiful baby boy. When that life changed, however it did, he tried to recapture it, first by having another child. But the baby cried most of the night, his skin splotched and tender. And so he wanted yet another child. Then another woman, years later, a fling. Jill had considered leaving him, but couldn't hate him, could feel mainly pity. And the fling ended, leaving Edward to try to remake those early years by winning Charley back.

And he was still at it, unaware his every gesture of reconciliation only pushed Charley farther away. Charley sensed the efforts were self-serving, that Edward's generosity grew out of selfishness. They only angered and alienated Charley more. Everything was clear to Jill now as it had never been before. The truth burned in her. She could see it, understand it, see that it was hopeless. She resented Edward for wanting to re-create the past, for judging their other children in terms of the first, for loving the young bride she had been instead of the strong woman she'd become.

He was weak because he believed in ghosts, the most paralyzing kind, the ghosts of himself, the ghosts of the people he loved. If Charley returned, she would have him arrested for arson. Regardless of what the others thought, she knew. Charley had burned down the house. He had lit the fuse years ago.

She didn't think he would come back this time. He was really gone, which was a relief. It was almost worth losing the house to be rid of him. Almost.

Ask and Cassie stared openly at her as she returned from the bathroom. Tom pretended to be caught up in the salad making, but he looked from the corners of his eyes. "He was sad," she said in explanation. "It was good for him to get it out of his system. He'll be fine." That she could come up with nothing better disappointed her. They deserved better.

"Salad's ready," Tom said.

"There's no bread." Cassie turned to Ask. "When is your stupid girl friend going to get here with the stupid bread?"

"Don't be a jerk, Cassie," Tom said, setting the salad bowl on the table next to the spread of meats and cheeses.

"This is a *party*," Jill said, wanting to spread her arms and pull them all in close to her, where it was safe, where she could make it safe.

TOM TOOK A BEER from the small white refrigerator. His father in the bathroom (crying? washing his face?) didn't bother him. He believed his mother was right, it would do him good. What bothered Tom was his role in all that had happened. Events revolved around him that he had no part in—Charley slept with *his* girl friend, then burned down the house on the day he knew Tom would find out. Only Charley could have done either of those things. The presumption amazed Tom, that Charley's troubles could be so great as to wreck the family, the house. That he would sleep with the only woman Tom had ever seriously dated, certainly the only woman he had ever loved, was an act of such huge selfishness that Tom envied him. How could he think himself so large as to be above the rules men respected, especially love between brothers? How could Eileen have let it happen? He wanted to hit her, to slug Charley in the face, to beat them both savagely. He drank a hard gulp of beer.

Charley, at least, was desperate, although why, Tom couldn't fully understand. He wanted out, but out of what? Fuck him. No one has the right to do this, he thought. He leaned against the refrigerator. It rocked slightly. It was bad for refrigerators not to be level. How did he know that? Why care about that now? Why wouldn't his mind stop harassing him? Or just let him break down, as Cassie had, as his father had. Why were there switches in his mind he could not control? Why was he asking all these stupid questions?

He guzzled the rest of his beer, tossed it into a brown grocery bag. The bottle crashed inside the bag. A piece of brown glass flew out. He picked it up, remembering Charley throwing the beer bottle through the window, remembering too picking up the nickel and tossing it in the Davenports' yard. *That was this morning*, he realized. It seemed long ago. Rita Davenport dead from breast cancer. It was such an adult disease and she had always been so childlike.

Altogether, it had been a lousy day. He looked over at Cassie, arms folded and grim in a kitchen chair; Ask, mixing more ugly drinks; his mother, rearranging the arranged meats; and his father, absent because he could no longer control himself. And the party hadn't even begun.

. . .

Ask took Tom by the elbow and pulled him near the row of drinks. "Try this one."

"I'm drinking beer," Tom said.

"Have a little sip. I've been working on it for an hour."

"I'll try it," Jill said. She took the glass from Ask's hand and sipped. "Why, it's good."

"Of course it is. I've been working at it for an hour." He watched Tom take a drink and smile.

Ask had decided to become a bartender instead of a lawyer. When Cassie jumped out of Julie's car and ran to the neighbors, he had just sat, staring at his father and Tom, who was bare-chested, walking through the ashes. Julie was crying. "I loved that old house," she said. "You must be so sad." She had been the one who looked sad. He hadn't felt anything but a certain wonder.

When he stepped out of the car, his feelings abruptly changed. He had left his iron on that morning. He had burned down their house. The idea struck him with such force and clarity that he didn't question it. He ran with Julie to the neighbor's to get Cassie, but she had locked herself in the bathroom and wouldn't come out. He'd wanted them all together so he could confess. The screaming and crying from the bathroom worried him. He ran across the street to his father in the ashes, and as he stepped into them, he sank to his ankles in the black muck, the wet and putrid remains of their home.

He could not confess. The black sludge convinced him. It was something too large to take blame for, to take credit for. It was larger than one person could do. Firemen yelled for him to stay out. His father waved a dismissive hand at them. "Just be careful," his father said. "Tom burned his arm." Blisters marked his arm like a relief map. Tom shook his head at Ask but said nothing, his bare chest streaked black. Ask stepped with his father and Tom into the room that had been Charley's. Two paint cans bubbled white. They stared at them as if they were a message, a promise. They reminded him of the drink his mother had made after his science project failed. A carbonated drink she had called El Volcano. "I'll get us something to drink," he said. He never told them that Cassie had locked herself in the bathroom. Julie had to do it. He began walking to a convenience store, although it was blocks away. He remembered then that he could take Julie's car, and walked to it. He had left his door open and the puppy was gone.

He searched the car, the neighborhood. Walking through the alley, staring at the scorched trees in what had been their backyard, he knew he could never really be a lawyer. It was too big a thing to be. Too much. A bartender was enough, was the right size. He wanted to tell Julie, whom he had resolved to drop but whom he now felt tenderness for. He wanted to tell her and drive to buy cold drinks and liquor for the party that was sure to come. He wanted to hold her and say, "It's too big. I can't be a lawyer." When he saw her, he held her shoulders and said nothing. He would not break up with her. He didn't want any more change.

He mixed another Firestarter to have enough for everyone. When his father returned from the bathroom and Julie arrived with the bread, he would make a toast and the party would begin.

CASSIE SAT on a wooden stool in the corner of the kitchen area. There were only three rooms, counting the bathroom. She was going to sleep on a roll-away in the tiny bedroom beside her parents' bed. There was only one closet, but they had nothing to hang there anyway. Cassie raised her feet from the lower rung to the higher on the stool. She put her elbows in her lap, her fingers to her mouth. On the counter was her purse, not the crocheted white one she loved—that had been lost in the fire—but a puffy blue leather one she'd left in the Ancient Mariner. Stacked neatly beside it were two clean pairs of panties she had insisted on buying before going to the motel, a new white blouse she had folded three times to make small, a Snickers bar, two plastic arm bracelets, and her key to the old house. The key was worthless, but she had so little, she was unwilling to part with it.

She didn't want to sleep on the roll-away bed, didn't like the way it looked, as if it might suddenly fold up on her. She didn't like the crinkles in the striped mattress. They looked dangerous. They might cut her. The bed scared her.

She wanted to eat, but they had to wait for Julie to arrive with the bread and for her father to come out of the bathroom. She was mad at Julie, who seemed responsible for a lot of the trouble, somehow.

She hated seeing her father cry, hated Charley, hated herself for sleepwalking into the van months ago. Charley was making her pay along with the rest. Her chest turned solid, the way it had when the puppy peed. She held her breath to force air inside. The puppy had let out that one squeak. Now everything sounded like that squeak—the TV next door, glass rubbing against glass when Ask poured a drink, his stupid shoes on the cheap tile floor, her breathing, when she let herself breathe.

To calm herself, she thought of the house. She imagined the first room with the dentist's chest and couch, the kitchen with the counters she had walked upon, her bedroom with one yellow wall, Ask's room with his pictures and papers, Tom's brown room with nothing but paint and a green jacket on the walls, her mother and father's room where she used to lie on the bed and talk on the phone, Charley's room where he had told her about his plans to get married. Thinking of the house made her feel better, and she exhaled quietly.

Earlier, her mother had smashed a spider in the sink. The spider was just a little brown one, but it had scared her. "Kill it," she had yelled and pointed into the sink. Her mother took off her shoe and slapped it. The spider was crushed, a smear on the aluminum. The smear scared Cassie worse than the spider had.

That had been hours ago; now she imagined people with eight legs, how wide halls would have to be, how hard it would be to get comfortable in bed, which made her think of the suspension of webs, of silver netting trailing out of her womb, following behind her like a wedding dress.

She turned to her belongings, rearranged the Snickers bar and the key, waited for Julie to come with the bread so she could eat. Then what, she wondered. What would happen next?

JULIE FINALLY ARRIVED, dressed in black, carrying two bags of Sunbeam bread and two white lilies. "I thought this would be like a wake," she whispered to Ask as he took the bread.

"It's a party," he said and held the Sunbeam above his head. "Let the festivities begin."

Edward walked out of the bathroom when he heard Julie arrive, smiling self-consciously. He went directly to her, the only one who hadn't seen him break down. "I'm starving," he said, grinning. "Let's start the party. Aren't you starving?"

"Where's Charley?" she said.

His name, finally said, froze them as if in an explosion, a burst of white light. Each struggled to come up with an explanation or a dismissal, but it seemed unexplainable.

"He's a prick," Cassie said and charged past everyone to the table to make herself a sandwich.

"IT'S TOM," he said into the receiver, glancing at the motel manager behind the desk watching wrestling on a tiny black and white. "Tom Warren, remember me?"

"You're alive." Marriet's voice was tiny, unreal, like the announcer for the wrestling match.

"You sound alive, too," he said. The announcer introduced the wrestlers. "Layeeedies and Gentlemen . . ." The motel manager shifted in his chair, a short man with a large sloppy belly. Tom turned from the scene, facing the cracked plaster wall. "I want to see you."

"You probably think I'm crazy," she said.

"No, I don't think that. Not at all."

"Then you just want to go to bed with me."

"I like you. I had a good time."

"Why haven't you called?" There was movement and rustling across the line. "I guess I made an ass of myself," she said.

The wrestlers, one in a black rubber mask, the other with peroxided shoulder-length hair, snarled at each other in the center of the ring. "Get him quick, Bingo," the motel manager said, softly, as if addressing a dog.

"I should have called you that morning. I wanted to. There were some things I needed to straighten out in my head," Tom said.

"Have you got them straight?"

"No." He would have to see Eileen again, he knew, but just to ask for an explanation and to tell her good-bye. "Look, let's meet somewhere. I want to see you and talk."

"My father's over here. He's doing the dishes right now. He's taking forever. Why is it so urgent now? I haven't heard from you for months."

"Move your feet," the manager called to the television.

Tom glanced at him again. "You could have called me, too."

"No. You should have."

"How about in the bar at Stag and Hound?"

"Is that the only place you know?"

"Practically. The Shanty then. After your father leaves. I'll wait for you."

"You pantywaist," the manager said, dismissing the screen with his palm.

"No, you can call me again. I'm not going to see you tonight."

"Get up," the manager yelled. "Get up."

"Where *are* you?" Marriet said.

"I'm in a motel lobby," Tom said. "Our house burned down."

She breathed heavily into the phone. "You can't stay here," she said, almost a whisper. "I'm sorry and all, but no."

"I'm going to be in the Shanty. I'll get us a table. I'll wait for you. Come by. As soon as your father leaves."

"God, Tom. He's spending the night on my couch. My parents are fighting. How did your house burn down? Was anybody hurt?"

"Charley's gone. Not in the fire—he's alive. He just disappeared. The truth is, he burned the house himself."

"Why?"

The manager jumped up and switched the channels rapidly. "That phone's for business," he said. "You can't live on it."

"I'll be at the Shanty," Tom said. "Just come. Find some way to come."

"Are you always like this?" she said.

"Lately," he said and said good-bye.

HE HAD TO FIND another chair for Marriet's father.

"Let me say, before we go any farther, I always thought you should have had more playing time. That coach of yours wouldn't know talent if it stood up and bit him." Mr. Shacterly put his hands on his hips and beamed.

"This is my dad," Marriet said.

Tom shifted the chair to his left hand and shook the extended hand of Mr. Shacterly.

"Look at that." Mr. Shacterly gestured to the raised chair. "It's good wrists that make a ball player." He stepped back to take in the chair and wrist at once. "I'd have made you the number one guard, that's what we old-timers call the point position."

"My God," Marriet said. "What happened to your arm?"

Tom set the chair at Mr. Shacterly's feet. "Burned myself. It's not as bad as it looks." He smiled and shrugged. "You look great," he said.

"I'm a mess." Marriet pulled at her hair and sat at the table. Her fingers went to her mouth. "So what happened?" She began chewing her fingernails.

"Our house burned down," Tom said.

"No, I mean about why you couldn't call me."

"Your house burned? I know your family. Your mother and my wife are friends."

"That's how we met," Tom said. "They introduced us."

"They set it all up. You should have heard them giggling about it." Marriet put her elbows on the table and leaned closer to Tom. "Now, why was it you couldn't call? Something about getting things straight in your head? Your family have a history of mental illness? Schizophrenia? Split personality? No personality at all?"

"Does your mother know about this? The fire, I mean?" Mr. Shacterly asked Marriet. He was still standing.

"You should call her." Marriet stood just as the waitress arrived. She was Tom's waitress, blond with braces. "Nothing for us," Marriet said and waved her hand to dismiss her. "Tell her about the Warrens' fire. Tell her about the blisters on Tom's arm. *Talk* for a while, then tell her you need someone to pick you up." She reached across the table for Tom's hand. "We have to go somewhere."

"Oh, of course, you two run along. Tell your parents we will do anything we can for them," he said to Tom, then turned to Marriet "You sure she'll buy this? She was pretty angry."

"Oh, Daddy, just call."

"Nice to meet you, Mr. Shacterly."

"Take care of that arm. We should talk basketball one day. I played for Northern Arizona way back when. Marriet ever tell you?"

"HOW DID YOU get here?" Marriet asked, turning the ignition in her Maverick.

"Tony Arzate gave me a ride. He's still in there drinking."

"I hope you don't mind. It seemed like a perfect way to get my dad off my couch and get out of that smoky room at the same time. How can you stand it in there?"

"I thought you used to smoke."

She pulled out into the street. "Will you get to the point already?"

"I like you. That's the point. Where are we going?"

"I want to see your house." She signaled and changed lanes abruptly, turning back and forth in her seat. "I want to see if it really burned down."

"I had a good time when we went out," Tom said. "You're a good dancer." He watched the familiar streets pass by them. "I have dreams about you. I should have called you and didn't, but now I have."

"What kind of dreams?"

"Do you know where I live? Used to live?"

"Yes. What kind of dreams do you have about me?"

"We do things together."

"Sex dreams?"

"Maybe."

"Oh my God." She stopped the car quickly and they rocked forward. In front of them was the rectangle of ash, blinking yellow lights on warning signs spaced around the perimeter, joined by clothesline. "It looks like a site. An archaeological site."

"Ruins," Tom said. One warning sign had a cardboard rectangle taped to it. "Drive closer," he said. Block letters in blue ink. CHARLEY, the sign read. EVERYONE IS ALL RIGHT. WE DON'T KNOW HOW IT HAPPENED. WE'RE STAYING AT THE OASIS MOTEL.

"Why do you think Charley did it?" Marriet said, reading the sign. "Somebody doesn't."

"My dad wrote that. He doesn't think Charley did it."

"Why would he?"

"Charley wanted to do something to get himself free of the family."

"He's never heard of nasty letters? Rude behavior?"

"He tried all of that first." Tom kissed her cheek. "Let's go for a drive."

"You seem to be taking this well." She lifted his arm, stared at the blisters, then shifted into drive. "Was he trying to kill you?"

"I got these in a food fight. With Eileen. It's complicated."

"I've got a full tank," she said.

He smiled at her. "Well, I know about a party."

BY THE TIME they arrived at the party, the family was slow dancing to music from Arzate's portable tape player. The furniture had been pushed against the walls, and they moved in a circle around the floor. "Dance?" Tom said as they stepped into the motel room.

Marriet took his hand.

Cassie and Ask immediately danced up near them. "This is Marriet," Tom said.

"Hi," Ask said, smiling and spinning Cassie.

"I don't usually dance with my brothers," Cassie said.

"Hi," Marriet said.

"You must think this is strange," Tom whispered in her ear. "Our house has burned to nothing and here we are celebrating."

"Unlike you," she said, "I'm tolerant of weirdness."

"That contract scared me," he whispered. "But I like you. I was just a little thrown off."

"You take a long time to recover," she said.

Edward stuck out his hand as he and Julie danced near them. Marriet shook it.

"This is Marriet," Tom said.

"How's your mother and father?" Edward said.

"I was talking to Julie," Tom said.

"They're fine," Marriet said.

"Nice to meet you," Julie said.

Jill, dancing with Arzate, bumped into Edward. "Gangway," she said and completed a faltering dip. She waved to Marriet.

"That was my mother," Tom said.

"We know each other," Marriet said. "Who was that dipping her?"

"Tony Arzate," Tom said. "Her lover."

She slapped his back. "You date a lot of gullible women?"

"He's a friend."

"Wasn't he a basketball player, too? I used to go to the games with my father after I graduated. Can you imagine that?"

"Your father seems like a nice guy."

"I guess he is. My parents are a mess." She put her mouth to his ear. "I didn't mean to scare you."

The music stopped. Tom looked her in the eyes and began applauding.

2

NO ONE QUESTIONED ASK when he said he didn't feel like going to school. After all, the party had run late. Once the Ancient Mariner pulled out of the Oasis parking lot, he got out of bed and dressed. Tom was waiting for him.

"This isn't something illegal, is it?" Ask said.

"What kind of question is that?" Tom opened the door and stepped into the parking lot. "We're going to see Eileen at the drugstore."

"Take me to school," Ask said, charging toward Arzate's Volkswagen. "I can still make first period."

"I need you, Ask," Tom said. "I may still love her. I don't know, but I do know that I can't see her anymore. It's not asking too much of you to come along and help me through this. I'll buy you a burger. They have the best burgers in town."

"It's seven forty-five, for chrissakes. You're going to ruin your stomach eating lunch food for breakfast."

"I was at the drugstore yesterday—it seems like a month ago." He climbed into the VW, and started the engine. "We had a big fight. That's how I got these blisters on my arm."

"You got those in the fire. Dad said so."

"I should know where and how I got the blisters on my arm." He shoved the shifter into reverse and backed out of the parking space. "Eileen threw hot grease at me."

"Is she going to throw things at me? What are you getting me into?"

"We made up. Sort of," Tom said, pulling into traffic. "That's the real problem. I don't want to make up with her. I want to clear up whatever happened between us and say good-bye. You know, get her out of my system. I like Marriet."

"She's a good dancer," Ask said.

"Eileen's married, pregnant." *With Charley's baby*, he thought. "Marriet is not married, not pregnant. And she likes me."

"A fresh start," Ask said.

"Yeah." Tom nodded and drove slowly through the morning rush hour.

"Did she throw the grease as soon as you walked in the door? Did she let you sit down first or what?"

"We got into an argument. She was happy to see me, then she got upset and threw a cheeseburger at me, and I tried to kill her."

"One thing led to another, you mean."

"She's not going to throw anything at you, I promise."

The aisles at the drugstore were straight and tidy. There was no evidence of their brawl. The store was empty, except for Eileen, whose hair was not tied back in a ponytail as it usually was but curled at her shoulders. She was wearing a green dress and made up as if she were leaving for a date. She focused first on Tom's arm. "Let me see," she said.

He lifted his arm to her in a gesture that, from a distance, might have been mistaken as romantic. "It'll be all right," he said.

"They're going to scar." She placed her fingers on his arm gently, near the burns. "Is that why you brought a bodyguard?" She nodded at Ask.

"Hi, Eileen," he said. "Your hair looks nice." He remembered Tom's advice.

"You always were the sweet brother," she said and put her arms around him, giving him a friendly squeeze.

"What did you tell your father?" Tom said.

"The truth. More or less. I said a maniac came in and had a seizure. Then I described you."

"Yeah," Tom said, "that's not the worst of it. Charley burned down our house."

"He did not," Ask said. "But it did burn down."

"I drove by last night," Eileen said. "I read the note your father left. I even drove by your motel room. I wanted to go in."

"I wish you wouldn't say Charley burned down the house," Ask said. "Rumors get started."

Eileen put her hand on Ask's shoulder. "Do you know how to run a cash register? There's nothing to it." She guided him behind a counter, then took Tom's hand and led him to the back, a storage room—shelves and cardboard boxes. They had used the room as a place to make out several times. Once, they had made quick and furtive love there, standing in a corner.

"Charley came by after you left yesterday. He gave me this to give to you." She pulled a key from her pocket. "It's to a locker at the bus station. He didn't tell me what he'd done, but I knew it was something terrible. Your mother must be going crazy."

Tom shook his head. It had been his father who had broken down, but he didn't want to tell her. "Did he say where he was going? I'd like to kill him."

"Because of the fire or because of me?" she said, leaning away from him, touching her perfect hair.

"The fire," he said. "I want to kill you because of you."

She extended her arm its full length and touched his collar. "You still love me, Tom. And I still love you."

"It doesn't matter."

"I made a mistake. He made me feel so sorry for him, and . . ."

"He got you turned on?"

"Don't be mean. Charley's the cruel one in your family. Don't horn in on his territory." She dropped her arm. "He used to come by to talk to me after you left. He came here, then sometimes he'd take me for coffee or a drink. It seemed harmless. We'd talk about you mainly. Then we started talking about him. He told me about his wife's miscarriage. His divorce. It doesn't sound like much, I know, but one night, we were at my house—my folks were in Phoenix. Well, he told me all of these sad things and I cried with him and held him and I can't explain it. He took my hand and led me. I watched him do it, but I didn't really feel a part of it."

"It *is* his baby," Tom said. "You're going to have Charley's baby."

She crossed her arms and slid down the wall into a squat. "He said he would be careful. I felt so distant from it, I wondered why he was talking to me. He wanted me to marry him. He's so pathetic. I married Sam so you wouldn't have to drop out of school, and so I wouldn't have to lie to you and tell you your brother's baby was yours." She had been staring ahead, but now she looked up to him. Was this lying, she wondered, telling part of the truth? Why should he have to know she slept with Charley several times? She felt she was telling the better truth, even though it was a story. "Sam is a friend," she said. "He's a nice boy."

"You're fucked up."

"Your brother never made a fool of you?" She rose from the squat with some trouble. "You never saw him make a fool of others?"

Tom remembered once when he was a kid, Charley testing the spark in the lawn mower by having Tom hold the plug and wire while he yanked the cord. The shock had knocked him onto his back.

Eileen took his arm. "You think that because I was in love with you that I should have been less vulnerable to him, but he got to me through you."

She leaned close, whispered in his ear. "I don't have to keep this baby," she said and waited, just a pause to let him stop her. He did nothing but glare. "I can go to Phoenix to have it, then give it up for adoption. Everyone will think that the baby died. Except my parents. I couldn't . . ." She shook her head. "But I could tell them something. Maybe even the truth. Everybody wants to adopt babies." She paused again, putting her hands on her ribs, then in her pockets. "Sam will divorce me without any trouble. He's just a friend. He's doing me a favor."

"And in return, he gets to sleep with you."

"Stop it. I'm talking about my child. I'm willing to give up my child to get you back. If I have to. If you make me. I want you back. Don't quibble with me about sleeping with Sam. I'm doing it for you."

"That's magnificent, Eileen. First you slept with Charley because of me and now you fuck Sam for me. I suppose if you loved me much more no man in Yuma would be safe."

"Go ahead. Say the worst things you can think of. Be the biggest jerk you possibly can."

"Why didn't you have an abortion?"

"You couldn't possibly understand."

"Try me."

"Your brother. I would have but Charley stopped me. Not by what he did, but he had told me about the miscarriage, and I know he lies, but he wasn't lying then, I know. I couldn't have an abortion. I thought it would kill Charley. Or set him off somehow. I thought he'd do something crazy."

"You're the one who's crazy," Tom said, but it came out a whisper, a wave of love for her hit him in the chest. It was just the kind of thing she would think, even for someone who had caused her all the trouble to begin with. This was the moment he was most susceptible to her, while she was explaining why she was having his brother's baby.

"I shouldn't have slept with Charley. And I'm sorry. I'm terribly sorry. Maybe I shouldn't have married Sam, but that made it a lot easier for me." She stepped close to him again, touched her cheek to his. "But it doesn't have to ruin our lives. That became clear to me as soon as I discovered I was pregnant. I sat here, in this room. I locked the door and sat for a long time thinking, and I realized that we just had to be rational. We just had to stay calm. That's why I didn't want you to drop out of college. Sam was here. He's a nice man." Had she already said that? She couldn't be sure. Her throat had gone dry and scratchy. She put her mouth to his ear and repeated softly, "It doesn't have to ruin our lives, Tom. Marry me. We can be happy. We can put this all behind us." She put a hand on his chest, another on his neck. "We can raise this baby and make the trouble into something good—you know, raising the baby that could have separated us, your brother's baby. It's an opportunity to be big, Tom. The truth is, we're lucky. Can't you see it? You don't get a chance like this often. It would be . . . it would be *noble*. Can't you see it? Marry me. This is our chance. I'm proposing, Tom. Marry me. Please. Marry me."

She pulled him close. The embrace was tender and tenuous, as she had touched his arm earlier. Her breasts pressing lightly against his chest, the restraint in her arms, her breath on his neck, the familiar smell of her hair touched him—he was moved by her and might have kissed her, might have lifted a hand to her breasts, might have said, "Yes, let's marry. Yes, we will make the baby ours," but a voice in his head, the one he listened to, the voice of his thoughts, spoke so clearly to him that he thought she might have heard. *You are not a noble creature*, the voice said, *and you can't pretend that you are.*

He stepped away from her.

"I don't feel the same way about you that I did," he said. "I'm not going to see you again."

"Don't." She tried to pull him back. "You're being a small-minded male."

"Maybe that's what I am," he said. She knew as well as he, he thought. She knew.

"You don't have to be. You don't. *Grow up.* It's not going to be perfect, but we can have a good life. We can be above all this other, this . . . *other*. We can, Tom. Please."

"There are consequences—"

"You think I haven't suffered for this? You think . . ."

"You're making a big deal over me," he said. "It's not me. You've made a mistake and now you think if you get me back, you'll erase it. You don't want me. You just want to clean the slate, elevate yourself above everyone else again."

She blushed, thinking of Charley wanting to get out clean, to be able to start over. Was she doing the same? Was Tom looking at her as she had looked at Charley? Did she sound as crazy and hopeless as Charley?

"You're making me out to be someone great." He was shaking his head. "I couldn't get through school. I don't have a job. You don't want me. Forget it."

"I love you, Tom," she said, but she had lost her conviction. If she were really being rational, why would she love Tom? But what did love and reason have in common? A clean slate was exactly what she wanted. She wanted out. Her fingers covered her eyes, her palms covered her lips.

Tom turned from her. "I suppose I still love you. But it's not enough." He spoke with his back to her, then waited for her to reply. "It's not even close." He took a step away from her, paused. She was not going to call him back, he realized, and began to turn to her, stopping himself before she came into view. "Good-bye," he said, waited a moment, then left her.

IN THE CAR, Ask began laughing. "This kid," he said, "came in and fumbled around for a while. I almost asked him why he wasn't in school. He said he wanted prophylactics. So I asked him what size he wanted. I really thought they came in sizes. How was I supposed to know? The kid got all shook up. He said, 'Normal size. Regulars.' " Ask pulled out a pocketful of rubbers. "I paid for these. It seemed like the perfect opportunity."

Tom smiled but pulled the car to the curb. "You drive," he said. "I broke up with Eileen." He opened the door.

"That's what you wanted to do," Ask said, sliding in behind the wheel.

Tom walked to the passenger door, fingertips touching the car the whole time, as if he were blind. He sat beside Ask. "Yeah, but I feel lousy." The car began to move again. "Why do you need all those rubbers? I thought you were giving up Julie."

"I had a change of heart. Yesterday. Breaking up looks like hard work."

"Unh," Tom said and let his head fall against the window. "Go to the bus station. We have a package. From Charley."

"Really?"

"You sure you like Julie? You're sure you're not just too lazy or too horny to cut it off?"

"I'm sure," Ask said. He began stuffing the rubbers back into his pocket. "I may have gotten a little optimistic."

"We're a weird family."

"No, we're not. You're just depressed."

"I am depressed, but we are weird."

"What's the package from Charley?"

Tom thought of Eileen's baby. He couldn't help himself. A package from Charley. "Oh," he said, "something we're better off without, I'd guess."

"We're *not* weird," Ask said and guided the car onto a new street. "Houses burn all the time. We wouldn't have fire departments if they didn't. And people sometimes go away for a while. That's not weird. Everyone has a temper. If we didn't have fights, *that* would be weird. What you think of as weird is really pretty normal. You have to adjust your thinking." And on and on he went.

THE BUS STATION reminded Tom of returning from Berkeley and his spirits sank even lower. It seemed to him that the world was full of ugly reminders of his failures and the failures of others, and these reminders kept seeking him out, returning to him one way or another to haunt and harass him. He had left Yuma planning to get an education at one of the best schools in the country, planning to continue his relationship with Eileen, and now he was back and discovering that landmarks in the city pained him like bruises.

Oh, why shouldn't a bus station be like a train depot or an airport? Why shouldn't there be large rooms with high ceilings and long windows? Why did the people who were surely on their way to somewhere new seem so static and lifeless? Why should every bus terminal smell of human urine and human sweat? Lockers the orange of a basketball rim lined one wall. Most of the numbers had vanished. They counted from the last marked locker to find the one to match the key. A bottom locker with a wide door, dented from several kicks, accepted the key and opened to them.

"What is this?" Ask said. Inside the locker were a long metal box, a suitcase, a framed photograph, a pocketknife, and an iron. "That's my iron," Ask said.

Tom turned the photograph up. He recognized it, a picture of his mother's brother, his namesake, in uniform, ready to leave for military duty. The knife was fat and red, the pocketknife Charley had given him when he'd come home from Berkeley. "Is there a note?" Tom said. "Any kind of message?" He ran his hand into the corners of the locker.

Ask clutched the iron to his chest. "He did burn it down," he said and sat on the concrete floor. "Charley burned down the house." He held out the iron to Tom. "He gave me this to let me know it was him and not me." He was nodding, his eyes red and moist. "These are gifts," he said.

The suitcase was stuffed with Cassie's sweaters, underwear, socks, blouses, butterfly salt and pepper shakers.

"He could have washed them," Ask said, holding a sock at a distance.

Tom pulled the metal box from the locker. It was long and narrow, with a locked drawer. "I've never seen this before," Tom said.

"It's the bills. Dad keeps the bills in it. He stores it in his closet," Ask said.

"Why would Charley save that?" Tom jerked on the drawer several times. "Maybe he left an explanation."

They searched the locker again for a note or a key to the box. "I've never seen him put any bills in here," Tom said, jerking on the drawer again. "He shoves them in the dentist's chest." He realized that the dentist's chest was gone, that he would be remembering other things they'd lost in the fire for the rest of his life.

"I saw him locking it up once," Ask said. "He said it was where he kept the bills for tax records."

Tom opened the red pocketknife to the thickest blade. He pried on the drawer.

"We shouldn't do this," Ask said. "It's Dad's box."

"I want to know what's in there. Charley burned down our house, I can break into this stupid box. If there's nothing but bills, then who cares? Why lock up bills anyway?" The lock gave, the drawer popped open. Inside were perfect white envelopes. There were hundreds.

"These aren't bills," Tom said.

"Should we look at them?"

They sat for a while on the bus station floor, surrounded by Cassie's clothes and the iron and their dead uncle's smiling face, looking at the box and at each other. Finally Ask pulled the front letter out of the file. It was addressed to their father in care of the high school. There was no return address. The letter had not been opened.

"What's the postmark?" Tom said.

Ask looked closely. "Last week. It's from Kentucky. We can't open it."

"See if there's one already opened."

The next letter was opened, the same postmark but a day earlier. Ask took the letter from the envelope. It was handwritten.

Dearest Edward, it began.

"I can't read this," he said and handed it to Tom, who pulled away from it, would not accept it, scooting back on the floor.

"Look to the end," he said, backing away still. "See who it's from."

Ask turned through three densely worded pages to the end. It said, *Always, Jennetta*.

"Jesus, God," Ask said.

"Fuck," Tom said.

THEY MOVED EVERYTHING to the car. There were hundreds, perhaps thousands, of letters dating back to when they'd first moved to Arizona, before the summer in Kentucky they'd spent going to

Hale's. They didn't read any of them but looked at the postmarks, returning them carefully to the same place in the file. Each was in the same white envelope. Many, more than half, were unopened.

"What'll we do?" Tom said. He started the Volkswagen and pulled into the street.

"We'll have to give Dad his letters at school."

"I say we don't give the letters to him at all."

"They're his," Ask said.

"What if Mom sees?"

"That's why we give them to him at school."

"Charley left these to humiliate Dad and to show that he knew about Jennetta. That's no gift. I say we burn them."

"No," Ask said. "Like it or not, we have to give them to Dad."

"We'll compromise," Tom said. "We hide them for a while and decide what's best."

They put the box under Arzate's bed, then drove to Lynn's Odds and Ends to find their mother.

AFTER GOING THROUGH several boxes of romance novels and two bags of cardboard masks, Jill came across an old photograph album. It pained her that they had lost all their photographs in the fire, but she refused to dwell on their losses. Each page of the album held only one black and white photo. The first was a man standing in a doorway, a typical family photo, except that the man was in white robe and pointed hood. A lit cigarette was in his right hand, a simple wedding band on his left, a curl of smoke, almost a question mark, just below his chin.

"Goodness," Frieda said. She reached over Jill's shoulder and turned the page—a dozen people in hoods milling about a hardwood floor, one staring directly into the camera. "What do you think these are?" Frieda said. "I mean, they must be a hundred years old." Jill looked up at her and said nothing. "That's just a saying," Frieda said, "but they must be old. Surely." She reached into Jill's lap again and turned another page.

A kitchen table. A woman in her thirties, hair pulled back into a bun, sat at one end. At the other end, sitting also, a man in a white robe but without the hood, a normal-looking man with short hair and thick eyebrows, a simple wedding band, a cigarette in his mouth, a pack of Winstons on the table beside a bowl of fruit. Another man stood beside him. The photograph caught him with his hands at his ears pulling the hood over his head, a silly smile on his face. On the floor, at the men's feet, a little girl in a brown dress with a white, lacy trim. A hood was over her head. Her tiny hands tugged on it.

Jill could not speak, could only look at the lacy trim on the girl's dress, the smile of the standing man, the woman's bun, her fingers laced together on the table. "That table is upstairs," Frieda said, pressing her finger against the photograph. "That very table. I was sitting at it. I was just sitting at it." She turned another page.

The car was a 1961 Chevrolet station wagon. Jill and Edward had owned one for seven years. It had been the first new car they'd ever purchased. The front door was open, the steering wheel visible. The road was not paved. There was a chain around the rear bumper. The links were large and light shone through the diamond-shaped holes, light from a flashlight held by a squatting man—white hood, white robe. The chain trailed the car like a tail. At the end, in a noose of chain, a man, dead, black or Hispanic—it was impossible to tell—lifted by the elbow by another man, white hood, white robe. The dead man was naked, blood from his raw neck suspended forever above the sand. And his tongue, too large now for his mouth, comically large, not something human, an enormous button.

"Goodness," Frieda said. Her voice squeaked. "Goodness," she said again. "Goodness." It sounded like a plea.

At that moment, a Volkswagen appeared out the window, Tom and Ask. "Take this," Jill said and handed the photo album to Frieda.

"I thought you were sick," she said to Ask as they walked into the building.

"I didn't say I was sick. I said I didn't feel like going."

"Since when did you just decide to stay home for the heck of it?" She turned her stare to Tom, who stood with his hands in his pockets, rocking on his heels—only he could convince Ask to skip school. Their house had burned to nothing, and here was Tom in his only clothes, rocking. "Do you want him to drop out, too? Is that it?"

He stopped rocking. He looked up to her as if to speak but turned and walked back out the door.

"We've got something to show you," Ask said.

She followed Ask. Who were these people who had once been her children? They were Jill's Odds and Ends, she thought. "Whose car is this?" she said.

"Tony Arzate's," Ask said. The three of them stood at the Volkswagen.

"Well?" she said. "What is it? I work. I have work to do."

"Charley—he left us . . ." Tom began.

"Gifts," Ask said. "Stuff he saved from the fire."

She felt a sudden and powerful chill. Her thighs, beneath her maroon dress, her only dress, turned to rubber. She was afraid she might lose her balance. A body. She envisioned a body in the car—bruised white thighs and swollen tongue. She could see the tongue with a clarity that sickened her.

"My iron," Ask said, opening the car door. "He saved it for me."

Tom pulled the knife out of his pocket. "He saved me this." He turned away from her and stepped from the car.

Ask reached into the backseat and gave Jill the photograph. Her brother. She felt a wave of relief. Smiling, in uniform, about to be sent away to die, her brother, still without a final resting place. She looked into the backseat. "What's in the suitcase?" she said.

"Some of Cassie's clothes," Tom said, his back to her. He kneeled to pick up a piece of gravel.

"All of it dirty," Ask said.

"What for your father?"

Tom looked over his shoulder at her quickly. "Nothing."

Jill paused a moment, then gave Tom the photograph. "I'm sorry I barked at you. Throw this away for me," she said and began walking back to the real estate office. She stopped. "The knife could have been in your pocket all along. The iron, you can say that it's new. Take the clothes out of the suitcase. Tell Cassie the truth. Edward will think they're clothes that had been wadded up in the car. I don't want your father to know there was nothing for him. See you two at five." She walked into the office, knowing what she had to do.

Everything in the building, all the odds and ends, even the clothes hangers, must be destroyed. Nothing would be sent to New Mexico but a lie—that there was water damage or thievery or some other excuse. If she could, she'd have the building razed and the earth around it plowed. As she stepped into the building, she heard Frieda say, "No. Absolutely not." Then the crackle of a page being torn.

She rushed into the adjoining room. "Yes," Jill said. "We're leaving here. I'm having everything destroyed. We don't have to do this."

Frieda closed the photo album. "I shouldn't have." She held photograph confetti in her cupped palms. "I just lost my head."

"I'm serious," Jill said. "I'm having everything destroyed. I've made up my mind."

"You can't do that." Frieda walked across the room and dropped the confetti into a large brown trash bag. "It's not yours to destroy, Jill. I've finished the files. We only have two more rooms besides this one."

"I am your employer," Jill said. She took a step toward Frieda but stopped. "Oh, I didn't mean that. I'm being just awful to everybody today."

"You can't destroy what's not yours. I shouldn't have torn that picture."

"I'll tell her thieves," Jill said.

"She won't believe that. Who would?"

"I wish we could tear the place down," Jill said. "Everything in here seems awful now. Those files, genealogical files. Even those. We could burn them. We could burn the whole place. She'd believe that. We shouldn't have to be a party to this."

Frieda touched Jill's shoulder. "People'd think you're a firebug," she said. "They'd think everything you touch turns to flame." She smiled. "You're just upset about your own fire. You shouldn't even have come in today. Jill, honey. Can I call you honey? My mother calls me that."

"Oh, you're right," Jill said. "Of course, you're right." Was this how Charley had come to burn their house, she wondered. Were they so bad? How could he make them out to be so bad? She would hate Charley, she knew, forever. "We don't have to do any more to this place. I'll hire someone to do it all."

"Do you think that the little girl in the picture—you remember?"

"The one with the lacy dress."

"And the hood," Frieda said. "Do you think she's the daughter who's paying us?"

"I don't know—yes," Jill said. "Yes, I think it's her. Yes."

"The poor thing," Frieda said. "That poor thing."

TOM EMPTIED the suitcase onto the back floorboard. He put the photograph in the suitcase to be destroyed. Ask put the iron in the suitcase as well. "It's best for the family," Ask said. Tom took the knife out of his pocket, tossed it into the suitcase, and closed it.

"We'll throw the letters out too," Ask said and climbed into the VW. "You were right. We should go to the dump now."

Tom shook his head. "I've got a job interview in forty minutes, believe it or not. I need to clean up."

"Oh yeah? Why didn't you tell that to Mom?"

He shrugged. "Security guard. Nothing to brag about." He started the car and began driving to the Oasis Motel.

Ask nodded. "I saw that in the paper. I didn't think you'd go for it."

"I noticed the red circle around it," Tom said. "I called this morning."

"What am I going to do for the rest of the day?"

"Practice bartending," Tom said. "Study. Watch television. Go buy a book and read it. Jack off."

"You think I can be a lawyer? There's no reason why I couldn't, is there? The speed limit here is thirty."

Tom accelerated. "You may be too interesting to be a lawyer. Part of the bar measures creativity and if you pass it, you can't practice law."

"I thought for a while I'd just be a bartender. There's no reason I can't be a lawyer." Ask put his hand on Tom's shoulder. "How would it look to get a ticket on the day of your job interview?" he said. "Pretend there's an egg under the accelerator."

3

"WE'RE LUCKY to be able to buy another house," Jill said, pulling and pushing on the front door to get the key to turn. It had taken a week for her to give in and accept the only house they could afford. "We've received nothing from insurance. Lean against this thing."

Tom and Ask leaned against the door. The key turned. "We'll have to get new locks," she said. "That's a good idea anyway." She withdrew the key, straightened her hair. The insurance company believed they had set the fire on purpose, to get a new house. The idea was so ridiculous it almost amused her. "You can't mention the insurance to your father. He's agreed to let me handle it. They may eventually give us something. If we could find Charley and have him put in an institution, they'd probably pay for everything," she said.

"We don't have any pictures of him," Tom said, "for the post office."

"Oh, come on," Ask said. He turned to her for support, but she looked away. "Let's go in," he said.

She wasn't ready, imagining Charley in a striped prison outfit. She thought prison might be good for him. But probably not. Prison was good for no one. She folded her arms and turned away from the house. "This yard is a mess," she said. Brown grass and green weeds, a darkened spot of earth where someone had changed the oil in a car, fast-food litter—crumpled food wrappers, a torn sack, a flattened Styrofoam cup with red lettering that said *Kentucky Fried*. She pointed beyond the yard to the shoe box triplex across the street. "Marriet lives over there."

"I know," Tom said.

Jill laughed. "Of course you do," she said, turning back. She believed it would kill Edward to know Charley had burned the house. He must have his suspicions, but as long as he could deny them, rationalize them away, he would be all right. He was the weakest, she reminded herself, placing her hand on the doorknob. He had lost the most. The knob groaned when she turned it, a sound that was almost human. "All our savings went into the down payment," she said. "We'll have to take out a loan to buy furniture. We're still paying for the old house, besides." She opened the door. "This is home now."

The gray walls mocked her. The room was dark and claustrophobic. She remembered showing it to the Stanleys, all the couples like the Stanleys. "It's very structurally solid," she said and knocked on a wall. She laughed at herself.

"I like it," Ask said. "It's secure. Like a fort."

Tom poked his head into the hall. "Or a bomb shelter." He turned back to her smiling. "It looks okay to me."

"We can paint," Jill said. "Maybe a few plants." Mirrors? Wall hangings? She couldn't imagine what would make it inviting. *A Neo-Alcatraz model.* She imagined now it was she who was in a striped prison outfit. Horizontal stripes made her look fat. She walked to the back room to open the door and air out the house.

Tom and Ask walked down the dark, narrow hallway. "It has a medieval quality," Tom said.

"I like it," Ask said. "It would have been bad to get a house like our old one. It would have made us homesick."

Tom opened a door into a tiny dark room. "This is different."

Ask stood in the doorway and measured the thickness of the wall against his arm. "This one won't burn. Look at that. It could survive a hurricane. This is the way houses should be built."

"A little light would be nice," Tom said.

"Big windows are dangerous in storms. Flying glass can take out an eye."

"You planning on a disaster? Another disaster?" Tom said.

"That's what we had, wasn't it? A disaster." Ask bit his lip to keep from smiling. "A tornado could blow through here, and this place wouldn't even shake." He turned to Tom. "Besides, Marriet lives across the street. It's perfect." He hit Tom on the back. "I say we let Cassie pick the room she wants. She's the picky one."

"I thought you were the picky one."

"No, Cassie is. You don't pay attention to the family."

Jill appeared in the dark hall. "Lamps," she said. "We'll brighten it up. Maybe we'll paint it yellow."

"Who's the picky one in the family, Mom? Me or Cassie?"

She kissed Ask on the forehead. "Come look at the fireplace." They followed her down the hall.

"Has Dad seen this yet?" Tom said.

"No," Jill said. "I told him it was the only big house we could afford. He said, 'You're the real estate lady.' " She laughed. "If I can sell the lot where we used to live, we'll be okay."

Ask walked to the fireplace and touched the stones where the fireplace bulged. "If I were the picky one, I'd say this fireplace is falling apart and will probably collapse on us and smash our skulls."

"It's a big fireplace," Tom said. "We could cook over the flames."

"You two have to help me with Cassie," Jill said. "Your father will like it fine, but I'm worried about Cassie. She won't care for it."

"She's the picky one, that's what I said."

Tom said nothing. He was worried about Cassie too. He had given her the clothes Charley had saved for her, and she'd acted strangely. "Why'd he do this?" she had said, holding up a white sweater.

"He wanted to give you something, I guess," Tom said.

"He's not giving me anything. He's just not taking everything. I hate Charley. He thinks he's the only one who matters." She straightened out a shirt.

"You can't tell Dad. Charley didn't leave anything for Dad."

"I wish he hadn't left anything for me. It makes it part my fault."

"He left stuff for Mom and me too."

"What? His autograph?"

"We threw our stuff away. Except for Ask. He threw it away, then got it back. His iron. He said we needed an iron anyway. He hates to be wasteful."

"What'd he leave Mom?"

"A picture of her brother."

Cassie gasped. "And she threw it away?"

He nodded. "He left me that knife with all the attachments."

"He gave you that to start with. But I can't see why Mom would throw away the picture of her brother."

"She doesn't want Dad to know, I guess."

"So what is Dad now, the baby? I hate all of this. I just want things back like they were. What am I supposed to do with these clothes? I can't wear these anymore. I don't like them anymore."

"Throw them away."

"Don't be stupid. You sound like Charley."

"No, you sound like Charley," Tom said. "Why are you angry with me?"

"I didn't say I was angry with you. Leave me alone."

She had stuffed the clothes in the motel dresser, which was practically empty. Later Tom had seen her walking home with the clothes from the laundromat, clean and folded. But he never saw her wearing them.

He had tried to talk to Ask about it but wound up hearing his explanation for keeping the iron a fourth time. "An iron is an iron," Ask said. "We have to go on ironing wherever we are. Dad will think it's new. The suitcase and knife and picture frame I gave to Arzate. There's no sense in throwing away things other people can use. The picture I tore up and threw in Arzate's trash."

"The letters?"

"They're still there. I didn't want to go to the dump for just a bunch of letters."

"You're hopeless."

"Oh, I am not."

Tom and Ask walked through their new home once again, then returned to the motel to pack their few belongings.

Edward and Cassie arrived twenty minutes after they left.

"We decided that you get the pick of the bedrooms," Jill said to Cassie. "Except for the master bedroom."

"I like it," Edward said, sounding almost exactly as Ask had earlier.

Cassie said nothing and walked down the hall.

"It's a little dark," Edward said after she left the room. He walked after Cassie, passing her in the narrow hall. He stuck his head in each of the bedrooms, the bathroom, then led Jill by the arm to the fireplace.

"I think we could do a little better," he said.

"We're lucky," Jill said. How many times had she said it? She stopped. "I know the houses in this town better than I like. There's no other house this size we can afford."

He walked to the back door and stared out the window at the barren backyard.

"It needs some work," she said, touching one of the great stones of the fireplace. "Some paint."

"I just don't think it's for us," he said. "I'm not questioning you. You know real estate."

"Some plants," she said, stepping next to him. "Lamps." The backyard was flat desert, a worn wooden fence. "Mirrors."

"Where's Charley going to sleep?" he said, almost a whisper.

In hell, she thought, but stopped herself, put her arms around him and looked out the door with him. "Ask and Tom can double up like they did as kids if we have to."

"They wouldn't like that. Those bedrooms are awfully small."

"We can put up a partition in this room, make it half living room, half Charley's room."

Edward scanned the room. "That damn fireplace is so big. I don't see how we could work around it."

"We'll figure something out if he comes back."

"He always comes back," Edward said. "I just don't want him to feel unwanted."

She held him close. "That was never the problem," she said softly.

"Well," he said and turned. "I guess we should move in."

They held each other like newlyweds and walked back to the hall. "Cassie," Jill called. "Cass." They walked single file down the narrow hall. Cassie lay asleep on the carpet in the far bedroom.

"Cassie's room," Edward whispered and closed the door quietly.

ONE WEEK AFTER APPLYING for the job, Tom began work at the Hidenall Construction Rental Plant, a huge aluminum barn surrounded by an asphalt yard and an eight-foot chain-link fence topped with barbed wire. Concrete mixers, flatbed trucks, tractor mowers, Caterpillars, backhoes, sewage snakes, pesticide sprayers, moving vans, forklifts, and one enormous crane sat on the asphalt in their designated spaces. The Hidenall colors were purple and yellow and the spacing was so exact, the machines looked like tokens in a giant board game.

Tom went to work at 6:00 p.m., closing time. For the first two hours, he sat in a peaked cubicle at the entrance gate and accepted late arriving machinery. He calculated rental fees and late charges, then parked the machines in their designated spots. In the floor of the cubicle was a safe with a slot for payments. At eight, Tom locked the cubicle and the front gate, then conducted a quick inventory of the lot, checking it against the rental list. He patrolled the inside of the yard and the outside of the fenced yard once each. His employer told him that he should be able to complete all of these functions plus have a half hour to eat and a fifteen-minute coffee break by the end of his shift at midnight.

Tom discovered he could complete everything by ten thirty. The first night, it worried him to be finished so early. He patrolled the outside fence again, then rested against the gate to wait for the end of his shift. At twelve, his replacement arrived, a German shepherd the size of a grizzly. The trainer accepted the keys from Tom, dumped the dog inside the fence, and drove off. Tom jumped into the Ancient Mariner, a working man. He started the engine, turned on the radio, lowered his window, and eased out onto the highway, his elbow out the window, a cool breeze in his face. He drove home thinking of his future, which suddenly seemed bright to him. When he turned down their street, the ashen lot lay in front of him. He had gone the wrong way, out of habit, and his happiness disintegrated.

By the end of his first week on the job, he realized that he was not only doing all right, he was the best night man they had ever had. The previous man had never understood how to inventory, the one before couldn't keep money straight, the one before him drank. Tom was exemplary by being merely competent.

By the middle of his second week, Tom found he could have all his work completed by ten o'clock if he delayed his meal. He then ate and read for two hours until the dog arrived and Ask came to pick him up. Tom enjoyed the time to read, although it occurred to him that he had had hours daily to read while unemployed and he had done very little. Being paid to read made a difference, or maybe it was just that having a job and having finally broken it off with Eileen freed him to think of other things. He couldn't consider fiction while the world clung so heavily to him.

Each night of his second week he sat on the asphalt, his back against the chain-link fence and read *Moby Dick*. The Hidenall Plant was in the valley, three miles out of town, and surrounded by fields of wheat and cotton. The yard was lit by tall lamps, but all around the plant was the darkness of the earth, which Tom found easy to imagine as the darkness of the sea; the lights of the town, the friendly but distant shore.

Monday of his third week, Tom forgot his dinner. He called home and asked for someone to bring it to him by ten.

Ask arrived at nine forty-five. "I decided to eat with you," he said. "I'm starving."

He had remade Tom's supper, which had consisted of a roast beef sandwich, a slice of dill pickle, two slices of tomato, a Coke, and a bag of potato chips. Ask's dinner, which he spread across the car hood, included two bowls of salad, each covered with Saran Wrap, a creamer full of Ranch Style Dressing, a bowl of mashed potatoes, another of creamed corn, hot dinner rolls, thick slices of ham, gravy, two pears, and two Cokes.

Tom sat cross-legged on the hood and began eating his salad. He surveyed the various bowls of food. "My earnings for the night won't cover the cost of this meal."

Ask sat on the opposite side of the hood, one leg folded under the other. He tucked his paper napkin into his collar. "It's an important evening," he said and bit his lip.

"Why's that?" Tom unwrapped a plastic knot of bacon bits. "I don't make enough to cover the cost of all the Saran Wrap you used."

"This afternoon Julie helped me move the new furniture into my room," Ask said.

"To furniture," Tom said and raised his can of Coke for a toast.

"Not that," Ask said. "We made love. Me and Julie. In my new bed."

"Yeah?" Tom said. He felt slightly deflated and sad without knowing why. "Well. Good. Good for you."

"I liked it," Ask said. "I liked it a lot."

"How'd she take it?"

"She liked it too. We were both in favor of it."

"Did you use some birth control?"

"I used one of those rubbers. It took me forever to get it on. They don't come with instructions. It was green. I thought that was appropriate for the first time. You know, greenhorn, new to something. Julie had done it before, she told me. I told her that didn't matter. That was right, wasn't it?"

"Why would it matter?"

"I didn't think it should, but I kind of felt like it might. I couldn't figure out exactly how it would play into things. She slept with some guy when she was a freshman. He was mean to her, she said. He wanted to take pictures of her while they were doing it."

"It was probably Charley," Tom said.

"That's not really funny, and it's not even accurate. Charley isn't like that. You can't make everything bad in the world Charley's fault."

Tom said nothing. They ate their salads and moved on to creamed corn, ham, and mashed potatoes.

"You know what I thought about?" Ask said. "I thought that I lived in that other house all those years and never slept with anyone . . ."

"What about me?"

"Okay, I shared a bed with you. But I never slept with anyone else and here in this new house, the first night I have a bed in my room, not even night, the first afternoon I have a bed in my room, I sleep with Julie, a woman. My first one."

"I've been usurped."

"It's almost like if we'd moved into that house three or four years ago, I could have been a playboy or something."

"The last thing we need is another playboy," Tom said. He ate his roll.

"Forgive and forget," Ask said.

"No." Tom said. "Why should I?"

"He's our brother."

"Listen," Tom said, and leaned forward. "There are some things I don't forgive. I can't and I won't. He's sick. Not insane. Evil, that's what he is. He's evil."

"He made a mistake. I don't like to hold grudges."

"You don't understand," Tom said.

"I understand every bit as much as you do. More. I can sympathize with Charley because I've made myself try to see the world as he does. Not that I really sympathize with what he did. Burning down the house was wrong."

"No kidding?" Tom cut into a slice of ham. "He slept with Eileen, Ask. *My* girl friend."

"No, he didn't. Stop exaggerating," Ask said.

"She's pregnant with Charley's baby. He slept with her as soon as I left town."

Ask stared at Tom. "Eileen wouldn't do that."

"She wouldn't but she did."

Ask wiped his mouth with his napkin, then folded it neatly. "You want to know something? I thought about Charley while I was in bed with Julie, while I was inside Julie. It bothered me because I knew nothing else should be on my mind, but I couldn't help it. I thought about him in the van, driving in some forest. It probably means something."

"Like what?"

"The van is white, so that would be like a semen and the forest would be a vagina," Ask said.

"That would make Charley the little sperm behind the wheel," Tom said.

Ask laughed.

"One little Charley sperm found its way through the forest to make Eileen pregnant," Tom said.

"I would never do that," Ask said. "It's one of my rules."

"Never to sleep with your brother's girl friend?"

"Not exactly. Number Six: Never to do anything with the sole intent of hurting someone else. Of course, he could have been in love with Eileen. Is she in love with him? Do you want more ham?"

"I don't think so," Tom said. "The hell with both of them."

"It's serious, this sex business, isn't it?" Ask said. "I'm sorry, Tom. I feel almost responsible. Don't you want more ham?" He reached for a crumpled paper bag. "There are pears," he said and drew the bag to his face, looking for something to give to his brother.

THE FOLLOWING NIGHT Marriet came with hamburgers and fries from Burger King. "I don't like Julie," she said. "Ask deserves someone better."

"He's happy. She's happy." Tom wore a white T-shirt and jeans. The short desert winter was over, the night, warm. His shirt clung to his chest.

"He deserves someone better," Marriet said. She also wore a T-shirt, navy blue, and tan shorts. They sat in the front seat of her car, a green Maverick, the white sack between them.

"That's probably what people say about you, that you deserve someone better than Tom Warren, the night watchman at Hidenall's."

"It would help if you'd make something of yourself. I, after all, am a retail salesclerk. It's hard dating below your social class."

"I *am* making something of myself. Before this I was a slug." He watched as she covered the french fries they shared with ketchup from a little packet. This was not how fries were eaten in his family. A communal glop of ketchup on a neutral site was provided for dipping. The advantages in his system were obvious—individual control of the amount of ketchup per fry, less danger of getting ketchup on your fingers. If Ask were here, he would have to explain all of this to her. Tom remained happily silent.

She lifted a fry, eating it in two bites, then licking the errant ketchup off her fingers. "What *do* you want to do? I've assumed that you have no idea, like me. But I guess I've also assumed that you want to go back to college, sooner or later, like me."

"And give up all this?" He swept his arms open, banging the windshield, rustling the sack.

"We've both given up a lot," she said, lifting and resettling her bare legs against the vinyl seat. "I left LA and you lost your house, your brother, everything in your house."

"Not everything."

"That stupid knife, but you threw it away." She ate another fry, licking her fingers again, slowly, distractedly. She left her fingers at her mouth to chew her fingernails. "Your mother threw the photograph away. Ask even threw his iron away for a little while."

"Ask is not one for giving up the past," Tom said. The manner in which she ate her french fry fascinated him. That probably meant he was in love. Signs were hard to come by.

"Is that why you did it? I thought it was so your dad wouldn't know it was Charley who torched the house."

"I did it, I think, because Mom did it. I don't know why she did it."

She reached across the sack and pulled on his T-shirt to clear the clinging wrinkles. "I left everything in LA, even my last month's rent and cleaning deposit. All my clothes." She chewed on a thumbnail.

"I remember you in a red sweater in high school."

She smiled. "I still have that. I didn't take it to LA. My mother has it in my old room."

"I remember you holding your books against your chest, running across the school grounds." As he said it, he saw her as she had been then—bleached hair, blue eyeshadow, lips the red of strawberries, fingers tucked away beneath the books—a kid.

"I never ran. You're embellishing. Why didn't you ever talk to me back then?"

"You were older. Pretty. Stuck up, I figured."

"I told you when I was in LA I was sleeping with my boss. He was about forty, and I knew I shouldn't be sleeping with him, but some part of me said, 'Quit being stupid about sex.' I didn't love him. I didn't even really like him. Maybe I shouldn't tell you this. It's pretty ugly."

"Go ahead," Tom said. He moved the sack to the floorboard and put his arm on her shoulder.

"I was staying at his house one night. He was married but his wife was always gone somewhere. That night we were in bed, asleep. God. He was fat. Not really fat, but he had this belly." Suddenly, she began to cry. She covered her eyes, then wiped them. "There was some noise outside, like someone at the door. It woke both of us." She looked out the car window as if it were the same outside, the same darkness as in her memory.

"He got up and took this gun out of the nightstand. It wasn't an ordinary pistol. He had shown it to me before. I hate guns. He was proud of it—an old-style pistol, a collector's item, he said. The barrel was long and round, like an Old West gun. You know the type.

"He went to the door and looked out, then checked all the doors—he was happy to have the chance to get out his gun, I could tell. Then he came back to bed. I was scared, partly because of the noise, partly because of the idea that the police might have to be called and the neighbors would find out I was there, but mainly because he seemed so awful, stalking around the house, naked with this long old gun and his fat belly. I thought even then that I would quit seeing him. I always used to think that, though, then never do anything. It's hard to break things off with your boss."

She paused and Tom thought that might be the end of the story. He didn't like hearing about a past lover, especially a fat man with a gun. He leaned slightly closer to her, planning to kiss her cheek, but she began speaking again.

"He came back to bed and saw the way I was looking at him and thought I was . . . oh, why am I telling you this?" She wiped her eyes again, tapped the dashboard with her fingers. "He crawled into bed and took the bullets out of it. Then he showed me it was empty, and he put the gun to my head . . ." She turned from Tom and looked again into the dark.

"I knew the gun wasn't loaded, but I was scared anyway. He made me . . . this is the awful part. He stuck the end of the barrel in Vaseline. And. Oh God, I left that morning in my car and drove here. I never even went back to my apartment."

She leaned into his chest and he held her.

"I didn't want any of that stuff." She spoke into his shirt, her breath warm against his chest. "I wanted to erase everything." She tugged on his shirt with her fist. "That's why the contract. I know it was stupid, but I didn't want to be frigid and I wanted some kind of protection."

Tom could think of nothing to say. He held her and tried to understand what she had felt—fear? humiliation? betrayal? He might be able to name it but he didn't think he could understand it, not in any real way. After a brief struggle and against his will, his mind turned away and offered instead an image of Charley, years ago, handing over his revolver and asking Tom to hide it. He didn't want to think of Charley; he wanted to make Marriet's pain his, or, at least, to touch it, to lay his hand on the quivering membrane.

He pulled her close. His hand moved gently across her back, and he tried again to understand, but his mind gave him Charley and Charley's black pistol, the look on Charley's face as he handed it over, his steady, serious eyes. Was this a failure of imagination? Cowardice? Did it stem from a poverty of compassion?

"Let's patrol the fence," he said finally and felt her head nod against his chest.

They stepped out into the night. A gust of wind blew Marriet's hair into her face. He put his arm around her shoulders. They walked together slowly, carefully, staring at the ground as if it might split open.

They stopped at the far side of the lot, fingered the chain-link fence, and leaned against it, into the wind. Trucks and tractors, sewage snakes and a crane—Tom knew all the equipment, but from the opposite side of the lot, the lights from the towers shining in his face, he could see only their silhouettes, dark and frightening shapes that resembled nothing he could name. And as he stared at them, they began to move—not with the mechanical precision of machinery, but with the awkwardness of living beasts just wakened, ancient and powerful beasts.

"The wind is shaking the lights," Marriet whispered into his ear, lacing her fingers around his neck.

Tom felt she had read his thoughts. The rocking lights had made the silhouettes appear to move. "Spooky," he said and kissed her, then looked again, happy, despite the explanation, that the shapes were locked within the fenced lot.

They returned to the car. Marriet pulled the front seat forward and crawled into the back. "Hey," she said and motioned with a crooked finger for him to join her.

He lowered the window an inch, stepped into the car, and locked the doors. Marriet, on her knees on the backseat, pulled her shirt over her head. Her hand moved first to her mouth then to a spot just below her shoulder. "I have a bruise," she said. A drop of perspiration fell from the tip of her nose to her breasts. She unbuttoned her shorts and wiggled out of them.

Tom took off his shirt. His jeans, damp with sweat, stuck to his thighs and were hard to remove. "Let me help," she said and pulled on his pantlegs. They struggled together to get them off. "This is work," she said and laughed.

He kissed her neck, the dark hollows beneath, her salty breasts. Her fingers moved through his hair. "You're getting paid for this," she said. "That makes you a prostitute."

"Gigolo," he said. He kissed her lips, thinking how many of the important events in his life had taken place in a car. "We prefer the term gigolo."

She pressed her face against his. "You're going to take me for everything, aren't you?" she whispered.

"No," he said, "that's not me."

They made love as slowly and carefully as they had walked together, as if danger were lurking near them, as if their love was as fragile as their bodies.

MARRIET OR ASK or both came every night at ten. It became Tom's favorite part of the day.

Cassie joined them one night, sitting with the others on the hood of the Ancient Mariner, eating from a bucket of chicken. Hidenall's disappointed her. She had wanted out of the house but sitting on a car in the middle of nowhere was stupid. The fields were invisible and only a portion of the highway was lit by the tall lights. There was nothing to look at but each other or the grotesquely colored machines in the lot. The hood of the car was hard and uncomfortable. Ask refused to play the radio, saying it would run down the battery. Tom told her to imagine that they were at sea and the city lights were a distant shore. Who was he trying to kid?

"This is the only joke I know," Tom said.

"I can never remember jokes," Marriet said.

"This guy is on vacation in Europe and he calls home to find out how things are. His brother answers."

Cassie knew the joke. It was one she liked. She looked through the bucket for a chicken leg, listening closely so she would be able to tell it herself.

" 'How's everything going?' he asks, and his brother says, 'Your cat died.' Well, he's shocked and he says, 'That's no way to give bad news. You should break it to me gently, say that the cat's on the roof and won't come down. Then next time I call, say that you got the cat down but he's sick. Then the next time I call you can say the cat didn't make it. By then I'd be ready for the news.'

"So the brother says he's sorry, and the other brother, the one in Europe, says, 'It's all right. Forget it. By the way, how's Mom?' His brother says, 'Mom's up on the roof and won't come down.' "

Ask and Marriet laughed. Cassie wondered why she had ever liked the joke. It didn't seem funny at all now. She could see the dead kitten lying on a rug, the dead mother in bed, a quilt pulled to her neck, her face the white of porcelain.

"Why is that funny?" Ask said, still laughing. "I've heard that joke a dozen times and laughed every time."

"They're such twits," Marriet said.

"I used to know a joke about monks and a Frisbee," Tom said. He held a chicken breast with both hands. "They had taken vows of silence and one was trying to show the others what a Frisbee was for. I can't remember the punch line, though." He took a bite of chicken.

"I never understood the idea behind a vow of silence." Marriet leaned against the windshield, tearing a biscuit in two. "What would be better would be to limit yourself to, say, fifty words a day. Then every word would be important. You'd never want to waste one. If someone said hi to you, it would mean a lot."

Ask shook his head. "You'd never hear any jokes. You'd use up all your words getting the necessities. Like, pass the pepper."

"Or who didn't fill up the ice trays?" Marriet said.

"No, really, pass the pepper," Ask said, extending his hand to Marriet.

"How about, 'Are we out of toilet paper?' " Tom said.

They looked to Cassie. She crossed her arms, disgusted with the whole line of conversation. "I hate being in that house every night," Cassie said. "It's like a morgue."

"Oh, it is not," Ask said.

"Morgues ought to be like that then," she said. She imagined a kitchen table in each of the dark bedrooms, a body on every one. Her mother, white and stiff, without breasts, her mouth crooked with bright red lipstick. Her brothers and father, staring straight up, tents over their middles to hide enormous erections.

The images made her sick. She dropped her chicken leg onto the car hood. She lay in one of the rooms, seemingly dead but really alive—paralyzed and cold, very cold.

"You've been in a bad mood ever since we moved," Tom said. "I'm sick of it."

"That's not it," Ask said.

Cassie glared first at Tom then Ask, wanting to picture them dead now, but her mind would not cooperate.

"You're right," Tom said. "She was mean while we were in the motel, too. Ever since the fire."

"That's not it either. I know what's bothering her," Ask said.

"You two are talking about her as if she's not here," Marriet said.

Ask turned to Cassie. "I know what's bothering you," he said. "I lost your puppy. I searched the whole neighborhood. I swear I did. I gave Mom my savings so we could get some furniture. But Julie and I are going to get you another one. I'm sorry."

Cassie softened almost immediately. She wanted to tell him the truth about the dog, but didn't want to admit she had drowned it. Feeling she should admit it made her angry.

"I don't want you to get me a dog," she said. It sounded harsher than she had meant. "Just leave me alone," she said and jumped off the hood to sit in the car. She slammed the door and locked it, then listened to them talk, asking her to come out, apologizing. She could hardly bear to hear people talk. Just the way a voice went up and down in a sentence made her angry. The chicken leg she had dropped on the hood had begun to slide, leaving a greasy smear. She watched its slow descent and crossed her arms, squeezing her chest to keep from crying.

DURING TOM'S SIXTH WEEK, Ask and Marriet came with the letters. They said they were on the way to the dump.

"She drives like you," Ask said, stepping out of the Ancient Mariner. The wind blew his hair across his forehead, and he ran his fingers through to straighten it. He tugged at the file of letters. "Help me with this," he said. Tom gripped the opposite end. Together they lifted it from the backseat and set it on the hood.

"She wants to look at them," Ask said, pointing at Marriet.

Marriet handed Tom a sack of fish and chips. "We already ate," she said and kissed him on the cheek. "Don't you have any curiosity about these?"

Ask opened the drawer and held an envelope up to the light given off by one of Hidenall's towers. The letter fluttered in the wind. "I don't think we should read them," he said. "I don't know what we should do with them."

"Let's read one," Marriet said. "Be human."

"I don't think we should," Ask said. He lifted another letter from the file, saw that it was opened, and pushed it back. "I'm not going to be the one who reads."

Marriet took a letter from the middle of the file.

"You didn't mark the spot," Ask said. "How are you going to put it back where it was?"

"I thought you were going to burn these at the dump," she said.

"We shouldn't fiddle with the order."

Tom put down his fish sandwich. "You act like they're specimens."

Marriet held the envelope up to the light. "It hasn't been opened," she said. "It's six years old and it hasn't been opened." She tore at the end of the envelope.

"Do one that's already opened, for chrissakes," Ask said. "At least open it the way the others are opened. Tear it from the flap. Don't tear off a whole end."

Marriet turned to Tom. "Do you have a leash for him?"

She held the envelope up again and began reading. " 'Edward Darling.' "

"Oh, for chrissakes." Ask slipped off the end of the hood and walked three steps away from the car, then came back, hands in his pockets, the wind whipping his shirt.

" 'You wouldn't believe the rain. Sheets and sheets. The sky just opened up. All the bottomland is covered with silt. Flat and brown. A few creases. Like an old mattress. I've been thinking about you all morning. When I was bathing. I thought of your soft red hair. The feel of it against my skin.' "

"Oh, come on," Ask said. He twisted violently from the waist, hands still in his pockets.

Tom stared into his sandwich.

"Should I stop?" She paused without looking at either of them, then pulled a strand of hair from her mouth and continued. " 'I thought how your smile centers your face. So perfectly. Sky has cleared now. A few puffy clouds. Little white pillows. I long for you. It centers my life. Does that make sense to you?' " She paused again and looked at Tom. "She has funny handwriting."

Tom nodded. Ask turned away and looked at the dark cotton field.

She read through the letter silently and stuck it back into the envelope. "It's mainly about the weather," she said.

"Read another one," Tom said.

"Why?" Ask spun to face him.

"I don't know. I just want to hear another one."

"No," Ask said. "There's no good reason . . ."

"I want to know," Tom said. "I want to know why she picked Dad." He lifted his sandwich but did not eat. "She could have had any guy who came in there. It doesn't make sense to me. One more. Read one more."

Marriet took another from the file. She skimmed the first page. "It's not all that romantic," she said and read another page silently. "Listen to this. 'I'm glad Tom made the freshman basketball team.' " Marriet looked at Tom, who blushed. " 'It means so much to him to be accepted. Ask isn't like that. He's my favorite. Doesn't need to belong to anything. But family. I don't really know that's true. What if you told me lies? What if your letters are make-believe? Their pictures line my dresser. Along with yours. I'm lucky to have you. Your boys. Cassie. I long for you. I . . .' " Marriet let her hand with the letter drop into her lap. She looked to Ask. "You're right," she said.

Ask turned, his eyes red, about to cry.

"Find the first letter sent to Yuma," Tom said.

"No," Ask said. "That's enough. You said one."

"Why?" Marriet said. "Weren't they all sent to Yuma?"

"We left Kentucky when I was nine and spent two years in eastern Arizona. Then we returned to Kentucky for just one summer. We had to move back because of Cassie. That was when we came to Yuma."

"You want to see if she told Dad about Charley," Ask said.

"What are you talking about?" Marriet looked through the file.

"You can do it," Ask said. "But I don't want to hear it." He began walking. "I'll be back in a little bit, all right? All right?"

"Yeah," Tom said and turned to Marriet. "Once," he said, "when I was eleven years old . . ." He told her the story of the summer in Kentucky, of Hale's Cafe, of Charley and Jennetta.

Marriet listened while she searched through the letters. When she found the first Yuma letter, she turned it up and listened to the end of the story. Then she handed the letter to Tom. He shook his head. "You read it," he said.

" 'Edward,' " she read, " 'I can't believe you're gone. I waited. I wrote letters. As if you weren't just across the highway. I worked day and night. If you had stepped down from the hill I would have been there. What am I to do?' " Marriet turned the letter over. "That's all there is. It's not even signed."

"Read the next one," he said.

Marriet had to read several to discover what Tom wanted to know.

Dear Edward,

Write me. Please. I miss you. I miss hearing from you. Call me. Let me hear your voice. I'm losing my mind. All summer the boys wanting me. Me only wanting you. Write me. Please.

Dear Edward,

The earth is black and hollow. I cannot stand to stay on it. My heart wells like a balloon when the mailman comes. I must hear from you. Tell me you hate me. Tell me I am nothing but a miserable pest. But tell me.

Dearest Edward,

Your letter brought me back. I was so carried away. I understand your reasons for not coming. I don't believe them. Had you come, I might be over you. The place I keep my love. A chamber of my heart. The size of a music box. It's locked. You could have opened it. And loved me. Or left. And let me love someone else. I tried to send you a message. You never got it. You never will. I love you. Still.

"She never told him," Ask said, back from his walk, behind them.

" 'A love,' " Marriet continued reading, " 'that can't grow. That can't quit. It's warped my heart. Like a bad record.' " She looked at Tom. "He never read this letter. The envelope was still sealed."

Tom shook his head. "Take them to the dump," he said. "Get rid of them."

Ask stepped to the hood immediately and lifted the file. "Let's go now," he said. The box slipped out of his hands, off the hood, the drawer flying open. Letters flew in the wind.

"Oh God," Marriet said.

The letters blew away in a spray of white, like light from a lamp. The fence caught dozens, envelopes papering over the chain links and dark holes, sticking in the barbed wire. More were swept into the cotton fields, the wheat fields, the desert, the black highway. Tom, Marriet, and Ask ran after them, throwing all they could retrieve into the backseat, until it was white with letters as if with snow.

JILL'S STORY

UNTIL I SAW MAY sitting alone at a picnic table, I thought everyone at the Tarrs' hamburger party was grotesque. Most of them were teachers—it was a teachers' function—and they knew about Edward's affair with a student. The affair was over and no one was talking about it, but they knew, and their knowledge made them grotesque. Those who weren't teachers, the spouses and dates of teachers and administrators, were just as bad. I could read the sentences on their lips, "Which one is she? The poor woman."

Mrs. Tarr, who threw the party, was vice-principal. Later that year she would die in an airplane. On her way to Hawaii with her husband, she would fall asleep and never wake. A heart attack, they said. I wondered if a bad dream had stopped her heart. A terribly bad dream.

Eva Horne was there with one of the new teachers. A woman older than I was, she dressed and acted like a tramp, or worse, like a teasing teenager. She came to the party in a low-cut blouse and miniskirt. Later, of course, we would become almost related.

May was also the girl friend of a teacher, one of the young

teachers. She had been a student of Edward's some time back, then worked for over a year with me in the real estate office as a receptionist. After she left I lost track of her until I heard about the accident, a head-on collision. The other driver and his passengers had been killed. May had gone into a coma, was kept alive mechanically, then miraculously, after a month, came out of it. I hadn't seen her since. It hadn't been long.

Her hair was very short and splotchy. Her scalp, ice white, showed through in places, but there were no visible scars. She had a large, pretty face. She had been plump, that sexy kind of plump that some men love. But she had lost weight.

"May," I said, as I walked to the picnic table, "you look wonderful."

She smiled at me and tilted her head. "I wondered if that was you," she said. She was wearing a mauve dress with little frills on the short sleeves and around her waist. It seemed to fit her funny. A size too large, I imagined, since she had lost so much weight.

She stood uncertainly, like a child trying to be proper. I hugged her. "You're so skinny," I said. In her ear I whispered, "It's so good to see you here. I didn't think there would be anyone worth talking to."

She giggled and sat on the picnic bench. "That's a good one," she said.

While she'd worked in the office, we'd been friends—lunches, a drink at five. She had been infatuated with Charley, but I had discouraged her from seeing him. Later, I told her to call him, thinking she would be good for him and that she was strong enough to deal with any of his doings.

I took her hand. Her arms were very thin. "We were all so worried," I said. "I'm happy you're all right."

"That's what Mother told me," she said and grinned, half shaking her head. "It's so funny. Everyone worrying."

I waited, thinking she would explain why that was funny, but she didn't. Instead she began playing with the napkin dispenser, the squeeze bottles of mustard and mayonnaise, the tall glass bottle of Heinz Ketchup. Her fingernails were purple. To match the dress, I guessed.

"You really do look wonderful," I said.

"That's what everyone says," she said.

What I wanted to ask her was what it was like to be gone, to be almost dead. I assumed she didn't have any recall, but I wondered if it might be like a dream where you remember nothing at first but later see a kite or the vapor of a jet and little parts of the dream come back to you.

She touched me on the arm. "Should we eat now?" she said. Her voice was low and serious.

I smiled at her seriousness. Mrs. Tarr had made little menus and run off copies on the school mimeo. There were several ways to order a hamburger. Burger à la Tarr came with soy sauce. The nuclear burger was smothered in mushrooms. There were a number of other cutesy possibilities.

May held her menu close to her face, her purple fingernails lining the sides. Finally I said, "I think the mushroom burger sounds good."

She dropped the mimeoed sheet, obviously relieved. "I'll have that, too."

This was the first moment I wondered whether she was damaged in some way. I wondered if she could read.

Mrs. Tarr came by, overdressed in a white blouse and skirt already spattered with hamburger grease. "You two gals ready to order?" she said, acting like a waitress in a greasy spoon.

May picked up the squeeze bottle of mustard, began fiddling with it, staring at the table. I felt, suddenly, that I needed to cover for her. "Well, ma'am," I said. "We girls'll have us two mushroom burgers."

"That's a good one," May said and laughed.

"Two nuke burgers for the sassy gals," Mrs. Tarr said and shoved her short pencil behind her ear.

"She's so funny," May said as Mrs. Tarr walked away. She set the yellow squeeze bottle of mustard down, touched the white squeeze bottle of mayonnaise, then brought the Heinz Ketchup bottle close to her face. "When did they start putting ketchup in glass bottles?" she said, laughing. "What will they think of next?"

The tenderness I felt at that moment was large enough to provide for the rest of the party members. I forgave them their knowledge, their grotesqueness.

I put my hand on May's. "Do you remember me, May?"

"Oh, of course," she said, and began turning the ketchup bottle in her hands, looking at the table.

"I have a terrible memory myself for some things." I smiled and she gave me a sidelong glance. "It's Jill Warren. We worked together for a while at a real estate office. You were the best receptionist we ever had. Well, one of the best." I didn't want to be condescending, although I felt it was probably too late to worry about that.

May leaned forward, her voice low and serious again. "Did I like that?"

I nodded. "For a while. I think you got bored with it."

She smiled. "I'm like that, aren't I?"

At that moment I remembered the dream I'd had a few nights before. I probably remembered it because I wanted to ask her about the coma, wondering if a memory of being in the coma would come back to her as a dream does. But what I had observed was that she was trying to recover her life, trying to recover little bits of her history.

In the dream I was an adult in the farmhouse where I grew up. I had just wakened, naked under a heavy white sheet. There was a bloodstain on the bottom sheet. I looked closer. The stain was a family crest. I knew, in the way one knows in dreams, that generations of my blood had marked these sheets in just this way. The crest was a buzzard with a long crooked neck and great wings. In the claws of the buzzard there was an enormous diamond and a steering wheel.

Then I was in the kitchen, heating water for coffee. The room was just as it had been when I was a child, white stove with curled feet, faded yellow wallpaper, hardwood floors that would be a selling point now. I began wondering, in the dream, whether the child I had been would care for the adult I had become. At that point, a girl walked into the kitchen. I realized instantly, with that recognition that marks dreaming, that the girl was me as a child. I became nervous, intimidated by the bone-thin child, me at twelve, with dark hair and a patient smile.

Steam curled off the pan of water. The girl approached me, her eyes twisting around my body. "Let me drink coffee with you?" she said.

I realized that she would like me if I let her drink coffee. It was that simple. Children don't judge in much deeper ways than that. I nodded to her, watched her swirl milk in her coffee to dilute the bitterness. I took mine black. We drank. She stared at my breasts. "These will be yours," I told her. She giggled.

Then our mother came in. I realized we'd been waiting for her. She told us our father was all right. This was news we were hoping to hear. I, as a little girl, ran to her. She swung me in an arc around her chest. I, as a woman, nodded in silence, approving.

May listened intently to my recollection of the dream. "I remember my dreams," she said. "Last night I was in a tool shed. There were two hammers and a rake."

Mrs. Tarr brought us our burgers. The black mushrooms oozed over the sides. She had dropped the waitress pretense. "Enjoy," she said to May. She set my paper plate in front of me and stooped to whisper in my ear. "You're holding up well," she said.

If I hadn't just spoken with May, I would have slapped her. "That's a good one," I said.

May stared at her mushroom burger. After Mrs. Tarr left, she said, "Do I like this?"

I laughed. "Maybe," I said. "Try it."

We ate slowly. I told her about the lunches we used to have when we worked together. "Was I there?" she asked. I nodded and continued. Some of the others had begun dancing on the Tarrs' patio. Edward was dancing with Eva, very close. He was drunk and liked to dance. Normally, I wouldn't have been annoyed, but with the affair unspoken on everyone's lips, I was angry.

Eva yelled to be heard over the music. "My best position is first base," she called out to a teacher dancing next to them. He was putting together a summer softball team. I had already passed on that opportunity. "Edward, here," she yelled, "has gotten to first base with me already." All the dancers laughed.

"We've got a first baseman—first baseperson—my wife." The softball coach pointed to the woman he was dancing with. "What's your second best position?"

Eva smiled. "The missionary position." The dancers laughed again. The music stopped. "I know what Edward's position is." They kept dancing without music. "I won't say, but his number should be sixty-nine." Edward smiled but tried to step away from her. Most of the party had crowded around and was laughing. "This team might be a little old for him, though," she said. The laughter stopped. "I hear he likes to practice his positions with a younger crowd." She ran her finger under his chin. "My Brenda has heard that he has a big bat and swings from the hip."

May laughed. Everyone else was quiet, dead quiet. Edward pulled away from her. "Come on, Ed," she said. She grabbed his arm but he yanked it away, pushing through the crowd. "I need a pinch hitter," Eva said and opened her arms.

May laughed again. "She's so funny," May said.

Then something extraordinary happened: I laughed with her. Just me and May. I was happy that Edward was already around the corner of the house. He would have thought I was laughing at him. I don't know how I would have survived that moment if I hadn't started laughing with May.

Mrs. Tarr put on some more music. People started moving, talking. I stood and May stood with me. She followed me around the corner of the yard to the fence gate. "Oh, you're leaving," she said. I kissed her on the cheek.

"Can you remember anything, May? From being in the coma?"

She shook her head. "I can't remember a thing," she said. "I can't remember your name."

"It's Jill," I said. "I'm your friend."

"I can't remember the funniest things," she said. I swung open the gate. "I can't remember sex. Oh, I know how you do it, but there was some other part. There used to be more to it." The space between the Tarrs' house and their neighbors' was narrow and shady, a single shaft of light shone on the yellow stucco of her home. "It's like I'm in a whole new world," she said, and we touched hands.

I looked up and down the street for Edward, then walked to the car. He was in the front seat, lying flat, undetectable until I was right on top of the car. He sat up when I got in. "I hate that woman," he said. I started the car and drove us home.

He was quiet and restless at home. He yelled at Charley to turn down the television. Charley, of course, turned it up. He stormed around the house, finally deciding to go to bed at eight.

I was sitting at the kitchen table, drinking tea. Charley joined me. He pointed with his thumb toward our bedroom. "What's with him?" he said.

"He had a bad time at the party," I said.

Charley nodded. He seemed concerned about his father, a begrudging concern, but real nonetheless. I realized I was concerned too. "Something awful happened," I said.

I told Charley the story. He knew about Edward's affair, everyone at the high school did, so I was sure he had heard. But acknowledging that he knew, acknowledging that my husband had had an affair with a high school girl, was a bit of intimacy that was rare between Charley and me. I told him the whole story and I felt close to my son.

The following weekend Charley had a date with Brenda Horne. When he saw how much it upset his father, he began seeing only her. Within a few months, she was pregnant, and they were engaged. I guess he really did fall in love with her. I'm sure of it. But if I hadn't sold out my husband in order to have a moment of intimacy with my son, it never would have happened. Maybe none of the terrible things that followed would have come about.

I forgave Edward his trespasses.

Years later, when the house burned, and I knew Charley was really gone, years after I had lost contact with May, I felt just the way she had in the narrow space between the suburban houses, between the laughter of the party and the sunlit street where my husband hid in our station wagon: I was entering a whole new world. It was frightening and sad, but full of possibility. And it became intoxicating. There were so many things to give up. I felt cleansed. And then I knew that was what Charley was looking for, too, a clean start. Only then did I know how much he must have hated himself and us.

I gave up the house. I gave up my past. I gave up Charley. I started anew, and I felt *lucky*.

When Tom and Ask brought me the photograph of my brother, I threw it away. I didn't explain to them. There were lots of reasons. But the main one was this: I had given up the past. My brother's disappearance was at last a death, finalized by the fire. I would not let him back into my life. I gave him up happily.

May was not so lucky in her new world. The teacher who took her to the party, a man everyone admired for sticking with her through her recovery, turned out to be an awful man, or maybe just typical. God, I don't know. When they pumped May's stomach, they came up with a pint of semen. She didn't know how many men there had been. She couldn't remember. And all I could think of was her saying, "Do I like this? Do I like this?"

HOUSE OF CARDS

I

Edward peeked through the part in the curtains each time he heard a car drive past. This neighborhood had more traffic than the one they'd lived in before, particularly at night. Cassie had gone to the movies with her girl friend and still hadn't returned. It was almost twelve thirty. Tom and Ask weren't home yet either from Tom's work. Edward had the feeling something was up. Jill was acting unworried, but she was still awake. It was Friday night, no reason for them to be in bed early, but the movie should have been over an hour ago, at least.

"What is that girl's name?" he said. He couldn't remember whom Cassie was with.

Jill had her feet curled in the secondhand easy chair they'd bought at Value Village. The entire room was made up of used furniture she'd scoured from stores and garage sales. She liked the room. She was reading a book about a detective who could not solve a murder because there were too many clues. She looked up at Edward.

"What is that girl's name?" he repeated.

"Cassie," Jill said, smiling.

"Aren't you the least bit worried?" he said, ignoring her joke. "Don't you think you should call the girl's parents?"

"Jennie Hargrove," she said. "Let's wait until one."

Another car approached, their station wagon at last. He could consult with Tom and Ask about Cassie. But the Ancient Mariner turned into the driveway across the street. The brakelights glowed red, dimmed, vanished. Why had they parked at Marriet's? It confirmed his notion that something was up. He wondered if Cassie was with them. Had some strange turn of events taken place? He often wondered if his children lived secret lives. His watch read 12:40. They were getting home much later than normal.

"Tom and Ask are back," he said, still staring out the window through the curtains. "They parked across the street at Marriet's."

Jill put her book down. "Cassie's not with them?"

He was elated by this question. They both had the same irrational belief that Cassie's being late was tied to Ask and Tom's coming home late, especially now that they were parking across the street.

"I wonder what they're up to," he said and felt suddenly less worried about Cassie, believing that she was with her brothers. Perhaps they'd gone to meet Tom after the movie. Now they were going to try to secrete her in through a bedroom window so he and Jill wouldn't know she was late, the way Tom had always done when he was in high school. Edward was tempted to turn off the lights in the front room to encourage this scenario, to give the impression they were asleep.

"I think I'll go over there," Jill said.

"I wouldn't do that," he said. "If they wanted us to be part of whatever's going on, they would have parked over here."

"Ask, I don't worry about," she said. "Tom, on the other hand, is capable of getting all of them into trouble."

"Tom's a good boy," he said. "So is Ask. Besides, they're with Marriet. She won't let them do anything stupid."

"Do you think Cassie is with them or not?"

"Maybe," he said. He turned away from the window. "We should call the Hargroves' and see if Jennie is home."

"I'll call her," Jill said. She got up and walked into the next room. "Cassie won't like us checking up on her."

"She's late getting home." He stared through the window again. Tom appeared from the side of the apartment with a large plastic trash barrel. Ask stood beside him. Wind whipped their clothes. Edward could hear Jill in the other room, apologizing for calling so late. Ask and Tom were squeezing the trash barrel into the back of the station wagon. Something blew out, small and white. Ask chased after it. Another blew out. The trash barrel wouldn't fit. Tom pulled it out and closed the door quickly, but not before two more white slips flew out.

Edward smiled. The boys together, trying to keep something under wraps, and failing comically. He felt rich and sweet inside watching his sons run together to retrieve the white slips. They threw them in the car and pulled the trash barrel back around the corner of the house. Charley should be here, he thought, in the middle of all of this with the boys.

Jill appeared in the doorway, phone still in her hand. "Jennie came home two hours ago," she said. Her face was white and severe. "I'll call around."

"I'm going over there," he said, already starting for the door. His happiness left so suddenly, his stomach was a vacuum. He hurried across the street, went directly to the car.

The backseat and part of the rear compartment of the Ancient Mariner were covered with white envelopes. He shielded his eyes and glared into the car. The letters were addressed to him.

He knew immediately what they were. The vacuum in his stomach dropped to his abdomen, which tightened and twisted. He felt a pain in his chest, a lightness in his head. He heard the front door of Marriet's apartment open. Instinctively, he jumped away from the car and stepped behind the end of the house, trying to catch his breath. Ask walked out of the apartment carrying two large trash bags. Tom followed. Edward ducked completely behind the building.

"You'd better hurry," Marriet said. Tom said something in reply.

"Don't tell him to do that," Ask said. "He's an awful driver as it is. I should drive whenever there's a hurry. You get in first. Both doors opening at the same time will cause an air sweep through the car."

One door opened and shut. The second opened and slammed. The car started up. Edward crouched in the shadows. As the car backed out of the driveway and drove off, he stood and watched it go, taking steps after it unconsciously. The world seemed stranger, darker. What did his sons know of him? What did the world?

"Mr. Warren?"

He had stepped into Marriet's view. She was still on her front step, watching them too. He looked to her, feeling sadder than ever. "Cassie hasn't come home. I was worried." He offered this as an explanation of his appearance. "Those letters," he said.

"Oh God," Marriet said. "I'm sorry."

"Did you read them?"

"Only to see who they were from."

He nodded sadly. He felt he should be angry. "You had no right reading my letters," he said but couldn't muster anger. Since the fire, he had kept the letters at school, in his desk. The new house was too uncluttered for a file of letters to go unquestioned. He should have known someone would poke through his desk, maybe as a prank. He sat slowly in the yellow grass of Marriet's lawn.

"Does Jill know?" he asked.

"No," Marriet said. "I don't think so." She sat beside him.

Their house, across the street, looked like a prison. He felt a surge of pain in his chest and shoulders. Real pain. "You must think I'm terrible," he said and looked at her. Her sad look calmed him. "I'm not really." He wondered whether he was trying to convince her or himself, but as he spoke he gained conviction. He told her the story of Jennetta and of the affair with the high school girl, who had been one of her classmates. To have excluded it would have only cast doubts. The story took longer to tell than he had imagined, but it calmed him.

"Tom loves you," Marriet said.

He didn't hear her. A car had stopped in front of their house, a dark blue Mustang with chrome wheels. Cassie jumped out from the backseat. The car sped away. She watched it go, waving.

"Cassie," he called. She put her hands on her hips.

"Can't I even get in the house?" she said and stepped into the road to walk to him.

"Is that you, Cassie?" Jill called from the doorway, receiver at her ear, phone in hand.

Cassie froze in the middle of the street and stretched an arm in either direction. "Which one of you wants me first?" she said.

"Get over here," he said. She trudged across the street. Jill watched her go, still talking on the phone, then closed the door.

Cassie walked as if on the side of a hill, unbalanced, weaving slightly.

"Where have you been?" he demanded.

"Hey, Marriet." She looked past her father. "Having a heart to heart with the old man?"

"You're not listening to me, young lady," he said.

"I went to the movies," Cassie said. She collapsed in the grass. "Then . . ." She paused. "Then I did other stuff. Don't bother me about it, okay? I'm not a little squirt anymore." She stood.

"We're going to talk," he said.

"You're so anal," Cassie said and began walking back toward the house.

He jumped up to follow her, leaving Marriet in the grass. Jill opened the door again.

"Don't you guys ever sleep?" Cassie said.

Was she drunk or stoned, he wondered. He wanted to hold

her mouth open and inhale her. She was at least drunk, he decided. As he stepped up the curb, something new struck him.

There were too many letters.

His knees buckled on the curb. He almost fell. The backseat had been covered in white. Cassie and Jill disappeared inside the house. The door stood open for him like an aperture of pure light. There were far too many letters.

He leaned against the doorway, shuddering. How could they not have burned? He had walked through the remains, looking for the box. The fireman had said the fire could have been hot enough to melt a metal box. But the paint cans in Charley's room had worried him. Why hadn't those cans melted? He guessed, rationalized, that they were farther from the heart of the fire. What other answer could there be?

His throat burned. His stomach turned to acid.

Jill had taken Cassie into the kitchen. "Go to bed," he said to Cassie as he entered the room.

"I think we should talk about this right now," Jill said.

"She won't remember a thing we say tonight." He felt dizzy again and leaned against the doorway.

This weakness in him was what convinced Jill. She sent Cassie to bed and put her arms around him. "She's testing us, pushing her limits some." Jill moved her arm across his chest. "She just needs some attention."

He draped his arms across her. "What do they think of us?" he said.

"Who?" Jill said.

"The children. What do they think of us?"

She laughed. "They think we're old farts." She held him closer. "And they love us."

He nodded and let her hold him.

BY THE TIME the Ancient Mariner pulled into the driveway, everyone but Edward was in bed. He smoked a Kent 100 and waited for them to enter the house. Impatient, he stepped outside. They were both almost to the door. He closed it behind him.

For a moment the three stood unmoving in the dark.

"Where did you get the letters?" he said. "My letters?"

They stared at him dumbly. Then Tom spoke. "What letters?" he said. "What are you talking about?"

Edward waved his cigarette dismissively. "I saw the letters in the car."

"Those were flyers," Tom said. He looked at his shoes, the barren yard. "Marriet works at Sears. There was a sale."

"Goddamn it, Tom. Those letters burned. Or should have. Look at me." He took Tom's chin and jerked it toward him. "What were you doing with them?"

"We went to the dump," Tom said, "to throw away some flyers for Marriet." He pushed Edward's hand away gently. "Let's let it go at that, all right? Let's forget it."

"Those letters burned," he said and felt the burning in his throat. "How did you get them?"

Ask stepped beside his brother. He looked funny, and Tom realized why. His eyes were like marbles.

"Before Charley burned the house," Ask began.

"Charley didn't burn the house," Edward said, pointing the cigarette at Ask.

Ask stared at the orange tip of the cigarette silently.

"Charley didn't burn the house," Tom said quietly to Ask. But it was no use.

"Before Charley burned the house," Ask said, "he saved things for each of us. Your gift was the letters."

"How can you say that about your . . ." The pain moved from shoulder to shoulder. Centered in his neck was not pain at all, but a lightness that lifted to his skull.

"We were throwing them away," Tom said. His son's head blurred as he spoke, as in a bad Driver's Education film, his voice slowed and stuttered. "We don't have to talk about them," Tom said in a new voice. Ask came near, began moving in a circle. Tom moved in the same circle. The Ancient Mariner joined the circle. Edward reached out to grab Ask, to stop him from moving—Ask, whom he could always rely on. His hand caught Ask's shoulder, the spinning stopped, the world became solid and still, his vision perfect, and a new understanding came to him with such a shock of recognition that he said it out loud.

"Charley burned the house," he said calmly. He turned, his knees weak again. He stepped toward the door, but it was a stagger. As he touched the door, it fell away, not a door at all. He almost fell with it but righted himself.

In his bedroom he stared at Jill's sleeping form as he undressed. The bed was not like the one they'd slept in for years. There was no headboard or baseboard, just box spring and mattress, sheets and pillows. He sat on the strange bed and pulled at his shoes. "Oh, Charley," he whispered. "My Charley." His chest hurt, then tingled, sharp then numb, as if stabbed with an icicle.

The bedroom door was ajar—Tom and Ask in the front room talking, a block of light on the gray wall and floor. The effort it took to remove his pants was enormous, but he folded them and pushed his shoes together neatly. Standing by the bed, he felt himself crumble, the shoes rising up to him, their openings elongated, so that they resembled nostrils. He turned his head, knowing now that he was falling. His hands reached out, found nothing, the floor suddenly gone, the walls gone.

"House of cards," he said.

An aperture of light appeared before him and immediately began to close.

2

TOM SAT in a plaid armchair in the corner of the hospital waiting room. It was close to four in the morning. He had been quiet since arriving, watching the other people in the room, the doctors and nurses, visible through two large windows, walking responsibly up and down the hall. This was just another night on the job for them, Tom thought. His family was no different from any other group of sufferers.

Marriet and Cassie sat on a couch at one end of the room. Beside them, a heavy man in thick glasses sat with his hands around his knees. He was pulled into himself, careful not to touch Cassie. Across the room from them, a family sat on a matching couch. A thin but jowly black man was at one end, very erect in a white shirt. A woman, apparently his wife, slouched against him. They looked to be forty-five or fifty. A pretty girl in her teens sat beside the mother, thin like her father. On the arm of the couch beside his sister, a young man with a thin mustache sat placidly. Tom realized that he could be her husband, although she looked too young to be married. He could be the husband of the person they were waiting to hear about. Tom had made them into a family when they could have been a church group, friends, neighbors, working companions.

Ask paced the room, pausing regularly at the big windows, the corner tables to look at magazines, which he quickly tossed down. He often sat for a moment in the chair next to Tom's, but he would be up again quickly, walking.

Jill was with Edward. As yet, they didn't know what was wrong with him or how serious it was. But Tom had lifted him into the car and his weight, his dead weight, had told Tom that it was serious. He had tried to tell a nurse this. "You should never move the patient," she had said. "Call an ambulance. You can do harm." Tom looked at his watch. They had been in the room over two hours.

Marriet, tired of the waiting, tired of the sorrow, decided to make conversation with Cassie. "Where were you tonight?" she said.

Cassie had been surreptitiously staring at the heavyset man next to her. "It's not my fault," she said to Marriet after glancing at Tom to be sure he wasn't listening.

"Of course it's not your fault," Marriet said. "You didn't make your father sick."

"Then why do you want to know?"

"I'm bored. We've been sitting together for hours, you could at least be pleasant. I'm putting up with your stink."

"What do you mean by that?"

"You're supposed to drink booze, not roll in it."

"I spilled a little. When I drink, I get spilly. I found that out tonight." She was feeling slightly drunk still, very tired, and there was a tenseness in her temples. "I just didn't want to go home. I hate that house. Jennie's mom dropped me off, but no one was in the front room, so I went outside again as soon as the car left. I went over to your apartment first, if you must know. You weren't home."

"We went to sit with Tom, Ask and I," Marriet said.

"I don't see what's so exciting about going out there and sitting on the car. When you weren't home I walked over to Toni's. She's this girl I've known for a long time but never been friends with before. She just lives a couple of blocks away. She knew about a party and we went. Her brother took us. It was a pretty cool party. This guy's parents were in Borneo or someplace for the week. He could have made that up, but they were gone."

"I used to love parties when I was in high school," Marriet said. "I always had the sense that something wonderful could happen. It never did, but it seemed possible."

"I like to dance," Cassie said. "Not so much with Ask or Dad at our parties. They think too much while they're dancing. There was one girl there . . ." She leaned forward, looked past Marriet to Tom. He wasn't paying any attention to them. "She kept asking about Tom, how he was doing, that kind of stuff. Real annoying."

"Uh huh," Marriet said. "Who was she?"

"This girl named Cathy Bowling or Boring or something like that. One of those quiet types who the boys all think are pretty and special because they don't ever say anything so you can't tell they're stupid."

"She was pretty but stupid?"

"I told her you and Tom were engaged and planning a big

family with a black and white sheepdog and you were the home-coming queen when you were in high school and you made two movies in Los Angeles."

Marriet laughed. "Those are all lies."

"I wanted her to leave me alone. Girls like that make me feel gawky and ten feet tall. And loud. Am I loud?"

"No, but you are drunk."

"I must get drunk easy. I was thinking about that because it makes me think I was adopted because that all comes from the genes and everyone else in the family drinks like a horse. Plus, this blond hair. My parents always joked about that. I think Mom knows I'm adopted but won't tell Dad because she thinks he'll have a heart attack." She stopped and looked around the room quickly. "I didn't mean that. You think that's what he's got? A heart attack?"

"I don't know."

"You think it's my fault?"

"I already told you that's silly."

"The thing that makes me think it's not my fault is that Ask always thinks everything is his fault, and I can always tell that he's being stupid or silly or with him it's just that he's being Ask. So I thought I was being Ask, instead of being me, but I wasn't sure. Maybe I did cause it by getting drunk and staying out late, but Charley and Tom did that all the time. The other thing is that even though I knew I didn't want to be acting like Ask, I haven't felt like I've been acting like me lately and everyone says I'm being mean or something like that."

"Impossible is the word I've heard. You've been impossible."

"That's what I've felt like. Impossible. That this is real and I am who I am, and all this is all there is. You know? That this is the world and I'm in it and I'm me and I'll always be just that, me, and all it adds up to is sitting in some stupid hospital room next to you and some stranger in glasses and Ask walking circles—*Will you sit down!*"

Ask, who was pacing by the windows, jerked his head around to her.

"Please," said the older black man in a deep, sorrowful voice.

Ask turned to the man and nodded. He sat next to Tom.

"So you get what I mean?" Cassie said. "I'm going to live my whole life and I can leave Yuma or even the United States, but I can never take a vacation from being me and that seems impossible when all there is is this and there seems like there's all that other stuff that I don't even know what it looks like or where it is or how to get there or if they have a name for it."

Marriet stared at Cassie and put her arm around her. "Have you ever been sailing?" she said. Cassie shook her head. "That works for me, a little. I knew a couple in California who had a catamaran and we went sailing around the bay in San Diego."

"I love San Diego," Cassie said.

"We wouldn't talk or eat—well, sometimes we would, but the part I liked best was moving across the surface of the water and forgetting who I was or why I was upset—that's not quite it. I just left myself for a while and I liked it."

"Were you in the big bay or Mission Bay?"

"Mission Bay. We could go sometime."

"Yeah," Cassie said. She looked down at her clothes and straightened them as best she could. "You think my dad's going to die?"

Marriet pulled her closer. "I don't know, really."

"I don't like *thinking* about it so much. I just wish someone would come and tell us something. Even if it was awful. What could be wrong with that family?" She stared at the black family across from them. "The father is nice with a deep voice. His wife loves him. See how she's pushed up against him? The girl is pretty. The boy can grow a mustache, and he has pretty hands."

Marriet looked at the young man's hands. They were unremarkable as far as she could tell.

"They seem like a perfectly good family to me, not like us. What could be wrong with that family? Why do they have to be here?"

"Someone is sick or hurt. That happens to every family."

"You ever watch 'My Three Sons' on TV? I used to think, What a good family. They have little problems that their dad solves and they don't feel bad toward each other and they have fun and they adopt that kid next door, the one with glasses?"

"Ernie," Marriet said.

"Yeah, then I realized their mother was dead and they never showed that and they never were sad about it, and I thought that was cheating. They shouldn't be able to have programs like that unless they showed the mother dying and how all the brothers and the father got sick about it. I couldn't watch it anymore after I thought about that, unless there was really nothing else on."

"You think the show should have a scene like this—everyone sitting in the waiting room in a hospital, waiting? You think people would watch that?"

"It's like a soap opera, I guess. I hate soap operas. The actors are all sweepy when they move and they wrinkle up their heads whenever the violins come on. If Dad dies, I think we should move. I think we should go to Borneo or Holland or someplace like that and fix up a tent or get an old house that has some windows, and make a new kind of life for ourselves. I don't know what, Mom has better ideas than I do, and then be other people, at least for a while. You could come with us. I like you."

"Thanks. I'll think about it."

Cassie started crying. She hid her face with her hands. "Don't let anyone see," she said. Marriet turned to block her from Tom and Ask. "I'd want Charley there," she whispered. "I've been trying to hate him like Tom does, like Mom does. But I'm no good at it. I don't like thinking about Borneo without Charley. It makes me crooked inside."

"You don't have to hate anybody," Marriet said.

"We're both behaving like Ask." She giggled and sniffled. "That sounded just like something he would say, 'You don't have to hate anybody.' " She giggled again. "You're already a part of the family. Ask isn't contagious to anyone else."

"Uh oh," Marriet said, and held Cassie until they both fell asleep.

FOR A LONG TIME Ask and Tom said nothing. They could hear Marriet and Cassie talking and laughing, but neither moved his chair close enough to join them. At four twenty, a young nurse dressed in white stepped into the waiting room. She had light brown hair and was pretty. Ask stood when she entered, waking Tom, who had been vacillating between wakefulness and sleep.

The nurse looked directly at Ask. "Mr. Willows?" she said.

The heavyset man beside Cassie stood, careful not to wake her. The nurse started to say more, but the man put his finger to his lips and looked to the sleeping figures on the couch. He walked to the door with her and they stepped into the hall. He turned the knob before closing the door so it would shut quietly.

Ask sat again. "It must be something really bad wrong with Dad," he said. "We've been here a long time."

Tom sat up in his chair. "I guess," he said.

"It might not be," the black man across the way said in his deep voice just above a whisper. "The hospital takes a long time for anything. We've been here longer than you."

"We don't even know what's wrong with our father," Ask said. "We were talking to him." He swallowed. "Then he was going to bed and he just fell to the floor."

The woman sat up straight at this. "My cousin Bob had that happen to him once," she said. "Remember that, Charles?" She looked up at her husband. "He was fishing. We all thought, heavens, what if he'd passed out in the boat, fallen in the lake and drowned? He was lucky to fall on grass."

"Ours fell on his shoes," Ask said.

"He hit the bed first," Tom said. "It pretty much broke his fall."

"Mmmmm." The young man sitting on the arm of the couch shook his head. Tom thought about how long he had been sitting on the arm of the couch, how uncomfortable he must be. Or, if he was feeling no pain from it, how worried he must be despite his calm looks.

"What was wrong with Bob?" Ask said.

"They never did discover," she said. "But he never had a thing like that happen again to him and had no ugly effects from it that any of us could tell. Just had the one spell—they did take away his license to drive."

The husband snorted and smiled. "Not that that stopped him. He'd rip up and down roads like he invented speed. That was his final doing in."

"He have an accident?" Ask said.

The young man with the mustache laughed. The girl on the couch beside him slapped his knee. The father spoke. "He had a passel of accidents and never got a scratch on him."

"Oh, Charles, he had plenty of scratches." The mother turned from her husband to Tom and Ask. "But he never got hurt like he deserved for driving like that until his wife left him on account of it. The first thing he did, the fool, was take to drink."

The door opened again. The same nurse. Ask stood. The man with the mustache stood. She looked at Ask, then turned to the family. "The doctor will see you now," she said. "Just the father, please."

"Oh God in heaven," the mother said.

The mustached man walked with the nurse out of the door. Ask remained standing, watching the closed door.

"If she was all right, we could all go," the mother said.

Charles put his hand on her head. "You don't know that." He looked to Ask. "Sit down, son. It could be a long night."

"It already is," the girl said. She lay her head on her mother's shoulder.

Ask sat and turned to Tom. "I should have taken those letters to the dump the very day we got them. I knew I should do it, but I didn't."

"Don't even start that," Tom said. "I could have dumped the letters." He crossed his arms. "I could have asked Arzate to. We could have not dropped them, or gone to some store to get garbage bags. Cassie could have come home on time. Dad could have been asleep. Charley could have not burned down the house." His voice had gotten loud and he stopped. Cassie and Marriet stirred but didn't wake. "It's nobody fault. Or it's everybody's fault."

"But all I had to do was get the letters . . ."

"Goddamn it, Ask," Tom whispered so fiercely it sounded like a hiss. "When you blame yourself for everything that goes wrong, you remind me of Charley. He made so much of himself he could burn our house, our house, just to make himself feel better. You, you think everything you do affects everyone in the family, everyone in the world. You think we all revolve around you. We don't. So don't blow yourself up thinking you killed Dad."

"Killed!" Ask jumped out of his seat. "You think he's dead?"

"No, I just said that. Sit down."

"Quit telling me what to do, for chrissakes." He sat again. "And quit telling me what to think." He crossed his arms and leaned back in the chair.

The door opened. Charles and his wife turned their heads quickly. It was Jill. Tom and Ask both stood and walked to her. Marriet eased Cassie's head onto the couch and stood. She hesitated, but Tom reached back for her. They stepped into the hallway, which had a different quality to it, louder, more businesslike.

"Your father has had a stroke," she said. "They're watching him. They don't know or aren't saying how serious it is." She stopped, saw that they were still waiting. "He's not going to die. His signs—whatever that means—are strong."

Ask felt the weight of the evening leave him. He smiled openly, so big it stretched his face. "Just a second," he said and stepped into the waiting room. He looked at the family on the couch.

"Dad is going to be all right," he said, biting his lip now to suppress the smile.

The mother reached out and took his hand. "I'm happy for you."

"I told you," Charles said.

Ask looked at Cassie. "Think I should wake her?" he said.

"Let her sleep," the mother said.

"No." The girl who had been resting against her mother lifted her head. "Don't leave her out."

Ask, for a moment, felt very close to the black girl. He nodded at her and walked over to the couch. He crouched close to Cassie. "Cassie," he said. "Wake up." She stirred, put her elbow over her face. "Cassie."

"Let them go home," Cassie said, still asleep.

"Wake up," Ask said. "Dad's going to be all right."

Cassie sat up, saying, "Then take your hand out of the blender." She looked around the waiting room. "What is it?" she said.

"A stroke," Ask said, "but he's going to live. They already know that."

Cassie put her arms around Ask. "What is a stroke?"

"It's like a heart attack, I think. Only not so bad. I don't know exactly."

"Son." Charles stood. He walked to the crouching Ask. "Did they say how serious it was? The stroke?"

"They said he's going to live. He's going to be okay. We were worried."

Charles opened his mouth to speak, to caution against such cheery optimism, but he didn't want to see Ask's face deflate. Let him have his moment of happiness, he thought, perhaps it was a very minor stroke. This was not a matter for a stranger to interfere in, not while his granddaughter might be dying in another room in this awful pastel building. He patted Ask on the shoulder and turned back to the couch.

. . .

JILL SENT the others home. She spent the remainder of the night in Edward's room, sleeping in a chair on rollers. The hospital permitted no one else in the room and encouraged her to go home as well. "Come back tomorrow at noon," they told her. "He needs his rest."

She believed he needed her. He was wakeful much of the time, but he didn't speak. Half his face, the right half, was flattened. His eyes moved around, focusing momentarily on her, then moving on. They were watery, red. They gave him sedation, and he slept. They told her she could leave now, if she wished. She couldn't bring herself to do it.

While Ask had run into the waiting room to wake Cassie, Jill had insisted to Tom and Marriet that all of them go home, get some sleep, and return at noon. She was gone before Ask and Cassie stepped into the hall.

Tom drove them home, and everyone went to bed, Marriet crawling under the sheets with Tom. Ask set his alarm for eleven thirty.

At eleven fifteen Jill called to say that Edward would sleep until three. They shouldn't come until then. If she had not been worried about Edward, she would have wondered why it was Cassie who answered the phone. She had been sleepwalking and answered the phone in her sleep, waking during the conversation, remembering just enough of her mother's directions to walk into Ask's room and turn off his alarm before returning to her bed and sleep.

At one, Jill called again. Marriet was up, making herself coffee, feeling mildly ashamed of herself for feeling so good while Mr. Warren lay in a hospital bed. She had enjoyed sharing a bed with Tom, sleeping with him without having sex. She had never spent the night with a man before without having sex. She was invigorated and feeling especially tender toward Tom.

Jill told her that the doctors wanted to spend some time with Edward after he woke. There were some tests. It was better that they wait until after he ate supper. They could come at six.

"How are you doing?" Marriet said.

"This is the dreariest room I've ever been in in my life. The man in the next bed moans about his back, the windows are covered, and Edward—I can see his chest rise and fall. He's alive. But he's been out for a long time. Don't tell them this. The doctors say everything's fine. Relatively fine. It's just dreary."

"Have you eaten anything?"

"They brought a breakfast tray for Edward even though they had sedated him. Jell-O was one of the things on it. Can you imagine? For breakfast? I should have eaten something more. I should have gone home with the rest of you. But I felt like I would have been abandoning him."

"Let me bring you something," Marriet said. "Everyone here is still asleep."

The phone went quiet and Marriet realized that she'd given away that she'd slept with Tom. She felt afraid and embarrassed. She didn't want to complicate anything more for Jill.

Finally Jill said, "A roast beef sandwich would be wonderful. You know that deli on Fourth and Olsen?"

"I'll be there in a few minutes," Marriet said, elated again.

"Leave them a note," Jill said.

Marriet stuck a note on the refrigerator.

Don't go to the hospital at three. The doctors will be through with your father at six. I'm taking a sandwich to your mother.
love,

She looked at the word *love*. Yes, she decided. It was the right word.

love,
Marriet

She immediately wrote another note.

Tom,
I'll meet you at the hospital at six. I hope this doesn't scare you, but I love you.
Marriet

She walked into his bedroom and put the note on his dresser. He slept with one arm off the bed. His hand, the fingers cupped, almost touched the floor.

TOM WOKE BRIEFLY each time the phone rang but fell back to sleep almost immediately. At four forty-five, he crawled out of bed. Marriet's note, folded like a tent on his dresser, reminded him that she'd slept with him, here in his room, his bed. Their mutual exhaustion had made sleeping together easy and comfortable. That she had written that she loved him startled and thrilled him. He took a long hot shower and shaved.

Cassie was slumped over the kitchen table when he walked in. He greeted her but she didn't lift her head. She waved to him and handed him the note from the refrigerator.

"Hung over?" Tom said.

"Is that what this is?" She lifted her head. She liked the misery better if it was a hangover. It was such a grown-up problem. Tom handed the note back to her. She read it again. "Does this mean he'll be home at six?"

Tom shook his head. "We can see him at six." He started to show her Marriet's other note but stopped himself. He couldn't, however, stop himself from smiling. "Marriet's going to meet us there at six."

"Are you *ever* going to marry her?"

Tom was surprised by the question. "What kind of question is that?"

"Charley always bounced from girl to girl except for Brenda. But you always see just one forever and never marry her, like with Eileen. And Ask never saw anyone until dopey Julie and he doesn't have sense enough to know what to do. So, you see?"

"No." Tom walked away from her to the sink. "Is Ask up?"

"He's gone somewhere in the Mariner."

Tom took a long drink of water. "I've only been going out with Marriet a little while," he said, but she had already grown tired of the conversation. "Get in the shower. We've got to be at the hospital in half an hour."

"Ask is probably there now," Cassie said, pushing herself up from the table, "pacing the parking lot."

WHEN ASK HAD NOT returned by five forty-five, Tom called Arzate and got a ride to the hospital. They couldn't find the Ancient Mariner in the parking lot. Arzate read *Sports Illustrated* in the waiting room while they went in to see their father.

Marriet and Jill stood side by side, arms around each other above Edward's bed. A bouquet of carnations and daisies in a cardboard vase sat on the table beside the bed, the wrappings of a sandwich beside the vase. They both turned to the door when Cassie opened it. Marriet stepped to Tom and hugged him.

"Where's Ask?" Jill whispered. Cassie shrugged and stepped to the bed, Tom just behind her.

"How you feeling, Dad?" Tom said.

Edward lifted his left arm slightly. He could see his son clearly, could see how he was concealing worry. Cassie, beside him, gripped her mother's arm. "I'm all right," he said, but he heard the slur in his speech. The words inside his head were perfect, but he could hear his spoken words, how they sloped into each other, a nasal hum.

"What is this?" Cassie said. She looked to Jill. "Mom?" She stretched the word into two syllables.

"It's going to take a while for him to recover." She sat on the edge of the bed and put her hand on his shoulder. "He begins therapy in a few days. Occupational therapy, where he practices arm and finger movements, and speech therapy."

"Back to kindergarten," Edward said, but the words fell in on themselves again. He didn't want to frighten them as he'd been frightened, as he'd seen Jill frightened. He lifted his arm and touched Cassie's cheek.

They began talking again, but the words didn't hold sense, only sound. His right arm and shoulder, the right side of his face tingled then fell silent again. He thought suddenly of a dentist anesthetizing half a body by mistake. The idea was funny to him. Then he realized someone was missing. There should be someone else in the room. He pointed with his strong arm. "Where's the other one?" he said. "Where?"

Jill couldn't understand him but knew from the way he said it, it was a question. "I can't understand you, dear," she said.

He kept circling with his hand, slurring the question.

"Ask," Tom said, understanding the feeling instead of the words, because he too was conscious of his brother's absence, the person least likely to miss seeing his father. "He got the times screwed up," Tom said loudly, and was embarrassed at calling out so loud. "They kept pushing back the time," he said in his normal voice.

Edward grinned a half grin, the right side uncooperative and dead. But the question was still unsatisfactorily answered and would have remained so, except that in the room was the person he'd shared most of his life with, who knew his worries now even better than he. Jill leaned closer to him and whispered, "Charley's out of town."

Oh yes, Edward remembered, Charley was gone. Charley had left him.

THEY SQUEEZED INTO Arzate's Volkswagen. Tom, Marriet, and Cassie shared the backseat. "Why didn't anyone tell me he would be like that?" Cassie said, squirming in place to make more room. "Move over," she said to Tom. "Why do I always have to ride on the hump?"

"Hush," Jill said. "Just shut up." She sat beside Arzate in the bucket seat, exhausted, with his box tape player in her lap. She tried to figure the number of hours she had been awake but lost count.

Traffic lights turned red as they neared them, cars slowed, trucks would not permit them to pass. The ride home took forever, Cassie squirming and grunting in complaint, the others silent and cramped.

Finally at the house, they climbed somberly out of the car and walked to the door, Arzate trailing to see if they needed anything more of him. It was Jill who opened the door.

The front room twinkled red, blue, green. Christmas lights were strung in loops from hooks in the ceiling that had once held hanging plants. The Sunday comics, stapled into long strips, hung from the ceiling, nearly to the floor. Across the hallway a banner read THE FALLEN SHALL RISE.

"A toast," Ask called out as he entered the room with a tray of drinks. Julie stepped in behind him. She was wearing a short party dress. "Where's Dad?" he said.

Jill covered her eyes. "My God, Ask." She walked into the hallway, ducking under the banner and into her room.

"He can't talk," Cassie screamed at Ask. "You told me he was fine. He can't even say my name." She slapped at the banner as she walked into the hall, tearing it nearly in two.

"What's going on?" Ask said. "I don't get it." The drinks began to slosh as the tray trembled in his hands.

"He's had a bad stroke," Tom said. His head began to shake. As he stepped closer to his brother, he saw that Ask was wearing a new shirt, with a Hawaiian design. A party shirt. "We went to his room at six. There was never any plan to let him come home today. You misunderstood. He could be there for weeks."

The drinks spilled. Ask's eyes watered. Beyond him, a tray on the kitchen table held an array of packaged meats. The plastic envelopes the meats had come in filled a paper sack beneath the table. Next to the tray was a loaf of Sunbeam bread. A bowl held big chunks of carrots, fists of cauliflower, broccoli, whole mushrooms, lettuce and spinach leaves.

The glasses on the tray Ask held rattled against one another. Tom looked into his eyes but couldn't get Ask to stare back. He took the tray from him and turned. "Arzate," he called and pushed the tray in his direction. Arzate stepped forward and took a beer.

"Get your blaster from the car," Tom said, "and some dance music."

"Tom," Marriet said, "your mother needs to sleep."

"I know," he said quietly. "Wake her, will you?" He kissed her and she took a beer. Julie took a glass of wine. "Hey," he said to Ask, shoving the tray under his nose. Ask took a beer. "Get Cassie," he said to Julie. "Tell her Kool-Aid is waiting."

"Strawberry," Ask said. He wiped his eyes. "I remembered that she was tired of cherry."

"Mom'll come," Tom said to Marriet. She kissed him on the cheek and went to get Jill, who lay exhausted in bed, too tired even for sleep.

Cassie trudged down the hall in front of Julie. "I can drink real stuff now. I proved that. I even had a hangover." She slapped her leg and took the glass of Kool-Aid.

Jill and Marriet stepped out of the master bedroom arm in arm, but the hallway was too narrow, and Jill stepped ahead.

"White wine," Ask said, taking a glass from the tray and handing it to his mother.

Arzate stepped in with Marvin Gaye on his tape player singing "What's Going On." Only a squat glass of Seven and Seven remained on the tray. Tom took it and lifted it into the air. "A toast," he said but couldn't for the life of him think of anything to say. They drank anyway and ate and danced and acted like a family.

3

EILEEN HAD THE BABY at nine in the morning on the first Saturday in June. By the time Sam called Marriet's apartment that afternoon, the temperature in Yuma had reached 107 degrees and the air was as still and dry as silence. Marriet and Tom had showered together before lunch to cool themselves, eaten BLTs and orange sherbet, then made love on her couch. She had showered again while Tom sat on the couch in his underwear watching baseball on a black and white Zenith. It was he who answered the phone. "Eileen wanted you all to know," Sam said.

"She's fine then," Tom said.

"Yes. She wanted you all to know that she was fine and the baby is fine. We named her Karla, after my grandmother," Sam said.

"That's good," Tom said. "I'll tell Marriet and my family."

"She wanted you all to know."

"She's fine," Tom said.

"Yes, we're fine."

Marriet walked in from the bathroom with a beach towel wrapped around her middle. "Who is it?" she said. Tom passed her the receiver. A trail of water trickled down her temple to her jaw, then dropped to her chest. "That's wonderful," she said into the phone. Tom couldn't sort out his feelings. Part of him was jealous. Part of him was still angry with Eileen and the ever absent Charley. Part of him was glad the baby was born and the waiting was over. Eileen was healthy. The baby was healthy. Marriet was here, with him, wet from the shower. "Congratulations," she said. That was what he should have said. *All the best,* he imagined himself saying.

On television Dave Parker lined a single over the leaping second baseman. "He murdered that ball," the announcer said. The outfield grass and infield dirt were reduced to being different shades of the same color by the black and white television. Parker rounded first hard, trying to stretch his hit into a double.

Marriet hung up the phone. "I have to get dressed. I'm going to go see the baby. Sam invited me. He sounds like a nice guy." She sat on his lap. Parker slid into second ahead of the throw, which skipped past the shortstop. "Who's winning?" she said.

"I'm not sure," he said. "I don't think there's any score." Her beach towel, wet against his bare legs, was red and white, a copy of the Budweiser label.

"He's safe," the announcer said. "Looks like he caught a spike.

No error on the play.'' Parker limped on the infield dirt, grimacing in pain. He bent over to touch his shin but rested his hands instead on his knees. *Never touch the area that hurts,* Tom thought. It was an unwritten rule. He pulled the towel loose and took Marriet's breasts into his hands. "Bring her lilies,'' he said. "She likes lilies.''

EILEEN, in a peach gown, her hair in a ponytail, was sitting on the hospital mattress when Marriet entered the room. Sam stood beside the bed, holding the baby, circled by grandparents. The circle opened. Smiling, Sam showed Marriet their daughter. Healthy, pink, and hairless, the sleeping baby moved her lips silently.

Marriet gave the bouquet of lilies to Eileen.

"I've always liked lilies,'' Eileen said. She accepted the baby from her husband and kissed her lightly on the forehead.

"She's lovely,'' Marriet said.

"Tell our friends, will you?'' Eileen said. The baby opened her mouth again, wide this time, a yawn.

At the car, Marriet slid into the front seat beside Tom. Ask and Cassie waited in the back, fanning themselves with city maps. "A pretty little girl,'' she said. "Eileen is fine, a little sore. Labor lasted almost nine hours. Sam looks happy.''

Tom smiled but wasn't sure whether it was a real smile or a forced one. "Let's get drunk,'' he said.

The suggestion found unanimous approval. They bought a case of beer and drove to the river. Everyone but Ask was wearing shorts and swam in their clothes. Ask stripped to his boxer shorts and sat in the river, drinking and watching a log raft, loaded with people, approach.

"Pilgrims!'' A middle-aged man with a beard stood on the raft, his hands cupped around his mouth, and called out. "Pilgrims! Ahoy there!''

Ask waved to them. Two adult women guided the raft with long poles. A teenaged boy stood beside them, and two naked children, a boy and a girl, kneeled on the raft's edge.

"Toss the anchors,'' the man called out as they came even with

Ask. The boy obediently threw the two kids over the side. The women erupted with laughter. They propped the poles into the mud to hold the raft against the weak current. The children splashed and shouted their way to shore.

"Are these friendly waters?" the man shouted.

"Aye," Ask said, joined now by Tom, Marriet, and Cassie.

The bearded man saluted and dove into the river. The women laughed and held up their hands to stop his splash from soaking them. The nearest woman smiled. "He's all wound up," she said and laughed.

The bearded man surfaced next to them, his face flushed and smiling. "Hail Neptune," he said, "queen of the waters." He beat his chest. "Captain Davey Jones at your service." He extended his hand.

"Davey Jones?" Cassie said. "He was a Monkee. The cute one."

Ask shook the man's hand. "Askew Warren, high school graduate. My brother Tom, sister Cassie, sister Marriet."

"And my crew," the captain said, turning and waving his arm toward the raft. "Narcissus, queen bee of the ship," he said. The nearest woman waved and smiled sheepishly, middle-aged and overweight in a dated one-piece bathing suit. "And beside her," the captain said, "Eleanor Rigby, sister of Narcissus, on her maiden voyage." The other, a much younger woman with the same face and a thinner body, waved. "To the aft, our first mate and general gofer, Ruby Tuesday."

"Nah, no way," the skinny teenager said, dismissing the suggestion with a wave of his hand. "I can't be a Ruby." He rubbed his hand over his bare chest, looking from Marriet to Cassie, stepping in place on the raft.

"It's the only first mate name I know," the captain said.

"Starbuck," Tom suggested.

The captain turned to him. "Magnificent! It's Starbuck you'll be," he said, twisting back to the boy. The two naked kids had reached the shore and were dipping their hands in the water and flipping them open in futile attempts to splash Ask and Tom. "And our anchors, Fannie Anchor and Lonesome George." The anchors applauded.

Tom offered them beer, and they countered with a bottle of tequila. Eleanor Rigby produced a joint, and the party moved to the raft. They smoked and drank and lay with their legs in the river. From underwater the raft would have looked like a huge multilegged water bug, or so Tom imagined, cupping water and rubbing it over his soaked shirt and burning face. A breeze floated over them, lifting shirttails, evaporating the drops of water from their arms and faces. They grew quiet.

Suspended between shores, drunk and high on pot, Tom felt himself lift off the raft and rise into the sky. The raft, the river, the earth receded, and Tom looked back on his family from the stratosphere. He saw his mother polishing silver, forks and spoons, then tossing them into the air. They rose, flying up past him, so quickly that they soon became nothing more than sparkles above him, daytime stars. His father stepped into view, twice as tall as his mother. He took one of the forks from her and pulled the tines off, staring intently to see what made the fork work. Befuddled, he took another fork and hurled it upward. The fork rocketed up a hundred yards, then fell back to earth, while his mother barely tossed a spoon and it rose to heaven.

Tom saw Ask and Marriet and Cassie on the raft below him, the others gone now, and they lifted their arms above their heads and held hands. The circle made by their arms became the center of the universe, as Tom could see it, a gyre of intense green light. Far from the center, on a dark cobblestone street, Charley stepped into view, skipping rocks on the air with a skillful submarine throw. There was something across his shoulders, something silver or chrome. Tom looked closer and might have seen had he not fallen from the sky back to the raft and to sleep.

"Hey," Ask said softly to the captain. "Who are you really?"

"You won't tell, mate?"

"On my honor as a sailor," Ask said.

"Why, I'm Huck Finn," the captain said. "Huck Finn grown old. Terribly old. Old as Medusa. Old as Captain America. Old as . . . as . . ."

"Paul McCartney," Cassie said.

"Yes," the captain said. "Old as the King of Sheba."

"As old as Lawrence Welk," Ask said.

"Old . . . old like Timbuktu," Starbuck added.

Narcissus lifted her legs from the water and turned on her stomach. "Old as those vegetables we found in the back of the refrigerator."

"Not *that* old," the captain said.

"Old as beehive hairdos," Marriet said.

"Old as those men who play checkers and wear those old-man hats," Cassie said.

Ask elbowed the sleeping Tom. "Don't you have one?"

Tom raised on one elbow. "Huh?"

"How old do you think our captain is?" Ask said.

Tom looked at the captain, who nodded encouragingly. "Forty?" Tom said.

"Wrong!" the captain said. "I'm old as memory." He took a swig of tequila and passed the bottle.

"Oh," Eleanor Rigby said. "I know. He's old as cafeteria food."

"Old . . . old like barbecue potato chips," Starbuck said. "The stale ones."

"Old as sin," Narcissus said, laying her head in the crook of her arm. "Old as betrayal. Old as murder. Old as death."

"Old as Dad's wingtips," Cassie said.

"Those are perfectly good shoes," Ask said.

"Old as water," Marriet said, splashing Tom, who was still sleepy.

"I know one," Lonesome George said. The little boy stood, walked to the edge of the raft, and peed.

JILL WAS READING a magazine in the front room when they stumbled into the house.

"Ma!" Tom said as he bolted through the front door.

Ask was right behind him. "Eileen had her Karla," he said.

Marriet and Cassie walked in singing, "Joy to the world, all the baby girls." They mixed the next lines, Cassie singing, "Joy to the babies in the deep blue sea," and Marriet singing, "Joy to the baby girls, joy to the baby girls."

"Who drove?" Jill said.

Tom and Ask looked at each other. "Was it you?" Tom said.

"Yeah," Ask said.

"No, it wasn't," Cassie said. "Marriet drove. Like aces, she drove. Like . . ."

"Like Mario Andretti," Ask said and laughed. "Eileen is a mom, Mom. Don't you get it?"

"You're wet."

"We went to the river," Marriet said. "We met the strangest people."

"A lot stranger than us," Tom said.

"Where's Dad?" Ask said.

"In the bedroom," Jill said. "He's had another spell." Having a spell had become a euphemism for the mild strokes he often suffered.

"Again?" Cassie said, exasperated and suddenly deflated.

"Again," Jill said. Near the end of March, Frieda had given birth to a little boy. His heart, the doctors said, was defective. He lived only a few hours. "His fingers," Frieda had said, "his little toes. You wouldn't have believed how tiny." Her voice had cracked and squeaked. "You're young," Jill had said, knowing there was nothing she could offer but the comfort of words. She folded her magazine and let it fall to the floor. "Eileen's baby is healthy?" Marriet and Ask nodded enthusiastically. "What's the baby's name?" she said.

"Karla," Ask said. "And it's . . ."

"She's," Cassie corrected.

"She's bald," Ask said.

"You were bald," Jill said to Ask. "Tom too. Cassie had thin, almost silky wisps of hair." She smiled at Cassie.

"What about Charley?" Ask said.

"Bald. All the boys were bald."

"Charley should be here," Tom said. He slumped into a chair.

"You're wrong," Jill said.

"No," Marriet said. "He's right. Charley should be here. Not this house, but here."

Jill stood quickly. "He should be in hell," she said.

"Mom!" Cassie said.

"Calm down, Mom," Ask said. "You don't mean that. That's not fair."

"Don't talk to me about fair. You are all drunk and sentimental. I am neither. Charley has no place . . ."

"It's his baby," Tom said.

Cassie dropped to her knees on the carpet. "I thought she was your baby."

Jill sat again in the chair, shaken. "That's ridiculous," she said.

Marriet put her arms around Tom.

"He and she," Tom began. "Anyway, he got her pregnant. You can't tell anyone. We shouldn't tell anyone." Jill stared hard at him. "It's true," he said. "He wanted her to marry him. He thought it would cut him off from us. It would have been a way out."

Jill thought of the party, telling Charley about Eva, and how he immediately started dating Eva's daughter. "I'm sorry," she said to Tom. "But you are still wrong. We're better off, Eileen is better off, the baby is better off with him out of here." She stood again, so quickly she was momentarily dizzy. As she left the room, she realized that she, this afternoon, had become a grandmother. The realization came so suddenly and with such impact that she lost her breath and her strength and had to lean on a kitchen chair for support.

Marriet hurried to her side. "I'm a grandmother," she whispered. They walked into the living room together and sat on the couch. The mammoth fireplace seemed, in the summer heat, to be a monument to stupidity. Jill wished the loose stones would fall, would finally come tumbling down. She began talking about the Tarrs' party. About Eva Horne. About May's accident. About Edward hiding in the car. She told Marriet the whole story.

CHARLEY'S STORY

TWO O'CLOCK, ten o'clock, my hands on the wheel, chest tipped forward, elbows out, eyes missing nothing—Mustang two cars ahead slowing down, slanting eastern barn the gray of hair, oncoming diesel crowding the center line, 209 miles to Philadelphia, quarter tank of regular, a drop of perspiration growing in my eyebrow, beech trees, birch, a canyon river crooked like a spine, grass the green of a fever—and no end to the driving—Arizona, New Mexico, Texas, Oklahoma, Kansas, Missouri, Illinois, Kentucky, Indiana, Ohio, Pennsylvania—sputtering through the Missouri mountain dark, on what road? in what mountains? driving north? south? west? east? I said to myself that I couldn't be lost as long as I didn't know where I was going, and saying it, I set myself free.

But out of the van—nothing—the dread of memory, a band of guilt around my abdomen, the pull of home. I called Eileen my second night on the road and every night for a week.

"Don't come back," she said. "You're out. You've got what you wanted. The place where you used to fit is gone; it's all ashes and anger. Don't ever come back. Their hearts have twisted against you, just the way you planned it. You have the new life you wanted, and we're here cleaning up your messes. Call me if you have to. Cry. Bitch. Worry. But don't come back."

She told me the house burned to nothing, that Tom would not love her, and, later, that vessels of blood in my father's brain were exploding like fireworks on the Fourth of July. I told her things, stories, mostly true, how I was molded into the image of my father, grounded by the betrayal of father to son, husband to wife. I was the beauty and I was the beast. I was the ugly witch and handsome prince. I was top-grade lumber cured in bile.

"Self-pitying jerk," Eileen said. "Just don't come back."

In Illinois the van turned south, a vehicle with a mind of its own, taking me to Kentucky, to the house that was my grandfather's, that was Aunt Hannah's, that was home for one miserable summer—a tiny house on a hill that overlooked a cafe.

Return with me now to the thrilling days of yesteryear: I am seventeen, senior in high school, uprooted to move to Arizona as a sophomore, uprooted as a senior to move back, and before the summer is out we will be in Arizona again in yet another town. I am seventeen, humiliated by my father through a cafe waitress—"I like you," she says, slipping her hand between the buttons of my shirt, rubbing the material between her fingers. "You're more mature than most the boys," she says, coy, sweet, coming on—but it's my father she wants, my father's body she needs to touch.

I'm seventeen in a tiny house with my parents, aunt, brothers, sister, and the room that was my grandfather's. The room is locked. Hannah can't move her father's stuff—it's not her place (his place is now six feet under), so I sleep on the porch like an untrained dog to please the dead.

Not me. I can move his stuff. Or so I thought.

Hannah is at work. Mother, Cassie, and my brothers are in Paducah. Father is interviewing for a job. I pick the lock to the locked-up room.

It's perfect. The bed is made, no wrinkles in the gold bedspread. The nightstand holds his reading glasses, a black wrap of tape between the lenses. A lamp grows out of a duck decoy, and beside it, a paperback western, a tapered comb. His dresser has an oval mirror held in place by four star-shaped buttons, a black and white picture of his wife clipped to the edge, beneath it another, he and his wife at the fair, she with a stuffed animal, an oversized rabbit. On the dresser, a doily with a phony floral design, hair oil in a clear jar with a little red cap, a thin pocketknife, flat can of shoe polish, picture frame with an inner oval of his long-dead son in uniform, a ceramic cup the size of a shot glass that holds several flat toothpicks.

And the drawers are full—thin socks and white boxer shorts, small collar shirts perfectly folded, suspenders, belts no wider than a finger, cuffed pants and overalls. A woven oval rug hides the floor. His dark shoes beneath the bed. A metal box with a sliding drawer, partially hidden by the bedspread. The drawer springs open when I yank it.

Letters. Two years of letters according to the postmarks, but it looks like ten. Letters to my father from his lover who told me I was mature enough to understand. Many of them are unopened—he betrays her even as he betrays my mother. Even as he has betrayed Hannah by putting them in that room. And all of them, even Jennetta, unaware how he betrays them. I wonder about all the other ways he must betray us daily, ways I can't imagine.

I'm seventeen and I decide my father will never know why I hate him until I'm gone and he can't be forgiven. I will cut his heart open. I am seventeen and will make it so.

I CALLED EILEEN and told her things I remembered, told her that I was nearing Kentucky, and more, something I had figured out about my marriage, about Brenda. "I've heard all of this," she said.

"I know how it happened," I said. "I know when it was my marriage went bad." I made her listen.

A day in October, a Sunday. I woke up before Brenda. When we were first married I used to lie there in bed and watch her sleep. That habit lasted about a month. This morning was a lot later. I got up and drove to 7-Eleven to get the paper and a box of doughnuts. Her mother was gone that weekend with some guy, a businessman. He'd taken her to LA to go fishing and to fuck. "This could be the one," she'd said to me, then pinched me on the ass to make me think she wasn't really serious, but we knew she was desperate to get married again. The house was different when Eva was away. She kept it filled up with noise and movement and a hairy kind of tension. Anything that went wrong between me and Brenda we blamed on Eva. When she was gone the house got really quiet, and we were careful with each other.

By the time I got back from 7-Eleven, Brenda was sitting in the living room in her nightgown, her feet on the couch, arms wrapped around her legs. "Did you remember coffee?" she said. I told her no. She sort of nodded, like that was what she was expecting. "You want me to go back?" I said. "Only take a minute." She said not to bother. I didn't drink coffee back then.

We spread the Sunday paper over the living room floor. She toasted some English muffins. There's not that much in the newspaper I like. The hell with sports, and I don't give a damn about who's killing who in Africa or South America. What I enjoy are the stories that aren't really news, like tips on how to get better mileage, stories on inventors and the gizmos that companies buy up but never use, columns where people ask for help. I even like the household hints, such as what to do with soap when it gets too little to hold in your hand (you stick it to the back of a bigger soap bar) or how to get out certain stains, like wine or chocolate or blood. That morning I read the Home section. Brenda had the Travel section. We read to ourselves, mostly.

My article was about a do-it-yourself house for under ten thousand bucks, the wiring, the plumbing, the whole works. Brenda read about Brazil. "We should go to Carnaval," she said, making the word sound as foreign as she could. "We should just up and go," she said. "Do something crazy." I told her that stuff costs money. She nodded and went back to reading. That's the way the morning went, her showing me a picture of a boulevard in Rio, a red brick house with bay windows and purple bougainvillea—me imagining a floor plan with kitchen and bathroom back to back to save on plumbing.

We went to an afternoon movie, but it wasn't any good, just people talking, making a mess of their lives with all their talk. Cassie and my brothers came over. They kept me up on the family news, which was one of my mistakes—you can't cut yourself part-way off. I should have shut them all out except for Cassie, who was young enough to have different memories. Anyway, we didn't have much to do. I changed the oil in my car before it got dark. Ask helped me. Brenda and Cassie made chocolate chip cookies. Tom watched a basketball game on TV.

When they left, it was just us again. She suggested cards, but I didn't feel like playing. We talked about the movie we'd seen. What was there to say? They should have shut up part of the time and they'd have been okay. Brenda didn't agree. She thought it had to do with fate.

We ate cookies and listened to an album of jazz her mother had bought. Neither of us understood it or why people thought it was great. Brenda felt a chill and wrapped up in a blanket. I checked the thermostat. I swear it wasn't cold. Something made her afraid. She had me check to make sure the doors were locked, the windows shut. I did. The house was airtight.

Brenda moved to the kitchen. She lit the oven and opened its door. I told her she didn't look well, but that wasn't exactly it. She didn't look sick, she looked funny, like she was trying to swallow a bite of lousy pie to be polite to the cook. You know that look?

She went to bed early. I walked around the house, through all the rooms but ours, where she slept. I started out looking for something, but I forgot what it was. I thought maybe when I saw it I'd remember. But it didn't work that way. All I found was the *TV Guide* on the kitchen counter and a six-pack of Budweiser in the refrigerator. I drank beer and slept on the couch while the TV filled the room with snow.

That was the night Brenda quit loving me, or started to quit. An ordinary day. Those are the ones that kill you.

THE VAN TOOK ME to Kentucky. Hale's Cafe was gone, a Jiffy Mart now. Only the checkered floor was the same, tiles cracked and missing. The house on the hill was abandoned, Hannah in a rest home since December. The house was smaller even than I remembered, green roofing tile, flaking white clapboards, plywood rectangles blinding the windows, television antenna hanging upside down from the peak of the roof like a Christmas ornament.

The van drove up the hill. The yard was brown, a patch of green by a stick maple. I parked behind the house and circled to the front, staring down at the Jiffy Mart, remembering the neon sign, now gone, even the pole gone, the hole that had held it completely filled. I walked around the other side of the house, back to the van, and leaned against it.

First I tried the rear door—locked. I walked to the front again, stepped up to the porch where I had lain when I was seventeen with my little brothers, the neon Hale's Cafe mocking even my sleep.

The door opened with my first push.

The front room where Hannah had slept on the couch, where Tom listened to baseball and Ask put together puzzles, was empty—spiderwebs, dust, a broken-handled broom. In the bedroom where my parents and Cassie had slept—everything gone, closet door on one hinge, falling forward from the top.

The door to the locked-up room was locked or jammed shut. I left it, moving to the kitchen, dusk approaching, light from the open front door and nowhere else.

On the kitchen counter, in the last light—a glistening rifle and serious cowboy hat, arched and stiff. Terrifying stuff. Was someone hiding out here? My whole chest shook.

I left the house quickly, drove down the hill, across the highway to the Jiffy Mart. Rainbo Bread, Hostess pies, beef jerky in a jar, Kools, orange drink in a milk carton, black Bic pens, fat packages of chewing tobacco, Virginia Slims, Barbecue Lay's. What kind of world has such things?

I bought a flashlight and two batteries, and crossed the street on foot. Up the hill, across the yard, I walked, my bowels turning, heart thumping against my Adam's apple, across the porch again, into the front room again, directly to the kitchen. The rifle, the cowboy hat in the harsh glare of the flashlight revealed themselves—toys. A BB gun so old it could have belonged to Tom or Ask, and a kid's cowboy hat. I left the kitchen for the locked door.

I tried to pick the lock but couldn't. I leaned against the door, but it wouldn't budge. I wanted to see the room covered in spiderwebs and dust, bare floor, bare walls. I wondered how long Hannah had left the room as it had been when her father was alive. How long did it take before she meddled with his forbidden possessions, before he was no longer her father and just a man, a dead man, a memory?

I took the BB gun from the kitchen and pried against the old doorknob until it popped loose. I kicked open the door to the locked-up room, and there was the gold bedspread, without a wrinkle—glasses, decoy lamp, paperback novel, and comb on the nightstand. One of the photographs had fallen, the one with the stuffed rabbit, curled and cracked, faded with age. Everything else, the hair oil, pocketknife, shoe polish, was the same. Only a coat of dust had been added. Even his shoes still yawned up at the bed. Why should this preservation have terrified me? Why should my stomach have twisted into a knot again? My bowels ache in fear?

The blades in my grandfather's pocketknife were all meant for cutting, but one functioned as a screwdriver anyway. I took the door off the hinges and left the locked-up room wide open.

I SCRAPED BRICKS in Pittsburgh, parked cars in Atlanta, washed dishes in D.C., polished new Chevies in Jacksonville, and had no sex, at least, no women—my hand and me on the van carpet, thinking of Eileen or looking at the foldouts in a magazine. Without my father to do battle with, I had no direction. In the past, things had an extra dimension, but now it was all flat, colorless—unless I was driving.

And one more thing.

When Brenda left me and we had our awful obligatory party, I said, "No dancing. No music," and there was nothing to talk about because I refused to talk about what hurt or to listen to meaningless crap. I took a chair outside and sat. There was no moon or clouds.

I had wanted to kill Brenda and her ugly lover. I was no good at it. I searched for my gun. I'd asked Tom to hide it—that's how I was, part crazy, part sane. I still don't know what he did with it. So I sat outside. The rest of them came out a few at a time, Ask first, of course, then Dad, Tom. When Mother came out with Cassie, she turned off the porch light, and suddenly, in the dark, the sky was full of stars.

Dad started telling a story. He said the stars made him think of it. I know that was just an excuse to tell it. He said the stars in Africa were like these, and pointed up. The sky was thick with them. Then he started in on his two friends during the war Somebody Aronson and Bill Henry. They had bought a bottle of Kentucky bourbon off some sailor they met in Morocco or some such place and were going to drink it the next day while they drove single file across the African desert. I think it was Morocco because they also bought silk scarves.

The next day, Dad got assigned to drive a jeep separate from the others, and he was pissed off because he wanted to drink the bourbon and knew they would finish it without him. He said the army never invested in decent shock absorbers and his ass was aching and he was yearning for the bourbon. They had to stop for some reason early on, and he ran back a few vehicles to his buddies and found that they had hidden the bottle under the seat. The rough ride had broken the bottle's neck. The bourbon was still in there, but there was no drinking it. Bits of glass sparkled in the dark liquor. He said they almost cried.

A couple of hours later, bouncing along single file, breathing everybody else's dust, he saw a jeep pull out of line and up next to him. It was Aronson and Bill Henry, laughing and holding the bourbon bottle, almost empty, up high over their heads. They had put one of the silk scarves over the bottle neck and were drunk. Their lips were scarlet with blood.

Ask laughed like crazy at that story. Even Tom and Cassie laughed some. I didn't laugh. I had just lost my wife, and it was enough that I put up with them at all. I had come outside to get away from them. Then Dad looked up at the stars again and said, "Neither of them left Africa," and he told how his friends had died.

I almost cried then. I felt close to him suddenly. I could have. I could have cried and let him hold me. But I steeled myself against it and against him and against them all.

Now when I think back to that night I remember sitting in the chair, Ask beside me, Tom and Dad settling near, the door opening. Cassie stepped out with Mother just behind, and how Mother paused to turn out the porch light, and how the stars suddenly became visible, how amazing it was that a 79-cent bulb could blot out the heavens.

A NEW DARKNESS

I

THE DOCTORS SAID the strokes would keep coming, no matter what. There was nothing they could do. Edward had had high blood pressure for twenty years. He smoked heavily, drank heavily, and ate too much salt. The blood vessels in his brain were damaged. They would continue to explode.

He came back strong after the first stroke, returning to school just before the end of the year, a slight drag to his walk, but otherwise fine. In the middle of May, while walking to the bathroom during a commercial in "The Mary Tyler Moore Show," he became dizzy and stumbled into the coffee table. Ask leaped from the couch and caught him. Cassie called an ambulance.

He recovered from the second stroke even faster than the first. It had been mild. He was weak but began walking in the mornings and afternoons to build up his legs. He lifted the dictionary ten times with each arm to strengthen his upper body.

The third stroke was also mild, coming in his sleep, blurring his waking. Only the tingling in his arm and the inability to focus on an idea let him know it was a stroke. He didn't go to the hospital.

By August, he knew he wouldn't be able to teach in the coming semester. By September, everyone in the house knew he would never teach again.

Jill's anger with Charley returned and grew. She held him responsible. With each stroke, Edward became less rounded, his interests more narrow, his inhibitions altered, fears magnified. He quit driving in early August, afraid he might suffer a stroke behind the wheel and kill himself or others. By September, he was incapable of driving a car, lacking the concentration and coordination. He used a cane to get around. He had fallen once, bruising his hip badly, and was afraid of falling again.

He quit reading in September, unable to focus on the printed words or concentrate on the material. He became bored and began watching television programs, especially game shows, and asking people to take him for drives.

A stroke in late October left him in bed for three weeks. He began using a plastic urinal, shaped like a milk carton except with an oval opening like the mouth of a bass. For a week after he was walking again, he carried the urinal with him and peed in it regardless of what room he was in or who else was there, until Cassie screamed at him and melted the urinal in the fireplace.

His speech was slurred most right after a stroke, cleared until the next came, then blurred again. He became incrementally narrowed in his topics, whining for a ride, asking for specific meals or where people were, especially Charley. He had to be reminded weekly that Charley was gone. When strangers came to the house, he introduced himself by standing, both hands on his cane at his crotch, and saying, "I'm a stroke victim." His mouth pursed in sorrow and self-pity, his eyes watery.

One Saturday in August he and Tom watched the Cardinals play the Mets. Edward began crying when Cardinal catcher Ted Simmons struck out with two men in scoring position.

"It's only the third inning, Dad," Tom said.

Edward shook his head and said something Tom could not understand. Tom thought he had said, "I'm not wrong on this word," and believed his father was trying to come up with the right words to express his sadness. Edward repeated himself, more clearly.

"I'm not long for this world," he said.

Tom became angry, yelled at him for being self-pitying, and walked across the street to watch the remainder of the game with Marriet.

Jill's anger had no expression. She sat through endless game shows with him after he became afraid to be by himself, hating Wink Martindale, Dick Clark, Bill Cullen, Peter Marshall, Gene Rayburn, thinking of ways to kill them and the sappy pseudo-stars and moronic contestants.

In September she saw Charley on "The Match Game" and screamed, "You!" scaring Edward. The contestant said his name was Luke and he looked very little like Charley. She saw him next on "Hollywood Squares," then "Dialing for Dollars," "Wheel of Fortune." On "Let's Make a Deal" Charley was dressed like a turnip and giggled when Monte Hall asked which curtain he wanted. Jill said a silent prayer that he would lose, the first time she had prayed since, as a child, she had asked God to take her soul should she fail to wake. On "Family Feud," Charley had a whole new family, a new prettier mother who had all the right answers, a dark heavy father who laughed easily, and three exotic older sisters who doted on him and rumpled his hair.

At the self-service gas station, the stupid clerk gave Jill change for a twenty when she'd only given him a ten. As she shoved the ten back to him, she saw the attendant was Charley. She kept the ten, backing away from the station in fright while the attendant called, "Ma'am, are you okay, ma'am?"

She saw Charley next at the 7–Eleven, behind the counter, smoking a mentholated cigarette, his arms crossed. For the first time in her life, she shoplifted, taking cigarettes, which she threw away, and three packs of pink bubble gum.

In late October, on a day she'd seen Charley driving a bus, selling doughnuts, and sleeping drunk against a tree in the library yard, she was pulled over by a city policeman for speeding. Ask and Cassie were in the car with her. "I was not," she said to the policeman. Afraid to look at his face, she stared into her purse and fumbled for her driver's license. She couldn't find it, couldn't even find the billfold she kept it in. She grew frantic. "I wasn't doing a thing," she said, dumping the contents of the giant rat-colored bag onto the front seat and Ask's legs.

"Calm down," Ask said.

Cassie reached over the backseat and picked the billfold out of the pile of things. Jill couldn't locate her driver's license among the credit cards, library card, pictures of her children. She gave the officer the entire billfold. "Take it," she screamed. "Take it." The policeman lowered himself to the car window, not Charley, but a gruff-looking man with a thick mustache. He wrote out the ticket. Ask drove them home.

Jill stayed in bed three days, crying and self-conscious. The morning of the fourth day, she rose early, made breakfast for everyone, and returned to normal.

Ask graduated from high school early in June, third in his class. He took Julie to the prom and was voted most likely to survive a nuclear accident. Julie missed her period in July, and Ask both researched the best and safest means of abortion and inquired about a loan to buy wedding rings. He vacillated until her period returned, but could not let the question go unresolved, finally deciding it wasn't his decision. He would support Julie either way. At the end of the summer, he enrolled in the local junior college and got an afternoon job tutoring math.

There was no party after Edward's second stroke, or after his third, or fourth, or after Jill's breakdown, or when Julie missed her period.

Cassie found a summer job at an ice cream parlor and kept it when school started. She knew, with her father out of work, that they needed money. His disability retirement pay was slow in coming and not as much as they had expected. She bought no new clothes for the summer and none for school until Jill insisted.

Tom took on a day job as a secretary for an answering service, typing up billings, assigning operators, handling new accounts. He kept his night job and continued seeing Marriet, who was becoming as much a part of the family as anyone; whom, he was quite sure, he loved.

On a cool, clear night in early November, Ask and Tom, sitting in the Ancient Mariner, staring at Hidenall's Construction Rental Plant, ate a chef's salad Ask had made. A car swooped off the highway onto the cleared siding next to the plant. They recognized it as Marriet's Maverick.

"She should put fluorescent markers on her speedometer," Ask said. "With Dad being a retired Driver's Education teacher, you and Marriet are embarrassing, driving like you never even heard of the rules of the road."

Marriet pulled up next to the Ancient Mariner and lowered her window. "Someone's prowling around the house," she said. "Twice I saw someone in the backyard."

"Our house?" Ask said.

"Yes, I called the police, but they said it would be a low-priority call unless I could see someone right at that moment, or I was alone or some such nonsense."

"I can't leave yet," Tom said. He looked at his watch. "Take Ask. Get Arzate to come over if you want. It's probably nothing."

"I want *you*," Marriet said. "*There.*"

Tom stared at her and what occurred to him was this: that it seemed perfectly natural to him for two people to be talking through car windows. "Let me call my replacement," he said.

He arranged for the dog to come early and hid the keys for the trainer. He rode with Marriet. "Why are you so upset?" he said. "It's probably some kid."

"No, it was a woman." She glanced at Tom. "I was afraid you wouldn't come if I said that, but it was scarier for me to see a strange woman in the backyard than a strange man. I mean, I figured she must be desperate to be a burglar—a junkie or a mother with starving kids or I don't know. Men seem to do that kind of stuff out of boredom. I was relieved it wasn't a rapist, but then I got scared again."

"Did you tell the police it was a woman?"

"I'm sure that's why it's so low priority. They don't even take women criminals seriously. I turned on all the lights outside. I thought that was good."

Ask arrived ten minutes after Tom and Marriet.

"You crawl down the road, you know that?" Tom said.

Ask paid no attention. "Did you see anybody?"

Tom shook his head. "I checked the backyard, the front, the alley."

"Let's roam the neighborhood," Ask said.

Tom smiled. "Let me get Marriet." With the house securely locked and Jill, Cassie, and Edward in the front room, they drove through the alleys and up and down the streets around their house. They circled back and covered them again. Ask was surprised that they were looking for a woman. "It's unemployment, I think," he said.

When they drove by their house the third time, Cassie ran out the front door. "The backyard," she said.

Tom began to jump out of the car, but Ask accelerated too quickly. "Hang on," he said. "I can go fast in emergencies." Ask flew to the end of the street, came to a full stop at the stop sign, then wheeled into the alley. A dark, squat figure was opening a gate and running into a yard several houses past theirs. Ask accelerated again. At the open gate, Tom jumped out and Ask hit the gas yet again. "Around front," he yelled. Marriet reached out and closed the door.

Tom looked the yard over quickly. He had no idea whose house it was. He ran to the side of the house and scaled the fence. He reached the front sidewalk as the Mariner's headlights were approaching. Ask pointed down the street and drove past him. A figure crossed the street in a run, then stopped, shielding her eyes from the headlights. Tom ran to catch up. By the time he got there, Ask and Marriet were standing next to a disheveled dark-haired woman.

"What's going on?" Tom said.

Marriet shrugged.

"It's you, isn't it?" Ask said. "It is." He turned to Tom. "Don't you recognize her?"

The short woman put her hand on Tom's shoulder, another on Ask's. "How's my little men?" she said.

THEY TOOK JENNETTA to Sambo's. The ride over was virtually silent. Tom, Marriet, and Ask shared the front seat. Jennetta sat alone in the back. "It's a surprise to see you," Ask offered. She only smiled.

Tom thought she had aged well, although she was heavier and the few lines on her face were deep. Her eyes, though, were still lit, still blue. Her face hadn't lost its shape. She wore a white blouse and dark skirt.

People were scattered sparsely among the tables at Sambo's, solitary men in coats, both hands held over coffee cups, couples sitting opposite one another, staring at the plastic tables. Tom, Marriet, and Jennetta ordered coffee. Ask ordered strawberry pancakes. "You can't get these everywhere," he explained. He said to Jennetta, "It's a surprise . . ." then trailed off.

Tom remembered Jennetta as she had been at Hale's, hair tied back in a red handkerchief, a few strands loose across her forehead, smiling, moving from booth to booth, balancing plates, pulling up a teenaged boy to dance. However, he could not picture her with his father. She could have had any man in the county, any man at all. The idea of them in bed together was ridiculous, but it had happened, he knew. "What were you doing in our backyard?" he said.

She folded her arms across the table. "The last time I saw you two, you were little spikes." She smiled. "Eleven and nine. I bet you wouldn't guess I'd remember such a thing." She smiled at them, then let it fade. "What's happened to your father?" she asked. "He's alive, isn't he? He has to be. The Wilson paper, they keep track of everybody's death even if the person lived there just a week. Edward, Mr. Warren, your father, was an important man in Wilson. An obituary like his . . ."

"He's alive," Tom said.

"Oh thank God," she said. "I had lost track of him, and I was more or less passing through."

"We know about the letters," Ask said. "I guess we know the whole story."

Jennetta dropped her head into her hands. "He was never too good at writing. Once a week for him was a lot." She took a drink of coffee. "I'm sorry for you all knowing. That was never my intent."

The waitress, broad-shouldered and blond with dark roots, filled the nearly full coffee cups. "She's very conscientious," Jennetta said. "I liked waitressing. She's pretty good." She sipped her coffee. "Why has he stopped writing me? Did Jill ask him to? Does she know? I can't believe he wouldn't at least send a note explaining. He's never gone this long without a postcard at least. Your daddy writes the funniest postcards." She looked at them, animated again, then was embarrassed.

"I am married," she said. "You said you knew the whole story, but I don't know if that's part of the story or not. I may be saying what you all already know. I've been married five years. I have a little girl, four. She's a mess, wants to be a rock and roll singer." Jennetta laughed, then touched her cheek. "I called his school. A foolish girl answered. She'd never heard of your father, said he wasn't on their list of teachers. I even called the newspaper. They thought I was some kind of nut. I didn't come to ruin his marriage. That's all I'm trying to say. I'm not like that."

The table fell quiet. Finally Marriet said, "He's sick. He's sick and he's not going to get better."

"He could live twenty years," Ask said. "He could outlive all of us. The doctors said so."

"He's had a series of strokes," Marriet said and began explaining his condition, that he didn't read, that he didn't write.

Tom did not like hearing it, although he knew it all. Hearing it gave it a definiteness that disturbed him.

"Well," Jennetta said, her face open and placid. "Well." She lifted her coffee cup, then set it down. "I've kept up on you all. And Cassie. Charley." She finished her coffee. "It's over then, isn't it?" She clasped her hands together. "Well," she said. "Well." She touched her face, put her hands flat on the table. "You boys still drink a dozen Cokes a day? What characters you were."

Ask smiled from his pancakes. "Do you still work at Hale's?"

"They closed it up years ago. You Warrens never visited once in all these years. Not once. Not since that one summer. I'm a projectionist in Paducah. It's a long drive at night but I like the job, seeing all the movies. I guess I've seen *Jaws* a million times. I like it though, the repetition, you know, how the good guys win every time." She touched her napkin to her mouth. "I will miss his letters," she said. "He's a sweet man, your father. Another man would have married me. Would have left you children with your mother and married me. It wasn't something he could do. He's a good man. A good one. My husband, of course, is too. How could I be here if he wasn't? An understanding man. He teaches junior college in Paducah. We both drive back and forth a lot. He asked me to marry him the first day we met. I said no. I was married as a little girl. I was seventeen. No age to start a marriage. Too young to know what a marriage is."

"Mom was nineteen," Ask said. "When they married. They've been married for a long time."

"Yes," Jennetta said. "Well."

The conversation lapsed again. Ask ate his pancakes, offering everyone strawberries, finding no takers. "I could write you," Ask said. "Let you know how the family is. Let you know about Dad. I mean, we all love Dad, right?"

Jennetta nodded in a half smile, drank her coffee.

"Why him?" Tom said. "Why Dad?"

She looked surprised. "Just because," she said and gave her head a little shake.

"No," Tom said. "I'd really like to know. Why him? He's just another guy, really."

"No, he's not," Ask said.

"Yes, he is," Tom said. "He's nobody—nothing special. To you he may be special." He pointed at Ask. "To us, I mean. But her, you." He looked again to Jennetta, who stared at her coffee.

Marriet touched Tom's shoulder and shook her head, but Tom could not let it go. "Why him?" he said.

"Why is the sky blue?" Jennetta said. She touched her earlobe, a turquoise earring. "How do birds fly?"

"They have hollow bones," Ask said.

"I guess I do too," she said. "Your daddy filled them in for me. He makes a body feel solid." She rubbed her hands over her arms. "It really is over, isn't it. It's really completely over." She laughed. "Life's funny, isn't it? Isn't it? Funny."

At the bus station Jennetta bought a ticket, then disappeared into the bathroom for a long time. Long enough for Ask to become worried. "She might kill herself," he whispered to Tom. Before Marriet could be convinced to investigate, Jennetta emerged in new clothes.

"Those stalls are so tiny," she said. "Like changing clothes in a coffin." She wore green pants and a matching blouse. "I can't stand riding in a skirt. And Edward, your father." She shook her head. "He never liked me in pants. He was old-fashioned that way. You don't have to wait with me."

"We don't mind," Ask said.

"I enjoy bus stations." She slipped the strap of her bag over her shoulder. "I rarely get out. It's nice just to walk around by myself. You kids, you . . ." She stared at Tom, then Ask, turned to Marriet. "They don't understand a thing," she said to Marriet.

"They're practically my own children, and they don't understand a thing. Take them home, will you?"

"Understand what?" Ask said. "I don't get it. Understand what?"

"Let's go," Tom said.

"No," Ask said. "I want to know."

"You explain to them," Jennetta said to Marriet. "Tell these boys."

Ask turned to Marriet. "Well?" he said.

"She's lonely," Marriet said.

"What my life's come to," Jennetta said, "is the man I love cannot read my letters and my own boys hardly know me." She turned and began walking away.

"We're not your sons," Tom said. She kept walking. "We're not your sons," he yelled. "We're not your boys."

She stopped and turned, her finger pointed at Tom like a weapon. "You don't know thing one. You don't . . ." She dropped her bag, opened it, and began looking through it. "You wait," she said, pulling at folded clothing. "Look here," she said and lifted from the bag a blouse, light blue with short sleeves and plain white buttons. "I was married in this," she said. "Five years ago. Now. Do you see now? Can you understand that? This is a part of my wedding outfit. Can you imagine? Can you imagine it?" She waved the blouse at them as they backed away from her. "This is the way I live," she said, and the blouse made a flapping sound like the sound of sheets catching the wind on a summer clothesline.

2

EDWARD HAD MOMENTS of clarity that came unexpectedly and permitted him to understand how much he had lost. He lay awake one night in bed with Jill, and the room suddenly became a complete room, the house a complete house. The blanket that covered their bed was green and blue, dark with shadows from the night-light. The blanket flooded him with joy, then sadness, and he sat up to see on the dresser the recent photographs of his children, the mound of clothing next to the picture frames.

He touched Jill's shoulder, a soft touch, a caress. He had not touched her that way in months, a touch full of mortality and weakness, a touch so full of who he had once been and no longer was that Jill wakened, startled, sure a stranger was in their room.

Edward, who could feel the moment passing, tried to tell her how he still loved her, how he'd had a moment where he knew irony and humor. He wanted to say, "I'm here now, and I know you are a miracle." But his tongue, made treacherous by the strokes, did not obey him.

"I'm hearing voices now," he said.

What could he do to tell her what he knew and would soon forget? To know and not be able to tell was worse than not knowing. He felt himself shrink away from his body. He stared out through his eyes as if through the eyes of another.

The clarity lasted long enough for him to see disappointment register on her face. Then the house shrank to the size of the room, and the room to the narrow blur of his vision. The blanket was just a blanket and he did not even think of blankets unless he was cold. The photographs of his children were faces again, familiar but blank, who stared at him while he went through the ordeal of dressing and mouthed questions he could not answer.

HE LIKED to be driven in a car, to see that the world outside the house was much as he'd left it, to be reminded of the precise color of the roof of the Ramada Inn, the specific snarl of one driver's complaint, the exact shape of a traffic light—things that he at once remembered, that created a peculiar warmth in his chest, a tenderness.

Desires came and went, some so quickly they left no residue, but most lingered. He wanted chocolate. He wanted beer. He wanted to smoke a cigarette. He wanted beautiful movement—a step in a dance, a boy throwing his head back to laugh, a silver car changing lanes on a freeway through a seam in traffic. He wanted to accumulate all the things that he had held dear so that they would become his again. He wanted Charley. He wanted ice cream to thrill him the way it once had. He wanted to go to work in the mornings, to read a book, to solve a crossword puzzle, to hear the harmony in a song, to tell a story. He wanted to make love with his wife. He wanted a lousy bit of conversation.

He had glimpses of the future, moments when he could make no sense of the physical world. Colors flashed around him. People came and spoke in strange tones, sometimes saying words he recognized but more often garbling language and snorting sounds into a rumble. And the world on the inside was not much better. Music and voices from his past entered randomly, the neurons in his brain crackling like firewood. These moments of terror passed, returning him to an easy chair in front of a television. A man smiled out from the set and asked him a simple question. Edward answered aloud and invisible people clapped.

He had glimpses of the past as well; a picture would suddenly form of his mother or his wife, a beach in Italy where he swam during the war. The one he liked best started on a train that was slowing, the green countryside beyond the window becoming less blurred. The train stopped with a lurch. He pulled a duffel bag from the rack overhead. Only a few people were leaving the train, but the woman ahead of him was very heavy and rocked as she walked, touching the back of each seat as if the train were still moving. He followed her, impatient, squeezing the bag against his chest.

And when he was outside, looking for his parents, imagining the sweet face of his mother, he would see a girl, a dark-haired girl, staring back at him, and his heart would bounce so that he would be propelled ahead thirty years to a dark bedroom and sounds of a woman sleeping, or to a room with an enormous fireplace and blaring television, or to the fractured vision and random clatter of his mind.

3

WHEN YOUR LIFE is at a crossroads, there will be an old woman who wants salt, a headache that will not quit, a mosquito whining about your skull. When you believe you understand a human, he will betray you at a party, curse your work, or forgive you more completely than you could have imagined. And when you think that the worst is over, the telephone ringing in the middle of the night, the neighbor walking slump-shouldered to your door, the steely smell of the earth will wake you to a new darkness.

Tom and Marriet lay against the windshield of the Ancient Mariner, their legs stretching down the hood. Ask sat with his legs over a tire well. His heels bounced against the whitewalls in a steady rhythm. The night was cool and breezy. Behind them, Hi-denall rental equipment rested darkly, making prehistoric shapes against the black sky. Ask was trying to explain something he had seen that day.

"There was this big prickly pear cactus against the side of the house, an old adobe house. The top ears on the cactus were almost as high as the roof," he said.

"Ping-pong paddles," Marriet said. Her hands were behind her head on the windshield. "Prickly pear limbs remind me of paddles. It's my favorite kind of cactus."

"They're called ears," Ask said.

"They look more like paddles though, don't they?" She turned to Tom.

He thought for a moment. "They look like shovel blades."

"Oh, they do not," Ask said, "for chrissakes. That's not what I was getting at anyway. I was walking by and this huge prickly pear was there and behind it was a fence about six feet high. An arm was sticking over the fence with a hose spraying water against the house and the cactus."

"Watering the cactus," Tom said.

"I know that. But it was strange, that arm just coming over the fence like that, the water spraying against the wall. I can't explain it. I stopped and stared at it for a long while. There was something to it, but I couldn't figure it out."

"I went with this guy once," Marriet said, "and he kept warning me about his father. He said his father was very conservative. Then the first time I went over to his house—it was a Saturday afternoon—his father was out in the yard working on the lawn. There was a hedge around the yard made of prickly pear, and his father was out trimming the cactus like you would a normal hedge—you know, flat."

"He was cutting the ears flat?" Tom said.

Marriet nodded. "The boy told me that, to his father, a hedge was a hedge."

"That makes me think of people who get Doberman puppies and cut their ears and tails so the dogs will look like what they think a Doberman should look like," Tom said.

"What I saw wasn't anything like that," Ask said. "I mean there was something in that hose and that hand, the cactus, the water. It was like a vision. Only I don't know what it means."

"Beats me," Tom said.

"Where did you see it?" Marriet said.

"It was just at this house." Ask kicked the tire hard with his heel.

Tom slid off the hood. "I've got to go around the fence. Anyone want to join the patrol?" he said, dusting off the rear of his pants.

"We'll wait here," Marriet said and waved to Tom as he walked off. She turned to Ask. "Where was this thing, this vision?"

"In town," he said. "I didn't want to tell Tom. We met this woman once who was breaking glasses and I went back to find out why. That was when I saw the cactus."

"Why was she breaking glasses?"

"It's a long story," he said, but he began the telling in his roundabout way. As he was finishing, they heard a noise—a scraping and a metallic creak.

"Think that's Tom?" he said.

Marriet shrugged and slipped off the side of the car. Ask followed her to the fence. A step before they reached it, the Hidenall light towers went dark. Ask stuck his fingers through the links of fence. "Call the police," he whispered and pointed to the little room by the gate, just visible.

She ran. Ask took several steps after her, stopping at the gate. He gripped the fence again, and tried to see through the dark. An engine started somewhere within the lot.

"The phone's dead," Marriet called. "Someone must have cut the line."

Ask looked past her to Tom, rounding the corner of the fenced yard, running hard, his flashlight bouncing white against his legs. The sound of the engine grew louder. Inside the lot—movement, something big and becoming bigger, as if it were sprouting from the asphalt. A truck, Ask saw, charging toward the gate. He jumped. The fence crashed open and slapped him against the ground. The heavy chain that had held the gate shut whipped him as he fell. The truck barreled past. As it entered the empty highway, its lights flashed—fields of gold and silver—then the truck rolled on in darkness.

"Are you all right?" Tom was beside him.

"Of course I am," Ask said. "Did you get the license plate?"

"It's a Hidenall truck," Tom said.

"Oh yeah," Ask said. He started to sit up, then fell back. "I'm dizzy," he said.

Marriet, next to Tom, put her hand on Ask's shoulder. "Stay down," she said. To Tom she whispered, "We shouldn't move him."

He nodded. "Go call an ambulance."

"I'll stay here with him," she said. "You go."

"No. I'm not leaving him. You go. There's an all-night gas station four or five miles down." He pointed. She ran to the car.

Ask lifted his head again, fell back. Tom caught him and put his head in his lap. "She drives like a maniac," Ask said as dust from Marriet's backing up floated over them. "You think I'm hurt bad?" He bit his lip to keep from smiling.

The car lights flashed across them as the Mariner pulled onto the highway. Blood shimmered across Ask's face. His shirt was black from blood. "No," Tom said. "You're not hurt."

"Oh, I am too. You never want me to do anything."

"Don't move around so much. Are you in pain?"

"Not really. I'm just dizzy. The truck threw mud all over me."

Tom nodded. "The ambulance will be here in no time."

"You could have just let me get in the car. You know how much an ambulance costs?"

"First you say I won't let you be hurt, now you want me to act like it's nothing. I'm not moving you until the ambulance gets here."

"That is what they said with Dad," Ask said. "You think I'm really hurt? What if I have a limp or something?"

"Then you'll limp."

"Julie would still like me even if I limped. You know what I'd like?"

"What?"

"Would you do my hair? You know, like Mom used to?"

"I could do that," Tom said. "Sure." He put his fingers in Ask's hair. "You've got some tangles," he said.

"Julie says I should use conditioner. She says I have split ends. That feels good. Why do you think that feels good?"

"You remember that night on Aunt Hannah's porch? When I started crying?"

"What?" Ask said.

"Ask?"

"Do my hair," he said. "Don't stop."

Tom ran his hands through his hair again and again.

"Of course I remember that night," Ask said. "I did your hair."

"Yeah," Tom said, and a gust of wind passed over them. He ran his fingers through Ask's hair for the ten minutes it took for the ambulance to arrive. It was this that the surgeon would notice, the perfectly combed hair, and wonder at human nature, the desire to tend to the commonest of details even when the boy's clothing was torn and blood streaked his arms and freckled his face. He would muse over all of this as he covered the blood-freckled face and perfect hair with a white hospital sheet.

ASK'S STORY

WE HAVE LIVED in five houses as a family, not counting hotels where we stayed from move to move: (1) the farmhouse in Kentucky, just outside of Wilson, where we lived while Dad was the principal of Wilson Elementary School, and where Mom returned from the hospital with Cassie, who, when three, forced our move to Arizona and our purchase of (2) the only new kind of house we ever owned (there were three other houses on the street that looked just like it), which we left after two years to live for a summer in (3) Aunt Hannah's little house on a hill back in Wilson, but Cassie got sick again and we moved to Yuma (back in Arizona) and (4) the big wooden house where we lived until it burned down and we moved to (5) the current bulky house, which is still in Yuma but on the other side of town.

(1) The farmhouse was two stories with an L-shaped corner porch and Corinthian pillars. There were doors at either end of the L-shaped porch, one leading to the living room and the other to the kitchen. The door to the living room was hard to open, especially when it rained, and when people came to that door, we

always waved them around to the kitchen. Mom said kitchens were friendlier than living rooms anyway. But when the Methodist minister came to see why we never went to church although Aunt Hannah put our names on half the donations she gave and I waved him around to go to the kitchen door, Mom said that was a mistake, that some people might misunderstand and think we wouldn't let their kind in our front door, and, I gathered, ministers and religious people of all sorts were the most likely type to take offense.

Charley had his own room and a door that led to the back porch. He had pictures of cars on his walls that he had torn out of magazines, some of which had come from the high school library and led to lectures from Mom about not tearing up public things, like magazines from the library, rest rooms at the park (a toilet at the park had been cherry-bombed, but we had nothing to do with it), and walls of the county building, which Tom and I had defaced with tick-tack-toes.

Tom and I shared a big room that held our twin beds, a couch, a piano (we all took lessons but none of us played), a long flat play table, and two dressers.

Cassie lived in a crib in Mom and Dad's room, which was in a corner next to the living room. She had a bunch of dooley-dads hanging up just out of her reach as an incentive to stand up, which she did in just a few months, and if we'd lived there much longer (Mom says), Charley would have had to move upstairs and his room would have become Cassie's because she was too old to be sharing a room with parents and because she was driving them nuts in there, talking in her sleep, walking around in their shoes, and spreading her clothes around the room in an even layer, like dust.

Nobody lived upstairs except all the broken or boring toys we had accumulated. The bottom portion of the stairs had been cut off by the previous owners and a wooden ladder had been nailed in place. You opened a door in the hall, climbed the ladder about four feet, then climbed the steps to the second story, which had four big rooms and a landing for the stairs (a little hall). Two of the rooms were complete; one overlooked the front yard, the oaks and mulberries, the other looked over the fields we leased out to real farmers and was where we kept our train set, race car set, construction set, army men, board games, stick ponies, and Cassie's less desirable dolls. The other two rooms were unfinished, the floors latticed with two-by-fours and fluffy insulation.

(2) The second house was too small for us and we all overlapped too much on each other, which is usually good but can be done to excess. Cassie slept in a closet, or what had been a closet at one time, that Dad had extended by a couple of feet. Mom made covers for a thick foam pad that became her bed. Cassie hung her dolls on hooks like they were prisoners and no one complained if it was messy. She liked it.

Charley's room was supposed to be a study, and the only way Tom and I could get to our room from the kitchen was to walk through his room, which, while he was in his model phase, was covered with primer-gray fighter jets and lipstick-red jalopies. The second year there he junked the models, listened to the radio until midnight, and wore turtlenecks.

Tom's bed was a foot away from mine, and I had to walk sideways through the crack between them to crawl into bed. He did his wall up with pictures of the St. Louis Cardinals (four Bob Gibsons and no Tim McCarvers because he didn't like catchers, which made the whole wall lose its symmetry, something Tom had little sense of), and I had my birthday pictures (we didn't have parties on birthdays but we did eat cake and the birthday person in question did get to choose what to eat for supper and there were gifts and, on my birthday, everyone stood in a half-circle around me and the camera ticked off the seconds on its timer and we giggled until it flashed, then when the picture was developed, Mom had it enlarged and I framed it in a 99-cent frame from the dime store, and hung it on my wall), and my daily checklists, which Tom was always joking around with and erasing "Floss Teeth" and putting in "Jack Off" *in ink*, which made me mad, and my various school awards (Blue Ribbon Speller, Math Master Certificate, Geographile, and so on).

Mom and Dad's room was normal in every respect, a corner room again, with Mom's picture of her brother, their same bed and dresser. Dad bought golf clubs and put them in one corner where they stayed for so long that the tile underneath them changed color.

The kitchen was smaller and didn't have as much light as the farmhouse, but all the appliances were new and there was a garbage disposal, which was a sign of progress. As was the carport where we parked the Ancient Mariner, which we just called the station wagon then because it was new, and on the front of the carport was a backboard and rim where Tom shot baskets and I shot backboards and Cassie shot air.

(3) Aunt Hannah believed that if people followed a certain routine every day they might not ever make anything of themselves but at least they wouldn't be slothful and undirected like some people we know, only she would never tell me who, and I asked practically everybody else in town and they didn't know either unless it was the Republicans or the damn northerners or outside agitators or the beatnik-hippie types (of which there were none in Wilson or, likely, in all of Ballard County).

Her little house was so neat that Tom claimed you could cut yourself on the furniture, which he often said he did, but really he had this one scrape on his elbow from roller skating in the gravel and he would pick the scab and say it was a new cut from the couch or end table or kitchen chair, each so clean as to pierce human flesh. I was never fooled.

Her kitchen was bright and the counter around the sink was green and the window over the sink was lined with dooley-dads that reminded me of Cassie's old crib. A big picture of Christ, his arms open and a halo giving him backlighting, was in the dining room (which was really just the other end of the kitchen) overlooking the table. The living room had a little couch where she slept while we lived there, an end table with a radio where Tom and Dad listened to the Cardinal game while I lay on the floor playing with Cassie or doing a puzzle with Mom and pretended to listen so I could be a part of their baseball talk. There was an old black and white TV that didn't work very well and made ghosts out of everybody, and pictures of her mom and dad and of her brother.

Then there was Aunt Hannah's bedroom, which became Mom and Dad and Cassie's room, but which looked more like an aunt's room because every surface was covered with frilly doilies and there were a bunch of lotions and liquids on the doilies that looked, smelled, and tasted (Tom and I conducted experiments) like Aunt Hannah.

All three of us boys slept on the porch, which was the only time Tom and I shared a room with Charley and it wasn't really a room since there was only one wall and the porch railing, but it was a great place to sleep. If Aunt Hannah didn't go to bed at the same time every night (to the minute), she developed a rash on her wrists and got cranky, and since she slept on the couch, we all hit the sack early, but being outside, we could stay up and talk, or play games, or slip off the porch and explore, which usually meant going to the edge of the hill and watching Hale's Cafe until the end of the summer when that quit being fun and we were ready to move somewhere else. Before the summer's end, though, we watched Hale's the way Mom and Aunt Hannah watched "As the World Turns," only we would have to make up most of the dialogue because we couldn't hear anything, unless there were boys drinking outside and then only scraps.

One night we were watching and a car on the highway had a flat right at the bottom of the hill, and a man and a woman got out and she was dressed up in dark clothes with a rose in her hair and another at her waist and a third right over one of her breasts, and she yelled at the man who was sitting on the ground staring at the flat tire. "Fix the damn thing, Maurice. Don't study it. What do I need with a man who studies flat tires? A dime a dozen are men of that rank. I need a man who can take action on flat tires and other such small and annoysome catastrophes of daily living. My sensibilities is too fine to be bothered and dallied with and . . ." She stopped in mid-blather when she spotted Hale's across the street and began staggering over there "to have a drink to calm my nerves," not knowing that the whole county was dry, and this man, Maurice, hadn't said a thing, just staring at the flat tire the whole time, and Tom and I were laughing and when she and her monologue were gone, he heard us.

He stood up, looking all around, and we tried to be quiet, but couldn't, and he said, "God almighty," and left, running back in the direction the car had come from, falling down twice. We wanted to see what would happen when the woman returned but I fell asleep three times and Tom finally had to sling my arm over his shoulder to get me back to the porch.

Then there was the locked-up room. Tom and I pressed our faces against its lone window to see in, but the curtains were complete and gauzy and all we could see were a few dark things in the white, like a mostly benign cloudbank with one or two small thunderheads. That didn't stop us from imagining, and when we got tired of counting cars or chasing lightning bugs, we talked about what could be in the room. Treasure was our first guess, doubloons and diamonds, gold masks, silver codpieces (Tom had found this word underlined in a book and looked it up), pirate chests or other treasure we couldn't imagine, things that would be important to Aunt Hannah and no one else.

Or maps, which led to treasures, could be in there, hidden in the woodwork, patterned into the wallpaper, or Tom suggested that the room itself was a map and that by memorizing the room you would have all the clues you needed to locate the loot.

On the other side of the doubloon, we also made up some pretty ghastly stories. One was that Aunt Hannah had never buried grandfather at all and he was still in his bed, head on his pillow, rotting away like old fruit—that was one of the good ones. What if he wasn't dead at all but hiding out from the mob who he had fingered as a young man, then got a new identity, lived happily for a long time, before he let slip a story after a bottle of corn liquor, and had to go on the lam?—this one was a little far-fetched. Or that his ghost was in there and not going to leave until Aunt Hannah got married or at least became friendly with a man (or woman, Tom tried to insist because he had just heard about homosexuality and I didn't know much about it and he liked to flaunt his knowledge, but I wouldn't hear of it and looked up the term he used, which was "less-men" and wasn't in the dictionary, and I said I'd quit if we included ideas we couldn't document and he gave in the way he always did—Tom and perseverance have never gone hand in hand). Or that he was a ghost but the reason he was back was that his son wasn't among the dead and he wasn't going to rest in peace before he found out what had happened to his son. That was my favorite one.

Tom also said that the room might have special properties, so that if we could get in there, we might be able to fly or look into the future or see the past as you see a movie. He said there might be a tunnel from the days of abolitionists that led to the river, or the woods, or to a trapdoor inside Hale's Cafe. He said that we might go in the room together and change bodies—me becoming him, him becoming me. I rejected these ideas, not because they weren't good ones, but because they didn't have anything to do with our grandfather.

We never saw what was inside the locked-up room but it became the biggest and most interesting one in the house.

(4) This was the house I thought of as home, not that the others weren't at the time, but this one was where I grew up a lot. We painted the whole thing just before it burned. Every room except for Charley's, which he left gray. All the others became off-white, except for Cassie's, which became part yellow, and Tom's, which turned brown as mud. I warned them about alternate colors. They didn't listen.

Cassie had her own room finally. We converted a den for her. What impressed me was that she managed to fill any room she had with clothes. If we had given her a gymnasium, it would have taken no more than a month for her to cover the bleachers with clothes, two months to reach half-court, and by three months she would have completed her personal style of carpeting from wall to wall.

Mom and Dad's room had two closets and room for their big bed and extra dresser, but otherwise it looked the same—the photo of Mom's brother, etc. It was a good room to make a phone call from, the only place you could talk without everyone else hearing—where I called Julie for our second date. Dad took me in that room to tell me about bees pollinating daisies. Mom took me in there to tell me about sex.

Charley's room was messy in a different way. He tore things up. Some night you might think everything's fine, and Charley would get up from the kitchen table or from watching television and walk into his room and tear apart a magazine or a shirt or he might smash a glass against his wall. At the time I didn't understand. Then one day I was with Tom and Arzate at the house of strangers, people we thought were friends of Charley's (it was one of the times Charley was missing), and the woman, Carol, started smashing glasses against the floor. I couldn't get any explanation for it from Tom or Arzate, and I couldn't make any sense of it myself, so I finally went back to the house.

Carol answered the door in a robe, the thin kind that always looks dirty. "Randy got a job," she said to me. "He's gone to work." She crossed her arms. Her hair was tied into a short ponytail. The skin of her forehead was pulled back tightly.

"I hope I didn't wake you up," I said.

She shook her head. "I've been up, but the kid's asleep," she said quietly. "I let him sleep when I can."

I nodded. "I just came by to ask you a question."

"Me?" She touched her face, her hair. She stepped away from the door, pulling the rubber band from her hair, shaking her head. "I don't know that much," she said, sitting on the couch. "I've lost touch with . . . things."

I crossed my arms. It made me uncomfortable to talk to someone who was sitting, but the only place for me to sit was next to her on the couch. There wasn't any other furniture. Even the bookcase filled with toys was gone. The other end of the couch was cluttered with folded T-shirts.

"You remember when I was here before?" I said.

"You were looking for your brother," she said. "You wouldn't drink any water."

"Yeah. He came home finally," I said. I didn't say anything about him burning down the house. I was surprised she remembered me at all.

She stood up and walked to the closet door, which was slightly ajar. She shut it. "That's good," she said. "Families are hard to keep up with. Mine is here in town, but I never see them. My mother drinks. It's no secret. I can tell you. My father lives with a bank teller. Everyone knows. Randy's brother . . ." She inhaled through her teeth, looked down the hall. She stepped into the kitchen, motioned for me to follow. "He's queer," she whispered. "That's a secret. He has a job but he does it with his roommate. They call themselves lovers, the way men and women do. But it's a secret. He would lose his job." She took a package of Camels from the kitchen table and stuck one in her mouth. "Randy beat him up. He hates queers. Do you have a light?"

I shook my head. "I don't smoke," I said.

"Oh," she said and threw the cigarette against the table. It bounced and rolled off the edge to the floor. There were three cereal boxes on the table. She picked up a king-size Frosted Flakes and shook the box. "You hungry?" she said. "You eat, don't you?"

I smiled because I thought it must have been a joke. "I've already eaten," I said.

She put the Frosted Flakes down and lifted a tall box of Cheerios to my face. I shook my head. With her other hand she lifted the red box of Cap'n Crunch. I shook my head again. She dumped a mound of Cheerios onto the table. "There," she said.

"I could drink some water," I said.

"Good," she said and walked to the sink, which had a stack

of dirty dishes and a greasy pan in it. She took a glass with the Jack-in-the-Box clown on it from the cupboard.

"What I wanted to ask you," I said, but I didn't go on because after she filled the glass with water, she stuck her finger in it. She had her back to me. She probably thought I couldn't see.

"Here," she said, turning. I took the water and she stuck the finger in her mouth.

I put the water to my lips but didn't drink. "Good water," I said. "I came to ask you why you broke those glasses when I was here last time. And. I guess. Why you poured the cereal on the table. And." I handed the water back to her. "Why you stuck your finger in my water."

She took the water from me, stared, and cocked her head the way a dog does. She turned and poured the water into the sink, put the glass back in the cupboard. "I want to show you something," she said and unbuttoned one button of her robe. She stuck a finger into the space and moved her hand in a circle. "Here," she said. She held her finger in one spot, then opened the robe around it.

Her stomach was pasty white. She lifted her finger. An oblong scar, brown and rough. "What is it?" I said.

"Cigarette burn," she said. "I burned myself with a cigarette."

"On purpose?" I said. I was getting a little scared.

"You want to see something else?" she said.

"No," I said. "I don't think so."

"I broke those glasses because I wanted you to go. Not many people stop by, and once I know you're not the one I want you to leave."

"The one what?"

"The one who's going to come save me," she said. "You're not the one, are you?"

I just stared at her.

"You're not the one, are you?"

"No," I said. "I just got out of high school."

"I went to high school," she said, turning and picking up a

plate from the sink. A blur of ketchup marked the plate and ran onto her hand. "I was nominated for homecoming queen but I didn't get it." She raised the plate over her head. "This is going to wake the kid," she said.

"Why don't I just go?" I said.

"We could do that," she said but didn't lower the plate.

I left.

I was walking back to the library, where I left the car, thinking about her and about Charley tearing up things in his room, and I decided that Charley had wanted us to leave too, that he wasn't able to leave himself, and wouldn't it be easier if we just left? Then I saw the house, the prickly pear cactus, the hand coming over the fence watering the plant, splashing the white wall. And that image seemed like an even better answer to the question, but I couldn't figure out why. What would that have to do with Charley? He didn't even like cactus.

But I did decide something, that Charley, my brother, was crazy. There was no way around it. I thought about it as much as I could stand. I even added two new rules to my list. Here. I'll read it to you.

1. Never make a complicated thing simple or a simple thing complicated.
2. Wear white at night.
3. Take care of Tom.
4. Eat from the three food groups.
5. Be consistent.
6. Never do anything with the sole intent of hurting someone.
7. Floss.
8. Always put the family first.
9. Clean even where it doesn't show.
10. Pursue the truth.
11. Wear socks that match your shirt.
12. Take care of Cassie.

13. Look up words you don't know.
14. Never put out electrical flames with water.
15. Get to the bottom of things.
16. If a person changes his or her hair, tell him or her it looks good.
17. Remember.
18. Forgive.

The other main thing about the house that burned was that Tom and I had separate rooms. We never had before. I think that was good. Otherwise we might have just grown inside each other.

(5) There's not much history to this house yet and even less furniture. Charley doesn't live here is the big difference. The house is solid and strong. The walls are thick. Except for the one in the front room, the windows are all small and safe. It's a good house to live in, and it will survive.

CROOKED HEARTS

AFTER THE FUNERAL, home again, her shoes off, drinking coffee in the living room, Jill watched low-riders. They passed by her window so slowly they hardly seemed to move at all—old cars, big and set close to the ground, their drivers slouched low, hats and dark hair. She propped her stockinged feet against the coffee table and counted the cars in the slow procession. They were painted in dark metallic colors or pasty greens and pinks. An Impala sedan, as old as their station wagon, entered her view, a somber blue like the dress she wore, driven by a skinny boy in a white T-shirt, who sat nearly erect, smoking a cigarette, turning a knob on the dash. He drove very slowly, very safely. The Impala's chrome bumper sparkled.

The casket had been open at Jill's request. Cassie hadn't seen the body, and Jill wanted her to be able to say good-bye to her brother. She hadn't realized how hard it would be again to see Ask dead, how her lungs would shatter like glass, and each breath would slice her insides open. Cassie ran out to the lawn of the funeral home, collapsing in the grass. Edward whimpered. Marriet wept into her hands. Julie had held on to Jill's arm, giving her someone to console, which had helped. And Tom had stared at Ask as if at an artifact from a ruined civilization. She had wanted to slap him, make him cry, make him lose his cool. No one should be in such control of himself.

The undertaker had used cosmetics to give Ask's face color (his hands were white as soap) and had forced his mouth into the shape of a smile, a smile that troubled Jill deeply. She'd seen it before—at Lynn's Odds and Ends, the obscene porcelain figures, black men, black women, humiliating stances, and all of them smiling. For a moment, her son, her dead son, became another obscene figure, a grotesque imitation of a living person. That, she thought, more than anything else, defined death: humiliation. She had closed the casket herself.

A hummingbird hovered outside the window, seeming to stare in, then flew away. Jill held her cup of coffee and waited to see if another low-rider would come by. The parade had seemed like a gift to her from someone who knew she was suffering. She hadn't called the others to see. It was her parade, her secret pleasure in a day of grief. It disturbed her that she could enjoy the cars, but their variety and gaudiness had pleased her very much. She drank from her cup. The coffee was hot and delicious, and again she felt guilty but drank.

Tom, Cassie, and Marriet had cleared the table of the casserole Frieda had sent, the various dishes friends had brought by over the past few days, and set up the Monopoly board. Tony Arzate, who had not come to the funeral, arrived at the house crying and joined them in a joyless game of Monopoly. They were only a few feet from her. She could hear them in the next room shaking the dice, moving their little symbols.

Edward was watching "Let's Make a Deal" and drinking iced tea. Twice he had walked carefully with his cane down the hall, looking into each of the bedrooms, then, returning to the television, he stared at her as he passed, the first time curiously, the second sadly. She couldn't determine how far he had slipped, how much he could remember, how deeply he could feel.

She finished her coffee and reached for the silver thermos beside the chair. She had made the coffee strong and filled the tall thermos, wanting to sit in one place but be wakeful. As she poured coffee into her cup, she thought what a comfort it would be to believe in God, to think that her son was in a happier place, at peace. She could not. She could only think what she believed to be true, that he was gone. To fall on some old beliefs would have blasphemed not God but the memory of Ask.

Another old American car approached very slowly. She leaned forward, set her cup on the table, hoping the parade was passing by again. It was green, less shiny, very old, with rounded edges, the kind of car she used to love when such things mattered to her. It moved very slowly, but there were no others behind it. The parade was over. This was just an old car.

It moved so slowly, she didn't notice at first that it had stopped in front of their house. She didn't want any more casseroles or cakes. Tom would have to answer the door. She was not going to move until she needed to refill the thermos. Even her bladder would have to endure her stillness. She looked forward to that small pain, a pain she knew how to find relief from, a pain she could enjoy for its shallowness.

The car door opened. A man stepped out. Sunlight shimmered off the door and turned his face into a white flash. He wore a green shirt and pants, like a uniform. Jill gripped the chair and eased out to the edge of it, losing her breath, catching it. It was happening just as it had in her dream, a dream she had almost forgotten—the car, the uniform. She jumped from the chair, ran to the door.

It was him. It was her brother. It was Tom.

She pulled the door open, ran into the yard. "Tom," she called, and ran in her stockings, her arms open.

As she ran, she saw him clearly, saw her mistake, but it was too late, her arms and heart had opened to accept home the lost.

She threw her arms around Charley, weeping and laughing and welcoming him home.

CASSIE, in the front doorway with Tom and Arzate, staring at the brother she thought she'd never see again, couldn't believe her mother's reaction—her mother who had been the angriest with Charley. Now she had run to him as if nothing were wrong, as if nothing had happened. It made no sense.

Marriet pushed past them and walked to Jill, who still held Charley. Marriet kissed her on the cheek, as if she were the daughter. It made Cassie angry, but she didn't move. She didn't know what she should do or how she felt. Arzate put his arm on her shoulder and said, "Your brother." He said it so sadly, she didn't know whether he meant the one before them or the one they had lowered this morning into the ground. Then her father was with them too, grinding his teeth, his head bobbing slightly.

"Who is it?" he said, staring out into the yard.

"It's Charley," she said. "Don't you have eyes? Don't you know anything?"

Her father gritted his teeth harder, snarling or smiling, she couldn't tell. "Charley's dead," he said.

Cassie shook her head. "Ask is dead," she said. "Charley has come home." She tensed her stomach, hardened herself against him.

"I know that," her father said.

Tom backed away from them and walked to the kitchen. There were circles of sweat beneath the arms of his white dress shirt. He should do something, Cassie thought. She shouldn't have to do anything.

"I know Ask is dead," Edward called out to Tom. He turned to Cassie. "Charley's been gone. It's been a long time, hasn't it?" He put his cane on the concrete. "Help me with this step," he said, and she held his arm. "Charley," he called out, "did you bring me anything? You've been gone a long time." He took several steps and stood in the grass, both hands on his cane. "I'm a stroke victim," he said.

Charley stared at Edward then past him to Cassie. "Yeah," he said. "I brought something for everyone." He turned and opened the rear door of the car. From the backseat he pulled out a large bowl covered with plastic wrap.

"A salad," he said.

Cassie ran to him.

TOM MIXED THE DRINKS. Marriet and Jill put away the Monopoly board and arranged casseroles and cakes on the table. Cassie selected the Doors for the stereo, then got out the silverware. Edward returned to the television. Charley put the salad beside the casseroles and made a telephone call.

"Who are you calling?" Cassie said.

"I want my daughter here," he said. Eileen was waiting for the call. "You coming?" he said.

"Am I going to be welcome?"

"If you're not, you'll never know," he said. "We're not the kind of family to talk about the unpleasant."

"Lucky for you," she said.

Charley stepped into the television room and sat beside the fireplace to watch "Jeopardy" with his father. "When did you start watching this crap?" he said. His father's condition had startled him. He hadn't expected him to be so distant, so changed.

"You win one of these and you're on easy street," Edward said. He smiled. "Most of the people they have are stupid." He looked to Charley and his expression changed. "I know Ask is dead," he said and was suddenly crying. "He was making me something, wasn't he?"

"What? What do you mean?"

"Sugar," Edward said, staring at the television.

On television, the camera focused on the patient host, then the contestant, who was concentrating, wrinkling his brow. Music ticked like a clock. The contestant, a middle-aged black man, said, "I think the number one export crop is . . . it would have to be sugar. What is sugar?"

"Is *right*," the emcee said.

Edward was no longer crying. He smiled again, although his eyes were red. "See, I can still do it."

"What were you saying about Ask?"

Edward looked blank and still for a moment. For an instant, Charley sensed that his father was going to say something important. The slackness in his jaw, the dulled glaze in his eyes left. But before he could speak, there was another answer from the emcee.

"What are the lungs?" Edward said to Charley, responding to the emcee. "The lungs are the first to go," he said, "then the heart, the liver."

"What the fuck are you talking about? You said there was something about Ask."

"Ask is dead," Edward said.

The contestant scratched his nose. "The arteries? What are the arteries?"

"No," Edward said. "He's stupid."

"What did you mean," Charley said, "about Ask making you something?"

The emcee shook his head sadly. "No," he said. "The correct question is: What is the heart? In almost seventy percent of the cases, according to the American Medical Association, the heart is first."

"Oh, the heart," Edward said. "I never could get that straight." He smiled as if he'd said something funny and adjusted himself in his seat.

"What are you getting at?" Charley said. "What's the point?"

"Stop it," Cassie said. She held a fork, a spoon, a knife in her hand.

Charley stood, pointed at Edward. "He was telling me something about Ask. But he won't get to the point."

"Let him alone, Charley," Cassie said.

"Charley?" Edward said and turned to him. "You were making me something, weren't you? Before you left?"

Edward's eyes, watery and blue, out of round, focused on Charley, and Charley felt a new and powerful anger shake him, the anger of having been abandoned. His chest shook with rage. "You," he said, but his throat had gone dry and his tongue had knotted. He made a dry rattling sound like the opening of an old book. He took a quick breath.

"What is Oklahoma?" Edward said to Charley, and for a moment, Charley thought it was a question that should be answered, that held the key to all their problems. The black man on television asked also, "What is Oklahoma?" Edward smiled and gritted his teeth as the emcee praised them both, and Charley's anger was gone.

"Please, Charley," Cassie said, banging the silverware against her leg. In the front room, Jim Morrison sang, "What was that promise that you made?"

Charley walked to her. "What is Oklahoma?" he said. "I took a turnpike through it. I didn't see a thing."

"Maybe they moved it," Cassie said. "Who cares?"

"I hate the Doors," Charley said. "They're no better than 'Jeopardy.' "

"This is a party," she said. "Quit complaining." She took his hand. "I'm glad you're back."

"Really?" he said. "Just like that? I thought you'd hate me."

"I thought so, too," Cassie said and led him into the kitchen.

JULIE BROUGHT colorful balloons that were impossible to inflate. She and Tom blew until their jaws ached, but the little balloons would not expand. The trying made them laugh, and that started the party. Eileen and Sam arrived wearing identical pants and shirts, although they claimed it was an accident. The baby could almost stand on her own. Frieda and Roger Stanley came at Jill's insistence. Roger brought an album of Elvis Presley's greatest dance hits. Tom, resuming control of the music, refused to play it. He played only current music—the Go-Go's, Talking Heads, Stray Cats. The dancing became intense and frenetic. There were no toasts.

Marriet, who had crossed the street to get a bottle of vodka from her apartment, stopped on the way back to talk to Charley. He leaned against his car, drinking a Budweiser.

"Jill really likes your car," she said.

He nodded and looked down at it. "I blew the engine in my van. I bought this in Alabama from an old woman. She'd let it sit in a barn for years. Or so she said. I had to put some money in it."

They stood together a few seconds staring at the car.

"Tom doesn't want to talk to me," he said. "He won't stay in the same room unless he's dancing."

"He likes to dance," Marriet said. "We went dancing on our first date."

"Bozeman's," Charley said. "I told him to take you there."

She was startled, reminded that he hadn't really been gone that long. Events had made the time go slowly. "He'll talk to you sooner or later. He's still upset. Ask died in his arms."

"He doesn't seem upset." Charley drank from his beer bottle and crossed his arms. "This house is . . . I don't like it. I feel funny here. I probably shouldn't have come."

She shook her head. "I'm glad you did. We needed a party."

"I'm not going to stay," he said. "I can't believe how they've let Dad get. Maybe that's why I feel funny. And the kid, my kid. You think she looks like me? The eyes? I don't like her eyes. That's mean to say about a kid, I guess. I always wanted a kid. A son. Or a daughter. It's not like she's really mine now. Diapers, throw-up, my hands smelling like baby powder or worse. Who needs it? Especially on the road. Did I tell you how I miss my van?"

"No," Marriet said, "you didn't."

"I liked that van," he said and began talking about driving it. His talk was rambling and long-winded, and by the time he was through it was late and he had told her his story, about Kentucky and the letters and his father.

"I still don't understand," she said. "Why you had to burn the house. I don't get it."

He drank from his beer but it had become warm. "You're easy to talk to," he said. "That's good. Tom always used to talk to Ask, you know."

"Yes," she said, "they were close. That's why the party is a good thing. Otherwise he might never get over Ask."

"I can't believe he's dead," Charley said. "Some things there's no explaining. Some things just are." He gulped the remainder of the warm beer. "Is he, my father, is he always like that? Like he is now?"

She shrugged. "He hasn't had a major stroke for a while. The little ones—it's hard to say. He watches a lot of television. Sometimes he surprises me. One day last week he told me I was wearing a pretty dress. He said red was becoming on me. Just out of the blue."

"You call that a breakthrough?"

"I'm just trying to answer your question. We should join the party."

"Yeah, one more thing. Have they cleaned out his room? Ask's room?"

"No one wanted to do that," she said.

"It should be done," Charley said. "I can do that much, then. I'm the one who should do it."

"There's no rush," she said.

"Yeah, there is," he said and started toward the door.

"Charley," she said, and he stopped. "I still don't understand why you burned the house."

"I know you don't," he said. "A person like you could never understand. You've never had a thing happen to you your whole life."

"That's not true," she said.

"I like you," he said. "I really do. All right, then here it is. See if you can understand this: I wanted to do it." He crossed his arms. "You get it?" He didn't wait for her to respond.

. . .

THE ROOM startled Charley. There was so little to clean out. As a kid, Ask had always covered his wall with photographs and little documents. These walls were almost bare, a few photos, his high school diploma. He tugged at the diploma first, then the pictures. One photograph showed Ask, Cassie, Jill, and Marriet surrounding a hospital bed and Edward in the bed, only his head and neck visible. Another was of Ask in a tuxedo with Julie next to him in a long pink dress. A third was of the Ancient Mariner, Tom and Ask on the hood, both smiling in the darkness.

"What are you doing?"

Tom was at the door. "I was beginning to think you weren't going to talk to me," Charley said.

"I want to know what you're doing."

"I'm cleaning out Ask's room. I don't want to leave it. You guys might never do it," Charley said and turned his back.

"Leave his stuff alone," Tom said. "I don't want you touching his things."

Charley turned to Tom again. "You know what I just remembered? She thought I was you," he said. "When I got out of the car, Mom ran to me but she called out your name."

"I was in the next room," Tom said. "She was just letting me know you were here."

Charley shrugged. "I guess," he said. "But it seemed like she thought I was you."

"Is that what happened with Eileen?" Tom said. "She think you were me?"

"If it'll make you feel any better, you can hit me or bash up my car or something."

"Go to hell."

"I felt trapped. I was trying to escape. I *have* escaped, that's why I'm able to come back." Charley looked at the photographs he held in his hand. "I thought we'd all be better off. I did it for all of us."

"Put those pictures down," Tom said. "Everything started when you burned down the house."

"No, when you came back from Berkeley. That's when I quit sleeping. Then after Cassie slept in the van . . ."

"Don't blame Cassie. This is your fault."

"I killed Ask?"

"I didn't say that."

"Who did kill him? Who was in the truck?"

Tom stepped into the room and closed the bedroom door. "They found the truck near the Mexican border. People take big machinery down there and sell it."

"They get caught?"

Tom shook his head. "They ran out of gas before they got to the border." He crossed his arms. "They saw me on the back side of the lot, I figure, because they didn't cut the lights until I was as far away from the gate as possible. They probably had no idea anyone else was there. There shouldn't have been anyone else. It was my job."

"So *you* killed Ask."

Tom stared hard at him. "Fuck you."

"I drove all night to get here," Charley said. "But I couldn't go to the funeral. I didn't want to see him dead. I was afraid then I'd just remember him as a corpse. I want to remember him alive."

"Just put the picture down," Tom said. "Leave his stuff alone."

Music from the front room drifted in. The others had begun dancing again.

"I'm going to clean out this room," Charley said. "It's got to be done."

"I don't want you touching his things," Tom said.

Charley turned and reached for the last photograph—Ask and Cassie and Edward in the backyard. Had his life here ever had that sunlight? Those colors? He turned to ask Tom, but Tom hit him in the mouth.

. . .

FROM THE FIRST PUNCH, Tom knew he could beat his brother. The punch caught Charley by surprise, and his knees buckled. Tom hit him again. Charley fell, head flying back, body collapsing against the bed and to the floor.

"Get up," Tom said and kicked him in the ribs with his black dress shoes.

Charley tackled him at the knees, knocking him down. The bedpost caught the small of his back as he fell, a sharp and sudden pain. Charley chopped at his face, bloodied his lip.

Tom wrestled the arms away, pinned them back. Throwing his weight forward, he knocked Charley off balance then crawled on top of him and raised his fist to punch him again, but the music in the front faded, and he didn't want to attract attention. He saw and felt Charley relax beneath him. They looked directly at one another those few seconds, out of breath, chests heaving, blood dripping from Tom's lip onto Charley's chest. Then the next song began and Tom slugged him in the jaw.

They rolled against the door, and there in the doorway, doorknob in his hand, was their father. He looked like he was about to cry. Tom felt like a guilty kid caught fighting, then the sensation dropped from his chest to his abdomen and he felt like a guilty adult. He stepped away from his brother.

"Won't one of you take me for a ride?" Edward said.

Tom laughed. He covered his face. He felt tears and wiped his eyes, but they were dry. He continued laughing.

"I'll take you for a ride," Charley said from the floor. "After the party."

Edward walked back down the hall.

"You sucker-punched me," Charley said.

"So?" Tom leaned against the bed and wiped his face again.

"So I thought you played fair."

"Quit thinking, will you? Everyone will be a lot happier." Tom considered his strongest punch, telling Charley that their father's strokes had begun the night he'd seen the letters. How would he handle that blow? "Leave this room alone," he said. "I will clean it out."

Charley stood. "You promise me that."

"I'll do it." Tom pushed past him to the door.

"We shouldn't go out there," Charley said. "It's going to upset Mom."

"What makes you think we have to protect her?" Tom started down the hall. "What makes you think we could even if we wanted to?"

The song ended just as they entered the front room.

Jill, who had been dancing with Sam, stared at the two of them, expressionless. Tom wiped at his lip.

"Which of you wants to dance with me?" she said.

Charley offered his hand.

Tom walked out the front door. He felt the urge to roll in the grass and dirt like a dog.

"What happened?" Marriet let the door swing shut behind her.

"I hit Charley."

"Did you get it out of your system?" she said.

"No, I didn't get it out of my system. I don't even know what that means. I hit him because he had it coming. He's got more than that coming."

"Don't get mad at me," she said.

Cassie slammed the front door as she ran out. "You hit Charley," she said. "You made him bleed. This is a party."

"I don't want a party. You didn't mess up a play. We didn't blow up a science project. Ask is dead," Tom said. "He's gone. He's dead."

They stood together on the lawn, quietly, turning slowly away from one another. On the stereo, inside the house, the Go-Go's sang "My lips are sealed."

"Why do you think it was Ask who got killed?" Cassie said softly, just above the muffled music.

Tom turned completely and walked toward the street. "I don't think there are reasons. Except the stupid ones, like he was in the wrong place at the wrong time. His number was up. He had bad luck."

Cassie sat in the sparse grass of the front lawn. "I want my casket closed," she said. "I don't want anyone to see me dead."

Marriet sat beside her. "Tom," she said, "we should do something to your lip. It looks awful."

"Charley's cheek is bleeding on Mom's blue dress," Cassie said.

"Remember when we were little?" Tom said, walking back to Cassie. He dropped to one knee, suddenly excited. "Remember, before we would go on trips, Mom would make Dad promise that if she died he would just pull over and bury her and keep on with the trip." Tom laughed. "Don't you remember?"

"I'm younger than you are," Cassie said. "I never heard Mom say that. That's disgusting."

Of course she didn't remember. The excitement drained out of him. It would be Ask who remembered. "She used to say it," he said. "It was a running joke."

"I don't like being the youngest one," Cassie said. "I always get left out of things. I'm younger now than ever. Ask was the next closest." She started crying. "He's always messing things up for me."

FRIEDA AND ROGER left first. Eileen and Sam and Karla left just after. Tom had hardly spoken to Eileen. "You have a pretty baby," he had said.

"I'm sorry," she said, "about Ask."

He nodded. "Me too."

"You want to know a secret?" she whispered. "I'm pregnant again."

Tom looked into her eyes a long while. "Things work out, I guess."

"What bothers me," she said, "about Ask, I mean, is the way it happened. It just doesn't seem right. I know it's never fair, death, I mean. But Ask? Hit by a stolen truck? It sounds so weird, so . . ."

"Funny," Tom said. "It sounds like a bad joke. I guess you're the one who told Charley about all this?"

"He calls me," she said. "He likes to keep up."

"You told him the bad joke of his brother's death. The bad joke of his father's sickness."

"I told him," she said.

Tom crossed and uncrossed his arms. "I'm happy for you. You and Sam. That's good."

"Thanks. I'm happy, sort of, for you and Marriet. She's a nice woman. Sometimes I . . ."

"Yeah," Tom said. "Sometimes me too." And that had been the end of it. He had gone to the bathroom when they began to leave and hadn't said good-bye.

At the last minute, Charley reneged on his offer to take Edward for a drive. After dancing with his mother, he washed his face and put alcohol on his cut cheek. He drank beer in the kitchen, watched the others dance, held his daughter briefly, and talked to Sam about cars and about Eileen and about Karla. Then he stepped out into the backyard and walked around to the front. He waited until no one would see him get into his car. The engine hummed quietly in the dark, and Charley drove away.

Tom had watched him go. He had wondered if there was one last thing he should say to Charley. But it was clear that Charley wanted to get away unnoticed, and Tom would not stop him. He watched him go as he had watched his other brother. What should he have said to Ask?

Ask had grown light in his arms. Tom had held him and waited. In the ambulance, slumped in a corner by Ask's feet, he had felt an awareness descend upon him. A doctor at the hospital, a stranger dressed in white, told him his brother was dead, and Tom did not cry. He nodded at the man. He already knew that he was going to leave the city. "I'm sorry," the doctor had said, and Tom had felt nothing but a sudden calmness: he was going away.

. . .

MARRIET OFFERED to clean out Ask's room, but Tom had promised Charley and it had become important that he do it. "I'll come over," he said, "after I finish."

She kissed him, held him. "Wake me," she said.

He put his arms around her, but she felt awkward there and he let her go, watched her leave the house, then stepped to the window and watched her cross the street.

Cassie was asleep on the couch. Tom slipped a hand beneath her head, an arm beneath her legs and carried her to her room. "Don't drop me," she said, and he didn't know whether she was sleeping or awake. He lowered her onto her bed. She immediately resettled herself. The sheet lay crumpled on the floor. He pulled off her shoes, then spread the sheet over her. It floated down and covered her face. As he folded it back, she grabbed his head and mumbled a sentence.

"Are you awake, Cass?"

She gripped his hair, rocking his head fiercely, and mumbled again.

"Cass?"

She pulled him close and wrapped her arm around his neck. "Ask is up on the roof," she said and let her brother go.

TOM JOINED JILL at the kitchen table. Edward slept in his chair in front of the television. They could hear his coarse breathing. Neither had any interest in moving him.

"I'm not drunk," Tom said. "I've had a dozen beers, I bet."

"I was," Jill said. "For a while." There were drops of blood on the shoulder of her dress. "Do you think, Tom, do you think we were so bad? Were we so bad as to deserve this?" Her voice had the flatness of reason to it, as it had years ago when she asked a speaker at a rally, "What were they like, the Vietnamese?" When the speaker, an army colonel, had answered by defining communism, she had interrupted him. "No, what were they like as people?" she had said. "Did they have big families? Who did they name their children for?"

"Were we so bad?" she asked Tom.

"Maybe," he said. "Maybe we were without knowing it."

She ran her hand over the table. "Ask wasn't a virgin, was he?"

"No," Tom said.

"I don't know why that worried me. And he didn't believe in God, did he?"

"No," Tom said.

"I don't think we deserved this. I don't think we had this coming. I don't see why we should have to pay so heavily for our mistakes. You're wrong, Tom. We weren't so bad. We weren't. I'm sure of it."

"Things don't work that way. Besides, it doesn't matter," he said.

"Yes, it does," she said.

"Why? How could it possibly matter?"

"Because Charley is gone again and your father is still sick and Cassie is only a kid and you, you and me, we're still alive. Nothing is over."

"I've got to clean out Ask's room," he said.

"I'm not making sense, am I? I'm rambling. I'm tired. Your mother has gone off the deep end." She smiled and her lip turned up. "I thought about my brother today. I had been sure I was finally free of him, then today he came back. Every moment becomes the past so quickly, but it won't stay there. I have no more control over the past than I do the future."

He stood. "I'm going to stay over at Marriet's tonight."

"Did you have a good time, Tom? This party, I mean. Was it worth having, do you think?"

He shrugged. "It's already done now."

She smiled a half smile. "You're not really a comfort—the party's over. The past is past. Do you think Charley will come back? You know what I think I'll do if he does?"

"Introduce him to some girl?"

"Sit down. No, if he comes back, I'm going to have him arrested. For arson." She took her head into her hands. "That's what I think I'd do. Maybe I'd be fooled again. Maybe I'd forgive him everything. My life is a mess. My life is a mess, and I don't know what I did wrong." She looked up at him. "Maybe I am drunk. I'm rambling. But you're wrong. We weren't that bad, aren't that bad. We're not. We're not."

He wished he could comfort her but could think of no way. He needed Ask. This was his department. What would Ask do if he were here? He thought about it several moments, then sat at his mother's feet with his back to her.

"Do my hair," he whispered.

HE FOUND THE BOX the new television had come in and dragged it down the hall to Ask's room. He collected the photographs that had been thrown about the floor during the fight and tossed them into the box without looking at them. The clothes in the closet were hung neatly. All he had to do was bunch the hangers together, lift them off the bar, and lay them in the box. A picture of Elvis Presley, torn from a magazine and framed with a cheap frame, he laid face down on the clothes. The remainder of the objects on the dresser he shoveled in without examining. The bottom drawer held T-shirts and underwear. The drawer came out of the dresser and Tom dumped them in. They had accumulated so little since the fire, even Ask. One box would hold everything.

The middle drawer was almost empty—a sweater, two knit shirts, a pair of corduroy pants. Tom lay them on top of the T-shirts. The top drawer held socks. They were made into balls and arranged according to color, dozens of socks, light colors at one end, dark at the other.

Tom felt the urge to cry but fought it. He fought although he knew it would be a good thing to cry and get it over with, but the urge to cry and the urge to fight crying were the same thing to him. He didn't know one without the other.

He pulled the drawer from the dresser, almost dropping it, the bundled socks rolling to the brim. The drawer felt oddly heavy and awkward; his movements, drugged. He staggered toward the box, each step a great effort. One pair of socks, dark blue, rolled against his shirt. He leaned forward to pin it there. His life had all led to this moment, he thought, carrying a drawer of his brother's socks to their container, trying not to spill them. He would never be able to retrieve them, he knew, if they were to spill.

The drawer rocked in his arms. He took another step, his knees weak, betraying him, the drawer unreasonably heavy. He lurched into a bedpost. A pair of black socks spun in the air but fell back into the drawer. He tried to steady himself, could not, and fell forward, balancing the drawer as best he could. A green pair, a yellow flew out but landed on the corduroy pants. He rested the drawer on a corner of the cardboard box, then dumped the socks in. They filled it. He had let none escape.

The drawer would not fit back into the dresser. He tried several times. It had grown too large, which was impossible. He left it on the floor.

All that remained in the room were the sheets, which he decided to leave, and the paper sack he had carried home from the hospital, which a nurse had called "the deceased's personal effects." The sack was torn. When Tom lifted it, it ripped open.

A belt. Shoes with socks knotted inside. A green, blood-spattered shirt. Bloody jeans that had been split open up and down the legs. Almost two dollars in change. Keys. A wallet. The photographs in the wallet were old school pictures—Tom as a sophomore, head cocked to one side; Cassie in the sixth grade, her hair pulled straight back; Charley as a senior in a black shirt, a white tie. There were three dollar bills and a ten. A driver's license, high school ID. A yellowed sheet of paper, folded neatly, which Tom unfolded. *Rules*, it said, and he knew what it was.

He would not read it, not now. He refolded the sheet and put it back in the wallet, which he threw in the box. He tucked the cardboard flaps under one another, then dragged the box into the narrow hall. Tomorrow he would get Cassie or Marriet to help him carry it away. Reaching back into the room, he flipped off the light, then knelt, slipped his hand under the cardboard flaps, and felt over the socks until he found his brother's wallet, which he put in his back pocket.

THE NIGHT SKY was clouded, although a few stars shone through the gaps. A car horn on another block sounded, reminding him that people were still doing their business and carrying on, even at 3:00 a.m., even on the night after his brother's funeral. Tom walked to the end of their yard. The house he looked at meant almost nothing to him, someone's ugly dream, someone having nothing to do with his family, long dead. He wished he could bring part of Ask back, that he could spot a lizard on the wall, see or hear something, but to imagine what could do it was to make it impossible.

He stepped onto the asphalt. Marriet would be asleep by now, or, unable to sleep, she would lie in bed waiting for him, the sheet on his side of the bed folded back like a page marker. The small of his back ached dully. His steps were slow, halting. He thought of his father sleeping in the chair, his mother sleeping or perhaps tossing in bed, and Cassie sleeping in her bed or on the floor or in a closet.

In the center of the street he paused, wavering. But what was there to question? What other kind of life was there?

The rough asphalt beneath his feet, the long rows of dark houses and parked cars, the silent windows of his parents' house seemed like answers if only he had the right questions. Just before the ambulance arrived, Ask had tugged him by the shirt sleeve and said, "Did you see that?" Tom had shaken his head. "What was it?" Ask didn't answer, never spoke another word. There was no use imagining. There were a million things he'd never know.

Several houses away, a parked car started its engine, which sounded to Tom like a horse neighing. He turned to the sound, half expecting a dark stallion. The car pulled slowly into the street, headlights shut.

It was Charley's car.

Tom didn't move, although his first thought was that Charley would run him down. The car approached slowly and stopped beside him.

The window lowered and Charley's arm appeared, his shoulder, his upturned face. "What are you doing in the middle of the street?" he said.

Tom shrugged. "I don't know."

"You need a lift?" He smiled. "I was waiting. Making sure you cleaned out Ask's room. It was the only light on the whole block. You like this neighborhood? I don't. I drove around it some. You get it cleared out? The room? You left the curtains up."

"I left the curtains and the sheets."

"I wasn't waiting for you. I didn't expect you to come outside and stand in the street. I wanted to get away clean."

"I guess you'll just have to get away dirty."

Charley laughed. "Yeah. Fuck it."

The knowing, the calmness that had first descended on Tom in the hospital, returned now. He would leave Yuma. He was getting out too, getting out dirty, terribly dirty. Marriet, he hoped, would come with him. They would make a break, but not a clean one.

"There is one other thing," Charley said. "Since you're here."

Tom lowered himself slowly to a squat and looked in the car window, his face inches from his brother's. "What? What else could there possibly be?"

"I had to put some money in this thing," Charley said, thudding the heel of his hand against the steering wheel. "Then I drove straight out when I heard—usually I find work as I go. I could use a loan. Not much—say, thirty, forty bucks."

Tom nodded and stood. He pulled his wallet from his pocket. He had eighteen dollars. From his other pocket, he took Ask's wallet and removed the ten, the three ones. Then, without questioning the impulse, he took the sheet of rules from the wallet, too. He rolled the bills and the yellow sheet together and handed it all to Charley.

"I'll send a money order to pay you back," Charley said. "Maybe I'll put a letter in with it." He shoved the roll in his shirt pocket over his heart. "If Ask was here, he'd say we were stupid talking in the middle of the street."

Tom shook his head. "If Ask were alive, he'd be asleep by now. He could never stay up for anything."

"I guess." Charley extended his hand. They shook, and he drove away, the car still without lights, disappearing finally into the darkness of the road and the night.

Tom's chest began to shudder, his face constricted. He wiped the tears from his cheek as they fell, but it was useless. He had locked his sorrow away too long, in a room too small.

He crossed the dark street in clumsy anguish and felt his way down the lit hall. From a corner of the bedroom, a fan emitted a steady hum. Marriet slept in the center of the bed, her hands folded beneath her chin, mouth slightly open. A short trail of hair, lifted by the fan, rose above her temple. Tom could not stop crying.

His sobbing rocked the bed and woke Marriet.

A NOTE ABOUT THE AUTHOR

Robert Boswell was born in Sikeston, Missouri, in 1953. He attended the University of Arizona, where he received an MFA in creative writing. He is currently an assistant professor of English at Northwestern University. The recipient of a National Endowment of the Arts Fellowship, he was awarded the Iowa School of Letters Award for Short Fiction for Dancing in the Movies, *and has had a story selected for the O Henry Awards Prize Stories collection. He lives with his wife, Antonya Nelson, in Evanston, Illinois.*

A NOTE ON THE TYPE

The text of this book was set in a digitized version of Janson, a typeface long thought to have been made by the Dutchman Anton Janson, who was a practicing type founder in Leipzig during the years 1668–1687. However, it has been conclusively demonstrated that these types are actually the work of Nicholas Kis (1650–1702), a Hungarian, who most probably learned his trade from the master Dutch type founder Dirk Voskens. The type is an excellent example of the influential and sturdy Dutch types that prevailed in England up to the time William Caslon developed his own incomparable designs from them.

Composed by Creative Graphics, Inc.,
Allentown, Pennsylvania
Printed and bound by The Haddon Craftsmen, Inc.,
Scranton, Pennsylvania

Designed by Peter A. Andersen